Creed grabbed Riana and turned her around to face him.

His lips pushed against hers hungrily, mirroring her own unbridled need. He smelled so good, so male, and he tasted even better. The warmth of his mouth felt like a balm on her heart. He slipped his hands into her hair and held her there, kissing her, until she wanted to scream with need, with relief, with sheer, raging want.

He made her feel so adored, and so very safe.

How could she have mistrusted him?

How can you trust him, knowing that part of him wants to kill you?

But that part was nowhere evident in his gaze. And she was way past reason now. Her lips tingled from his kiss, and her body tingled from wanting his mouth, his hands. She wanted him inside her, and she didn't want to think about anything else.

"Take me downstairs," she whispered. "Now."

BOUND BY SHADOW

A NOVEL OF THE DARK CRESCENT SISTERHOOD

ANNA WINDSOR

BALLANTINE BOOKS • NEW YORK

A Ballantine Books Mass Market Original

Copyright © 2008 by Anna Windsor

Published in the United States by Ballantine Books, an imprint of The Random House Publishing Group, a division of Random House, Inc., New York.

BALLANTINE and colophon are registered trademarks of Random House, Inc.

ISBN 978-0-345-49853-3

Printed in the United States of America

www.ballantinebooks.com

OPM 9 8 7 6 5 4 3 2 1

To Cheyenne McCray.
This book—and my career—exist because
of your help.

(1)

"Sixty-third. Sixty-second." Andrea Myles squinted through oversized sunglasses as she wedged the Crown Vic through New York traffic. "We're here. And I didn't say Riana was weird. I said she was unconventional."

Creed Lowell struggled to keep the growl out of his voice. "She's some kind of psychic, isn't she? Riana Dumain. Sounds like a television tarot reader."

"She's not a tarot reader." Andy braked and slipped into a rare parking space alongside Central Park. "She's a scientist who studies ... unusual things. She and her two cousins. They're like private investigators."

Creed's gut tightened at Andy's I'm-holding-a-few-things-back tone. "And?"

"And she's my friend, so you better be nice to her."

"And?" He drummed his fingers on two thin, unmarked folders stacked between them on the Crown Vic's front seat.

"And she's not like the women you're used to." Andy rubbed a hand across her forehead, moving a shock of red curls. The other hand twitched on the steering wheel as she shut off the engine. "Ri won't be a sucker for your good looks."

"And?" He gave the unmarked folders another meaningful tap.

She sighed. "All right, all right. I think she'll be able to help on the Latch killing."

Creed groaned. "That's not our case, Andy."

"But maybe Ri can tell us more about the knife wounds on the boy's body. Those blade marks the M.E. can't identify, and the freaky symbols all over the floor, too."

Cabs, buses, and cars whizzed by on the crammed street, sending plumes of exhaust into the morning air. Creed glared at the bits of smoke as they drifted over the sidewalk.

A psychic. Great. Rats and roaches are more useful.

He'd never met a real psychic, but that didn't mean real psychics didn't exist. Creed avoided anyone who claimed any kind of mystic title, anyone who might have the slightest bit of enhanced perception, and he advertised his sarcasm as often as possible so the NYPD wouldn't stuff a psychic down his throat.

No mediums. No seers. No sensitives.

I don't need that kind of risk.

But here he was, taking that risk because of Andy. He couldn't say no to the woman. Well, actually, Andy didn't hear the word *no*, didn't understand the concept of *no*. Maybe it was her Southern upbringing, or maybe she was just crazy and he had to humor her. Most days he wasn't sure. Next to his own solve rate, Andy had the best record in New York's low-profile Occult Crimes Unit. So, crazy or not, it was usually a good idea to listen to her.

Creed sucked air through his teeth in frustration. "The FBI came up empty with the blade marks and the symbols. How can Riana Dumain possibly one-up the federal databases?"

When Andy didn't respond, he added, "The OCU can't touch the murder of a senator's kid—especially a senator who almost ran for president last election. The press would murder *us*."

Andy glared over her sunglasses. "It's not out yet, and you know it. The press is busy covering the break-in at the Met. That Russian history exhibit that got torn apart—Volgograd, or something like that? And get over yourself, Creed. Ri might help us find a child-killer while the trail's still red-hot. Who cares if we have to stay off the grid and give credit to Homicide?"

"She's a psychic and you're just not telling me," he grumbled as he got out. Cool morning air chilled the sudden sweat on his face. While Andy fumbled with the folders and keys, Creed stretched and gazed across the sidewalk, over the stone wall surrounding Central Park.

Autumn hues shimmered in the fresh, early sunlight. He stared at the reds, yellows, and greens, stilling his mind, turning loose his formidable senses. Time seemed to slow, but Creed knew it was only his thoughts getting faster, speeding out of normal human rhythms.

His nostrils flared at city smells, morning smells, park smells, building smells. The pungent sweat of the horse hitched to a nearby hansom cab made his eyes water. Light and color forced him into a squint, and his ears wanted to shrink from the cacophony of traffic and birds, footsteps and talking. He could taste car exhaust on his tongue, feel the rush of passing cars and crowds and the wind on his face. New York. The Upper East Side at rush hour, yes, but nothing unusual. No twist of reality. No scent out of place, at least not in the few miles he could sense most clearly.

Fighting to keep his balance and his sanity in the onrush of sensory information, Creed turned to face Andy. To his unleashed perceptions, she seemed to be moving at one-quarter speed, extending the remote to arm the sedan's locks.

Creed looked past Andy, to the brownstone matching the number Andy had given him—the place where Riana Dumain lived. Five steps up to the front door. Three floors. White curtains.

Odd, but the energy around the building felt flat—or rather, dense. Thick, like the bark of an ancient tree. Even more odd was the fact he couldn't see through those white curtains, even though they appeared to be lace. He narrowed his eyes and increased his focus, but he still couldn't see through the openings in the lace.

On the third floor, one of those lace barriers twitched. A shadow moved past, just a flicker of darkness, so fast it almost escaped Creed's enhanced scrutiny. The signet ring on his right ring finger hummed against his skin, hot and urgent.

He glanced down at the ring.

A hot, solid wave of energy slammed against his expanded thoughts.

Creed's head snapped back from the rush of power. His mind folded in on itself and his perceptions screeched down to normal speed so abruptly he almost stumbled. His ears rang. His jaw ached from clenching his teeth—and from—from what?

A mental slap?

Had somebody really slapped him?

He rubbed the space between his right eye and his chin. Damned if it didn't burn.

What the hell?

Some kind of barrier. Some kind of elemental protections?

The beast inside him wanted to snarl and retreat, but he couldn't let that happen. He was here in New York City with his partner Andy, poking around on the ritualistic murder of a senator's kid. He was Creed Lowell, a detective in the modern world, and he had to do his job. He had to atone, and keep atoning, for as long as he lived. Forever.

He looked at the brownstone again as he hitched up his jeans and adjusted his leather blazer.

The curtains lay still against the windows, as if the house had its eyes closed, pretending to be asleep.

Andy tucked the folders under her arm. "You coming?" she asked when he looked at her.

Creed scrubbed his hand against his stinging jaw, then followed her as she wove through cars, cabs, and buses on the busy street. Andy pushed her sunglasses to the top of her head and raised her hand to use the big brass knocker, but the door eased open before she grabbed it.

"Nice touch," Creed muttered, twisting his ring, still try-ing to get his mental balance. "Thought you said she didn't play psychic."

Andy's sharp stomp on his toe helped him focus.

The door opened a little farther, and a woman stepped into the morning sunlight. A tall, striking woman who looked like she'd just walked home from a fashion photo shoot.

Creed found himself grateful for the aches in his toe and jaw. Without the pain, his teeth wouldn't have been clenched, and he would have let his mouth drop open like a stunned schoolboy.

Soft, tinkling music seemed to play from somewhere in-side the brownstone. Maybe a radio with classical music, though it sounded more like distant church bells. The woman's polished-jade eyes captured him completely as her loose black hair billowed in the breeze. Gentle curls brushed her lightly tanned cheeks, and the full shoulders of her brown cashmere sweater suggested an athletic build. The sweater tapered to a snug fit at her waist, and her black slacks and boots matched the sensuous, silky shade of her hair. Around her neck hung a long chain with a silver-and-gold crescent pendant. The sunlight glittered on the crescent moon and on the deep red of her nail polish. Her enticing lips, the same deep red and beautifully curved, parted ever so slightly, as if she was immediately aware of her effect on him.

He was only dimly conscious of Andy saying hello to her friend—*God,* what a friend—and then the woman spoke. Her words came out in a rich, slightly accented flow, that enticing kind of voice more appropriate for dark restau-rants, candlelight, and fine wine than bright city streets at bright, early hours.

"So this is your infamous partner." Once more, Riana Du-main's jade eyes caught him in some invisible net. Creed felt the sound all over his skin, like gently traveling fingernails. "I was beginning to think you made him up."

Creed knew he was supposed to say something. He tried not to look at her prominent cleavage and the obvious swells of her breasts, failed, then managed to gather himself enough to extend his hand and say, "Creed Lowell. Nice . . . uh . . . to meet you."

Riana's dark eyebrows lifted and she took his hand confidently in hers. When her fingertips brushed against his signet ring, she didn't jerk away, but she sure as hell let go in a hurry. As the gold band warmed and vibrated against his finger, her open, curious expression turned shrewd, then guarded, and those relentless green eyes seemed to drill into his very essence. Creed leaned back before he caught himself, straightened up, and returned her stare.

She knows, he told himself, and the thought made his chest tight.

Since his grandmother died when he was a teenager, the only living soul who knew about Creed's true nature was the man who shared it—his twin brother Dominic—and he hadn't seen Dominic in five years.

But she *knows.*

The beast inside him—the *other*—stirred in response to the threat, but Creed forced it down with a ferocious inner snarl. Riana flinched as if she heard the sound. For a long second, her eyes blazed. Her hands twitched as if they wanted to grab for weapons.

Creed actually found himself glancing at the ample curves of the woman's hips for purely self-protective reasons. No holster. No unsightly bulges. His gaze traveled to her boots. Could be daggers in there, he supposed, but he could move faster than daggers.

Andy seemed cheerfully unaware of the tense undercurrent. When Riana Dumain stepped aside to let them in, Andy bustled past her without hesitation. Creed clenched his fists, feeling the warm, sharp pressure of his signet ring. The weird vibrating had stopped. Still, he didn't want to walk past Riana Dumain and enter her sanctuary. Everything inside him, especially the *other,* screamed for him to back away, to leave this woman as he found her.

Her crystalline green gaze intensified, and her mouth opened slightly again, daring him to come inside and daring him to flee at the same time. She knew what he was, or at least that he was different, potentially dangerous—and she didn't care. Not even a little bit.

Who is she, really? What is she?

There it was again. That same dare in her expression. Come in, Creed Lowell. Find out for yourself.

He felt his lips curl at the challenge.

A split second later, he drew even with her and paused to drink in her heady aroma of fresh rain and lavender. Then he moved past her into possibly the strangest room he had ever seen. The only normal things in the room, in fact, were the doors at the back and sides, and the broad staircase on the right, leading into dark reaches of the brownstone. Competing aromas blended—sage, he knew that one. And jasmine, and vanilla, and something like cherries or apples, all light, all swirling to form an unusually pleasant departure from the typical antiquated must of most old dwellings.

Andy had already flopped down on a comfortable-looking overstuffed sofa, camel-colored and covered with mahogany pillows. Four matching chairs formed a circle in front of the couch. A massive oak table sat dead center in the circle, laden with papers, pens, plates, cups, a couple of incense burners, two socks, one blouse, a nylon footie, and a high-heeled shoe. A red one. Creed could just make out that the knee-high table's edge was actually a carved lip with a trench in it, lined with what looked like silver or lead.

Damn. That table's big enough to hold a dance contest. Bet it weighs like a bastard, too.

There was no other furniture save for a few musical instruments leaning against the back walls. The walls themselves

were covered with various antique mirrors hung at seemingly random heights, interspersed with spare sculptures
that looked like Slavic runes. Wind chimes dangled from
the ceiling. A lot of wind chimes of different sizes and
lengths, but all the metal-pipe kind, some silver, some
coppery-looking, and one, up near the door, a bright polished bronze. The bronze chime danced in the light breeze
flowing through the front door, sounding again like distant
church bells.

Creed studied the wind chimes and then the instruments,
and thought he recognized the prominent body, intricate
markings, and distinctive drone string and handle of a real
koliosnaya lira, also called a Russian hurdy-gurdy. The
thing functioned a little like a mandolin combined with a
bass guitar, as far as he could remember from the few times
he had heard one played. There was also a Greek cithara
that looked so old the Olympic gods might have played it,
and if he wasn't mistaken, the third instrument was a good-
sized Celtic harp. His eyes almost watered as he imagined
the unusual noise all three would make in combination
with the wind chimes.

As Riana closed the front door, the bronze chime rang
again and the door at the back of the room sprang open. In
came two more women. The first had hair as red as Andy's
and legs almost as long as Riana's. She seemed taller because of the spiked heels she wore, along with tight-fitting
leather pants and a loose white tunic shirt. As she came
into the room, she pulled back her hair, fastened it into a
ponytail with a leather tie, and slowed to stare at Creed.
The second woman was a little shorter but no less fit, with
cropped blond hair and bare feet showing beneath the
frayed cuffs of her jeans. She held a bag of potato chips and
a bunch of soft drink cans crushed against her black
sweater. She, too, stopped to stare at Creed.

He had the uncomfortable sense of being probed and dis-
sected. Both women narrowed their eyes. Their gazes

moved from his face downward to his signet ring, which once more decided to quiver.

Christ. What is this, psychic central?

Was he sweating yet? Damn them. Damn Andy! What had she gotten him into?

"Riana's cousins," Andy announced. "I told you before, remember? The redhead's Cynda and the blonde is Merilee. Cynda and Merilee, this is my partner, Creed Lowell."

The women nodded at him in eerie unison, as if they were well accustomed to acting and moving in concert.

He returned the gesture, wishing he'd stayed in bed, wishing he'd never come to work, wishing he'd tied Andy up and stuffed her in her locker instead of letting her drag him to this bizarre brownstone full of—of whatever these women were.

"Sit down, Creed," came Riana's low, sexy voice from too close behind him. "We don't bite."

He turned slowly back to the beautiful woman with the bright jade eyes and let his expression say it all.

Yeah. Right.

She didn't smile at him, but he thought he saw the barest shadow of mirth cross her hard-to-read features. His body responded so fast he almost couldn't stop a menacing growl. As it was, his senses flared, showing him the brilliant colors of Riana's natural energy. Lavender like her scent, and powerful. God. He had never seen such a halo around a human before. He wanted to touch it, thought it might feel solid. Hell, he wanted to touch her. Wanted to see if her skin felt as soft as it looked, if her lips really were that full and moist. Blood thrummed in his ears. His cock got hard in record time, and he had to close his eyes and think of his grandmother's smile before things got totally out of hand.

By the time he positioned himself beside Andy on the couch, hoping in the distant reaches of his mind that she would shoot her friends to protect her partner if necessary,

Cynda and Merilee had joined them around the table. Merilee dropped the chips in the middle of the table mess, then distributed soft drinks to everyone but Creed. She gave him a guarded but apologetic look, gestured to the cans, and started to ask if she should get him one, but he shook his head.

Meanwhile, Cynda shoved the shoe and socks and footie onto the floor beside her chair, along with a bunch of the maps and diagrams. Creed caught a glimpse of what looked like sketches of hallways and doorways arranged in a vaguely familiar pattern before Cynda pushed them farther away to make room for some dirty dishes. He was tempted to let the *other* come forward a little bit, to risk a few seconds of reduced control in order to get more information off that scrap of paper, but one look at the array of women staring at him killed that idea in a hurry. He settled for committing the details to memory, along with the rune sculptures between the ancient-looking mirrors, and some of the odd designs carved into the mirror frames themselves.

Riana kept up her determined surveillance. Creed fiddled with his ring but refused to shift under the woman's fierce gaze as Andy moved aside some candles and notebooks to spread out the photos from one of her folders.

Andy had cropped them, removing identifying information. Only the strange markings found around the body were visible, along with the dead boy's unusual wounds—and morgue markers showing the pitifully small size of the victim.

"Same rules as always, ladies." Andy tapped the first photo with one square-tipped nail. The clear polish stood out against the lurid details of the photo. "Nothing leaves this house, and I'll never put your names on a piece of paper, so you won't get called as witnesses. These came in last night, and I need you to take a good look."

Slowly, Riana's attention turned from Creed to the photos. Cynda and Merilee also focused on the pictures, freeing Creed from the weight of their scrutiny. Before he could enjoy the relief, however, the photos pulled him back to the larger, darker issues at play in the universe.

What maniac had carved up a senator's ten-year-old boy and left him to bleed to death inside a set of weird, nonsensical designs—and why?

"The FBI can't find a match for the blade pattern," Andy was saying. "And nothing on the markings around the vic. Some of the symbols were drawn in his blood, but others were there before the blood, scratched into piles of something white and grainy. Some kind of powder."

"Sea salt," said the blonde. Merilee. Creed glanced at her. She had an accent, too. Something Italian or Mediterranean, and an innocent face, but her blue eyes held the detachment of a longtime scholar of death. "I wonder if the salt's processed. Store-bought, or if somebody harvested it, or purchased it straight from a harvest. It's white, so it would have to be from France or Ireland, or maybe China or India. If it's fresh and from the U.S., it would have to be from Maine, or up around Cape Cod."

Creed had pulled his little notepad out of his gun belt, and he was writing furiously. He didn't look at Andy, who would have a see-I-told-you-so expression.

When Merilee stopped speaking, he glanced up, impatient, anticipating, but the blonde only shrugged. "A guess. You'll know when your tests come back—but some ancient cultures used sea salt in rituals, to purify. If it's processed, then it's just some player imitating stuff in books. If it's fresh, somebody really intended to purify that space."

Cynda, the redhead, leaned forward in her chair. "Purify," she murmured, "or keep something pure inside the circle. Maybe use the elements to protect it." Creed noticed her decidedly lilting accent, and that she didn't reach for the photo in front of her. In fact, she seemed to be keeping her hands away from it on purpose, as if touching the picture might be dangerous. When Cynda looked up, she said, "You know elements can be locked, right?"

Creed shook his head, feeling clueless. He felt a bit relieved to see Andy looking just as confused as he felt.

"Someone who knows what they're doing can call the energy of one of the elements, or two, or all of them, and force it into a stable pattern," Cynda said. "We call it locking, but really it's more like . . . stacking. Like the stones in an Irish fence." She moved her hand in a straight line across the air, making Creed think of pictures he had seen of the Irish countryside. Miles of winding stone fence, nothing more than perfectly stacked stones, held together by form alone—no mortar.

He nodded, and saw Andy nodding, too.

"Depending on how much elemental force is used," Cynda continued, "you can coat an object with a certain kind of energy—or even build a barrier as strong as an actual stone wall, though nobody can see it." She pointed to the photo of the salt patterns. "Salt could have been used to lock a really strong elemental barrier, to protect something precious."

"Protect, trap." Riana had a picture of the wounds in her lap. She spoke without looking up, and she sounded infinitely sad. "Not much difference, unfortunately."

The emotion in the woman's voice surprised Creed. He'd taken her for a hard-ass. Some kind of psychic/private-detective/cowboy who kicked out teeth and took stupid risks, like letting a supernatural creature into her house when she didn't fully understand its nature.

Then he looked at her again. This time, he considered her solid, secure posture, and the way she had taunted him with her expression.

Or maybe she does understand my nature, and knows just exactly how to kill me. Fast, bloodless. Probably painful. What the hell am I doing here?

He kept his mouth shut and his pen busy, and otherwise he sat very still as the women mumbled to themselves and each other, took sips from their soft drinks, scrounged up

their own notebooks, and exchanged pictures. All but Riana. She kept that first picture in her lap. As her graceful
fingers traced the edges of the dead boy's larger wounds,
she took a deep, even breath, the kind Creed sometimes
used to center himself.

Was she finding her center, too? Did photos like this hurt
her down inside?

If they had been alone, Creed might have asked her.

Andy picked up the potato chips and munched noisily.
Creed grimaced. Nothing much disturbed his partner's appetite.

"Did you bring me a sample?" Riana asked quietly, still
absorbed by the photo and her rhythmic tracing of the
wound pattern.

"Yep." Andy stopped eating long enough to shove the
other folder toward her. Creed saw the corner of a plastic
evidence bag slide sideways through the flaps. "The M.E.
trimmed some of the smaller wounds. Here's about an
inch. Is that enough?" To Creed, she said, "Down boy. He
thinks I took it all up to Trace—and I only lifted one edge
out of a dozen. They've got plenty of skin to analyze."

Riana finally looked up, but only long enough to snag
the folder containing the bag. When she extended her arm,
Creed caught sight of a tattoo on the inside of her wrist.
His ring heated up as he let the image sink into his mind.

A mortar, a pestle, and a broom, in triangular points
around a dark crescent moon.

The woman didn't seem to notice his interest in the blue-
green mark. He sketched it in a hurry, pretending to be finishing his notes.

"Give me tonight with the sample," Riana said. "I
should have something for you this time tomorrow. A
guess at the blade type, too."

"Aww, you're not going to show Creed the lab?"
Andy's disappointment didn't keep her from cramming
another handful of chips in her mouth and crunching

loudly as Riana once more tore her attention away from the photos.

Her green eyes fixed on Creed, and she came up with one of those sultry almost-smiles. "Not on the first date, sailor." She winked. "Maybe next time."

Creed ground his teeth and thought of his grandmother.

Andy's cell rang with the special ring Creed knew meant the captain was calling. She washed down her last load of chips and answered with a quick, "Andrea Myles." Then she frowned. "Okay. Fifteen minutes."

She was already getting to her feet as she closed the phone. "The press got a whiff of the Latch case. They're mobbing the senator's house and the nearby precincts. All hands on deck. Ri— Call me if you find something urgent."

Riana stood as Creed did. Cynda and Merilee stayed seated, but they nodded at Andy and Creed before taking out notebooks and beginning to scribble furiously.

It was all Creed could do to stop looking at Riana as she shifted her necklace to center on her cashmere sweater and waited for him to follow Andy to the door. He wasn't quite sure how he separated himself from her, or how he walked across the littered floor as the wind chimes began to ring. His head was spinning from Riana's presence, from whatever real psychic talents she and her two cousins possessed, from the risk they might pose, even from the systematic way they attacked those photographs and sketched their theories.

Professionals. Seasoned. Fearless.

He had been working OCU for almost six years now, but until this moment, this day, Creed had never sensed the real workings of power, of supernatural energy outside his own. OCU crimes were committed by psychotics and psychopaths, by religiously obsessed nut-jobs of every faith. He was used to that. This brownstone, these three women—they were something else entirely. Something new.

He wished he could talk to Dominic the way he did in the good old days, when his brother had worked OCU right next to Creed.

Riana gave Andy a hug at the front door, then turned to Creed. He offered his hand and expected her to shake it again, but she took it and used it to pull him close instead. Before he knew what was happening, she wrapped her arms around his neck.

The shock of her warm, soft body against his electrified Creed. He put his hands on her waist, reflex more than conscious action. The firm curve of her hips, the press of her breasts against his chest, that intoxicating blend of rain and lavender—the woman was killing him. She had to be doing it on purpose. She had to know. Any second now, his erection would rip through his jeans.

Instead of smiling and kissing him on the cheek as she had done with Andy, Riana stood on her toes and rubbed seductively against the hard swell of his cock. His back was to Andy as Andy headed down the outside steps, hiding the progress of Riana's hand—the one with the mysterious tattoo—as it traveled down, down until her long fingers brushed the notable bulge. Her green eyes sparkled with appreciation and a deep, almost disturbing amusement.

"Nice," she said, one eyebrow raised, and gave his cock an intimate, mind-blowing squeeze. At the same time, she pressed her lips against his ear. The heat of her breath and the unbelievable feel of her hand made his gut tighten with helpless need.

Just then, her fingers moved again—this time in a sharp, painful backward thrust.

His breath left in a rush and his eyes watered from the agony of her sudden forceful grip on the most tender parts of his manhood.

"I don't know what you are," she whispered sweetly, her exotic accent taking on fresh menace, "but if you hurt Andy or anyone else, I'll kill you. Do you understand me?"

Creed nodded to save his life and his balls.

Over her shoulder, he saw Cynda and Merilee smiling at him with that same horrifying sweetness as those infernal bronze pipes over his head chimed and chimed.

Riana let him go, and he made himself walk slowly out the door, which slammed behind him. He heard the distinct clink and rattle of locks sliding into place.

When he joined Andy on the street corner, trying not to walk funny because of the miserable ache between his legs, she grinned at him.

"I think Riana might like you, partner."

"Yeah," he grumbled as the light changed. Andy started into the crosswalk, and he hobbled along behind her. "She might like me, all right. Dead in a display box, with little pins through my wings."

2

Riana's triad sisters made it to the window before she did. Cynda and Merilee both spoke at once, so fast she could barely discern who said what.

"Goddess, he's delicious. Did you see those *muscles*?"

"Look at that ass in those jeans."

"Was his cock huge?"

"I bet it was huge."

"I love a dark-haired man in jeans and leather."

"I love a man with a gun."

"But who is he, really?"

"*What* is he?"

"Not an Asmodai. He could talk and his features were too stable."

"Hush." Riana put a hand on each of them and watched Creed Lowell's departure through a tiny slit in the lace curtains. "We'll probably have to stick a dagger through his heart."

The man—or whatever he was—cut a figure, even limping with a bad case of bruised balls. Riana had meant to intimidate him, she had tried to intimidate him, but her fingers still tingled from touching him so intimately.

Definitely not an Asmodai.

In all of her years of fighting the man-made demon servants created by members of the Legion, she had never encountered an Asmodai with normal male parts. The demons were solid enough, but without definition. More like life-sized clay models of humans, built from an element, a talisman, and energy generated in perverted rituals.

Creed Lowell was gutsy. She had to give him that. He

had realized she spotted him, knew something was off about him, but he still entered her home, her most protected zone. He still let her put her hands on him—*it*, she reminded herself. *The creature.* Something she'd likely have to kill without mercy when the time came.

But damn, did that creature ever have a hard body, never mind those gorgeous eyes. Onyx filled with dark fire, like the flame of a black candle burning in some hot, sweaty underground ritual. She especially liked the way the sun glimmered off his midnight hair. It was longer than cops usually wore it, just above his shoulders, but pulled back at his neck.

Like some Celtic warrior. Goddess help me.

When Riana had tracked Andy Myles to her health club, joined it, and intentionally struck up a friendship with the woman a year before, she had planned to gain the detective's trust enough to get a little information on OCU cases. Riana had hoped Andy's work would lead the Upper East Side triad to a few real supernatural villains.

But Andy's partner?

Not in the plan.

In the months Andy had been in Riana's life, she had become one of the best friends Riana had ever known. Riana put her hand over her crescent pendant, which had been a gift to her from one of the Russian Mothers—one of the ancient women who trained her to be a warrior—on the day she was chosen to form her triad. Her group of fighters. The only people she truly cared about—other than her friend.

She would *not* let that creature harm Andy.

As always, Cynda was the one to start putting dark thoughts into words. "Did you see that signet ring on his right hand? Was it really a coiled serpent?"

"It was," Riana confirmed as Creed and Andy disappeared into their Crown Vic across busy Fifth Avenue. "Like the ones I've seen on ancient coins. I'm sure of it."

Behind the car, the trees of Central Park swayed gently in morning breezes. Merilee's fingers dug into the windowsill. "Then he could be one of those bastards who make the Asmodai! Finally one of the Legion—and we let him walk away?"

"We can get him back," Riana said with more confidence than she felt. She had a sense that Creed, that the creature, had survived for many years among humans, and he hadn't done that by taking foolish chances. "Besides, we couldn't very well trap him, grill him, and execute him in front of his police-officer partner, could we?"

Merilee's angry hiss put a question mark on that assertion.

For a graduate of Motherhouse Greece, the training facility most known for its peaceful, academic approach to the powers of the air, Merilee could be surprisingly violent.

Wind is made from air, Riana reminded herself. *And tornados.*

Merilee hissed again. Air gusted through the brownstone, randomly ringing the communication chimes.

"Hurricanes, too," Riana said aloud.

"What?" Cynda glanced up at her, bright fire in her green eyes. Real fire that threatened to break across her freckled skin. It had happened before. A lot, actually.

"Nothing." Riana sighed. "Enough spying. We have a lot of work to do."

The two younger members of the triad followed her back to the table without arguing. Merilee spread out a detailed street map of Manhattan as she mumbled a repetitive prayer to the old gods of Olympus, something about patience and perseverance. Riana didn't know the words for sure. Her Greek was rusty.

Cynda sang a folk tune about a cutty wren and John the Red Nose. No doubt she learned the song in a pub in Connemara, the town nearest Motherhouse Ireland. In time with the lilting tune, Cynda retrieved the diagrams and maps she had shoved off the table so casually, to hide the papers from their guests. Soon, schematics of the Metropolitan Museum were once more laid out on the tabletop, resting across the carved, lead-lined indentation that marked the table's edge.

Riana chose an old Russian song to help her focus and relax. She had learned the tune at the oldest and grandest of the three Motherhouses, the one near Volgograd in Russia. As she sat and spread the autopsy photos in front of her on the table, she hummed the comforting melody, letting the words unfold in English in her mind.

Dark eyes, passionate eyes, burning and so beautiful eyes—

Merilee snickered, then laughed outright. "Isn't that one about grief in the soul and sacrificing everything for ardent eyes?" She moved her compass and used a blue pencil to trace a pattern on a piece of paper she had slipped over her map. "Bad choice."

Cynda let out a snort of agreement as she compared pamphlets, lists on ancient papers, and the museum's floor plan.

Merilee pushed one of her papers forward. "The Met and Senator Latch's residence are too far apart to make it likely the same Asmodai was involved with both crime scenes."

"Is there a third point on the map?" Riana looked up at her pretty Greek triad sister. "An origin point?"

With a flourish of warm air, Merilee held up a second piece of paper. "The only equidistant point would be the U.N. headquarters. Possible, but not likely. Maybe Grand Central?"

"Grand Central's big, but I don't know if there are enough private places to do the ritual it would take to make an Asmodai." Riana chewed her lip for a moment. "I'm betting my tests will show that the boy was killed with a ceremonial blade—maybe from the robbed exhibit?"

Cynda kept a finger on the Metropolitan Museum schematics as she studied Merilee's colorfully marked plot. "How much are we going to tell Andy? I hate holding back on another woman who fights evil the best way she knows how."

Riana shook her head. "Andy's not trained."

"So that makes it okay for us to use her," Cynda grumbled.

Riana thrust out her arm and let her tattoo show. "We protect her."

Cynda started to snap back, seemed to think better of it, and hung her head instead. After a few moments, she studied her own tattoo. Merilee did the same.

Broom, mortar, and pestle—the sacred triad in flight across a dark crescent moon.

The mark of the Dark Goddess.

The triad tattoo was the sign that identified the Sibyls, member of the Dark Crescent Sisterhood, female warriors with a lineage almost as old as time, not to mention years of training in a Motherhouse. Riana was proficient in seven languages, seven different styles of traditional hand-to-hand combat, and all known close-proximity weapons. The women she had chosen to complete her triad—Cynda, the pestle, and Merilee, the broom—had skills to complement her own.

Andy could use a gun, sure, and she had excellent law-enforcement instincts. But without the powers of a Sibyl passed down through generations and controlled by training, Andy could never stand against *real* supernatural foes.

Cynda scooted the Met schematic in front of Riana. "Motherhouse records don't show a ceremonial dagger as part of the traveling Volgograd collection, but there is mention of a mortar and pestle, one of those six that might have belonged to the Dark Goddess. It's not on the museum manifest, and not listed in the exhibit, but it could have been there." She pushed forward a snapshot of the destruction left behind when the collection was wrecked. "Whoever broke in did so much damage, we may never know. It could be dust on the floor."

"It was an Asmodai," Merilee said. "It had to be, to trip no alarms until it knocked down an entire wall. Look at all that char. The thing was probably made of fire."

"It could have been made out of air," Cynda countered. "A powerful fire-Asmodai would have burned down the whole building and split the stones."

Riana raised both hands. "The Asmodai could have been shaped out of earth, air, fire, *or* water. There could have been more than one, from more than one source. That's not the issue. We need to know if it took an object of power."

"My instincts say yes," Cynda said at once. Merilee nodded.

Riana checked the sensations in her own mind, in her own belly, that subtle but accurate intuition granted to her by her heritage and training as a Sibyl, and she had to agree. The Asmodai, whatever form it had taken, had managed to steal an object of power from the Metropolitan Museum and carry it back to its creator.

She pulled together Cynda's diagrams and Merilee's maps and stacked them beside the autopsy photos. "So, we have Asmodai activity at the Met, to steal an object of power. And we have Asmodai activity at Senator Latch's house, to murder a child. By timing and location, they're unrelated—but we can't be sure of that."

"The Legion usually ignores contemporary politics, and they hardly ever attempt a public crime like that museum theft." Merilee leaned back in her chair and steepled her fingers. "Why the Met? Why that kid?"

Cynda frowned. "And did somebody try to protect the boy with that circle—or just trap him to make the Asmodai's task easier? Do they have human dabblers working for them now, or has the Legion begun to expand?"

Riana found her master notebook and wrote down the

lingering questions. She tried to remain calm, practice the detachment she had learned from the Mothers, but her stomach churned no matter what she tried. Her mind kept flashing startling images of the dead boy, the utter devastation of the museum exhibit—and a pair of dark, burning eyes filled with confusion and pathos.

Is Creed Lowell one of the Legion?

Did I let the only chance we've had to stop these bastards just walk out our front door? Damnit. *I have to get him back.*

She chewed the tip of her pen. Sibyls used pen and paper instead of computers to help their thinking process through the meditative act of writing. Also, notebooks couldn't be hacked from distant locations—and supernatural energy tended to play hell with electronic devices anyway. Low tech just worked better, except for Internet searches and retrieving other public-domain information.

Cynda leaned over and smacked her arm. "Quit eating the equipment."

Riana dropped the pen on the table next to three or four other previously chewed pens and pencils. "Okay. Action. Merilee, we need current information on Senator Latch. Everyone in his family. Everyone he knows."

The Greek historian and archivist blew her a kiss. "I'm the broom. It's my job to know everything, to sweep it all up and pile it in neat little stacks."

Before Cynda could say something about pestles being able to crush brooms, Merilee got up and hurried up the stairs. The third floor of the brownstone was entirely her domain. It was higher than everyone else, of course, where wind-lovers liked to be—though hardly a breeze could stir up there with all the shelves and stacks of books and notebooks, and the impressive array of computers.

Riana stretched, feeling tired though it wasn't even noon yet. "Cynda, can you let the Mothers know what we've got so far?"

"Sure." She smiled as she stood. "You going to test the skin while I ring the chimes?"

Riana nodded, then felt the weight of her next words. "After that, we'll figure out a plan for our new friend Creed."

"Oooh. Good." Cynda wiggled her butt as she hurriedly cleaned off the big round wooden platform that doubled as a worktable. "I hope it involves full physical examination."

Irritation surged through Riana, catching her off guard.

"I bet you do," she managed clumsily as Cynda took off her shoes and climbed on the platform.

Riana's hands shook as she picked up the folder from the floor and removed the bag of trace skin evidence. Her crescent pendant bounced against her sweater as she straightened herself again, and she thought of Mother Yana.

A waxing moon, she had told Riana in Russian the day she gave it to her. *Small, yes, but growing stronger every day. Trust yourself. Believe in your instincts. Leave behind your losses, your tragedies, and you, too, will grow to banish darkness.*

It had been a long time since Riana almost lost control of her emotions, even for a moment. If an earth-loving Sibyl let her feelings get away from her, the results were invariably disastrous. Damage from wind and fire could be extreme, but only an earth Sibyl could break the foundations of the ground itself. Early in her training, Riana had been made to visit chasms and pits that once boasted cities, not to mention caves and faults that once were solid mountains. Imagining that level of destruction drove home the need for rigid self-discipline.

"I am the mortar," she whispered to herself. "The stone bowl that holds us all."

Merilee and Cynda needed the stabilizing force of her earth energy. She couldn't fail them. She couldn't fail the Sibyls—her only family.

Motherhouse Russia graduates always worked with the earth, always chose and led the triads. She would not allow herself to be distracted by a strange creature with black flame eyes. Not now, with Asmodai activity coming into the open in her city, and the Legion changing tactics for the first time in the century they had been tracked and engaged by the Sibyls.

Cynda apparently hadn't noticed Riana's consternation. The Irish communications expert had raised her arms and started her chant to reach the Motherhouses. She danced a circle slowly on the table, her image reflected in their collection of projective mirrors, as the wind chimes rang softly over her head. At first, her movements produced only little tinkles and a musical clattering. Then, slowly, slowly, drawing off the heat of Cynda's inner fire, the noise became more rhythmic. Sparks danced along the table's carved and lead-lined lip, and little flames licked upward. Good pestle that she was, Cynda let her fire grow until her strength ground open the ancient channels of sound, and she began to ring the chimes.

Like a conference call, Riana thought. *Only this one can't be hijacked or overheard.*

They all had the skills to send basic messages through their tattoos and through objects that rang, but only Sibyls from Motherhouse Ireland could handle complex communications—and do so reliably, in such grand fashion.

Mist shrouded three of the projective mirrors. After a few more seconds, students from each Motherhouse stepped forward to receive Cynda's messages. Riana saw Motherhouse Ireland's green robes first, followed by Motherhouse Greece's cerulean blue. The brown of Motherhouse Russia took longer to become distinct, because protections were much stronger and older along those lines.

As the chimes transporting Cynda's messages to the Mothers began to ring, Riana headed into the kitchen, then down the marble stairs into the waiting embrace of the earth. She felt instantly soothed by the dark, quiet pressure behind the concrete and marble walls, and pleased by the peaceful earth tones of her own choosing. She stopped first at the right of the stairs and went into her bedroom to change into lab clothes, then headed to her small private kitchen for a bottle of water. After centering herself and managing to go five whole minutes without thinking about Creed Lowell or his eyes, she left the bedroom, opened the door on the other side of the stairs, and stepped into the expansive reaches of her underground laboratory.

Sibyl Motherhouses spared no expense when it came to archiving, communication, or research, the three pillars of their main duty in the world: saving the untrained, the weak, and the innocent from the supernaturally strong. Riana had access to the fastest and most modern equipment available. She even had access to machines and procedures not yet discovered or perfected by the untrained. Soft gleams of silver and glowing green-and-red displays gave the laboratory a secret light all its own. She almost hated to ruin it by turning on the overheads, but time was short. She had samples to analyze, and later, no matter what she thought about it, a dangerous creature to capture and interrogate.

3

The last work session after nightfall didn't start well. The Sibyls weren't on recon duty, but Riana knew they had more than enough to keep them busy.

She settled herself on the sofa, still a little full from dinner, armed with a sheaf of lab values and analyses. Cynda had a stack of communications notebooks spread on both sides, and Merilee was late coming down from upstairs. When the historian made her appearance, her olive skin looked distinctly pale.

"We've got problems," they all said at once.

"Me first." Riana handed copies of her salt analyses and skin sample analysis to her triad sisters, who dutifully glanced at them. As Merilee scribbled an archive number on her copy and made an entry in her archive log, Riana summarized the first part.

"The salt was definitely fresh, purified for ritual. From what I can tell from the metal deposits left on the skin, the dagger was a double-S curved blade, made of treated silver and locked by all four elements, so regular police forensics won't be able to analyze it." She paused, took a breath, and waited for Merilee and Cynda to look at her. When they did, she added the rest of the uncomfortable information. "I estimate the blade was made in the fourth century or before, Proto-Slavic, and it was an object of power. I bet it was stolen from the Volgograd collection, maybe parts not on display. And according to printouts I got from Motherhouse Ireland, the cuts on the boy were made in a classic containment pattern. When he died, his blood would have flowed in a circle around him and stayed close. Worse, his essence, his life energy, wouldn't have been able to leave his body. Somebody could have . . . collected it somehow. The energy and the blood."

"Shit," Cynda said.

At the same time, Merilee said, "So the Legion didn't just steal an object of power. They probably *used* it—and to collect the blood and life essence of an innocent."

"What the hell are they up to?" Cynda thrust her notebook forward. "The Mothers reported other child-murders, in at least fifteen countries. Probably more we don't know about yet. They want us to double recon runs and take out as many Asmodai as we can, and pull out all the stops in trying to capture a member of the Legion. We've *got* to get more information. And, they want us to get into the Latch case, to find out every possible detail and report back as soon as we can. For some reason, this murder, our murder, troubles them the most."

Merilee sat up straighter. "Did they say why?"

"Of course not." Cynda snorted. "Do they ever?"

Riana scratched her shorthand version of these latest instructions into her smaller, portable notebook, and numbered them for importance—Legion capture first, Latch case second, Asmodai recon and destruction third. She flipped a page, and she had started notes on a plan to lure and trap Creed Lowell when Merilee said, "I think I know why they're so upset about this murder."

Riana glanced up, then put her notebook down.

Merilee was definitely pale, and she looked both perplexed and miserable.

Cynda tapped her pen on her own portable notebook. "Well? Spill it!"

Merilee offered three sets of documents, one at a time. "According to the latest press releases, the main suspects in Jacob Latch's murder were one of Latch's employees, an assistant—and the boy's own father, Senator Davin Latch. Then we have his wife, Raven, and Latch's chief opponent in the senatorial race. It's Alisa's husband, Ri. It's Corey James."

"Alisa from the North Bronx triad." Riana didn't miss Merilee's subtleties, and her anxiety climbed a notch. "You said *were*. These *were* the suspects. Have they narrowed the list?"

After a deep breath, Merilee slid a fourth set of documents across the table, this one amazingly thick. "Here's the last dossier, the one on Alisa."

Riana felt the color drain from her own face. She grabbed the dossier and flipped to the first photo—well, a photo of a painting, on a blurry reproduced page. Merilee would have pulled the information from her set of master volumes. Each triad archivist had a set. In the old days, pages had been hand-copied. Now they did, at least, allow the convenience of copy machines—when they could get the stupid machines to work properly. The one in Merilee's library always made blurry pages, but there could be no mistaking the powerful lines of Alisa's aristocratic face.

Merilee's expression turned unusually sympathetic. "I know she trained with you in Russia. Graduated a few years ahead, got permission to marry about ten years ago . . ."

Cynda whistled. "They've got a Sibyl for a suspect."

"She can't be involved." Riana's fingers clenched on the dossier, wrinkling the pages. "A murder, for the sake of the Goddess. There's never been a recorded case of a Sibyl participating in a perverted ritual."

"The police questioned the Latch's assistant, but let him go because he was out of town. Alisa admitted to being at the house, and they matched her prints to some at the scene." Merilee sounded like she was apologizing instead of informing. "Prints in blood, I mean. I found it in the headlines from this afternoon, and hacked this out of NYPD's intranet." She held up what looked like an e-mail and shook it. "They found some additional partials they couldn't identify, also in the blood. They're running tests on the type of sea salt used—Alisa just got back last week from a trip to Cape Cod." Merilee lowered the paper. "They've arrested her, Ri."

"What?" Riana shot to her feet and dropped the paper-clipped stack. Pages scattered in every direction as her face heated to fine blaze. "We need every trained Sibyl on the streets killing Asmodai and tracking the Legion. Alisa's one of the best fighters in New York!"

"Raven Latch is throwing a fit and saying the NYPD made a horrible mistake," Merilee said. "She wants bail set right now so she can pay it."

Cynda's eyes sparkled as she grinned and rubbed her hands together. "What are we going to do? Bust her out? I've always wanted to break into a jail. I bet I could use their phone and electrical systems to—"

Riana's tattoo suddenly warmed and moved against her skin, demanding and urgent. Cynda and Merilee grabbed their own wrists as Riana grabbed hers.

The simple communication came through forcefully.

Danger.

Danger.

At the same time, the bronze chimes near the front door began to ring.

All other sound in the room ceased immediately.

Riana did her best to slow her racing heart, to concentrate. She only picked up a few words, but Cynda translated almost immediately.

"Asmodai in our quarter. The South Manhattan triad picked it up. They think it's heading straight for us."

"For our house?" Merilee was stripping off her jeans and shirt in record time as she hopped toward the closet to get their leathers. "Creed Lowell! Has to be. He sent one after us."

"Tell South Manhattan to back off," Riana said. "If the Asmodai's bent on destroying us, it may succeed. Tell them to watch, but don't put themselves in harm's way. We can't risk losing too many in one fight. Not now."

Cynda gave her a look but complied, then quickly changed into the black leather bodysuit, boots, and gloves that would protect her from some of the Asmodai's energy. She belted on her sword while Merilee checked her bow and slung her quiver over her shoulder. Riana tucked her hair into her face mask. She belted on her knives—elemental iron containing trapped fire, air, earth, and water—just like Cynda's sword and the tips of Merilee's arrows.

Without discussion, they all rolled down their masks until only their eyes were visible. The masks also had small perforations around the nose and mouth, but exposed flesh was vulnerable flesh. The holes were very small.

Riana saw Merilee fight back her instant panic at such confinement. It was harder for air-lovers. Cynda had no reaction to the bodysuit one way or another.

I'm not afraid of anything that burns, she had told Riana the day they met. *And that includes you.*

Riana felt protected by her leathers, as if she had slipped into a glove made of the night itself. Indeed, when they eased out of the now-dark house to take up positions on the street, none of the untrained passersby even noticed them.

Communicating through hand signals, Cynda said, *Alley.*

Asmodai kept to dark, unnoticed places and concealed their movements. The alley made the most sense for an approach, unless the thing was bold enough to barrel across Central Park.

Riana nodded her agreement and saw Merilee begin to move toward the alley on the left of their brownstone. Riana signaled her to stop, to take up watch in the tree directly across the street, just inside the park's wall. Merilee changed course immediately, darted unseen through moving cars, and catlike climbed into the tree's waiting branches.

Air-lovers fought best from aboveground, and archers had the best chance of taking down a foe with a single shot.

They usually led battles—or swept up the mess. Riana couldn't risk any messes, so she left Merilee—the triad's broom—there in the tree, in that last protective position.

Cynda, giving off a subtle but definite smoke, led the charge into the alley. She moved so fast Riana had difficulty catching up, but she managed to pace her after a few running steps.

The alley, long and dark, had a few dumpsters and a handful of fire escapes. Otherwise, it was a collection of service tunnels joined by smooth, black pavement. Two service lights illuminated either end, leaving the center shadowed.

After a quick gesture to indicate her plan, Cynda pulled down the lower steps of a fire escape, climbed up, then pulled up the steps while Riana pushed them from the ground. Nimble as always, Cynda hopped from iron staircase to iron staircase, until she reached the center of the alley. Riana stayed where she was and faded behind one of the dumpsters to wait for warning of the Asmodai's approach.

She didn't have to wait long.

The service lights at the far end of the alley flared, then went out.

Riana narrowed her eyes and allowed her trained perceptions to take over, sifting through the darkness, through the suddenly distant sounds of the city, until she found . . .

There.

A scrape. An off-kilter rustling. Sounds that didn't quite belong, that felt wrong to her powerful instincts.

The faint smell of sulfur drifted through the alley.

Goddess. It's made of fire.

A soft, low "Shit," from Cynda, somewhere above, confirmed that perception.

At that instant, a blue-black jet of fire erupted from below Cynda's fire escape.

It struck the metal, heating it to red almost instantly.

The bottom stairs pinched off like wet clay and sizzled onto the alley pavement.

Riana barely had time to register Cynda swinging desperately up, up, to get out of range before a hot jet struck the other side of the dumpster.

Riana propelled herself headfirst away from the melting metal, flipped, rolled to her feet, and drew her daggers. Heart pounding, she called on the trapped fire inside the weapons, and both daggers blazed in response. Fire ran along the iron, outlining the wicked curve of the blades.

The light cast by the burning daggers illuminated a man standing, arms raised, dead center in the otherwise dark alley. A normal-looking man in a normal-looking black overcoat, nice slacks, a silk shirt, decent tie, and polished shoes—except this man's body seemed to shift in and out of different features. One second a thin, tall being. The next shorter, fatter. The next, more feminine. Riana knew if she got close enough to see its face, she would want to scream. Human, yet not human. Purposeful, yet utterly slack and vacant. And the eyes. If she looked into the eyes of a fire Asmodai, she would find only burning hollows.

When the creature fixed on Riana, black fire shot from its hands.

She ducked and let the heat slam against the bricks behind her.

The gut-punch sound of cracking stone made her wince.
Son of a bitch.

This thing *had* been sent to destroy them. If it had been on some other mission, it would have ignored them even as they destroyed it. Somewhere on its person, then, would be things the triad had touched, along with the talisman left by the creature's maker to keep it under control. If it completed its task without being destroyed, it would use that talisman to return to its maker.

More fire shot in her direction.

She feinted left and the fire slammed into the melted remnants of the dumpster.

Cynda picked that moment to leap down behind the

Asmodai. Her sword blazed with brilliant orange flames, the height and intensity of the fire outlining her body.

So much for another leather jumper.

"Hey, hell-breath!" Cynda yelled.

The Asmodai whirled at the sound of another one of its targets.

Riana charged up behind it as Cynda parried a blast of fire with her long double-edged sword.

Deflected flame cracked another chunk of bricks, and a few loose pieces rained down on the Asmodai.

It covered its head.

Riana reached it and rammed one of her daggers deep in its back.

A little to the right. Missed the heart!

She jerked it out and jammed the second blade home just as the Asmodai started to turn.

Her second dagger struck the man-thing full in the ribs.

The hot impact of her dagger against a fire Asmodai blazed up her left arm and she had to let go of the dagger hilt.

The creature struck at her and she barely got her remaining dagger up in time to absorb some of the blow. Heat coursed over her bodysuit, melting layers of protections into so much twisted, lumpy char. Another couple of hits and it would cook her like bacon.

Cynda had taken her stance. Riana saw and dropped low to give her triad sister a clear shot at the Asmodai's head.

Riana also reached within herself, to that core of power and connection to the earth, to her legacy. Her awareness of her feet on the ground, of the stones and dirt all around her doubled, tripled. Cautiously but deliberately, she loosed a controlled fragment of her own earth power, rattling the ground beneath the creature.

It stumbled. Fell to its knees.

Cynda's strike would be easier than a practice-hack.

At that second, something slammed into Riana and knocked her down. Her dagger went flying. Pain ricocheted through her hands, wrists, and knees as she fell hard on the asphalt. Her control slipped. The ground rattled hard, then rumbled and bucked.

What the hell?

A second Asmodai?

A human helper?

Why hadn't her instincts warned her?

A full-blown earthquake built under New York's Upper East Side.

"No, no, no!" Wheezing from the shock and strain, Riana fought to focus, to calm her mind and fold the energy back under her conscious control.

She was dimly aware of a large, dark shape grappling with the Asmodai. The damn Asmodai still had its head. Cynda hadn't been able to take her swing.

And Cynda—where was she?

Screaming and swearing, that much Riana could hear.

Good. At least she was still alive.

A few seconds later, Riana managed to quell the tremors in the earth, to pull back the power she had accidentally released. The sensation almost suffocated her, but she did it.

"You've got to be kidding me," Cynda yelled. "You can't just punch the thing in its nose, asshole!"

Fire cracked brick.

More fire turned a piece of fire escape into a molten puddle.

The air smelled like sulfur and burned hair.

Riana lunged forward, grabbed her dagger and renewed its flames, then staggered to her feet just in time to see Cynda kick the hell out of something and send it slamming against a hot, chipped brick wall.

Then she found herself almost nose to chest with the Asmodai.

It raised both hands to crush her skull and burn her to death at the same time.

"Not happening." Hand shaking, she drove her dagger

up, up into its chest cavity. She felt the blade strike the drumming center, the heart, right where she had intended.

At that same second, the flaming tip of a whistling arrow drove between the creature's eyes.

Riana had only a moment to process this before Cynda yelled, "Fore!" and the thing's head went flying off.

Instantly, the mass of the creature evaporated. Merilee's arrow and Riana's trapped dagger clattered to the alley pavement, but she kept hold of the other dagger in her hand.

The thing's clothing—some pieces of it draped over Riana's arm from the instant the thing vanished—caught fire.

"Bastard!" She yanked her arm back and sent a rush of earthy energy over the sizzling spots, with immediate effects.

She pulled up her leather face mask as the rest of the clothing, some of it no doubt the talisman used by the creature's master to control it, burned in seconds. Little blue-black flames danced until there was nothing left except her dagger, the arrow—and a slightly charred soda can.

She kicked the dagger and arrow to the side, bathed the curved blade on the ground with a little cooling earth energy, then tended to the dagger in her hand. When she finished, she sheathed both weapons.

Cynda pulled off her nearly ruined face mask. Freckled skin peeking through the holes burned in her bodysuit, she leaned down and tapped the blackened soda can with her still-glowing sword. "Diet, with lipstick on the rim." She looked up at Riana. "It's yours. Motherfucking Legion gave the Asmodai our *trash* to target us? Come on. That's cheating."

Merilee, face mask dangling from one hand, came running up chanting, "My kill, my kill, my kill."

"Excuse me?" Riana turned on Merilee as Merilee retrieved her arrow. "I got it first."

Cynda said, "You're both dreaming. That was my kill."

Something groaned.

Riana and Merilee turned toward the alley wall.

"Oh, yeah." Cynda pointed her cooling blade toward a dark shape lying on the ground. "That freak charged in here and tried to fistfight the Asmodai, if you can believe that. Help me get him inside."

"No rest for the weary," Merilee muttered.

Riana's heart gave a strange buck, not unlike the ground she had accidentally rattled too hard.

She knew that black hair, that leather blazer. She'd been thinking about them all day long.

Creed Lowell stirred and let out another groan, this one louder than the first.

Cynda nudged her shoulder. "Come on, fearless leader. You can moon over the cute demon-man's eyes *after* we tie him up."

(4)

Creed dreamed that he was standing naked in a forest. Standing on some sort of smooth, polished wood. His knees gave, and he stumbled forward. A warm wind caught him, caressed him like dozens of fingers, gentle enough to make him groan, yet firm enough to hold him upright. A soft, teasing breeze lifted his cock oh-so-slowly—

Knock it off, Merilee.

But it's got to be eight inches, Cynda. Eight inches and he's not even aroused. Look at it.

Don't make me burn your hair again.

Confused, Creed twisted away from the breeze as best he could. He didn't like the touch. It wasn't . . . right. Not the right scent, either.

The breeze dropped Creed's cock and grew stronger, lifting his arms high above his head and crossing them.

Metal cuffs snapped shut around his wrists.

Handcuffs.

His handcuffs?

His ring started to vibrate. The wind stopped.

He fell forward and jerked against the cuffs, but his arms stayed in place. When he tried to open his eyes, his head throbbed. Were his lids glued shut? He moved his thick tongue against the grit in his mouth. He felt like he had eaten a brick whole, only bothering to chew the bigger bits.

Roots and vines—no—colder—harder—chains? Chains snaked around his ankles and pulled his feet sideways, in opposite directions. This time when he lost his balance, Creed barely moved. He was standing in some weird parade-rest position, hands high, and he couldn't open his eyes.

What the hell?

Unbearably warm sunlight licked across his back and his ass.

Cynda. You'll hurt him.

So? I swear you've gone soft, Riana.

Whatever he is—

It. We don't know that it's human.

Fine. Whatever it is, don't cause him—it—pain for no reason. Get off the table. I'll handle him myself.

I bet you will.

Creed's ass quit burning. The pounding in his head doubled. God, he wanted some water. Better yet, a cold beer. Two or three of them.

Hands prodded his neck, his chest, his arms, lingering on the thick scar that ran from his left shoulder to his left elbow.

Creed's skin started to burn again, but this time the fire came from inside.

These were the right hands. Yes.

Fingers brushed his scar again, and the smell of fresh rain and lavender washed through his senses. Spring storms. Flowers in a field, just after a summer downpour.

A band stretched first around his head, then his neck. Something tickled as it drew along the length of his arms, then ringed his chest, then his ass, then his left thigh, and the right one, too.

Measuring tape?

"Are you measuring me?" he muttered.

The band whipped away. All tickling stopped.

"Not yet," a woman said from behind him. "We're not ready."

"Then get ready," said a second woman. "Hurry!"

Creed jerked against his cuffs, and metal clanked on metal. He tried to ask for water, but only coughed.

A hand—a soft hand with very, very sharp nails—closed around his cock.

Wind chimes tinkled softly, seemingly from everywhere at once.

Wind chimes.

Shit!

His ring seemed to buzz against his skin.

Creed forced his eyes open.

Light stabbed into his awareness. He squinted and swayed against his bonds, and the fingers on his cock tightened. The *other* inside Creed tried to rise, but its energy seemed oddly thick and restrained. Creed snarled and yanked against the cuffs.

"Give it up, cowboy," said that sultry voice Creed had been thinking about since the moment he first heard it. "You're grounded. Literally."

The hand on his cock moved, slipping like silk from tip to base, then cupping his sensitive sac. Creed's mind cleared in one big hurry.

Riana's crescent pendant came into focus, then her bright green eyes, along with her nose and those red, red lips, close enough to kiss. He would have kissed her, too, on impulse, if he hadn't been chained to her ceiling. She was smiling in that knowing way.

Once more, she had him by the balls.

Which, by the way, were still tender from his earlier encounter with her.

This time she wasn't squeezing them until they hurt. She toyed with his sac instead, kneading gently, gently, leaning so close he could smell leather and fire from the battle he vaguely remembered charging into—and getting his head busted.

Despite his pain and confusion, Creed's cock got hard so fast his teeth clenched. His back tensed. He wanted to thrust forward, feel her fingers on his throbbing shaft again.

Riana seemed to read his mind.

With a smile that would have killed a lesser man, she gripped his cock. Eyes locked on his, she palmed the soft underside, then ran her fingernails down his swollen length. Creed could swear each nail left a trail of fiery sparks. All the moisture in his body dropped southward, engorging his erection.

When she brushed her nails across the tip, he almost came like a schoolboy.

At that second, he became aware of someone else in the room. A woman. Two women. And something was burning his ass.

Actually burning. God!

His eyes watered from the pain, but his erection refused to wither.

"Done," said the redhead, Cynda. As she stepped around the table where he could see her and lowered her hands, the flame-hot feeling on his ass died away. "You can quit distracting him now, Riana."

Creed's gut dropped as Riana let go of his cock, but she held his gaze for another mind-wrenching second. In that moment, no matter how firmly he was chained or what she planned to do to him, Creed wanted Riana more than he had ever wanted anything in his life.

I have lost my mind.

As if in agreement, Riana turned her back on him and stepped over a ring of wet earth and flames no higher than her ankles.

A ring of fire burning in a metal-lined groove on a platform.

No. A table.

Creed realized he was standing on the big wooden table in the candlelit living room of Riana Dumain's brownstone. The ring of earth and fire were contained in the metal-lined trench around the table's lip.

Another step took Riana down off the table, so that her head was level with his cock. When she turned around, she eyed him from head to foot. He imagined her climbing back on the table, walking over to him, kneeling, and taking him deep in her silky throat. His erection went from painful to unbearable.

At least whatever was burning his ass decided to back off.

"Look, I don't know what's going on, but you don't want to do this—whatever it is you're planning, I mean." Creed noticed candlelight flickering in mirrors on the walls, but a lot of the mirrors had been covered. "I'm not as safe as I look."

Weird. A lot of the chimes had been tied with a single cord, too, rendering them silent. *Closed,* his mind corrected, though he had no idea why.

"You don't have to be safe," Riana said, her voice almost a purr. "We like dangerous."

Creed's cock bucked.

I might be in trouble here.

His besotted senses slowly processed the blond woman, Merilee, to his left and a little behind him. On his right, also a little behind him, was Cynda. All three were dressed in black leather jumpsuits, though Cynda's was more melted shreds than real covering. Her wild smile made him wish he could cover his cock. Women like Cynda liked to bite. Hard.

All three women stared at him, but Riana's gaze was so intent he felt it like fierce, sweaty strokes all over his body.

He groaned and his cock jerked again. The chains around his ankles rattled, and the shackles above his head clinked together. When he looked up, he saw that his hands indeed had been secured by his own handcuffs, which had been passed through the links of a formidable chain secured to one of the ceiling beams.

Talk about a wet dream gone completely wrong . . .

Grounded. That's what Riana had told him. So the

table's little groove had been packed with earth, water, fire, and a little air for good measure. And yeah, that was probably lead in the groove, to contain all the elements.

If he got loose, he could cross it, since he was mostly human.

Maybe.

This is not good.

Real power. That's what Creed saw in that ring of damp dirt and fire. After all the years of searching for something supernatural outside of himself and Dominic, everything was happening at once. The Latch murder, the weird museum break-in, Riana and her tattoo, her freaky friends, that—that—whatever it was in the alley . . .

"Be careful what you wish for," he said, voice cracking in his parched throat. "I mean it—you need to get me down from here before something bad happens."

"Oooh. We're afraid." Riana winked at him and folded her arms. "Tell us what you are, and we'll get you some water."

Creed stared at her. This was not good, for real. His perceptions started to speed up and expand. Bad. Very bad. They had no idea what he kept inside him, and he didn't even know how to tell them.

"What are you?" Riana repeated.

Creed's fists clenched, and he wanted to rip himself free. With his senses heightened, he could smell her lavender scent and her woman's musk like he had his face buried in it. He wanted to switch places with her, send the other two packing, peel off that leather bodysuit, and take his time running his tongue over every perfect inch of Riana Dumain.

Goddamn. My friggin' cock is going to fall off if I don't stop.

He did his best to swallow and prime his throat. "What are *you*? Some sort of witch? A Siren, maybe?"

Riana sighed and moved clockwise away from him, until

she stood where Merilee had been. Merilee's reflection replaced Cynda's, and Cynda stood directly in front of him. Her green eyes took on the color of fire itself, and the flames ringing the table grew an inch or two.

Creed wished Riana would move back into his line of sight. He needed to convince her that he was serious, that this little interrogation was a potentially fatal idea. But he felt a heaviness in his feet, a lightness in his head and hands, and heat spreading upward from his cock, through his gut and chest.

"What are you?" Cynda asked. Only, to Creed's enhanced perception the sound of her voice was more like the crackle of fire blazing out of control. Unsettling. Infuriating. The *other* clawed at the inside of his skin, wanting out, wanting to rage, but it fell back as if something had struck it between the eyes. Creed's mind screeched back to normal speed, normal senses, normal understanding of the absolute weirdness around him.

At least the unnerving sensation finally deflated his cock. Creed had no time to enjoy the relief, however.

Cynda moved.

Merilee stood in front now, Riana to the right, and fire-bitch on the left. Merilee's tanned skin gave her an aura of delicate beauty, but a wicked flicker in the depths of her blue eyes told Creed that this one might be the most dangerous of all.

Riana. Where was Riana? His dizziness got worse. His head—God. Any second now, it would snap off his neck and float to the ceiling.

"What are you?" Merilee asked. Or did Merilee actually say the words? It seemed like the wind made the sound. The wind roaring in his ears.

Another shift. Riana again.

Total relief. Creed tried to focus on her, to speak up about the very real danger inside him, but he felt such a heaviness he wondered if his wrists would tear through the cuffs suspending his arms. Riana stared at him, her gaze at first distant, then knife-sharp and piercing.

Did he see uncertainty in those beautiful green gems?

If so, it vanished quickly.

The table shook beneath his heavier than heavy feet.

"What are you?" Riana's mouth asked, but Creed heard the question in the deep, terrifying bass of the earth itself, groaning as it turned, turned, turned under the sun's blazing gaze.

Creed's thoughts crumbled. His muscles convulsed. His throat worked against his will. "Creed Lowell. NYPD. OCU. Detective Second Grade."

His vision blurred.

A harpy made out of fire stood in front of him. Then a creature made of air, and finally, a woman-shaped being sculpted out of dirt and leaves.

What are you?

What *are* you?

What are *you?*

He feverishly gave his address. His birthday. Repeated his name and profession. Said he was dangerous, told them they needed to get him down and get him out of their house. Told them his relationship to Dominic. He even gave the name of his dead mother Grace, and his grandmother Delilah. And still they asked.

What are you?

"Human," he muttered, even though he didn't mean to. "And something bad. Something *other*. Don't know—can't explain. Let me go before it gets out."

The pressures on his body and mind eased. Gentle hands caressed his shoulders and face. "Stay awake."

Riana's voice and touch roused him, brought him back from the edge of some dark, twisted place. He forced his eyes open, tried to hold her gaze, but she was gone before he even got oriented.

The questions started again.

Stop, he pleaded in his mind, as if Riana could hear him. *This won't end like you think. In the name of everything sane, stop!*

Did he say any of that aloud? The *other* was rising again, getting stronger now, like an unstoppable wave of bile and heat and hatred. If it broke loose, if it changed him, would the grounding circle be enough to stop it?

Fuck.

Would Riana be inside the circle when it happened?

His ring hummed and jerked against the skin of his finger. Everything got louder, brighter. Colors flowed from the women—lavender around Riana, red around Cynda, and golden around Merilee. The colors shimmered and twinkled until he almost closed his eyes to get away from them.

The room around Creed swam and rippled. He stopped paying attention to anything other than controlling the energy inside him. The *other* had only ripped free against his will a few times before, always with the ring off, and oh, God. He had to keep that from happening.

"Don't," he tried to say—did he? Could he? "Dangerous. I'm bad. It's bad. You don't understand—"

Creed couldn't make sense of much else, until someone gave him another drink of water. Someone with sweet green eyes, who gazed at him with mercy and horror all at once.

His heart crashed against his ribs.

"Riana." He tried to reach for her, but his hands were still bound. "You have to stop. And get out of the circle. I'm not safe."

He took another gulp of the water she offered. "I don't know if the grounding will hold it—get away from me."

She looked down, then climbed off the table again. But she didn't go far enough. Not nearly far enough.

"Move!" Creed bellowed, struggling with the unnatural energy rising through his body.

"We're perfectly secure," said someone from behind

him. Probably Cynda, but he didn't know for sure. "You're the one who should worry."

The women started to move clockwise, walking, walking the room into a spin, and Creed sank into confusion once more. New questions came, along with more heat, more dizziness, more heaviness, until the voices joined, stronger than time, older than reality.

What kind of other? they demanded. God, so loud. It hurt his head. Pounded his brain.

"A bad one," Creed mumbled, and he knew he couldn't refuse to answer. He wasn't even sure he was still standing up, but he had to be, right? The *other* flailed, and Creed imagined himself holding that untamed energy by the throat. He would not let it out. Not now. No way.

Does Andy know what you are?

Andy. Protect Andy. "No."

Who sent you?

"I sent me." He needed more water. He needed to lie down. Was he lying down?

Why did you come here tonight?

Creed blinked at the distant shapes of mirrors. Colors swirled from one piece of glass to the next, surrounding him, holding him inside the brilliance, forcing him to speak. "To see Riana."

Riana. Yes. Riana. Control the *other*. Don't let it harm her. That's what he intended—to control himself, and keep her—keep all of them—safe.

Did you make the Asmodai?

"Asmodai." Colors. Too many colors. Was the water drugged? "What's an Asmodai?"

Are you one of the Legion?

"I'm NYPD. OCU. Detective Second—"

Are you one of the Legion?

"Legion of what?"

Who was talking to him now? Which woman? Was Riana still in the room? Creed fought to regain his mental balance, but reality shimmered at the edge of his thoughts. The *other* shredded at his gut, charred his throat, his blood, his consciousness, but he had it contained until one question stabbed into the center of his mind.

Where did you get that ring?

The *other* surged forward so fast and so hard that Creed lurched into full awareness.

He was still on the table. Fire still burned atop the earth in the lead groove on the table, and someone had added a bit more water. A breeze made the tops of the flames twitch, and the light seemed to blaze in the few uncovered mirrors reflecting the room and the women who had him captive. A single wind chime in front of the door tinkled softly, like a faraway admonition.

Riana stood inside the circle, only inches away from him. Her face shimmered in the candlelight. Sweat glistened on her forehead. "The ring," she repeated. "The crest of the Legion. Where did you get it?"

Anger and fear dug at Creed, wounding his insides almost as much as the *other*. His mind speeded up again, and his senses spread out across the room. Merilee smelled like the ocean and fresh rain. Cynda, like fire and smoke and light sandalwood. Neither woman was aroused.

Riana was, but she was holding herself back. Creed breathed deeply, taking in the rich aroma of her juices, the hints of jasmine clinging to the dark curls around her face. He tried to speak, his heart to hers.

"Go." He jerked away as far as he could move. "It's always been mine. Don't touch it."

His voice, but not his voice. The *other* was coming.

Riana stepped even closer to him.

"Get back," Creed heard himself snarl. "Now!"

"Take the damned thing and get it over with," Cynda said. "I'm tired. And way past hungry."

"Leave . . . the . . . ring . . . alone," Creed managed through clenched teeth. Between exhaustion, increasing pain in his wrists and arms, the muddling questions, the spinning room, and the roaring of the *other* in his mind, he thought he might crack down the center.

Riana once more locked her eyes on his.

She seemed to be considering. Weighing his statement. Perhaps doubting herself a fraction.

Creed did his best to put all of his emotions into his gaze. "Don't, Riana."

Her lips trembled into a frown. "I'm sorry," she said at last, her pained voice so quiet he barely heard it. "I have to."

Riana stretched up on her toes, reached forward, and gripped his manacled hand. Her leather-covered chest pressed into his neck. Her chin brushed his lips.

So soft. So beautiful. God, he didn't want to kill her.

Creed tried to jerk his hand back, but the chains held him fast. Before he could think of a way to stop her, Riana grasped his finger and tugged at his signet ring.

In absolute desperation, Creed lifted his head and crushed his mouth against hers.

Sweet, incredibly sweet.

Feminine, angry, powerful.

He could taste so much in her. He wanted to taste so much more. The hot shock of the kiss rocked him, and as she tried to pull back, Creed captured her bottom lip with his teeth and wouldn't let her go.

Riana's mind reeled.

The exquisite pleasure-pain of his bite nearly made her senses explode.

She couldn't help but lean forward, couldn't help but give her mouth back to Creed, and Creed really kissed her then, pushing forward, pressing his naked flesh against her body as his tongue found hers. She felt him everywhere at once, like bone-deep lightning. He tasted like salt and sex and smelled of cedar and mandarin and sweat—one-hundred-percent male, and completely human.

Riana moaned and pressed one hand against his shoulder. The other hand found his incredible erection.

Still, he kissed her. She couldn't breathe. Didn't want to breathe.

Dizzy, she dug her nails into his neck as people yelled at her, seemingly from thousands of miles away.

Wind buffeted her back. Heat bit at her fingers, and Creed tore his mouth away from hers, cursing.

A jet of flame receded, and a veritable tornado of wind calmed instantly. The smell of singed hair lingered in the air.

"I swear to the Goddess," Cynda yelled. "Get the ring, Riana!"

Riana stepped back from Creed, grappling for her focus and balance. She tried to ignore the strain of her nipples against the leather of her jumpsuit. She tried to pretend she wasn't so wet the leather chafed her thighs when she moved. This man *wasn't* completely human. He was something *other* by his own admission—but she couldn't convince her body of that simple truth.

His cock had felt like molten steel in her hand, and the way he had kissed her, like he wanted to drive that cock into her until she screamed . . .

She had almost moaned again, just at the thought.

After an hour staring at his chiseled chest, watching the way the wild locks of his hair dusted his shoulders, tracing that interesting scar on his left arm with her eyes, studying the perfection of his rock-solid thighs—and now, after that kiss—damn, that kiss! It actually hurt her to do what he asked her not to do.

Cynda started ranting again, but Riana couldn't fault her. Cynda was right. Enough bullshit.

Riana shook her head, then clamped her teeth together. In one fast, deliberately harsh motion, she slammed herself against Creed, stood on her toes, and got hold of the ring.

It felt hot to the touch, and she could swear it was vibrating.

She pulled at the thing, but Creed pulled back. His black eyes smoldered.

Another fierce tug, and Riana slipped the ring over his knuckle and into her palm.

Instantly, the tattoo on her arm got so hot she thought it might be scalding her. She shouted and grabbed her wrist, almost dropped the signet ring, but managed to keep hold of it. Cords tore off the wind chimes and their tuned pipes clattered and smashed together. All the uncovered mirrors cracked down the center. Metal groaned and stretched, and the table started to shake.

Riana cried out, then Cynda and Merilee had hold of her, yanking her out of the circle, dragging her off the table, falling with her to the floor. When she managed to get her head up and look back at Creed, she saw that he had broken the cuffs on his wrists and the chains on his ankles. He clenched his fists. His eyes closed and his teeth clamped together, as if he was spending every fiber of his being holding back something inside him.

Something awful.

The tense muscles of his chest shimmered.

And parted.

He literally separated along all the major lines of his body.

White-gold light blazed from every crack. He shouted once, a bass note of absolute frustration.

Riana couldn't get a full breath. She felt as if the brownstone's walls were crushing in on her, forcing all the air out of the world. Cynda and Merilee went absolutely still on the floor beside her as Creed Lowell changed—no—*transmogrified*—into a being made completely out of light and energy.

He—it—was still man-shaped, still muscled, like some sort of god who stepped from the clouds onto their living room table. This *other* was so tall its head brushed against the remnants of the cuffs and chain it had destroyed.

It reached up and gripped the chain. The metal links melted into a puddle at its feet.

"Oh, shit," Cynda whispered.

"Give him back the ring," Merilee said immediately. "We don't need it that badly. Fuck. My arrows are across the room."

"No arrows." Riana gulped air. Her hands dropped instinctively to the belt holding her daggers. A rattle and clatter told her Cynda had drawn her sword before even bothering to stand.

"No sword, either. Don't kill him—I mean, don't kill it—unless we have to."

"Yeah," Cynda muttered. "Sure."

The *other* made a noise in between a growl and a roar and bent down to examine the melted metal on the table.

Caught between a wish to run and a strong desire to cower, Riana made herself get up. Her knees shook as she moved, and she knew her hands were shaking, too.

She checked the grounding circle. It was still intact,

flames, water-soaked earth, and all. Somehow, Merilee was keeping a breeze weaving in and out of the flames. All secure. It should hold.

Right?

The *other* stood again, its golden head nearly touching the ceiling beam.

Riana glanced at the hardening puddle of metal that used to be a chain and some handcuffs. Her heart skipped and squeezed, and she swallowed again and again.

Fear.

No, terror.

She wasn't used to terror.

She squeezed the signet ring in her hand. The mortar, pestle, and broom on the inside of her arm burned hot enough to keep her mind from fragmenting, and the dark crescent moon in the center of her tattoo literally squirmed against her skin.

"Goddess, my arm hurts," Cynda murmured, then let out an amazing string of curses as Merilee pointed toward the door.

"The warning chimes. She's ringing them, but not for us."

Cynda was setting off chimes for other Sibyls, warning them away.

There's mortal danger here. Riana stared at the gleaming golden god-thing. She searched its face for some hint of the person she had met, the human being she had touched, the man she had wanted only a few minutes ago. *There's death in this house.*

The *other* seemed to be studying them as hard as they were studying it. It had no definite facial features, no eye color. And it didn't seem to know her at all.

"I always thought death would wear black," Riana said, almost to herself.

The *other* cocked its head.

It moved.

The table groaned beneath it, and the whole brownstone seemed to shake. The *other* stuck out its arm and knocked three covered mirrors off the nearby wall. They plummeted to the floor and shattered, leaving a dark, smoldering mark on the wall where the creature's hand—did it have a hand?—made contact.

"Stop!" Cynda leaped up and thrust her flame-ringed sword forward. Merilee reacted next, charging around the table to pick up her bow and nock an arrow.

The *other* paid them no heed. A single step took it off the table and out of the circle.

So much for grounding. Riana's thoughts fired automatically, offering her no comfort. *So much for the fearsome powers of the Sibyls. If this creature sneezes, our roof will fall in.*

The god-thing landed on the floor in front of her.

It was close enough to touch, and its energy vibrated across her skin until her teeth chattered. The floors shook. The remaining mirrors on the walls shook, too, and glass fell from the cracked ones.

Cynda cursed as she dodged a big shard. Merilee stood on the other side of the table without moving, bowstring taut, arrow aimed at the *other*'s head. The being smelled eye-wateringly sharp, like the air just before a devastating thunderstorm.

It wanted to kill her. Riana could tell. It wanted to tear her apart, eat the pieces, then clean house. Completely. Before its presence could overwhelm her, Riana drew one dagger and kept the signet ring tight in her other hand.

"Get back." She gestured with the dagger. "Now!"

To her immense surprise, the *other* shot backward as if she'd shoved it. Well, as if some giant three times her size had shoved it. It flowed more than leaped onto the table and changed size—first smaller, then taller, then thinner, then wider. In seconds, it became fully manlike again, tall and muscular, like some artist's marble sculpture of Apollo, bathed in electric sunlight. Only, Riana could tell by its almost-expression that it still wanted to tear her head off.

Something held it back.

But what?

Merilee adjusted her aim, keeping the deadly tip of her arrow trained on the thing's shimmering head. "It acts like an Asmodai," she said.

"With no human body, and lots bigger." Cynda positioned herself beside the table, sword raised for a lethal strike. "Honestly, Merilee, have you ever seen a golden Asmodai?"

"It's not an Asmodai," Riana said, though in truth, she wasn't sure. It did have some features in common with the demons.

And a little while ago, it was Creed. And a little while before that, I had my hand on its cock.

"I think it's doing what you say because you have the ring." Cynda shifted her weight back on one foot. "Tell it to do something, or let me cut its head off."

"Sit," said Merilee. "Stay. Roll over. Nice demon."

The *other*, still godlike in its form and size, let out a wall-shaking roar.

"Shut up, all of you!" Riana kept the dagger in front of her. Based on what Cynda said, she held out the ring, too.

The room had gone silent at her command.

To the *other*, she said, "Can you speak?"

It made no response.

"I should shoot it now," Merilee said. "It's dangerous."

Cynda stiffened. "Beheading's more certain."

Riana glared at them for a moment, then returned her attention to the *other*. "Sit down on the table."

The glowing god-thing hesitated, gave her another murderous almost-expression, then lowered its powerful shape to the table's surface. Hatred emanated from it as it stared at her hand, the one holding the ring. She sensed other emotions, too. Jumbled, indistinct—confusion? Fear? Resentment?

Cynda and her sword flamed and crackled. A breeze stirred constantly in Merilee's hair, aggravating the damaged wind chimes. Riana found herself holding her breath and counting to keep from allowing any of her power to escape. If the brownstone shook any more, the walls would crack. The neighbors might have called the police already, or the news media might be surging toward them to explore the earthquake focal zone at Sixty-third and Central Park.

She had no idea what to do next, and that pissed her off. She was never without answers. She couldn't be. She had to lead. She had to think of something before Cynda and Merilee killed the *other*—if they even could—or before it killed them.

I will not *lose my triad. I will* not *lose my family.*

The crescent pendant felt like a lead weight on her chest, and she felt the harsh, wary eyes of Mother Yana evaluating her, prodding her, even now.

The signet ring dug into her palm.

She glanced at her hand, then at the godlike golden creature.

"Put out your right hand," she commanded. "Let me see five fingers."

It seemed to glare from its constantly shifting eyes, but it complied.

Riana edged forward. She sheathed her dagger and held the ring on either side, with both hands.

The *other* growled.

"What are you doing?" Cynda shifted her weight again, looking all the more ready to whack the creature's head right off its shoulders.

Merilee stood still as a Greek carving. "Ri, don't give it the ring. Are you nuts?"

Riana shook her head once to silence them. Her heart pounded so hard she thought it would jump to her throat and choke her. If she was right, she would diffuse the situation. If she was wrong, the thing—Creed—would die—or it would eat her triad whole.

"Spread your fingers," she ordered.

The *other* grunted and spread five golden shafts of light.

"Riana . . ." Cynda sounded genuinely uncertain.

Riana kept her gaze squarely on the creature. "Be still," she told it. "Don't move until I give you permission."

The *other* gave off a wave of disgust and frustration, but it didn't so much as twitch.

Riana lunged forward and jammed the signet back on the thing's right ring finger, where Creed had worn it.

As Riana jumped back, Merilee sucked in a breath and muttered, "Oh, Goddess."

Cynda came around the table slowly, sword raised, until she stood beside Riana. Merilee moved around the other side of the table. She had lowered the bow, but her arrow was still at the ready.

Riana knew what they were thinking.

If we're about to die, let us die together.

She put one hand on Cynda's shoulder and the other on Merilee's arm and watched as the *other* began to shift.

Tall. Short. Wide. Thin. Manlike. Godlike. Huge, then tiny, huddled on the surface of the table like a child. A buzzing sound rasped against Riana's ears. She felt the vibration in her teeth, like the hum of powerful electric wires.

"Please," she whispered, even though she knew she had given up her command power with the ring. "Come on, Creed. Please."

The *other* stood and took on its more definite man-shape. Apollo again, only more normal in height, translucent and not quite real.

As Riana watched, the golden light began to fade. Bones showed through the light, like a radiographic image. Muscles attached to the bones. Skin formed and joined. More human. Then totally human. Well defined and handsome, with normal man-parts. The scar on Creed's left arm and his silky black hair came last.

The second he seemed completely solid, Creed fell to his knees on the table and bent forward, arms folded, left hand clasped around his right, covering the signet ring.

He seemed too weak to stay alive.

Riana ran forward and climbed onto the table, heedless of the dwindling fire and scattered earth that once formed the grounding circle. As if from a great distance, she heard Cynda and Merilee warning her to be careful, urging her to stay back.

Were they insane? Couldn't they see Creed couldn't even lift his own head, much less hurt her?

She knelt beside him on the table and touched his shoulder. Her palm rested against that thick, straight scar. He smelled like himself again, his human self. The cedar-mandarin scent comforted her even though his skin was clammy. He started to shake as if he was freezing to death.

"Get him a blanket," she called to Merilee, who was still standing with her bow and arrow in hand. Cynda gazed at Riana but didn't lower her sword.

"Put down your weapons and get him a blanket!" Riana turned back to Creed. "I think he's going into shock."

What have we done?

She stroked his arm, like that might keep him from changing or vanishing or dying right there in front of her. She wanted—needed—to apologize, but when she opened her mouth, she asked the same question they had started with, what seemed like a dozen years ago.

"What *are* you?"

Creed looked up at her, and the dark, haunted depths of his eyes tore at her heart. His quiet, agonized answer tore at her even more.

"I don't know, Riana. God. I don't even know."

(6)

Did you call her, Riana?
Yes. I woke her up. It's early, but she's coming.
Are you sure it's a good idea?
She has a right to know.

Creed's perceptions swam. He had never had the mercy
of forgetting what he did when the *other* was forward, but
it was damned hard to come back to his human self. He sat
huddled and his skin burned as if he'd been dipped in oil.
Blood hammered hard against his temples, and he was covered with sweat. He couldn't stop clenching his jaw, because he wanted to shout. He wanted to smash the dirty,
wet wooden table beneath him with his bare fists. How
could he let himself lose control like that? How could he
put a room full of women in jeopardy, even if they *were*
psychics?

Or witches.

Or something.

His mind frothed.

Stupid. Weak. Dangerous.

Why did he even try to live among *real* humans? When
would he give up the fantasy he could be "normal" and do
what Dominic did? Run away from New York and the
NYPD and join a cult of the "enlightened mind." Those
freaks probably thought he was some sort of god. At least
in a cult full of drugged-out junkies, he might not hurt anybody.

Dominic seemed happy enough in the few untraceable
e-mails he had sent Creed. They were rambling letters that

talked a lot about purpose, power, and destiny. Dominic had asked Creed to agree to join him two or three times, but Creed had always refused.

Yours in enlightenment,
Nick.
Yeah, right.

Maybe the next time Dominic sent him a missive and an invitation, Creed should go for it.

Morning sunlight streamed into the brownstone. *All night.* Whatever they did to him, it had taken all night. Creed crushed his fists into his eyes and wished the pressure would stop the pounding in his head. The only sensation connecting him to sanity was a surprisingly comforting touch on the arm that bore his birth-scar, the line of knotted tissue created when his grandmother used a kitchen knife to cut him free from Dominic as their mother lay sobbing, damaged and dying.

I've been a killer since the day I was born. I almost killed people today. Riana, for God's sake. As if God has any use for me.

Normal babies had no real memories of birth, but Creed remembered his, and everything that happened afterward. Creed remembered almost everything he had ever seen or heard, especially when his senses were heightened by the *other*. Even the devastating, horrible things the *other* had done.

For now, the beast lay dormant inside, as it always did after coming forward. It was just a hot, sleeping weight in his chest and belly, present, yet as distant as a star in some faraway sky. Creed wondered if it was exhausted. He was always exhausted after a transformation, so much so that he suspected if the *other* ever managed to stay forward for longer than a few minutes, it might utterly consume his human aspects.

"Are you all right?" asked a low, sexy voice.

The firm but definitely feminine grip on Creed's scarred

arm made him take his fists out of his eyes. He blinked against the stabbing pain of light and motion. Riana Dumain was kneeling on the massive table beside him, dressed in a form-fitting black leather jumpsuit that had big holes burned through it. In several places. She had hold of him, her long fingers clasping his biceps as if to steady him, while with the other hand she adjusted a green blanket covering his bare shoulders. A blanket that, if he wasn't much mistaken, was smoldering, as if someone had almost set it on fire.

Creed's thoughts settled slowly as he stared at the vision of a woman who tended him so gently. How could she be kind to him after what she saw? After what he—well, the *other* that was part of him—almost did to her and her friends?

An uneven breeze stirred the air in bursts, and wind chimes clanked, off-key, as if they had all been broken. The tangy odor of smoke mingled with wet dirt and burned wood. Creed caught a whiff of lavender and spring dew that made his body want to respond, but behind Riana, he could see piles and pieces of shattered glass, smashed mirror frames, and wind chime pipes scattered on the floor. The sight of the destruction he had caused quelled his interest, at least temporarily.

Damn, but he had done this mess up right. Even the walls had been ruined by sprays of dirt and blackened streaks of soot. One piece of a mirror dangled from its hook, showing him flickering images of the rest of the room, which didn't look much better.

At least there weren't any bodies. But . . . he was naked. He looked back at Riana, tore his eyes away from the tempting bits of soft, tanned skin he could see through the holes in her jumpsuit, then had to fight not to stare into her worried green eyes. Despite the acid churning in his gut, despite his humiliation and frustration, naked was going to be a problem next to this woman—and fast.

He tried to swallow, but his throat was so dry he coughed instead. His voice came out in a thirsty rasp. "At least nobody's dead, right?"

The big wooden table, the one he remembered from his first visit to the brownstone, shook slightly beneath him. The hair on the back of Creed's neck stood up, but he was too weak to turn and face the threat he sensed.

Cold steel pressed against the side of his neck and smashed the blanket against his shoulder.

Creed went so still he didn't even breathe.

Riana glared upward as his attacker said, "Nobody's dead, you bastard. No thanks to you. What the *hell* was that—that thing you turned into?"

Creed recognized the redhead's voice. Cynda. And she wasn't holding a knife to his throat. She was holding a friggin' sword. Merilee came into view and stopped beside Riana. With a pointed frown in Creed's direction, she tucked a strand of blond hair behind her ear and handed Riana a glass of water. The water's surface rippled from the strange wind inside the brownstone.

With my luck, that water's poisoned, or the glass will explode when I touch it.

"Back off." Riana kept her intense stare leveled on Cynda. She added, "Please," like she didn't really want to say it.

Cynda moved the sword a fraction of an inch away from Creed's neck, enough that he felt comfortable reaching for the water and taking his chances about whether or not it would kill him on the first swallow.

It didn't.

Creed gulped the cool liquid, letting it loosen his throat enough to say, "I'm sorry." He chanced Cynda's reaction time and turned more fully toward Riana, who let go of his arm. He missed the touch instantly and wanted it back, but he settled for wrapping the blanket around himself, at least enough to shield the important parts. "I would never hurt you on purpose."

She studied him for a moment, long enough for the heat of her gaze to make him glad he had a blanket over his cock. Then she shrugged. "You did try to warn us, at least."

Cynda swore. The sword retreated another inch, resting on his shoulder now, but still perilously close to his neck.

Merilee stood on the periphery of his vision, arms folded—and he thought she might have a bow slung over her shoulder. She asked Cynda's question again, and when she did, the breezes in the brownstone gusted. "What did you turn into when we took off your ring? Tell us now, if you want to walk out of here alive."

Creed addressed his response to Riana. "I really don't know. I've always called it the *other*." Out of habit, he almost let go of the blanket to touch his ring. "I try to keep it inside."

Silence answered him.

Riana's green eyes narrowed with an emotion Creed couldn't read. Anger? Suspicion?

Fear?

"My twin has one, too," he said, hoping she believed him. "An *other*. Only I think his is worse. Maybe that's why he went missing."

More silence. More scrutiny from Riana. A twitch from the sword resting on his shoulder. A hiss from Merilee, followed by a hiss of wind that chilled his damp face.

Shit. These women didn't need any psychic abilities or rituals to make people talk. They should have just left him handcuffed and naked, and let Riana sit a few feet from him, staring at him the way she was staring at him now. He would have spilled his guts in a heartbeat.

"We've had the *others* inside since we were born," Creed said lamely, hoping it would be enough. It had to be enough, because he didn't know anything else to tell her besides a list of the things he blamed himself for doing. And he'd rather not share that, now or ever.

"Did your mother have a creature inside her, too?"

Riana's question was logical and innocent enough, but Creed felt his expression darken. "I don't know. She . . . died. When I was a baby. And I never knew my father."

The redhead snorted and finally took the sword away from his neck. "You don't know what you are. You never knew your father. Your brother is missing, so he can't tell us anything. And your mother is dead. How convenient."

Creed clenched his fists, then made himself relax his fingers. "If you want to call it that."

Merilee gestured to the destroyed room. "Excuse us for having no compassion."

"We should have killed him when he was a god-thing." Cynda brushed past him and got off the table, the melted shreds of her bodysuit flapping against her belt and scabbard as she jumped. She kicked a piece of broken glass against the wall as she took her spot beside Merilee. The two women flanked Riana like a pair of trained Dobermans showing their teeth.

Not without effort, Creed made himself look away from the attack dogs. Riana settled back on her knees, staying on the table an arm's length from him. He wanted to reach out and take her hand in his, talk quietly and gain an understanding of her and why she had trapped him and questioned him, but he didn't want her bodyguards to bite off his fingers.

Instead, he leaned forward to hide the cock-bulge in his blanket and asked the one question that made sense to him. "So, Riana. And Cynda and Merilee. What are *you*?"

"As if you don't know," Merilee said.

Cynda snapped, "You don't have the right to ask questions," at the same moment.

A beat later, Riana answered with, "Sibyls. We're Sibyls."

This stunned the guard dogs into silence. They both stared at Riana with open mouths.

Okay. So, Riana seemed to be the leader of this little

coven, or whatever it was. He gazed at her as he searched his memory. "Sibyls were ancient women, crones or something, who lived nearly forever but didn't stay young. Oracles from Greek mythology, right?"

"Sibyls came before Greek mythology." Riana rubbed her leather-clad knees with both hands as she shook her head. Her dark hair spilled over one shoulder, accenting the clean, beautiful line of her jaw. "Every culture has a myth about wise women who serve the Mother—Sibyls, in whatever form. The word comes from *Cybele,* the Goddess, the oldest deity in human history. The Greeks used a similar term to refer to some of their priestesses, and eventually the word got associated with elderly women who could see fate and the future."

"We aren't those Sibyls." Cynda gripped the hilt of her sword as if daring him to argue. "Some of the Mothers and Sibyls see the future and give prophecies, but we aren't fortune-tellers or weak nellies who hide out in caves." Smoke rose from her shoulders. If looks could kill, Creed figured he would have died five times in the last thirty seconds.

"We're warriors of the Dark Goddess," Merilee said in a tone every bit as icy as the breeze that whipped past Creed's ears. "Initiates of the Dark Crescent Sisterhood. Highly trained in the use of weapons and fighting skills. We can take you out in whatever form you choose to attack us."

"Easily," Cynda agreed.

The floor trembled. Just a little, but enough to make Cynda and Merilee clamp their mouths closed.

Creed felt a rush of surprise and discomfort. Riana did that. He was sure she did. Riana made the house shake—or had it been the ground beneath the house? Either thought was disturbing.

"Sibyls work with the elements." Riana tilted her head to the side to indicate Cynda and Merilee. "Fire and air." She touched her own chest. "And earth. We're a triad."

Damn. She did *make the ground shake.*

"What about water?" he asked numbly, gripping the edges of his blanket in tight fists. "Water's an element, too. Shouldn't you be a quartet?"

Riana gave him a sad smile. "We all do a little work with water, but the water Sibyls didn't survive. A disaster wiped out Motherhouse Antilla in the Atlantic, west of the Azores, in ancient times."

"A natural disaster," Merilee said before Creed could ask.

Cynda added, "Yeah. A tidal wave on top of a flash flood. Imagine that. The whole island sank."

The brownstone shook again. A broken mirror crashed to the floor and finished splitting into a few dozen pieces. Riana clenched her teeth and closed her eyes, and the shaking stopped. Tense lines formed across her forehead, and she looked utterly exhausted and vulnerable.

Creed fought an impulse to grab her and kiss her until she opened those eyes in surprise, then closed them all over again, lost in the pleasure of his touch.

Bad idea. She probably knows how to snap my neck with her knees.

He remembered the sweet sensation of kissing her before she took his ring. He remembered biting her lip, tasting her as she surrendered her mouth to his, and he almost groaned.

Robberies and a murdered kid. Weird beings on the loose in NYC. Getting handcuffed to the ceiling. Letting the other *get loose and almost killing people. Remember that, too? Snap my neck with her knees . . .*

After grinding his teeth for a few seconds, Creed said, "I think we should work together."

Cynda burst out laughing as Merilee's gaze dropped to his newly invigorated erection, which he had forgotten to cover with his hands when Riana started shaking the brownstone.

"I'll just bet you do," she said. "Exactly what kind of work did you have in mind?"

Riana opened her eyes then, and the exhaustion seemed to fade into mild amusement as she watched him scramble to cover up the blanket bulge again.

So much for cool dignity.

He sighed.

She smiled.

"What the hell?" Creed met her gaze and moved his hands out of his lap. If she wanted to size him up—literally—then let her. "Look at me if you want to. A man would have to be blind, deaf, and stupid not to notice how beautiful you are."

As Merilee and Cynda laughed and hooted, he continued. "We should work together. Whoever murdered the Latch kid had real supernatural abilities. I think you know something about the killers, too, so you can help us get the bastards."

When Riana didn't answer, Creed went a step further. "I can behave myself. If you want me to."

At that, Riana's cheeks flushed a brilliant scarlet. She started to lean toward him, seemed to catch herself, and leaned back instead.

Creed didn't really care that Cynda and Merilee were in the room laughing their asses off. He felt like he was fighting for something he couldn't quite name. It couldn't have been Riana's respect for his wisdom and self-restraint, though, because the next thing that jumped out of his mouth was, "What, you want me to bare my soul again?"

He jerked off the blanket and stood.

The only wind chimes still intact, the ones by the front door, rang.

Riana froze. If she'd moved an inch, his stiff cock might have brushed her face.

Cynda choked mid-giggle, swore, and drew her sword.

Merilee snatched her bow from her shoulder and nocked an arrow in the time it took Creed to blink.

At that moment, the door to the brownstone burst open.

Creed turned toward the sound.

Bright sunlight outlined the unmistakable shape of his partner Andy, her Big Apple sweatshirt wrinkled and stained, and her jeans frayed just above her untied sneakers. She pulled off her huge sunglasses, then stood as still as a redheaded rock in the entrance, taking in the scene in front of her.

Creed followed Andy's gaze around the destroyed room. To Cynda, half-naked through her burned bodysuit, holding her sword in a fighting stance. To Merilee with her bow and arrow. To Creed, wet and dirty and bruised, and absolutely naked, standing on the huge messed-up table. And finally, to Riana, dressed all in leather, on her knees in front of Creed's cock.

Andy put her hands on her hips and cleared her throat. When she spoke, her words came out in an uncharacteristic soprano. "Okay, now. Y'all have some serious explaining to do."

An hour later, Riana wished she could collapse on the splinter-strewn sofa occupied by Cynda, Merilee, and Andy. Had she ever been so tired? And hungry. Up for twenty-four hours, starved except for a few handfuls of potato chips—and she needed to change clothes. Her torn bodysuit felt hot and tight, and the thing had holes burned in it everywhere.

She rubbed her forehead. What had possessed her to be open with Creed Lowell about the Sibyls? Did she really feel a bit of trust for this creature who had almost killed her triad?

It made sense to talk to him. There's something about him . . . and he's right. We do need to work together.

Riana bit at her bottom lip, which was still sensitive from Creed's passionate bite when he kissed her. She didn't like how dizzy that memory made her feel, and she really didn't like the twist of uncertainty in her belly.

Sibyls were discreet, of course, as they had been throughout history, but there was no code or rule that forbade them to reveal the existence of the Dark Crescent Sisterhood. Many people in Russia, Ireland, and Greece, especially those who followed the ways of the Goddess, knew about the Motherhouses.

But was her judgment affected by the schoolgirl jitters she experienced whenever Creed looked at her? She had known her share of men in every sense of the word, but few could boast such an immediate and powerful effect on her.

She couldn't stop thinking about Creed's bold admission of his attraction to her, either. Riana bit her tingling lip again, this time harder, wishing for one of Merilee's pencils to chew.

Did he have to be so frank, so open?

How did he know she would admire that? A man not afraid to want a woman. A man willing to pursue what he desired.

He's not a man.

She glanced at Creed, who had wrapped Cynda's green blanket around his waist. He was sitting in the chair closest to hers, an intense look on his handsome face as he spoke to Andy. Riana's gaze drifted from his dark hair to his muscled arms to his well-defined chest, and lower, to where the blanket hid his cock.

Sweet Goddess. He's more man than anything else.

He respected Andy, too, and treated her with a kindness and deference Riana associated with protective older brothers. Andy clearly had no idea there was anything unusual about Creed, beyond his tremendously accurate instincts on the job.

They had explained about Sibyls and Creed's *other* to Andy, and explained again, and explained a little more. Cynda had produced flames in her palms. Merilee made the wind blow three times, and Riana had rattled the brownstone once to convince her. Andy had asked to see Creed without his ring, but everyone refused.

"You could have told me," Andy said to Creed. The hurt in her tone made Riana wince. "What did you think—that I'd turn you in or something? You're my partner, you big idiot. We should be able to tell each other anything. And you three"—Andy turned to the women, focusing on Riana—"are you really my friends, or did you just want information on OCU investigations?"

Cynda and Merilee took turns gazing at the floor, but Riana couldn't afford that luxury. "At first, that's exactly what we wanted." She fought the urge to stare at her toes like a chastened child. "It didn't take much time to like you for yourself, though. And even less time to learn to respect you."

"We've come close to telling you about us," Merilee mumbled. "A bunch of times."

A piece of Cynda's bodysuit gave off a burst of smoke as she cut her gaze to Riana. "I wanted to spill everything, but our exalted leader thought we should protect you."

Merilee let out a breath. "Any time you're ready to be the pestle, sweetie, you just step right up and tell the Russian Mothers. I'm sure Mother Yana would just love to welcome an Irish fire-bitch into earth training. Right before she fed you to her wolves."

"Are they always like this?" Creed asked Andy.

The low rumble of his voice made Riana shiver.

"Sweetie, this is mild." Andy eyed the thin line of smoke rising from the leather on Cynda's shoulder, then Merilee's hair, which was dancing in a light inside breeze. "But I've never seen the special effects before. Riana, I still don't get who you're—well, I guess who *we* are—supposed to be fighting. Are the Legion some sort of devil-worshipping group that summons these Asmodai demons?"

"Not summon," Riana said. "Create. Asmodai have human shapes, but they're really made of one of the four elements. Their maker controls them with a talisman." She gestured to the sword Cynda had placed on the floor at her feet. "We destroy them by cutting off their heads or piercing their hearts or brains with the element that powers them. If they survive their mission, they take off their talisman, hold it in their hand, and return to their masters. And I don't know what deity those masters worship, but it isn't the Goddess."

Cynda and Merilee had relaxed against the sofa's over-stuffed arms, and Merilee had actually closed her eyes. Riana seized her chance. "And I agree that we should work together, the five of us, to catch whoever really killed the Latch boy, because it wasn't Alisa. She would never do something like that."

"You know her?" Creed asked softly, making Riana shiver again. Then, "Oh. I get it. She's one of you. She's a Sibyl."

Merilee had jerked upright at Riana's suggestion of collaboration. So had Cynda, but it was Merilee who spoke. "Never in the history of our existence has a Sibyl turned to perverted rituals. We don't kill good guys. We try not to kill humans at all, and we would *never* kill a child."

"And we need our warriors," Cynda cut in, managing to keep her inner fire under control. "The Legion has stepped up its attacks. We have no idea what they're up to."

Andy nodded. "That much, I understand. How many Sibyls cover New York?"

"We have ten triads here," Cynda said. "Two in each borough."

Creed gave a soft whistle. "Thirty women to look out for eight million people. That doesn't seem like enough."

"We aren't an endless resource." Riana looked at him, tried not to stare into his dark eyes, and failed. "Fewer Sibyls are marrying these days, and even fewer have daughters to pass on the gift."

Creed gazed back at her, and Riana felt the air between them sizzle. She had the heart-melting impression he was thinking about the kiss they shared. A rush of heat made her cheeks blaze, and she couldn't shake the sensation of his hard body pressed against hers. She shifted in her chair, trying to keep her cool, but it was a short step from that image to the memory of his hard cock in her hand, straining to meet her eager touch.

"So being a Sibyl, it's a bloodline thing," he said. "I wondered."

"Not always." Merilee twirled a strand of her blond hair around her finger. "Sometimes the gift shows up spontaneously, but that's not common. Plus, it's hard to convince the parents to surrender the girl for training."

"Until she accidentally burns down her house," Cynda

said sleepily, then looked stricken. "I mean, if she's a fire Sibyl and gets mad, or something like that."

Riana was startled by Cynda's candor, and distressed by the tight look on her triad sister's freckled face. Before Cynda fumbled around any more to cover her drowsy admission, Riana stretched and yawned. "I think we've all had enough. We can get started this evening, but right now, I need a nap. Merilee and Cynda and I didn't get any sleep last night. Creed didn't, either."

Cynda gave Riana a grateful look.

"And y'all woke me up at the ass-crack of dawn, thank you very much." Andy rubbed her stomach. "I'm starving."

"God, me, too." Merilee sprang up and headed for the kitchen without so much as a kiss-my-butt or a goodbye.

"Don't throw out any trash!" Cynda called after her.

When Andy and Creed looked confused, Riana explained about the soda can the Legion used to direct the fire Asmodai to them. "We'll have to take our trash elsewhere, or risk making life too easy for the Legion."

Andy shook her head. "What a pain in the ass." She gestured to Creed. "Well, Tarzan, I suggest you get up and find a way to tuck in that long loincloth. I'm parked a block away."

Riana stiffened. "I'm sorry, but no. He's not leaving."

Cynda's hand twitched as if she might reach for her sword, but she stayed still. Her sleepy stupor gave way to a sharp, wary frown as Andy said, "Excuse me?"

Riana stood and made herself face Creed, who sat forward in his chair, his body rigid. "The signet ring that controls you—we told you it bears the Legion's crest. A coiled serpent like I've only seen on ancient Greek and Roman coins. You and that ring are the only connection to the Legion we've ever been able to capture. You understand that we can't possibly let you go. Not until we can contact the Mothers again." She gestured to the broken mirrors, hoping they would understand. "Not until we learn more."

"I don't know anything about the Legion." He squeezed his hands, obviously battling his temper. Riana wondered if he was battling the *other*, too. "And this is out of the question. It's not safe. I'm not safe to be around you."

"We're grown women," Riana shot back. "We'll decide what we can and can't handle. And we'll do better with protecting ourselves now that we've seen the *other*."

Creed twisted his signet ring, his expression clouded. "What if I don't agree to stay? Are you going to chain me up again?"

"Absolutely." Cynda stood and bent to retrieve her sword.

Before she got the blade raised, Andy had drawn a shiny black Beretta from her ankle holster and trained it at Cynda's head. "Fr—" she started, but an arrow whistled between Andy and Cynda. It struck the pistol with a *thock*. The shaft snapped in two as the pistol sailed out of Andy's hand and spun into the air.

Andy grabbed her wrist as Riana caught the gun. Both women whirled toward where Merilee stood in the kitchen doorway, half a sandwich hanging out of her mouth, fresh arrow already nocked. Somehow, she actually managed to chew and swallow without dropping a bite or the arrow.

Andy groaned and rubbed her wrist again, drawing a look of sympathy from Riana, who had been on the receiving end of a few of Merilee's well-placed strikes in the past. She popped the Beretta's magazine without really concentrating on the weapon, and tucked it inside her bodysuit. Then she tilted the gun on its side, pulled back the Beretta's slide, caught the chambered bullet and tucked it against her skin with the magazine. When she finished, she offered the gun back to Andy, grip first.

Andy shook out her hand before accepting the pistol with a quiet, "Shit on a shingle."

"My decision isn't open for discussion." Riana took hold of Andy's wrist and examined it for injuries. The other woman didn't even struggle. "You're free to remain or come and go as you please, but Creed stays here. He won't be harmed. You have my word."

As Riana let go of Andy's wrist—no doubt sore, but not bruised or damaged—Andy glanced from Riana to Merilee to Cynda. Cynda lowered her sword and said, "Sorry. She's the boss."

"Mortar, pestle, broom. Right. I remember." Andy looked at Creed with a questioning expression. "We aren't on the clock until Monday. Should we fight our way out of here, or do you just want me to break into your place and bring you some pants?"

To Riana's shock and relief, Creed's frown slid into a devastating grin. He turned those blazing black eyes on her, showing her that he was still angry, but also intrigued, and cooperating only because of his interest in her.

How am I going to handle this? How am I going to handle him?

Hesitating just long enough to make her tremble inside, Creed shrugged and said, "Who am I to refuse a grown woman's invitation?"

(8)

If Creed had known Riana lived in a dungeon with a mad-scientist laboratory *and* an eight-by-eight elementally locked jail cell in the back corner—complete with cot and toilet, no less—he never would have agreed to stay.

Too late now.

When Riana had showed him the cell and asked him to get inside, he had thought about telling her to go to hell. In truth, though, after a few hours of being behind the elementally treated lead bars, he had relaxed a little and felt more confident that the *other* couldn't escape his control and menace Riana or the other women again. He had the ring firmly in place, after all. The ring had always given him more control and stability.

At first, Creed settled down on the cot with only the singed green blanket Riana had loaned him. He tried to sleep away his captivity, but his mind knew it was daylight outside, and he had cases to solve, like the vicious occult murder of a little boy. Despite his exhaustion from trying to fight some kind of man-made demon, getting his head bashed, staying up all night handcuffed to a ceiling beam, and spending time as the *other,* he couldn't seem to drift off. Instead, as he lay on his back on the cot in his cell and stared at the stone ceiling above him, his brain picked through details of the Latch case. Over and over, he added together what he knew with what Riana and her buddies had told him the day before. He also added in the detail of Alisa James being a Sibyl.

"Riana's damned sure Alisa couldn't be our perp," he said aloud, as if Andy might be hanging out across the room, taking notes. "But Merilee said something about sea salt, right? Used in rituals to purify. Did somebody purify the kid before they killed him? And if so, why?"

And Cynda had told them the salt could be used to keep something inside the circle and protect it—but protecting it would trap it, too, according to Riana. So had Alisa James tried to save the child but accidentally doomed the boy to murder? And why *that* boy? Who targeted him? Did some psychopathic bastard use a bit of the kid's trash to send a demon after him, like some jerk had done to the Sibyls?

And again, if so, why?

Why . . .

Creed kept coming back to that question, and his instincts told him that was the key. Find out why, and he'd find out who.

Instincts. Yeah. He glanced around his little cell. *Your glorified cop instincts let you walk into this house. And into this mini-prison. Great job so far.*

Did Riana know real practitioners of the occult? Did she know why someone would sacrifice a child?

Definitely the next question he needed to ask her head-Sibyl-ness, whenever she showed up again. A small part of him acknowledged that Riana might not show up, that she could leave him in the cell as long as she wanted to. She didn't have to come around, she didn't have to bring him food, and she didn't have to talk to him.

But somehow, he thought she would.

No, he hoped she would.

That had to be worse, wanting something from a woman who might not want anything to do with him. Creed sighed and shifted on his cot. The squeak of bedsprings echoed through the dark, cavernous laboratory.

Riana did want something to do with him, though. He had seen the attraction in her eyes, tasted it in her kiss. Riana was interested in him, even though she had seen the *other*. Could he really have a chance with a woman who knew all of him, and wanted him anyway? A woman who excited his mind *and* his primal desires?

With that fascinating thought, he finally dozed off for a while.

Soon after, he woke to the smell of food. When he sat up and swung his legs over the edge of the cot, he saw a plate with a steaming sandwich and chips resting on the floor just inside his cell door. Beside it sat a metal pitcher full of ice water, a metal cup, and a few napkins.

Yeeaaaah. Great cop instincts. Great cop senses. A beautiful woman slips me a hot roast beef on rye, and I don't even jerk an eye open. He yawned and adjusted his blanket. Then his stomach growled like some monster in a B-grade horror flick. He glanced up to see if Riana was still in the lab.

She was, standing on the far side of the room, with her back to his cell. In the soft lighting, he could make out her shiny black hair against the bright white of her lab coat.

He cleared his throat.

She didn't turn around.

Well, fine. Lock a guy in a cage, then ignore him.

Creed could play the I'm-not-interested game just as well as she could, and better than most. He'd eat the sandwich and chips, drink about half of the pitcher of water, and rest to get his strength back. Maybe then she'd feel like talking. In the meantime, the bars would keep his mind at ease, even while he watched the woman who had begun to menace his sanity.

Riana's laboratory-and-jail took up most of the brownstone's downstairs space. When she had brought him down, he saw one other door on the opposite side of the stairs, and he suspected that door concealed Riana's private bathroom and bedroom.

Bedroom. Shit. I don't need to say that word and her name in the same sentence.

He stopped eating long enough to allow himself the fantasy of Riana in that bedroom, which he imagined to be lit by candles, not to mention full of unusual scents and sculptures and patterns. Maybe runes and mirrors on the wall. He envisioned her naked, stretched across a white fur bedspread designed to highlight her tanned curves. Would her nipples be pink and tight, or ample and wine-dark? His money was on dark. And his cock was on high alert.

Gotta stop. Knock it off. Concentrate on the roast beef. And what kind of mustard is this? It was sort of nutty and rich and sweet, but so spicy his eyes watered and he had to breathe deeply each time he took a bite. He'd had it before, he thought. Some kind of hot brown mustard. European. *Sarepta,* maybe?

Russian mustard. So sweet you want the whole jar, so fiery it'll burn you inside out if you eat it. Figures. Just like her.

No matter how hard he tried, he couldn't make himself stop watching Riana. He enjoyed the way she flowed around the big room, silent and graceful, seemingly focused on nothing but work. He had dated a lot of smart women, but the way she worked hinted at genius combined with resolve stronger than the lead bars forming his cell.

Riana spent time at several silver-barreled microscopes that looked powerful enough to examine strands of DNA, and he studied her, bemused, as she took notes on a thick white pad. All of this modern equipment, but these women seemed to prefer working out problems in longhand. What was with that? Was it like talking things out with Andy, that saying or writing the words sometimes made pieces fit together? Another question he stored for later, when Riana once more sat down to talk with him. He found himself looking forward to that almost as much as touching her. He usually didn't look forward to talking to women other than Andy.

It wasn't just the cock-grabbing sound of Riana's voice, either. It was the sharpness in her eyes, the way she seemed to see everything, and notice and understand bits and pieces other people would blow off as insignificant. She could have been a cop, easy. She'd have made a great detective. Even without the training and experience he'd had, Riana stayed about a half step ahead of him and Andy.

Riana drifted over to a computer that appeared to be wired into a closed hood, probably monitoring some experiment or other. Several handheld devices lay nearby, on some of the half-dozen stainless steel countertops. Next to the PDA-looking machines were an assortment of burners, tiny hand-tools, boxes, beakers, and shelves. The names of about a dozen complicated pieces of equipment eluded Creed, but he thought he recognized a spectrometer, a gas chromatograph, and even a massive top-loading centrifuge. A few of the machines looked so futuristic and alien that he was almost certain most regular scientists—most *human* scientists—had never seen them, except maybe in whatever passed for genius-geek wet dreams.

One workstation definitely had genetic testing equipment, and in the opposite corner of the room from Creed, beside an industrial sink, a steel table with a morgue scale, saw, and tray of surgical tools looked frighteningly like a setup to perform autopsies. Creed's neck prickled as he realized that the big silver "freezer" next to the table was actually a four-drawer morgue refrigerator.

Does she have bodies on those four-by-eight trays inside? What the hell have I gotten into here?

His gut told him she wasn't a criminal. His gut also told him to leave the rest of his sandwich untouched and drink the other half of the pitcher of water before spontaneous combustion became a risk. His mouth burned. He put down the plate, guzzled a little water to calm the flames in his throat, then stood.

"Do we have company?" he asked as he tried to adjust his green blanket, noting the spice-pained rumble in his own voice. The blanket wouldn't wrap right, and he was too distracted to keep fooling with it. He just held it like a gun belt, making sure it didn't fall.

Riana startled at the sound of his voice, almost dropping a silvery two-sided telescope with something like a tiny spaceship in between the tubes.

He nodded toward the morgue refrigerator and autopsy setup. "I asked if we had company. Anything—er, anyone—in those morgue drawers?"

She glanced in the direction he indicated, then turned back. Even though she was at least thirty feet away from him, he felt a wave of heat from her gaze as she ran her eyes from his face to his bare chest, and lower, to where he still gripped the blanket wrapped around his waist.

"Not yet."

The silk of her words slid against his cock like she was standing in front of him, ripping off his blanket, and breathing against the sensitive, pulsing skin. His jaw clenched from the need to kiss her.

For a moment, he made himself focus on the dozens of drawers and cabinet doors facing him. Dark hardwood, about half of them sporting digital or manual locks. And the walls. Stone. Probably too thick to let out any noise, screams or otherwise. No mirrors on these walls. Instead, he could make out charts, bulletin boards, graphs, and posters, all neatly arranged and neatly labeled. Most of them looked like they'd been drawn by hand instead of by machine—and expertly drawn, at that.

He risked asking another question. "What are you working on?"

Riana put down her weird silver pistol-thing and came closer to him. Twenty feet. Fifteen. Ten. Five. She had changed clothes after locking him up and taking her nap. No more leather bodysuit. Her lab coat protected tailored brown slacks and a tight-fitting ivory blouse that showed every curve and dip, including a mouthwatering bit of cleavage decorated by that odd crescent pendant.

Worse than the bodysuit. Christ. How can she be even more beautiful in a friggin' lab coat? If he gave her a pair of glasses, she'd look like Wonder Woman in disguise. The image of Riana spinning in circles as lightning flashed and her clothes fell away to reveal a form-fitting leotard—with gold cups to hold her breasts high—almost made Creed sit down on the stone floor.

"I'm running about six procedures right now." Riana pointed to a pad and pencil on the nearest countertop. "Some are related to the Latch case, like determining the origins of that salt sample and a more detailed exploration of the skin sample—and the one I'm planning to start next is about you, though it might take a while."

Creed felt his eyebrow arch before he could gain control of his reaction. Shit. Is that why she had locked him up? Did she intend to cut off body parts and stir them up with chemicals to see what reacted?

He ground his teeth, then forced himself to relax his jaw. "What are you testing about me?"

She came closer. Four feet. Three feet. Two. Creed knew he could reach through the bars and touch her if he wanted to, and he thought about it.

"I took a mouth swab when we had you handcuffed earlier." Riana leaned toward him, so close he could smell that rain-and-lavender scent that made him want to groan. "I'm starting your advanced genetic profile—Sibyl-style. It takes much longer than the tests you use, but it's far more detailed and specific than what you're used to requesting to solve crimes. We can compare it to all the genetic databases in the world, as well as information we've collected on all known supernatural species." Her eyes flashed. "I want to see what you're made of, Creed Lowell."

The beast stirred in Creed's depths, a snarl amid the pounding of blood in his ears. He smashed it down, hard and fast. Not now. This woman was his, only his, and all his. No sharing. He felt irritated, intrigued, and aroused all at the same time. Invaded—yet oddly hopeful that this woman might actually be able to find some answers about his true nature.

"Don't tease me, honey," he said, only half jesting. Did she know what she was doing to him? His body, his mind?

Her gaze didn't waver. "I never tease."

Creed let go the blanket, then grabbed it again when it threatened to unwrap. "Do you really think you can map my insides under a microscope?"

"It's a start." Riana's eyes blazed at him. "With the kind of analysis we do, your genes will show me things you can't imagine."

Bullshit you never tease. Bullshit!

She liked torturing him.

Not that he minded.

He pushed aside thoughts of learning more about his heritage and winked at her. "If I show you mine, will you show me yours?"

Riana's smile made every muscle in Creed's body tense. "We can discuss that later. Much later, perhaps."

"I want to discuss it now." He could barely rasp out the words. "Come another step closer. Let me touch you again."

Her smile shifted to a look of shock, then heavy-lidded desire. Her hand trembled, and she tried to hide her reaction by straightening her lab coat.

Too late, beautiful. I saw that.

"Come here," he demanded. He let go of his blanket and gripped the bars with both hands. The blanket unwrapped, and he crushed it between his gut and the bars, keeping it up, though barely. He felt a tingling from the elemental lock, but in his human form, it was mild. The space between the bars was just wide enough for his face, and narrower than his head.

Riana didn't say anything, and she didn't move, but she stared at the blanket. She seemed to be thinking about taking him up on his offer.

"You have me trapped." He leaned forward, pressing his chest into the bars. "I can't do anything you don't want me to do, can I?"

"This needs to wait," she murmured, but the throaty whisper gave away her desire.

Creed's hands tightened on cold bars, doubling the humming sensation until it felt like a gentle current across his palms. He felt it through the blanket on his gut, too, and his thighs, and his swelling cock.

"A horde of Asmodai could attack tomorrow," Creed countered. "Don't wait. Come here. Now."

He held her gaze, wouldn't look away, wouldn't temper the raw desire he knew had to be showing on his face. More than that, he wouldn't turn loose the almost tangible rope of attraction connecting them. In his mind, he yanked on that rope, harder and harder.

Come here . . .

Come here . . .

With the sexiest little sigh, Riana stepped toward him.

Riana had time to think, *What in the name of the Goddess am I doing?*

She couldn't form a coherent thought after that, because she was kissing Creed again. Their lips met with a hungry force, and she tasted the lingering, burning spice on his tongue as he thrust it into her mouth. She let him in without hesitating, answered his tongue with her own, felt her breath leave in a rush as she gave herself fully, totally, to the fire of the kiss.

Did he growl?

Did she?

He forced his arms through the bars separating them, grabbed the lapels of her lab coat, and pulled her closer, closer, until the cold bite of the lead on her cheeks and shoulders seemed to give way to the heat of his hard, muscled flesh. Only the thin fabric of her blouse and silk chemise separated her nipples from his bare chest. And that blanket shielding his body from hers, it was gone. She felt it brush her ankle as it fell to the floor.

In the next second, she was reaching through the bars, too. Her hands found the thick, corded muscles in his back and she couldn't help digging her fingers in, deeper, deeper. Then her hands slid down to his firm, hard ass.

This time, she was sure he growled. He kissed her harder, crushing his mouth into hers. She gasped for breath, but couldn't stop, couldn't let him go. He thrust forward, and she felt the steel of his erection against her belly. God, but she wanted to take his cock in her hands, her mouth. She wanted him deep inside her. She wanted him to burst out of those bars, tear off her clothes, throw her down on one of the counters, and drive into her until she screamed.

Creed had his arms around her now, as best he could manage with the bars. Delicious. The man tasted delicious. That spice, and salt, and something so utterly fresh and powerful and male. And he felt even better. She squeezed the flexed muscles in his ass.

He broke off the kiss and stared into her eyes with such intensity she answered with a little moan. Damn, she wanted him. Her whole body tingled. Her nipples ached, and she knew she was wet. She didn't lose control of herself like this, not for any man—especially a man she had only known for a handful of hours. But she was losing control over Creed Lowell. She wanted to see those black eyes burn for her, and never stop. She wanted him to kiss her again, and again, and again.

As if she had shouted her thoughts for him to hear, he did kiss her again. Just as passionately. Just as deep. She lost herself in the firm but yielding pleasure of his lips and tongue. So demanding. So insistent.

Then he seized her ass, squeezed once, and lifted her straight off the ground.

Riana let go of Creed's ass and grabbed the cell bars out of reflex. She tried to move back from the kiss, but he had her bottom lip in his teeth again. Her eyes flew open to see his, see that mocking, teasing, dancing light flickering in the endless black depths. Urgent, yet patient. He wasn't desperate the way he had been when he kissed her to stop her from taking his ring.

Those eyes said, *I know you could get away from me if you wanted to, but you don't want to. I'll take you right now, right through these bars . . . and you'll let me.*

Her eyelids fluttered, then closed.

She could escape. She was more than trained in escaping any hold, in any situation.

But she didn't want to.

Not even close.

She was lost again, letting him kiss her. Letting him take her just like he wanted, Goddess help them all.

His hard cock pressed between her legs now, moving heat, stroking her sensitive center through her slacks and the thin strip of her panties. He had unnaturally good aim. He might as well have had her naked, lower lips parted. He might as well have been stroking her with his thumb, rhythmic, persistent, refusing to stop no matter how hard she bit him.

She was biting him.

Shit.

She realized she had stopped kissing him and pressed her face against his neck, and now she was biting him, tasting him. A lead bar had to be six inches inside her right ear, and she didn't even care. Riana made herself ease up on his neck, but he only pulled her closer.

"I like you crazy," he said in her ear, his voice so low she shivered all over just from the sound of it. "I want you wild."

Riana felt as if her mind was expanding like a balloon pumped with helium. She had the mad urge to jam her legs through the bars and ride Creed like a wild stallion until she had taken every bit of energy he had to offer. Instead, she clenched her thighs against his erection and felt his groan of approval more than heard it. She was so sensitive, so ready she almost screamed with need each time the man moved.

That's it. Enough. I'm going in that cell, and we're getting this out of our systems right now, before it gets any worse.

She stopped kissing his neck, opened her eyes, and pressed her hands against his shoulders. "Let me go."

He swore and thrust his cock forward and up, sending electric shocks through her whole body. "No."

"Put me down," she insisted, only the words came out in a hoarse gasp. "I want to come in there with you."

Creed slowly stopped the maddening, delectable thrusts between her legs. Her clit ached instantly, and she wished she could wave her hands and make the bars disappear. Her clothes, too, but she had a feeling Creed could take care of them fast enough once she got in the cell.

He lowered her to the floor so gently, like she was some fragile treasure he might break if he handled her too roughly. All the while his night-black eyes bored into her, searching for something she couldn't identify.

Truth?

Emotion?

Passion?

Plenty of all three, without question.

Creed turned her loose, obviously hating to do it. Riana hated it, too. She pulled away from him and turned toward the cell door, already fumbling in her lab-coat pocket for the keys. Her hand shook as she did it. She had never re-sponded at such a primitive, basic level to any man, much less so fast and so totally. Why him?

Her fingers closed around the keys.

Riana looked up at Creed, feeling the heat in her cheeks. The intensity in his gaze rattled her down deep inside, and heated her body even more. Another few degrees and her skin would catch fire, she was sure of it.

She should turn around and walk out of the lab right now. Get away from him for a few minutes or hours. A week. A month. Goddess. Go take a shower. Go sit in a vat of ice cubes. Something. She did not need to go into that cell and give herself to a man—a supernatural creature—she hadn't even known for a week.

I'm insane. I'm confused. What if that's one of his abili-ties? I need to find my center, get my thoughts together. Talk this out with somebody.

Both of her hands were shaking now, and flames seemed to touch her skin everywhere she wanted Creed's hands. Her breasts felt heavy. Her nipples tightened like his mouth was already fixed on the responsive tips, and her core throbbed like his cock was poised for entry. Had she ever been so aroused?

Riana took a step toward the lab door.

Creed jammed his arm through the bars, caught her by the shoulder, and spun her until her back was to him. She caught her breath and dropped the keys on the floor in front of her, out of his reach, as he pulled her backward until she was once more pressed against the cell bars. This time he held her around the waist and pulled her up until she was standing on her toes. She frantically gripped the bars again for balance.

Instantly, she felt his teasing bite on her neck, sending chills straight down her spine and doubling the ache in her clit. His lips moved to her ear, and she shivered again and again, nearly over the edge from the ragged warmth of his breath, from the thrust of his cock against her ass.

"Sorry," he said, his bass voice making her insides vibrate. "Not waiting."

Riana's heart hammered in her throat as he used his free hand to rip open her blouse, push up her silk chemise, and cup her breast. His fingers closed on the hard nipple and pinched. Molten pleasure erupted from the spot and flowed all over her body.

She actually screamed. Not loud or long, but enough. Enough for him to know he was free to do whatever he wanted.

Damn. Damn!

"Yeah. Like that, honey. Get as wild as I know you want to."

Oh, sweet Goddess . . .

She was still on her toes, but he had his hands on both of her breasts now, pushing up, pressing, kneading, rubbing her pulsing nipples between his fingers like he knew exactly how to drive her completely out of her mind.

"So soft." His voice drove her to new heights. She bit her

lip, trying to salvage some control, and failed completely. "Made for my hands. Made for me."

Riana's shoulders scrubbed against the bars. Creed nibbled at her ear, her neck. She was ready to climax. How could she be ready to climax?

Her mind spun.

He worked her breasts without mercy, pausing only to lick his fingers and get her nipples wet. The cool air in the laboratory ruffled across her, chilling them, doubling her sensations. All Riana could do was moan and rub her ass against his cock. So hard and ready, ready like she was.

"I can't," she whispered, not even sure what she wanted to say. "I can't. I can't."

One of his hands dropped lower, rubbing across her belly. "I think you can. I think you want to."

He found the button on her pants. "I think you need to." He ripped the button off and forced the zipper down in one motion.

Italian slacks. Torn to hell. Did she care? She could smell her own musk, mingled with the tang of sweat and that sexy cedar-mandarin scent that seemed to be uniquely Creed's.

His teeth found her neck again as he pinched her nipple and pushed his palm beneath the lacy band of her panties. She moaned louder as he cupped her, forcing his fingers upward, into the damp, aching flesh. Almost inside her. Almost where she wanted his cock.

Goddess. She didn't care about the slacks. She didn't care about how long she had known him, or what he was, or anything else. Her world consisted of the short distance between her core and her swollen clit.

Creed covered that distance in the time it took her to beg.

His touch was rough and adamant as he pressed two fingers against her clit and started to rub in tight circles. Back and forth, back and forth.

Riana heard herself swear, heard her breath jerk in and out of her throat in little half screams. Her emotions spiraled upward faster than she thought possible. Her eyes clamped shut and her mouth opened. She let out a shriek of need, followed by, "Now, please! Now!"

Some wild woman's voice. Not hers. Not her.

But it was her, jammed up against those cell bars, holding on for dear life, her clothes torn open, a dangerous stranger massaging her stone-hard nipple and her wet clit even as he kissed her neck again, again.

"Come," he whispered between bites. "I want to feel you shake."

Riana's whole body shook on command, wave after wave of orgasm making her buck against the bars so hard she'd probably have vertical bruises on her back.

Then the room shook. Literally.

"Turn it loose, honey. Let it roll."

No matter what he said, she couldn't do that. Not totally. Riana clung to the bars with one hand, trying to salvage a shred of mental control and awareness. The shaking subsided. At least the shaking in the earth. Riana couldn't stop the shaking in her body. She couldn't even stop the urge to make it worse.

With her free hand, she reached down and behind her, until she found Creed's cock. Velvet and steel. He was thrusting forward as she wrapped her fingers around him, squeezed, and pulled him hard against her ass. He let out a surprised groan, then thrust himself into her grip.

It only took a few strokes to make him roar, to bring him with her, right over the edge. Riana felt a rush of satisfaction and power. Then she lost her mind again.

Creed squeezed her breast as he bit her neck harder and his fingers slipped down and thrust upward into her core. Two fingers. Three. Four. Her walls expanded to take most of his hand. She yelled as he lifted her to her toes again and again with the force of his thrusts. Goddess. She yelled louder as she pumped her hand up and down his throbbing cock. His thumb rested against her clit and he rubbed it even as he drove his fingers into her. The heat of his seed flooded against the fabric of her lab coat and slacks, warming her back and ass. Her walls contracted and squeezed his fingers like she planned to keep him inside her forever.

She didn't know who shouted louder as she came again, her or Creed.

Riana stroked his cock until his spasms stopped, then refused to turn him loose even when he sagged against the bars. He pressed his mouth against her ear, kept her breast cupped, and left his fingers buried deep in her channel, creating mind-twisting aftershocks every time he took a breath.

When she didn't think she could stand it anymore, she said, "Turn me loose now."

His laughter made her shiver and twitch from the pressure of his hand inside her. "You first, honey."

They stood like that another few seconds.

Riana relented first and let go of Creed's spent cock.

Reluctantly, slowly, making sure to spread his fingers and cause her to convulse from the combined pleasure and pain, Creed slid his fingers out of her core, then out of her panties. He pulled his hand back through the bars, and Riana's cheeks blazed as she realized he must be tasting her.

The next thing he said was, "Sweet."

Riana pushed his hand away from her breast and turned to face him.

He grabbed the lapels of her lab coat and pulled her to him again.

This time when he kissed her, she could taste herself on his lips, feel his bare chest and the lead bars tingling against her sensitive nipples, feel the heat of his cock pressing into her belly just above her exposed hair. So easy to get lost in this man. Too easy. Her body ached for more. Her body ached for *him,* and she imagined herself in the cell, lying on the cot with her legs around his shoulders as he pumped into her until she shook the whole house down. Hell, the whole neighborhood, probably.

When Creed pulled back from the kiss, Riana moved away in a hurry. She almost tripped on her torn slacks, which fell down around her ankles. Then she almost tripped over the keys she had tossed out of Creed's reach. He laughed as she kicked out of her soiled pants and took off her lab coat, then made an appreciative noise when she bent over to pick up the keys, breasts swinging free.

Riana glared at him as she pulled off her ruined blouse, then tugged down her chemise to cover herself. She had to adjust her panties, too, but they were too wet and stretched to give her much cover. She stared at the trapped man, gave him a wicked grin, and rubbed her hand and the keys up and down, right where he had cupped her.

Creed's eyes widened. "Cheater. No fair. Let me out of here, or come in."

"I don't want to get in that cell with you." Riana kept touching herself, enjoying her ability to return a bit of the insanity he brought out in her. "I'm satisfied now."

His grin was every bit as wicked as hers. "Liar."

He stared at her hand. With one hand, he grabbed his cock. With the other, he took hold of one of the cell bars. His features shifted. With a loud curse, Creed let go of both in a hurry, as if the lead bar had shocked him. His face tightened as he stared down at his fingers.

Riana went still, hand and keys frozen between her legs.

Had Creed just . . . just . . . shimmered?

Did she imagine that?

He looked up at her, his expression a mix of frustration and horror. Then he turned his back on her, put his hands against the stone wall over the cot, and stood there taking long, slow breaths.

Riana still couldn't move.

Creed looked like a sculpture, carved to perfection, posing just for her. Yet she sensed his distress like a bitterness in the air.

She finally pulled her hand from between her legs and

walked toward the cell, kicking the keys as she went. "What's wrong?"

"Nothing," he said. Too loud. Too tense.

"Now who's the liar?" Riana reached the cell and touched one of the bars. Nothing unusual, at least not to her senses.

"Riana, take the keys and go. Leave me for a while."

Even though her skin still hummed from their encounter, even though she was only half-dressed and staring at the backside of the most gorgeous naked man she had ever seen, Riana's scientist-mind clicked into gear. "The *other*. Have you had problems with the *other* in sex before?"

For almost a whole minute, Creed didn't say anything. Riana watched as his muscles bunched, tighter and tighter.

Her heart thumped, and she backed away. If the *other* came forward, would the cell hold it? It had to. The lab—her analyses! She looked at the ceiling. The house. Cynda and Merilee.

What kind of chances had she been taking with everyone's life?

"No," Creed said, and it sounded like he said it through clenched teeth.

"What?" Riana looked at him, confused.

"I haven't—had trouble with the *other* during sex before." Another deep breath, then his muscles relaxed. He turned toward her, glanced at the floor, reached down, picked up his blanket and fastened it back around his waist. When he finished, he raised his eyes to hers again. His face was bathed in sweat.

"If I thought sex would make the *other* come forward, do you think I would have risked your safety like that?" He touched the bars with both hands, as if testing them, then visibly relaxed when he was able to keep hold of them this time. "Do you think I would have let you think about coming into this cell?"

Riana stared into Creed's eyes, earnest and more haunted

than ever. "I—no. I don't think you would have put me in jeopardy. Not on purpose."

He nodded. "Maybe you should go get dressed, and we'll talk a little more about—"

The ceiling shook from some sort of blow.

Riana jumped. Was it the wall? What the hell?

Thud.

A big puff of smoke sucked under the lab door, driven by a massive gust of wind. The air filled with a wavering gray haze.

Riana cut her eyes to Creed, who was staring at a spot on the far wall—the spot right below where Riana thought she heard the first noise. Another thump made the ceiling rattle. Then two.

Riana's tattoo burned, right on the pestle.

"Shit." She grabbed her arm. "Cynda! Something's wrong with Cynda."

"Let me out!" Creed said as she started to run out of the lab. "Hey, don't leave me here like a sitting duck. Let me help!"

Riana hesitated.

Creed had almost changed to the *other* only seconds ago. Was this some kind of diversion? Some kind of trick?

More smoke rushed under the door, this time with a gust of wind big enough to shove a beaker off a countertop. The fragile glass shattered all over the stone floor.

Riana ran back toward him, shook the keys loose from her fingers, and threw them in Creed's general direction. Then she turned, raced to the lab entrance, tested the handle for heat—none. Good. That much, at least.

She threw open the door and plunged into the waiting cloud of smoke outside.

(10)

Creed dropped to his knees and crammed his arm through the bars. Pain shot through his shoulder. Damn! Close, but he couldn't reach the keys where they had clattered to the stone floor in front of the cell.

Smoke billowed through the open door. His eyes stung and he coughed.

What had Riana charged into?

And he was here, friggin' locked in a cell, unable to reach the keys she had thrown at him. He let out a stream of curses, ripped the blanket off his waist, stuck it through the bars, then flicked one end over the keys.

They didn't snag.

"Fuck!"

He tried again as he heard pounding on the upstairs door. Riana yelled for somebody to open it. Great. Whoever was attacking the other women had locked Riana out.

The keys still didn't snag. Creed flipped the blanket out a third time. The floor shook. He pitched into the bars, banged his head, and managed to snag the keys all at the same time.

The upstairs door opened with a heavy thump. Creed imagined Riana charging into the living room to take on half a dozen freak-demons like the one he had tried to punch in the alley. He jerked the keys into the cell, snatched them off the stone floor, and lunged to the cell door. The smoke in the lab seemed to be thinning out, but he figured there was no time to lose. He crammed the first key into the lock. Nothing.

"*Son* of a . . ."

Second key. Still no match.

There were five more keys.

Riana shouted.

He thought he heard a woman scream, "No! Don't touch it!"

The fourth key fit.

Creed turned the lock, swung the cell door open—and felt the *other* flare through his insides, raging and huge and seemingly unstoppable. The damned thing screeched inside his mind like it had never done before. Creed stumbled out of the cell and fell to his knees, holding both sides of his head. His skin strained and burned, and he felt as if the *other* was about to rip straight through his skin.

What the hell was making it so insane? It felt more powerful, more determined than ever before.

He clenched his teeth and strained against the *other*'s furious energy. It wanted to storm and destroy and rip things apart. It wanted to kill the women. It really, really wanted to kill Riana. Creed felt driven to get up from the floor, charge out of the laboratory, grab her by the throat, and choke her to death. When he shook off that image, he got another, even worse, involving knives and lots of blood. Then swords. Then simply cooking her by letting his energy envelop her.

The signet ring sizzled against his skin. He yelled and grabbed it, started to rip it straight off his finger, but caught himself just in time.

"No!" He leaned forward and bashed his head against the stone floor. At the same moment, he imagined himself slugging the *other* right in its hateful, ranting mouth. Pain—from inside his head and outside, too—made his vision swim to a sick, hazy gray.

The *other* fell back, howling its frustration, then went eerily quiet.

Riana shouted again, this time from the living room, and Creed forced himself to his feet. Vision blurred, he staggered out of the lab to the marble stairs, which seemed steeper than he remembered. He felt half-blank and rattled from the pain in his head and the *other*'s bizarre, forceful activity. Something was fueling the beast. Something upstairs, Creed just knew it. Whatever the women were fighting—was it some sort of key to his origins?

Or was it just some monster trying to kill Riana and her friends?

With a snarl to match the *other*'s temper, Creed launched himself up the steps. He lurched into the kitchen—which was surprisingly intact and smoke-free—then banged open the swinging door to the brownstone's big living room.

The scene he found was absolutely not what he expected.

Instead of being destroyed or splashed with monster blood, the room was neater than when he last saw it—except for the four arrows sticking out of the walls. All the broken glass and wood had been cleaned away, and somebody had washed the soot off the paint . . . but there *were* four arrows.

Four arrows sticking out of the walls.

Remnants of smoke curled lazily around the fletching, as if trying to coax the arrows to fall to the floor.

Creed's partner Andy was standing by the overstuffed sofa, patting a singed piece of her pulled-back red hair with one hand, holding a bow in her other hand, and saying over and over again, "I'm sorry. I'm soooo sorry." Her jeans had soot on them, and her sweatshirt, too. Even her sneaker laces looked singed. A quiver full of arrows lay at her feet.

Creed followed her gaze forward, to the big wooden table with the heavy iron base that took up most of the living room. Riana and Merilee were on their knees on top of the table, struggling to hold down a swearing Cynda. The redhead was dressed in blue-jean shorts and a green blouse with one sleeve burned clean away.

And, clearly visible even to a man half-stupid from banging his own head on a stone floor, was an arrow sticking out of her right ass-cheek. A small red stain spread around it, and every time she swore, a flame burst out somewhere. Almost as fast, some force—presumably earthy in nature—smothered it out.

"Get hold of yourself," Merilee snapped. "Jesus, you big baby. It's just a flesh wound. A flat-head trainer tip stuck in the fat part."

Three flames popped out, two beside the table and one on Merilee's shirt as Cynda screamed, "My ass does *not* have a fat part!"

"I'm so sorry," Andy said again as the flames got doused. Then she looked at Creed, first at his face, but second at his chest. Her eyes started to slide down his naked body.

Creed covered himself with both hands, in a big hurry.

"I—uh." Andy shook her head, then pointed her bow at one of the chairs, which had something in the seat. "Um, brought you some cock. I mean, clothes. A shirt and sex, too. Shit. Socks. Socks! And some shoes. Couldn't find any underwear, though." She turned a brilliant shade of maroon, closing her eyes and rubbing both hands over her face.

Creed glared at her. "I don't wear underwear. Thanks anyway."

Andy somehow turned even redder.

"You've been shot before," Riana was telling Cynda in a brusque but calm voice, as Creed walked to the chair, careful to keep his hands over his cock. "You know we have to take it out—unless you'd rather just live with it?"

By the time he got his jeans, sleeveless T-shirt, and socks on, Cynda still hadn't stopped swearing and threatening Merilee's and Riana's lives if they touched the arrow. Creed worked to put on sneakers as Andy said, "Look, I don't think I'm going to get this arrow-and-sword stuff. I shoot guns. Aim and pull the trigger, bang." She put the bow on the overstuffed couch and jerked her hand away as if the thing might have acid dripping from it. "We have to figure out a way for me to fight with bullets, okay?"

"Whatever," Cynda moaned. "Just get these bitches off me."

Riana ignored her and focused her attention on Merilee. "Why?"

Merilee looked put out. More than usual. "You said she wasn't trained. We were just starting her training, that's all."

"You can't train an adult woman with no elemental talent to be a Sibyl."

"Hey," Andy said, wounded. "I told you. I have talent. I can shoot things. There have to be some human bad guys, right? Bullets will do just fine for them."

Cynda thrashed on the table and added, "She has more talent than you give her credit for!"

Riana didn't answer either of them, instead keeping her conversation directed at Merilee. "What element did you use to lock the tips?"

Merilee looked miserable and didn't respond.

Riana pushed down harder on Cynda's shoulder and leaned toward the blonde. "You used air, didn't you?"

"Screw you!" Cynda tried to buck off her captors, then set them both on fire, albeit briefly. "We were just trying to make it easy for her!"

Creed chanced a glance at the four arrows jammed into the walls, then looked back at the one in Cynda's ass. He hoped the Sibyls never tried to make anything easy for *him*.

Andy babbled about guns and shooting and how well she did at target practice.

More fires broke out and got snuffed just as quickly.

Riana glared from Cynda's back to Merilee's face. "I can't believe you did that. Air? Air?!" She shook her head. "Even air Sibyls have trouble controlling air weapons locked with air! That was irresponsible."

"Hold on." Merilee took her temper out by cramming Cynda's head farther into the table. "You're the one who came out of the basement with a naked demon-man, Riana—wearing just your underwear. And you smell like sex, so let's not start measuring anyone's responsibility, okay?"

Instinctively, Creed braced for the earthquake. He figured they'd lose their last half-dozen mirrors and the arrows might even fall out of the walls.

But . . . the earthquake never came.

About fifteen fires started, with one impressive jet shooting out of the biggest, heaviest mirrors still hanging on the wall. Riana's attention shifted to the streams of fire pouring out of the mirrors. She stared at them, eyes wide, and Creed knew Riana was going to do something to put out those blazes. He smelled the light odor of fresh dirt even though he didn't see anything other than a shimmer in the air between Riana and the mirrors.

The flames winked out before they cracked the glass.

Creed blinked at her. "Impressive."

She jumped at the sound of his voice, spared him a brief glare, then concentrated on the rest of the fires. Her cheeks flushed crimson, and she spoke to Merilee through her teeth. "Just unlock the air in her ass, please. It's fanning her flames, literally."

When Merilee tried to take her hand off Cynda's head, the redhead started to get up.

Riana turned to Creed, then Andy. "A little help, please?"

Creed got up, and he and Andy jogged to the table. Andy put her hand on Cynda's head and apologized four more times while Creed held her legs, trying not to react to the unnatural heat charging into his hands. Riana encouraged Cynda to act her age, and Merilee made another comment about flesh wounds and fat asses as she grabbed the arrow. Then the blonde closed her eyes and said something in Greek.

Creed saw Riana tense.

A loud *pop* hurt his ears, and the arrow wiggled in Cynda's ass, as if it was trying to pull itself free.

Cynda shouted and seemed to set the entire world on fire at once.

Riana handled that as fast as she could, but not in time to save Creed's shoelaces. He thought he might have a nice set of blisters on his palms, too.

Merilee took hold of the arrow, snapped the shaft in half, and tossed the crest and fletching over her shoulder. It burst into flames in midair, and Riana didn't bother putting it out.

Andy mumbled, "Temper, temper," but Merilee just ignored the cinders forming on what remained of the shaft. She pressed her fingers on either side of the entry point, rocked the shaft a couple of times as Cynda called her everything but a nice girl, then in one smooth action, pulled out the bloody tip of the arrow.

Creed saw nothing but flames for about three seconds, but thank God nothing burned him to death before Riana got the situation under control. Merilee, her blue shirt and shorts sooty from that last onslaught, kept her fingers pressed against Cynda's bleeding ass for about a minute, then said, "If you'll stop setting shit on fire and come upstairs, I'll flush it and put some ointment on it. I don't think it'll need a bandage. She didn't shoot you that hard."

"Hard enough," Cynda muttered. Creed let her go at the same time Riana and Andy did. "And my ass absolutely does not have a fat part."

Andy started to apologize, but Cynda got up from the table and cut her off with, "Don't worry about it. Wasn't your fault."

As Merilee and Cynda reached the stairs to the upper level, which were situated about halfway between the kitchen door and the front door, Merilee stopped and looked back at Riana, with a gesture toward Andy. "She shoots things. So, is it possible to cast her some pure lead bullets and lock them?"

Andy answered before Creed could speak. "My father

was a gun nut. He used to make bullets, and I still have his old swaging equipment. Would that work? Creed and I could try." She glanced at Riana. "You are going to let him go home soon, right?"

Riana let out a breath and got off the table. She answered Merilee instead of Andy. "If she's going to work with us, she needs weapons she can use comfortably. We need to make sure the lead is pure, or we won't be able to lock in enough elemental energy to make them lethal to Asmodai." To Andy, she said, "Real bullets will have contaminants, so they won't work. I'll have to get the proper molds for your ammunition and cast the bullets myself. Swaging is a cold-forming process, and I can't get rid of contaminants without heat. Casting should work, but we won't know if the bullets will be effective against Asmodai until you use them the first time."

"Well, I'm *not* going to be the guinea pig," Cynda announced before stomping up the stairs. Merilee followed her, renewing her teasing.

To Andy, Riana said, "I can't make any promises or projections about when I'll release Creed. I've just started my analysis, and we haven't spoken to the Motherhouses for their input. It might take weeks."

Creed inspected his hands. *Analysis. Experiment. Input. I'm just a piece of data to her, right?* He studied his hands harder. No blisters on his palms. That was good. Other than wounded pride, a few char marks, a couple of small holes in his T-shirt, and his fried shoelaces, he'd come through that little nightmare pretty well. He looked at Andy, who had a lot more burn holes in her shirt than he did, and said, "I can't believe you shot her in the ass with an arrow."

Andy tucked a wild bit of red hair behind her ear. "Shut up. I can't believe I found you naked with one of my best friends. Christ. It's like catching your brother fucking."

They both looked at Riana, who turned red all over

again. She glanced down at her chemise and panties, turned redder, and said, "I need to go downstairs for a minute. Maybe longer. Can I trust you?"

Creed wanted to tell her to go to hell, that he and Andy were leaving, but he couldn't make himself do it. "Yeah," he said. "I'm not going anywhere."

Andy grunted, and he was tempted to elbow her.

Riana looked at her bare feet, then back at him. "Okay."

Her eyes said, *Don't make a fool of me for taking you at your word. Please.*

And he knew he wouldn't.

"I—I need a shower. Or something." Riana spun around and almost jogged out of the room.

Creed watched her go, savored the way her body moved, and thought about touching her. He had to fight to keep from smelling his fingers to see if Cynda had managed to burn away the sweet musk he had so enjoyed before all hell broke loose. His cock stirred in his jeans, and the *other* stirred in his gut. He clenched his jaw, then took a step back in shock.

Riana.

Riana set it off. The *other* reacted to her.

No. No. Not to her. To his feelings for her.

"Shit," he muttered to himself.

He had been attracted to his share of women, but he had never felt anything like what he was already feeling for this one. And he had never had trouble with the *other* responding to his physical sensations or emotions.

It could be because she had paranormal abilities, some sort of psychic signature, but Creed doubted that. His instincts told him the stark truth. The *other* was reacting to Riana because Creed was reacting to her at such a deep level.

So the more he wanted her, the more he cared about her . . .

The beast inside him snarled again, and Creed's gut

twisted into a knot. This was one hell of a complication he hadn't expected.

Stop it. You don't know for sure. You don't have evidence.

But he had enough. He knew he did.

Enough of a hunch that he knew he shouldn't take any chances with Riana's safety.

He turned to Andy and meant to tell her that she needed to buy about a dozen pairs of shoelaces, just in case she kept accidentally sticking projectiles in Cynda's ass. He meant to get that out of his mouth, and sound lighthearted about it, too.

Instead, he stared past Andy, wordless, and imagined he could still smell Riana's fresh, feminine scent. He wanted to reach inside his soul and rip out the *other*, and beat the thing to death with his bare hands.

When Creed finally made himself focus on Andy, he couldn't tell her anything he had planned to say. He couldn't look her in the eyes, either.

After a few moments of silence, what came out of his mouth was, "I'm in deep shit here."

Riana ran down the marble steps to her bedroom, raced inside like something was chasing her, locked the door behind her, and stood there shaking, clenching her crescent moon pendant in her fist. Candlelit earth tones met her eyes, along with her refreshingly clean and Zen-like environment. Bamboo mats. Mattress on the floor with a spread that incorporated autumn shades. A single wooden dresser, Mission style. A single chair, also Mission style. Several mirrors reflected the light from candles floating in little bowls of water, some on the floor, some on her dresser. The bowls of water were a must, what with the . . . occasional shaking that went on wherever she lived, accidentally tipping candles over and the like.

Yellow flickers danced off her yoga mat in the corner and picked up highlights in the glass eggs in the bowl on top of her dresser. Her incense burner winked in the dancing light, too. She hadn't burned a stick today, but yesterday's lavender and jasmine, her favorite combination, lingered in the air.

The door to her bathroom was closed. Her one indulgence, an Oriental tapestry of a peacock, hung on the bedroom door. The picture usually comforted her, but today her insides hopped and danced and she had to fight back panic.

She felt as if her head was going to explode. Or her heart. Riana rubbed her pendant against her chest and tried to breathe. The smooth stone floor felt cool under her bare feet, but that only reminded her that she was barely dressed. That she'd let down her guard in her own haven, her laboratory, and given herself to a man who could have killed her and her triad, too.

When she had heard the noises upstairs and sensed that Cynda was injured, Riana had been sure they were screwed—and not in the fun way. She thought her triad had been compromised while she had been busy giving in to her selfish desires.

Never again. She had a responsibility to her friends, her triad sisters. They were the most important things in her life. The Sibyls were the only family Riana had ever known. Like many earth adepts, Riana was the product of careful breeding. The Mothers selected certain Mother-house residents for the task, and chose nearby men to mate with them. It was an honor for the men and the chosen Sibyls. No doubt one of the women who had helped train Riana was her biological mother. Her blood-grandmother and even her great-grandmother might have been at the Motherhouse, but they never revealed that information.

We are all your mothers and grandmothers, Mother Yana had told her late one night, when she came to comfort Riana after yet another round of nightmares. *We are all your sisters, your family of the heart. We will keep you safe, and help you learn how strong you can be.*

"But I'm not strong," Riana mumbled to herself. "I'm not a good mortar. Never have been, never will be. I still don't know how to do it!"

She was letting down her true family. Letting down Mother Yana and all the years of careful training.

Cynda and Merilee thought she was an idiot because she lost her head over Creed. She could tell by the way they looked at her, by the jeering glint in their eyes. They had lost respect for her, in part, if not entirely.

How had she ever thought she could hold a triad together?

Fatigue struck Riana like a blow. She leaned against the door of her room and gazed at her own reflection in the mirror. Even softened by candlelight, she was pale and shaking, wearing a dirty chemise and stretched, ruined underwear. Her hair was a wreck. Soot and grime covered her cheeks, and she had streaks of Cynda's blood on her hands and arms.

Yep. A real fashion plate.

You smell like sex . . .

Merilee's smart remark rang in her mind, and drove her thoughts back to the feel of Creed's hands on her, his fingers inside her. The way he claimed her nipples, her neck. The way he brought her to climax so fast, so hot, so easily. Riana's body vibrated from the memory.

She rubbed her chest again to make herself start breathing.

Then, head down, she slipped out of her bedroom, padded into the lab, and picked up her ruined blouse and pants. She picked up her lab coat, too, and on her way back out the door, she peeled off her chemise and hurled it and the lab coat toward the industrial washer and dryer that occupied the far corner of the big room. The shirt and pants and panties she tied into a trash bag and tucked into her closet. They had to haul off their trash from now on, and she didn't want the clothes lying around in plain sight to taunt her—and get her taunted.

Riana's next stop was her shower, a copper creation with frosted doors that took up most of the space in the little bath chamber, leaving only a few feet for her toilet and sink. Inside the shower, the smooth jade tile felt perfect and soft as she stroked it, like three walls full of ancient worry stones.

She was acutely aware that Creed and Andy were on the ground floor, probably alone and unsupervised, if they were still in the brownstone at all. Cynda would be in her room beneath the stairs that led up to the third floor, with her headphones on, ignoring the world.

Riana couldn't get enough of the hot water massaging

her shoulders, her neck, her head. She soaped herself and rinsed three times, then washed her hair twice for an excuse to linger in the water's heavenly pulses. Her nipples felt sweetly sore, and each time she moved, Riana felt a gentle, painful twinge between her legs.

That was just his hand. What would his cock feel like?

With a groan of frustration, she thrust her face under the water again, hoping it would wash away the temporary madness that seized her every time she thought about Creed. She knew it had to stop, right now, today. She couldn't give in to her fancies and sexual urges again, not with him. Too dangerous. Too destructive to her relationship with Cynda and Merilee.

Still, when she got out of the shower, toweled off, and walked back into her room, Riana couldn't help looking at her body in the mirror.

Riana had never been insecure about her body, but it pleased her to know Creed liked the way she looked. He didn't make any secret of that. He didn't make any secret of anything.

She ran her hands over her breasts, her belly, her hips. Then she touched her lips, remembering the taste of him, the feel of his mouth crushed against hers. Her skin tingled all over with the thought of making love to him—not just a quickie against the bars of a cell, but all night long, over and over.

"Not lovemaking. Sex. I need to get a grip. It was sex!" She turned away from the mirror and stalked to her dresser.

A few minutes later she had on her pendant, a comfortable pair of khakis, a white blouse that didn't show too much cleavage, and her favorite jazz shoes, the ones she usually wore to do yoga. She hoped the shoes would remind her to keep her feet on the ground.

Something needed to.

She rubbed her forehead, took a deep breath, and headed

back up the marble stairs to see if Creed had kept his word. When she got to the kitchen, she realized the sun was already going down. It was almost nighttime. Almost their busy hours, and she hadn't had near enough sleep. A snarling rumble from her stomach reminded her that she hadn't had enough to eat, either, and she grabbed a handful of almonds as she passed the basket of fruit and nuts on the kitchen table.

Swallowing the nuts in a hungry gulp, Riana pushed open the door to the living room. She was surprised to find Creed sitting on the couch talking quietly to Andy. Both of them fell silent when she entered the room, and Creed looked at her like he could see straight through her conservative clothes. Like they turned him on even more than a leather bodysuit or panties and a chemise.

Riana's body heated up and started to tingle. She felt the instant flush in her cheeks, and she almost groaned as her tender nipples tightened against the soft cotton of the high-necked tank she had selected to put on under her blouse.

Then Creed looked away and doubled his fists.

Riana felt a moment of relief, followed by a moment of frustration.

Was he suddenly ashamed of his attraction to her? Had Andy dressed him down and made him think twice about what he was doing?

From the look on Andy's face, sisterly concern mingled with worry, she might have done just that. Riana didn't know whether to be grateful or pissed. She picked grateful right about the time Cynda and Merilee came downstairs.

Merilee had changed into black shorts and a black shirt, as if she was taking precautions against another fire, ash, and soot attack from Cynda. As for Cynda, she had on a very loose shirt and an even looser pair of shorts, and she walked with a notable hitch. When Cynda looked at Riana and rubbed her ass, Riana couldn't help commenting.

"At least Andy didn't shoot you intentionally. When

Merilee sticks an arrow in your ass, she does it on purpose."

Merilee glowered and flopped into one of the chairs.

Cynda, who seemed to be past her ill humor—for the moment—snickered and did not flop into a chair. She didn't look ready to sit on anything, anywhere, in any way. She grinned at Andy and said, "No worries, okay? I've been shot before." She tossed Merilee a smart-ass look. "More than once, I might add. And I heal fast. This'll be history by morning."

"That's good." Andy let out a breath. "I really didn't mean to." She patted Creed's knee. "Creed told me where to buy lead. Riana, if the lead isn't pure, can you—uh, fix it in your lab, or do whatever it is you do to make it pure enough?"

Riana nodded.

"Okay, then." Andy smiled and stood. "I'll head out and pick up everything we need. Creed tells me he'll be staying for a bit?"

Without looking at Cynda or Merilee, Riana said, "Yes. My initial analyses take about eighty-six hours, and I don't even know what the next steps might be."

Merilee grumbled something about camping out in the lab to chaperone and make sure shit got done as fast as it could be done.

This time, Riana didn't look at Creed when she said, "Whatever you want to do. I could use all the help I can get."

Merilee looked up, startled by the invitation to actually go down in the "pit of earth-hell," as she called the lab.

Cynda's mouth came open, but she closed it in a hurry. She stared at Riana, obviously making sure she wasn't kidding or being sarcastic.

"I mean it," Riana insisted. "I've got a lot of work to do, and Creed isn't exactly safe to be my lab assistant."

She risked a glance in his direction. He looked tense, but not upset.

Riana's stomach dropped.

What the hell? Had she wanted him to be upset about not getting more time alone with her? Had she wanted him to stand up and grab her and kiss her, and demand that they finish what they started?

Yes, said a tiny, pathetic voice in her head. Goddess, she hated that voice.

Andy rubbed her eyes, yawned, apologized to Cynda once more, and took her leave with a promise to come back after eating the contents of her refrigerator and getting a good night's sleep. She started for the door, but before she grabbed hold of the handle, the wind chimes started to ring.

Merilee was on her feet and moving before Riana could react. Silently, swiftly, she reached Andy and put her hand on Andy's arm to keep her from opening the door. When Andy opened her mouth to ask what the hell was going on, Merilee put her finger to her lips.

Cynda studied the chimes, shook her head, then turned her right ear toward the sound and massaged the tattoo on her wrist. Riana recognized the gesture. Cynda was having trouble interpreting the message, probably because the chimes were slightly out of tune from all the wind and fire and rattling, and whatever Creed's energy had done to them.

The chimes rang again, and a third time, the pattern shifting slightly with each ring. Riana picked up *Bronx, Long—no, wait. Court? Something about a court?*

Cynda's head snapped up and she whirled to Riana. "It's Alisa's triad. The North Bronx group. They're on the run from three Asmodai on the John Muir trail at Van Cortlandt Park, up near the aqueduct. It's the South Bronx group transmitting. They're closest. North Queens is responding, too—and South Manhattan's joining up with Queens. They want us to hold the fort in this borough."

"We should go," Merilee said. She let go of Andy and ran for the steps, presumably to change and grab one of her bows and some fresh arrows.

"If we respond, we leave Manhattan uncovered." Cynda turned to Riana. "Right?"

Riana felt like her stomach was tearing in two. Alisa's group, in trouble. If Riana were in jail and Alisa heard that the North Manhattan triad was under attack, she'd be there in a heartbeat.

But Alisa had a history of being impulsive like Merilee, even if she had earth training. Cynda, for once, was thinking with her head instead of her battle lust.

"Right," Riana agreed. "Suit up. We need to spread out and hit the streets in a hurry. This might be a distraction for something bigger."

"What do we do?" Andy's fingers twitched as if she wanted to draw her gun. "And how do we do it?"

Riana did her best to smile. "You let Cynda take you to Creed's place, and then to your apartment, you stuff your face, and you get some rest. The Asmodai aren't after you—they'd have no reason to attack."

"Don't tell me you're putting me back in the cell." Creed's statement came out low and direct. A challenge.

"Of course not." Riana tried not to lose her temper. "But you don't have any proper bullets yet, and you can't use fists or guns on Asmodai. Stay here, please. Protect our home if you can, but if something breaks in, lock yourself in the cell. No Asmodai can get through those elementally locked bars."

Creed's mutinous expression set her teeth on edge, but he didn't say anything. Riana ran to the closet, grabbed a couple of bodysuits, and tossed one to Cynda, who disappeared into the kitchen to change. Riana followed right behind her. They dressed in a hurry as Cynda complained that she hadn't had a chance to rub her blade with choji clove oil after beheading the last Asmodai.

"It still has brown, sooty streaks. I'm losing my touch."

Riana zipped up her suit. "We just haven't had time."

"God I'm starving." Cynda grabbed an apple. Riana did, too. They could eat and walk if they had to.

She followed Cynda out of the kitchen to find Merilee standing alone in the living room. As was typical, she didn't have her face mask down or her gloves on, but otherwise she was ready.

Riana glanced from the door to the couch and chairs, which were vacant.

"Shit!" Cynda whirled around and glared at Riana. "The bastard's gone, and he's got Andy with him."

"Creed wouldn't hurt Andy," Riana said. "They probably left together."

Merilee looked confused, then outraged. "I thought you had them with you." She turned around and smacked her hand against the closed door. "What the hell do they think they're going to do out there, other than get themselves killed?"

Riana retrieved a set of her daggers from the closet.

Cynda cursed some more and grabbed her sword. "You know they're headed for the Bronx. For the trail. You know they are, Riana."

"I know." Riana wanted to slap Andy and kill Creed. And she had to agree with Merilee—what did they think they would accomplish? It was suicide, going after Asmodai with conventional weapons.

"They've got five minutes on us," Cynda pointed out. "Maybe six or seven, and more each second we stand here and bitch."

Merilee popped the door another good one, then turned back to Cynda and Riana. "Should I get the Jeep?"

Riana blew a long breath through the tiny opening in her face mask. "Yes. Get the damned Jeep. Let's go."

(12)

Andy laid tracks up the Major Deegan Expressway. Outside the Crown Vic, the lights of the Bronx flashed by at record speed. Creed clenched his fists against his knees and tried to focus on the darkness. Riana would probably think he'd lied to her when she found him gone. He hoped he'd get the chance to explain that Andy had come unglued, that he couldn't let his partner plunge into weird shit with no backup. And Andy wouldn't have called for backup. They were off their turf, out of their area of authority, and about to be friggin' out of their league.

"Are you sure you want to do this?" he asked again, keeping his voice as calm and quiet as he could.

"Shut up." Andy squinted so much Creed wondered if she actually closed her eyes while she was driving. "You've seen one. Thing. Monster. Whatever I'm going to see. You don't have to take a bunch of unbelievable bullshit on faith. And you didn't just find out all your best friends are witches or wizards or voodoo queens."

"Sibyls," he supplied, then regretted it when she banged her hand on the steering wheel. The Crown Vic swerved.

Creed decided silence was the best option.

Andy drove without speaking for another few minutes, breathing heavily, then said, "And you. My partner. The man who knows *everything* about *me*. When were you going to tell me you just happen to be a—a—whatever you are? Next week? Next year? The twelfth of never?"

"Never, but not because I don't trust you." Creed grimaced as Andy swerved around an 18-wheeler and cut off an SUV. The driver blared the horn. "I don't talk about my . . . uh, problem. Never have. Never intended to."

"You told Riana and the girls, and you hadn't even known them a day."

"Chrissake, Andy, they had me naked and handcuffed to a ceiling beam—and they pulled off my ring. What the hell was I supposed to do?"

Andy hit the Crown Vic's blinker and swerved toward the West 230th exit and Van Cortlandt Park South. He thought he saw her face slacken, and she wasn't crying anymore. Either she was intrigued about what they were about to find on the John Muir Nature Trail, she was considering forgiving him, or she had finished leaping into a pit of total batshit craziness.

Clearly, Andy didn't handle shock well.

Creed had to give her a break on that one. It was a lot to find out your best friends worked as leather-clad paranormal warriors by night and your partner was some kind of demon. All in less than a day.

"So," Andy said a little too calmly as she made the turn onto Bailey Avenue. "Are you just going to fuck Riana, or do you plan to get serious?"

Creed felt the *other* stir as he thought about Riana against the bars of that jail cell, writhing with pleasure as he touched her. About the way she felt in his arms, the heat of her juices on his fingers. God, she tasted sweet. All woman. It took him a moment to calm his thoughts and the beast inside, and when he opened his mouth, he intended to take a turn telling Andy to shut up. He wanted to tell her he didn't want to talk about a woman the *other* wouldn't let him have.

Instead, he laughed.

At least Andy wasn't losing her mind after everything she'd heard back at the brownstone. She was being a total bitch, yeah, but total bitch was one hundred percent the partner he knew.

"Because if you're just planning to fuck her, you might be

in trouble," Andy went on, for once keeping her eyes fixed on the road. "I don't think Ri and the girls do casual, past the random gym sex toy."

Creed gave her what he knew was a blank look, because he was trying to keep all expression off his face. "Random gym sex toy?"

Andy shrugged, then jerked the Crown Vic's wheel to the left, making the corner on two wheels, three tops. "You know. Muscle hunks from the gym. They're good for one-night stands when the battery-operated boyfriend just won't cut it. Good exercise, too. Extra cardio."

"That's, uh, probably too much information." Creed watched signs for the Van Cortlandt Golf House flash by. He didn't like the image of Riana cruising for muscle hunks at the gym. He resisted the urge to check the definition of his biceps.

Andy ended up getting turned around trying to find a good place to leave the car, exiting the park, and barely listening to Creed when he told her the best place to reenter. He knew the park better than she did, since he had run cross-country events in Van Cortlandt before. She swore a lot as Creed directed her onto the Henry Hudson, then back off at Broadway, so they could get to the Riverdale Equestrian Centre.

"It's closer to the trail," he said over her swearing.

She swore some more and griped about losing valuable time.

As she pulled into a parking space, Creed said, "Andy, if I hadn't gotten knocked out in the alley, that Asmodai would have killed me. I know you need to see things for yourself, but I don't want you to get hurt."

"I won't get hurt." She threw the Crown Vic into park, jerked the keys from the ignition, and opened her door. "You'll protect me. I have faith."

Creed got out in a hurry as Andy circled around to her trunk.

Powerful scents of grass, water, and moist, fertile dirt washed over him, carried by the chilly breeze. The air smelled sharp, too, almost acrid, and Creed's skin crawled with the sensation of unnatural energy rippling through the dark fall night. The big red buildings of the riding stables seemed too dark, too quiet, as if the horses knew to be absolutely silent.

Andy dug in the trunk, jerked out two NYPD standard vests, and handed Creed his body armor. He automatically shrugged into the padded straps and jerked the Velcro closings tight over his T-shirt at the sides.

While she fastened her own Velcro, Andy said, "We don't have the right weapons, do we? Pistols probably won't make a difference with these things."

"Pistols won't make a difference." Creed grabbed two black flashlights out of the trunk, and tossed Andy one of them. Before he even got his flashlight switched on, she had started toward the stables. "Hold up a sec," he called after her. "You're going the wrong way."

She stopped and looked back at him, obviously annoyed. "So which direction is the John Muir trail?"

"Stay back a step or two." Creed got his flashlight on, and he jogged east toward the trail entrance, intending to keep Andy behind him so she would at least have a human shield. "The aqueduct's about halfway down—a mile? Maybe not that much."

As he made the slight left turn onto the John Muir trail, he couldn't see the stone bridge abutments from the old Getty Square spur of the New York Central, but he knew they were there. His super-bright beam splashed against about three hundred feet of oak, tulip, and hickory trees crowding the white curb running at the edge of the pavement. In the few tree breaks, he could see city lights glowing against the sky like beacons, summoning them back to safety. Ahead of him, the trail seemed to stretch into oblivion. Definitely not safe. Van Cortlandt Park had over a thousand acres of ball fields and playgrounds and thick forest, with a golf course and streams and even the biggest freshwater lake in the Bronx. Tonight, it had Asmodai, too. Creed doubted they would do much for the ambience.

Andy's sneakers ground against the pavement as she ran to keep up. Creed didn't bother to slow down, to ask her the plan, or to come up with one himself. No way to plan for the unknown.

Just charge in and hope we kill what's trying to kill us. Before *it kills us.*

He crossed a bridge, then headed past the spot where, in the daytime, trail walkers could look across the Henry Hudson and see the big Fordham Gneiss rock formation on their left—a piece of the ancient bedrock that held up New York City. Creed hoped that bedrock was as strong as it always looked to him. There was enough going on in the Big Apple to rock the city right down to that gray, flinty core.

The night felt wrong. The air smelled wrong. He couldn't put his finger on it, but the *other* coiled in his gut, snarling insistently.

His ring started to vibrate.

Okay.

Bad shit. Dangerous shit. And really close, too.

He jogged forward, faster now, pushed by the *other*, forgetting more and more about caution and sanity. The flashlight beam danced off the trees, the pavement, and ultimately, the high metal mesh fence separating the trail from the Van Cortlandt Golf Course. Nothing unusual. Nothing out of place.

Yet.

Was that a rustle in the leaves?

A scraping, a thump?

Something growled.

Then something up ahead, something in the endless darkness of the vines and plants and trees between him and the natural staircase, let out a feral roar.

A woman shouted, then screamed.

"Shit!" Creed doubled his speed and heard Andy pounding along behind him. The staircase had to be just ahead. Creed swept his light back and forth, searching for the stone steps. Hard to see. Made to look like part of the landscape. There. There!

Another scream tore the air, followed by a curse.

Those sounded familiar.

Had Riana's triad reached Van Cortlandt and joined the battle while Andy was driving all over the Bronx?

The *other* made a charge inside Creed, turning his gut and making his ribs ache. His skin pulsed. He clamped his teeth tighter and gripped the flashlight. One of his eyes closed from the effort of keeping the thing contained.

Too much uncertainty.

Too much strange shit.

He never had this much trouble with the *other* when he was on his own turf, in his own element.

The reek of sulfur and burned flesh filled the air. Turned dirt. Burning leaves. A breeze bashed into Creed as he stumbled over the first of the natural stone steps leading upward toward a rough stone building that once belonged to the old Croton Aqueduct. Seconds later, Andy plowed into him from behind. Creed bounced a knee off the next rock ledge but didn't slow down or turn around. If Andy fell backward and came up the steps more slowly, so much the better. What the hell was she planning to do?

What the hell am I planning to do?

But he went up, scrambling for each step, trying to keep the flashlight beam in front of him. He crested the hill and pelted down the path toward the melee he could hear near the aqueduct building. Grunts and curses rang out, along with the crack and spark of metal striking stone. Jets of fire blazed upward and sideways, too. An arrow whizzed by his head and buried itself in a tree with a sickening *chock*.

"Down!" Shouted a woman's voice. "Left. Left, Bela!"

A wall of dirt slammed into Creed. Dirt and rock rained on his head as he lunged toward the aqueduct building and trained his flashlight forward. Something heavy crashed against his arm. Electric shocks traveled all over his skin. He shouted as his flashlight went spinning into the night. He tried to jump away from what hit him, but rough hands grabbed him by the sides of his vest and jerked him off the ground.

In the bouncing light of Andy's fast-approaching beam, Creed found himself looking into the face of a big-boned man with drooping jowls and a thick, ridged brow. For some reason, he couldn't get a fix on age or nationality, or any of the features beyond basic shape. He grabbed the bastard's wrists—and shook from what had to be a serious electric shock. Cursing out loud and even louder in his mind, Creed let go. The man held on to the sides of his body armor, dangling him just off the ground like a toy.

Creed drew back his fist to punch the guy, then froze again when the man blinked. An eerie gray light came from the freak's eyes, and Creed thought he saw swirls of black inside that light. Like tornados, getting closer and bigger. The man opened his mouth. A sound came out like the rush-roar of a hurricane, and wind stronger than a g-force simulation slammed into Creed. His hair and clothes swept backward. His body armor flapped and tugged against his waist. He thought the skin was going to peel right off his face.

The *other* flailed inside him, roaring right back at the freak. Creed felt his fist moving forward, then swinging forward, powered by his own rage and the rage of the creature inside him. The wind's resistance shattered. Lightning crashed through every muscle in Creed's body when his knuckles made contact with the thing's nose, but the freak let him go.

Flying.

Back down the trail, away from the aqueduct building.

He crash-landed into something that fell heavily to the

ground beneath him. His ears rang from the roar of the wind that thing had thrown at him, but he could hear well enough to make out Andy's muffled threats and insults. As fast as he could manage, fighting to keep control of his senses and not let the *other* run away from him, he rolled off her, facedown in the dirt of the trail. He got a good mouthful before he pushed up on his hands and knees.

"Jesus H. Christ on two fucking crutches" came Andy's voice from beside him. She sat up and snatched her flashlight off the ground. Creed winced as its beam blazed into his face.

"What are those things?" She swept the light up the path, toward the aqueduct building, at least fifteen yards ahead of them. "And are those the Sibyls? The chicks in the leather bodysuits?"

Creed nodded and spit out dirt. His right hand throbbed from hitting what had to be an Asmodai. He felt like his friggin' fingers were going to burst into flames and burn right off the end of his wrist. Worse, he couldn't stop snarling, because the *other* was snarling so powerfully in his chest. His skin seemed to be tearing off his ribs each time the beast thrashed inside his gut.

Andy scrambled up and waited for him to get to his feet.

It sounded like the world was coming down around their ears.

The Sibyls shouted to each other and roared frustration as they waded in closer and closer to the small army of powerful demon-things. More blasts of fire and wind roared through the night. Creed's eyes watered from the stench of burned clothes, burned hair, scorched dirt, and sulfur. Dark curtains of earth swelled from the ground, then crashed back to the forest floor.

Andy's flashlight revealed five Sibyls. No, wait, more. Eleven women in those tight black bodysuits. Some had swords. Some knives. Some bows. And one was throwing what looked like small silver disks. They were battling five men. Only not men. Things. Asmodai.

Creed narrowed his eyes. The Asmodai kept . . . changing. Two of them threw fire out of their palms. One was pushing up chunks of earth and rock and hurling them like baseballs. The other two kept opening their mouths—mouths too big to be human—letting wind roar out and buffet the women fighting them.

"I've seen enough," Andy whispered.

Creed noticed her flashlight beam was shaking.

They should leave. They had to leave. But how could he just walk away from a fight—a horrible fight he wasn't sure the good guys—uh, girls—would win?

"Gotta do something," he muttered. "Keep the light trained, okay?"

Andy grabbed his arm. "No way! That thing threw you halfway back to Manhattan!"

"I punched it, didn't I?" Creed started forward, saw what was coming, and barely managed to whirl and tackle Andy before a jet of flames roasted the air where she had been standing. The flames sizzled against trees and leaves and vines, filling the path with a swath of gray smoke.

"Stay down!" someone shouted, but the voice brought Creed immediately to his feet.

Riana. Somewhere in the middle of all those killing machines.

"They're coming out of the stone building!" another woman yelled, and Creed thought it was Cynda. "It's full of holes. Look!"

Andy recovered her flashlight, and the two of them ran forward, shining a blistering white light on the mayhem.

Three to one, the Sibyls started taking the bastards out. First, one of the monsters took an arrow between the eyes and just seemed to evaporate. Turned to air and blew away, clothes and all. Little bits of metal and glass streamed to the ground where it had been standing. Before they reached the cleared spot in front of the aqueduct building, a wall of earth buried another Asmodai not five steps away from

Andy. Two women charged up the mound, dug its head out to the neck, then stepped aside as a third used her sword and sent the head flying. The Asmodai burst into flames even as the women who killed it tried to grab a piece of its clothing, something, anything. Creed and Andy reached the mound and glanced down. Nothing left except a metal tin that might have once held tuna or canned chicken, a bottle, a can, and other pieces of junk he couldn't make out.

"Pieces of trash, just like with Riana's triad?" Andy sounded incredulous, but Creed thought it made sense. If it worked once, why not again? By the time the Sibyls stopped putting out trash, the bad guys—the Legion—had already collected what they needed. And they cranked these demons up with multiple targets. Maybe all the Sibyls in New York, wherever they might be, whenever the demons might run across them.

The three Sibyls who had killed the first Asmodai had already joined their fellow warriors, hacking and slashing and firing arrows at the three remaining monsters. The Asmodai used fire, earth, and wind to deflect the attacks.

Creed tried to figure out which Sibyl was Riana. There were four women fighting with daggers.

The stone building shuddered. Part of the wall gave way, and another Asmodai staggered out, this one bigger than the rest and dressed in a long brown trench coat. Fire blazed off its shoulders.

"More," Merilee shouted from somewhere. "Did they have a demon-building party?"

An arrow struck the new Asmodai in the neck. The shaft caught fire and burned to nothing. It hesitated, nailed a Sibyl with a wicked stream of blue-hot flame, then swung toward Creed and Andy.

Riana ripped a sheet of earth from the forest ground and doused the flames, but too late. Goddess! Woman down. And the way she fell, she looked to be down for good.

Riana pulled away from the side of the stone building and ran toward the fallen Sibyl, Cynda and Merilee right behind her. The injured woman's fighting partner let out a howl of rage and jumped to protect her triad sister, curved blade blazing against the dark backdrop of trees and sky. Riana recognized Camille's blade. Camille from Alisa's triad. The fallen woman must be Bette. They had been fighting without their mortar, without their strength—and fighting like hell, too, but now they were paying the price. Even though Riana knew Bette was most probably already dead, they couldn't let Camille face that reality on her own. She would likely die defending Bette's body.

"Riana!" Creed's worried shout rose over the cursing and roaring and gouts of flame.

Riana had no time for Creed, no time for Andy, though her belly burned at the thought of any harm coming to them. She knew where they were, right below the stone building. She could track them because of the flashlight beam, which was more hindrance than help to the Sibyls, who saw fairly well in the darkness. For now, they would have to fend for themselves.

Goddess help them.

Riana's triad formed a triangle around the fallen Sibyl and her half-crazed defender, intent on preventing any Asmodai from getting near to what was left of Alisa's group. The other three triads would have to do the fighting. Damn, but that last Asmodai had been huge. And the demons seemed to be targeting *all* the Sibyls, not just one group.

How was that possible?

She didn't have time to wonder.

A rotten, earthy scent filled her nose, and she spun to face a tall, slimy-looking monster with mossy teeth and lichen-covered skin. Earth Asmodai. Its eyes blazed a sickening, dead-looking brown, and ripples of energy made the ground rumble with each step it took. Rocks pelted Riana's head, and she barely got her dagger locked with earth energy and directed her own power to shielding Camille, Bette, and her group before a steady stream of dirt poured down on top of them.

Deflected by her answering earth energy, the dirt piled all around them like extra fortification.

Riana tried to open a rent below the charging demon's feet, but it leaped toward her and grabbed her by the shoulder. She slashed at it with her earth-locked dagger and the thing's arm fell off and crumbled into mushrooms, snails, and black dirt. Before Riana could get in a clean stroke to the heart, Merilee fired over Camille's head and caught the thing with an arrow in the cheek—but that only enraged it. It swung its remaining arm like a club and caught Riana in the side.

She went down hard, gasping for breath.

Did it break my rib?

It was on her again, and she slashed its ankle off.

It roared and hobbled back.

The ground shook a little as Riana got to her feet, side aching. Earth Asmodai could do a little rattle-and-roll, but nothing like a Sibyl. Riana taught the creature that lesson, buckling the earth beneath its maimed leg and foot. It crashed to the ground. Riana ran forward and planted her earth-locked dagger deep in its chest, which caved into bracken and sour dirt. Its clothes writhed with what looked like insects and maggots, which consumed every thread in an instant before burrowing into the newly turned earth.

"That thing smells like shit," Cynda called. She had her hand on Camille's shoulder.

Camille still had hold of Bette, and she wouldn't look up.

"Riana, I think our favorite idiots are in serious trouble." Merilee's shout barely blocked the ragged sound of Camille's sobs.

Riana turned toward Creed and Andy's flashlight, winced from the pain of moving her body—and realized the flashlight beam was shining up at her from the ground.

She squinted against the light as the other three triads swarmed two of the remaining Asmodai and worked to shore up the stone building so no more monsters could break out of it.

The third Asmodai, the big fire demon, was moving away from the clearing.

Chasing Andy and Creed.

"No. No way it's targeting humans." Cynda's movements gave the lie to her words, because she was already leaving her protective position, pelting down the trail toward the Asmodai.

Merilee ran, too, and Riana didn't call them back.

"Camille!" she shouted over her shoulder as she pressed her hand against her throbbing side and ran after her triad. "Get a grip and pay attention! We have to leave you to make this kill."

Behind her, the sobbing stopped abruptly. Riana hoped the woman was alert again, ready to protect herself in the name of protecting Bette until they got back.

"Son of a bitch!" Cynda yelled as the fire Asmodai knocked Andy into a tree, caught Creed, and lifted him off the ground by his throat.

Merilee hit the demon with three arrows in his back, all a little off, all already burning to nothing. Riana reversed the earth-lock on her dagger, locked it with fire, almost dropped it in her desperation and pain, but got it thrown to the left of Cynda, at just the right angle. It struck the As-modai in its head.

Damnit. Not deep enough! It would burn Creed to ashes and Andy, too. They couldn't get there in time!

Creed's clothing caught fire.

Then his hair seemed to blaze.

Only it wasn't his hair. It was his whole body.

His unearthly bass rumble of surrender echoed through the trees as his body armor blew apart and the *other* emerged.

Cynda stopped so hard and fast she actually kicked up a spray of dirt. She jumped off the path, taking shelter behind a mound of dirt stirred up by the battle. Merilee didn't reverse course. She plunged forward, jumped around the battling demons, and threw herself over Andy's prone form. Riana stopped running, too, and dodged behind the nearest tree.

They couldn't attack now, not without risking killing Creed instead of the demon. And if they killed the demon, what then? She didn't have Creed's ring. She couldn't command the *other* at all.

Sulfur stung her eyes and nose, and she coughed. Murmurs and shouts from back around the stone house told Riana the Sibyls had noticed what was happening. She glanced back to be sure no other Asmodai had emerged from the building, and felt the briefest relief for that shred of good luck.

A shriek brought her attention back to Creed-as-*other* and the Asmodai, who appeared to be locked in a combat to the death. As Creed finished taking on his alternate form, Riana saw that he towered over the big fire Asmodai.

Another shriek made Riana look down near the smoking feet of the Asmodai, where she saw Merilee had dragged Andy out of immediate danger, behind a big oak near the trail. Merilee was standing and waving crazily.

Creed-as-*other* crushed the Asmodai's head between his big golden palms, tore the smashed head right off the demon's neck, and flung it into the brush even as it caught fire and burned away to nothing. At the same moment, Merilee hurled something small and shiny directly at Riana's head.

She snatched the object out of the air on reflex, then opened her palm to discover Creed's signet ring.

The towering golden god-shaped creature turned on the dirt mound protecting Cynda, thrust out his hand, and swept the pile of earth back toward the stone house in one fluid motion. Riana covered her head to keep from being pelted by rocks and sticks.

Cynda jumped into battle stance, sword blazing. "Don't make me," she shouted. "I swear I'll do it!"

She pulled back to swing.

The other nine Sibyls who had been fighting Asmodai burst back onto the path. They charged forward, a blur of black leather, raised swords, sailing daggers, flying arrows, and deadly, whirling *shuriken*—"ninja stars" to people who watched too many movies.

"No!" Riana drew deep on her earth energy, reached into the ground with her power, and yanked a thick, long wall of dirt and rock skyward. The dirt wall blocked flying daggers and arrows. *Shuriken* struck rocks and dirt clods, knocking them to the ground. The earth itself rumbled and groaned in protest, but Riana's dirt wall did its job. The charging throng of Sibyls stopped, shocked.

"I've got the ring, Cynda! Don't kill him!" Riana ignored the nine pairs of eyes glaring at her. She sank to the ground holding her side, her muscles little more than weak rubber after expending so much effort creating the earthen shield between Creed and the triads.

Cynda dropped to one knee to dodge the *other*'s first roundhouse punch. "Well use the fucking thing already!"

Riana propped herself against the trunk of a hickory

tree, held up the ring in both shaking hands, and yelled, "Creed, stop! Be still!"

The *other* let out a jaw-clenching roar of anger. It wheeled on her, then went still, glaring across the path, its eyes flashing wild, furious gold.

Riana kept the ring in one hand and used the other to brace herself against the hickory tree and stand. "Kneel," she commanded, trying to sound stronger than she felt.

The *other* radiated hatred and refusal, but after a few seconds, it complied, dropping to the ground on both knees.

The three other earth Sibyls temporarily held back by Riana's dirt wall managed to open the ground and return the curtain of earth to its origins. As a result, three other triads watched Riana instruct the *other* to put out its right hand and spread five fingers. They were still watching when she jammed the ring onto the creature's right third finger and stepped back.

The *other*'s golden light faded. As had happened in her living room, the creature's shape became more definite, then gradually stopped glowing. Bones and muscles appeared, followed by skin, scar on the left arm, and finally Creed's black hair. Naked. Splendid. But pale and shaking. Eyes closed, he fell forward, then curled into a ball.

Riana ignored the pain in her side and ran to him. She dropped to her knees and put her hand on his shoulder. He was saying something, so she bent forward to hear the words.

"Had to," he whispered. "No other way. No other way. Had to save her."

Her heart squeezed like it might stop beating. She wanted to curl up behind him and hold him, protect him from the prying gazes of all the people staring at him. Women who didn't know him or understand him.

Like you do?

"What the hell?" Bela Argos, leader of the South Bronx triad, pulled off her leather face mask and turned on Riana. She had pulled her dark hair back in a tight bun, giving even more emphasis to the natural slant of her exotic eyes. The woman was hard as forged steel and utterly unforgiving, which Riana knew all too well from previous encounters. "Did you bring this *thing* here, Dumain?"

"What is it?" one of her triad asked.

"Exactly what I want to know." Bela folded her arms. "Why did you defend it? And why are we letting it live?"

"Look, bitch." Andy elbowed past Merilee and Cynda and walked right up to Bela, not seeming to care that Bela's saw-toothed sword was still drawn and smoking from battle. "This is my partner Creed Lowell. He's an NYPD detective and a good man, who just came here to keep me from getting my stupid ass killed. Which he did, in case you didn't notice."

"NYPD." Bela snorted. "The bastards who arrested Alisa? Please give me an excuse to kick your ass."

A chorus of grumbles agreed with her.

Andy got even closer to Bela and pointed her finger in Bela's face. "Don't give *me* an excuse, because I have a gun. I bet bullets work against your skinny ass just fine."

Bela opened her mouth to say something, seemed to think better of it, and clamped her lips together.

Cynda and Merilee both turned around suddenly to keep from laughing in Bela's face. Andy's unrelenting attitude silenced the other Sibyls, too.

"We're trying to clear your friend, by the way." Andy swept her angry gaze over the group of warriors. "If she's innocent."

"She's innocent," Bela said immediately, then looked back at Creed. "Can you say the same for him?"

"Creed—and what he is or isn't—is my problem, and I'll handle him," Riana said quickly, letting her eyes dare anyone to challenge her. Goddess, but her side hurt. She hoped she didn't have to slug it out with anybody. "We need to see to Bette. She was injured—I think killed—and Camille's with her up by the stone house."

It took almost an hour to make certain no more Asmodai were getting ready to pop out of the old Croton Aqueduct stone house, and to determine that the Asmodai had used trash to target all of their biological signatures—Creed and Andy included, though the Goddess only knew why. Riana meditated for a few minutes to ease the pain in her side and start the healing process for her deep bruise. Nothing seemed seriously injured when Cynda checked, except of course Cynda's ass, which was still wounded from Andy's arrow-strike.

When Riana could move comfortably, she helped the group repair the damages to the area as best they could, and calmed Camille enough to prepare Bette's body for transport.

After a brief discussion, they decided to send Bette's remains and Camille home to their Motherhouses, with the help of the South Bronx triad. Cynda volunteered to accompany them to assist. The complexity of the communication necessary to open the ancient channels to transport living beings—even if the Mothers willed it and assisted on their end—was formidable. Most pestles could accomplish such a feat, but Cynda was the best of the best, and everyone knew it. Tonight, nerves and wills had been frayed to the breaking point, so no one even thought to refuse the offered help. Not even Bela.

Bela had, in fact, been remarkably quiet since Andy had threatened to shoot her, and since she realized Creed and Andy had been targets of the Asmodai, too. In fact, once they had found Camille huddled over Bette's burned body, Bela had done what she always seemed to do best—offer motherly comfort to the younger, less stable Sibyl. Camille had always been troubled. She had barely made it through her fire training in Ireland, but Riana knew that Alisa thought the girl was worth the risk and took her as the third member of her triad. Bela treated Camille with kindness, speaking to her tenderly and guiding her gently through the grounding and wrapping of the corpse, using sheets that they retrieved from Camille's nearby apartment.

As for Creed, he slowly returned to himself, but he remained seated on the ground with his face averted from the group. Riana figured he was being quiet because he was exhausted, not to mention naked except for a towel, also borrowed from Camille's apartment at the edge of the park, and unarmed in a large group of women who had recently tried to kill him. She sensed that he realized he was a liability, that his presence had placed Riana in a tenuous position with the other New York Sibyls who saw his transformation. She appreciated and respected him for minimizing the damage. Not every man knew when to keep his mouth shut and his participation at a minimum.

In the end, Merilee went with Camille, too, as did the other air Sibyls, an honor guard for Bette's final trip back to Motherhouse Greece. Riana watched Camille and her triad sisters go with a hollow ache in her chest. How would she feel if her chosen family had been ripped apart, jailed or killed? She didn't know how Camille would survive such blows. If she lost Cynda or Merilee, she would lose part of her own heart.

And yet . . . hadn't she taken such horrible risks only a day or two ago? Hadn't she brought Creed into her home and kept him there?

He stood, as if sensing her attention had turned to him. Andy came up beside him. The three of them remained in the clearing, a quiet trio, until the other Sibyls were well on their way. Then Andy said, "I'm so sorry. I never should have come here. Creed kept saying it was a bad idea, but I just had to . . . I thought I needed to see things. For myself, I mean."

She covered her own mouth and looked at the ground.

Then she pulled her hand away, took a deep breath, and said, "I got her killed somehow, didn't I? She wouldn't have died if I hadn't been here."

Riana shook her head and gripped Andy's elbows. "Sibyls die, Andy. We're soldiers in a war, and we get killed. Bette never even knew you were here."

Andy wiped her eyes, nodded, then started crying again, and Riana held her until she got control of herself. When she finally felt like Andy was okay, she stepped away, only to notice Creed's dark eyes appraising her tenderly, as if he wanted to hold her the same way. Riana felt flutters in her belly, then pushed the feelings away. She couldn't let that continue, even though she had to deal with Creed and keep him locked away until they understood more about what he was and the danger he truly posed.

"I'm going home for a shower," Andy said shakily.

"Too dangerous," Riana countered. "You've been targeted by the Legion. Pack some things—fast, don't linger—and come back to my place. Use your cell if you run into trouble."

Andy looked like she wanted to argue, but she glanced back in the direction of the stone house and shivered instead. "Ooookaaaay. Going home to get my suitcase." She flicked the edge of Creed's towel, making him slap it down to keep his cock off display. "Guess you're going back to sex-jail, so I'll head by your place and get you some clothes. Uh, maybe a lot of clothes, partner. I'm sick of staring at you naked."

"Shoelaces," Creed said instead of telling her she didn't know how lucky she was. "Don't forget extra shoelaces."

Andy gave him the eye. "Right. You planning to garrote the monsters next time?"

Creed shook his head. "I'm planning on pissing off Cynda a few more times. You probably will, too. Shoelaces burn fast."

In any other situation, Andy might have laughed her ass off over that. This weird night, however, she just nodded, and he saw her making a mental note. "Shoelaces," she muttered. "Gotcha."

Creed and Riana walked Andy to her Crown Vic, then cut back through the park to reach Riana's Jeep. Creed remained silent most of the way, wary and tense, darting glances at the shadows over and over again. Riana felt stupidly safe with the big man next to her. She couldn't get over the sight of the *other* destroying an Asmodai with its bare hands. Even though she knew Creed had no control over that aspect of himself, she couldn't help thinking that he—it—did it for her, at least on some level. For her, for Andy, for the rest of the women.

Not just for its own survival. I hope it isn't that feral. She cut her eyes to Creed's watchful profile and sighed. *Even if it is, Creed isn't. He took that ring off to save Andy. To save all of us—even though he knew the other Sibyls would probably kill him.* She stopped walking. *Goddess. Did he want them to kill him?*

Creed turned back to her. His expression allowed no interpretation except that he was a cop on alert, ready for anything, even if he was wearing nothing but a towel.

Faint moonlight spilled onto the trail, giving the impressive cut of his muscles a silvery sheen. Riana's heart raced as she stared at every gorgeous inch of him, caught between the urge to kiss him and hit him.

"You wanted them to kill you, didn't you?" Her voice came out with a quaver that grated on her nerves. "You intended to save Andy, save us, then figured they'd take you out. Easy solution for everybody, right?"

Creed stood very still. His expression didn't change, and his lack of denial answered her question.

"I don't ever want to hurt you," he said quietly, keeping his eyes fixed on hers.

Riana launched herself at him. "You son of a bitch!" She swung her fists and hit him in both shoulders. "Nobody kills you but me, understand? Nobody!"

He stood still for her assault, then simply took her in his arms and kissed her long and hard and deep. Riana didn't fight his embrace. She returned it and held on to his neck like a drowning woman. His tongue found hers, blending, pushing, and he tasted so incredibly hot and powerful and male. She dug her fingers into his shoulders. Every muscle in her body ached, and she thought her sore side might split open. Still, she wanted to rip off his towel and ride Creed until morning, feel his cock thrusting inside her until they couldn't begin to move again.

How dare he think about dying?

How dare he think about leaving her?

I'm getting in trouble fast. Real trouble.

Creed broke off the kiss and pushed her gently away. Instantly, she hated the loss of his body against hers, and almost cried out in frustration. His nostrils flared and his fists clenched, and she could tell he was struggling with himself.

With the *other*?

"This isn't safe," he said in rough, gravelly tones. "Not here, not now. This thing in me—it's making everything crazy."

Riana didn't know what to say. Her body pulsed and throbbed. Her arms wanted to be filled with him again, and her mouth, and the rest of her.

When he looked at her, she saw agony etched across his face, and she didn't want to do anything other than kiss him again.

"Take me home and put me back in that jail," he instructed. "I'll go to work as usual, but I'll come back every night until you've figured out what I am—and how to control me."

(14)

Creed lay on the cot in his cell with his hands behind his head, actually grateful to be behind bars—and under a sheet Riana had given him to replace the towel that covered him on the ride back to Manhattan from Van Cortlandt Park. Thank God it had been too early for most people to be out on the street when they got to the brownstone. Steely gray light had just begun to push aside the darkness, and not even a cab had driven past as they hurried inside from Riana's Jeep. He hadn't been up to facing strange neighbors wearing nothing but a prissy pink towel. And a little towel, at that.

Most of his muscles still burned and ached, but he couldn't rest. He couldn't stop thinking. Mostly, he was stuck on the fact that Asmodai didn't attack at random. They had to be targeted—and an Asmodai had attacked Andy and him.

What did that mean?

Somebody saw us enter Riana's house and didn't like it. Or Andy told somebody about the Sibyls and word got around. But who? And once again, why? What difference do we make in the big picture?

Creed didn't fully understand what Asmodai were, but one of the monsters had tried to kill him. He had killed it instead. The memory of crushing the thing's head still played through his mind, and he didn't know whether to feel sick or elated. Mostly, he just felt exhausted—and Andy was taking forever to get back with his clothes. He knew he could sleep if he could just make himself close his eyes, but with Riana in the lab, that was hard.

Every time he heard the rustle of her clothing, he could

swear he smelled that enticing spring rain laced with lavender. It reminded him of everything beautiful, and he had already fused the scent with the image of her beautiful face and blazing green eyes. The smell alone made him want her now.

Everything made him want her.

"Are you sure the Asmodai won't jump Andy while she's alone?" he asked, trying not to look at her, but unable to help it. She was sitting about ten feet from him, working on that double-barreled science fiction pistol he had seen before Andy shot Cynda in the ass with an arrow. "If they have pieces of our trash, they have our biological signatures. They can attack us wherever, whenever, right?"

"Asmodai don't move in the daytime," Riana murmured without looking up from the telescope lens she was adjusting. "Only at night. The ritual to create them has to be done at night, too, and the demons only last a few hours before they disintegrate. Whoever sent that mob figured a bunch of us would answer the call for help, that we'd be overmatched and lose a lot of fighters."

She leaned to grab a small screwdriver, giving him a delicious side view of her curves outlined by form-fitting slacks and a white blouse. Her lab coat was missing. As for the lab, it smelled fresh and clean after a night of sucking in dirt and wind and that sulfur-stink from the fire Asmodai.

Creed forced himself to study the bars of his cell. He didn't know if the elementally locked lead would really contain the *other*, but the *other* seemed to think it was trapped. It hadn't stirred since Riana slammed the cell door. As for his cock, well, that was another story.

Above them, the brownstone seemed unnaturally quiet and still. No Andy yet, and Cynda and Merilee were still assisting with Bette, the Sibyl who had been killed.

"So, this Legion," he said, more to avoid the weight of the silence than anything else, "what do they want?"

Riana put down the pistol-thing and seemed to consider

her response. "Money. Power. Impunity. We're not completely certain." She tapped one of the pistol's barrels with the tip of the slender screwdriver. "Best we can tell, the Legion considers its members a higher class of human being, physically and intellectually superior. We think they want a return to feudalism—lords and serfs—with themselves as the new-age nobles. The rest of us would be chattel."

"That's nuts." Creed found himself shaking his head. "Something out of a *Batman* movie, or some old comic book. They can't possibly expect to pull that off."

"They're patient and well funded, Creed, and the leaders are as brilliant as they think they are." Riana sighed. "Never underestimate rich megalomaniacs with genius and persistence. They've been around a long time, and we still have no idea who they are—just Asmodai evidence that points toward their general locations and a vague sense of the group's internal structure."

She related that structure to him, using almost corporate terms—a council that controlled the flow of money and guided the overall plan. On the smaller, more local level, a director, assistants, and simple foot soldiers the Sibyls called "employees."

At last, she glanced in his direction, the troubled look in her eyes digging at his insides and making him want to kiss her until she smiled again. "We don't know if Legion members have innate abilities like the Sibyls do, or if they've found and handed down powerful ancient rituals. Maybe it's both. But for the last couple of years, the game's been steadily changing. We barely have time to attend to any other type of supernatural crime."

That made Creed sit up. He yanked the sheet over his lap to cover his ever-present erection. "Other types of supernatural crimes?"

"Sure." She turned back to the pistol-thing again, shifted on her stool, and picked up the device. "Like an out-of-control voodoo *houngan,* or idiots who get mixed up in perverted rituals." She gave the screwdriver a final twist and placed the little tool back on the countertop. "Last year we had to contain a woman who found a way to turn cats into rabid bats and sic them on people she hated."

Creed's cop-alarms gave a faint ring in the back of his mind. "Define *contain*," he said as lightly as he could manage.

"We took her cats away and sent her to Motherhouse Russia." Riana's tone was almost chilling. "The Mothers— especially Mother Yana—have ways of destroying perverted powers, or, if necessary, people who wield them."

Not for the first time, Creed thought that he would prefer never to meet one of those Mothers, or set foot anywhere near a Motherhouse. He was particularly disinclined to deal with Riana's Motherhouse, or that Mother Yana person he had heard about one too many times. She sounded pure evil, that old woman, and no doubt she'd be happy to wear his balls for a necklace.

Creed cleared his throat. "Andy and I have been working OCU all this time, and we haven't seen a single real supernatural event . . . until you, that is. Until all of this."

Riana's fingers traveled over the pistol in a way that completely captured Creed's attention. "You have to know where to look for power. You have to know how power smells, how it tastes, how it feels."

God, but she was killing him, stroking that contraption and talking about power, and tasting and smelling and feeling. . . . Any second now, his aching cock would give up and just fall the hell right off his body.

"People always talk about *magic*," she said, distracted, her voice dropping lower, into that range that made him want to throw her across one of those countertops and take her wild and hard. "What we deal with isn't magic. It's a connection to natural forces and awareness of energies that aren't human. It's ability—and knowing how to use that ability."

Yep. Cock's falling off.

He winked at her to save himself. "I've got to know this, then. Are vampires real?"

A half smile.

He smiled back at her.

Riana closed her eyes, and when she opened them, her face went serious again. "Creed, I like talking to you, but I have work to do."

Shit.

At least she stopped caressing the pistol. Creed took a breath and tried to look relaxed. "Shouldn't keep your jail in your lab, you know. Convicts get bored."

"Mmmm." Riana went back to whatever she was doing to the weird machine, but now and then, she cut her eyes toward him.

Every time she did it, he had to bite his tongue to keep from teasing her or trying to seduce her, or just talking to her. He liked talking to her, too, a lot. And he couldn't stop thinking about the fact that they were alone in the house.

Don't go there.

But he couldn't help going there.

After the crazy night and everything that had happened, he wanted to wrap his arms around her and make her his until morning. Maybe a lot longer. He wanted the relief. He wanted to give her the relief. And he wanted more than anything to keep her safe, to never see her in another battle like the Van Cortlandt Park fight. Seeing Bette crumpled on the ground, burned too badly to survive, it made his gut twist. That could have been Riana. He could have watched her die like that.

"What—uh—what will happen to Bette now?" The question came out before he could censor it. "How do you avoid all the attention from her death?"

Riana gave a little shrug and didn't look at him. "She wasn't a public figure, not like Alisa."

Creed thought about the attitude of the other Sibyls

toward the arrest and the NYPD in general, and he grimaced. Maybe Bette would be alive if Homicide hadn't locked up the North Bronx earth Sibyl. Shit. Even if he didn't have an *other* threatening to tear out of his skin, those women would have wanted his balls on a platter just for that.

"Cynda will help send Bette home to Motherhouse Greece." Riana kept her attention focused on the two telescope barrels attached to her weird pistol. "Merilee and the other air Sibyls will go with her as an honor guard, but I don't expect them to stay very long. The important part is getting Camille to her Motherhouse before she completely falls apart."

"How will they send her home? Do you have to book passage on a plane?"

"What?" Riana put down the pistol, but still kept her face turned away from his. "Oh—oh, no. That would take days and cause questions. We have other ways. Older channels of transport that Sibyls like Cynda can open."

Creed thought about the broken mirrors all over the brownstone's main room. He figured the Sibyls had some fantastic, impossible-to-believe way of moving through the glass, but he didn't press. The thin, tired sound of Riana's voice had troubled him. He studied her, and realized she was holding her crescent pendant in both hands, keeping her pain to herself.

He got to his feet, tugging the sheet around his waist, and cursed his own stupidity for not really considering what she must be feeling, losing a friend like that. "You knew Bette pretty well, didn't you?"

Riana nodded. "Cynda and Merilee are like my sisters. Sibyls in other triads so close by, they're like cousins. We help each other. We look out for each other." Her voice broke. "I didn't do a good job of that tonight."

"You did all you could." Creed leaned into the bars. "If you hadn't been there, that other one, Camille, probably would have died, too."

Riana folded her arms and lowered her head, and looked so utterly fragile that Creed came undone. "Come here. Let me hold you, honey."

Riana looked at him then. Her expression was startled, but soft. "I—I don't think that's a good idea."

"Neither is hurting with no one to comfort you." He wished he could pull the bars apart with his bare hands. He couldn't stand to see her like that, needing him, but just out of reach. In the short amount of time he had known her, he had realized she was made of steel—but only partly. The rest of her was soft and wounded and absolutely giving. He wanted to be the one to give to her, heal her, protect her, and he wanted to do it now.

"Riana, let me out, or come in here with me." His words came out in a husky growl, obvious and unmistakable, but he didn't care. He knew she wanted him, and he wanted her just as much. He could see it in the way she stared at him, in the tense lines of her body, in the way her mouth opened just a fraction, as if to let him inside. She wanted him to take her and close her away from all the pain, to remind her how good it felt to be alive, even in grief, even with so much worry.

When she started toward the cell, Creed clenched his fists around the bars to hold himself in check. Riana was breathing fast, like a little bird trembling before a panther.

Am I so dangerous?

He had a fleeting thought about the *other*, but the beast had gone dead inside him. No stirring, no sign. Maybe being forward wore it out as much as it wore Creed out. He didn't really care, so long as it stayed dead.

The sight of Riana walking toward him made blood pound through his body. She was so graceful, every step a glide. And the way her slacks molded to the curve of her hips—she was perfect. He could almost feel the silk of her hair in his fingers, taste the heat of her juices on his tongue.

Less than a foot from the door, she stopped and grabbed

one of the bars as if to hold herself upright. She turned her back to him then, so he couldn't see her face.

On impulse, he covered her fingers with his. So warm. So soft. Just making physical contact caused his jaw to clench with need. She gasped as if he had shocked her, and when she turned back to face him, the raw desire in her crystal green eyes made him groan. She leaned toward him—then pulled up short and touched her shining silver-and-gold pendant.

"This can't happen," she whispered.

Before he could argue with her, she slipped her hand from beneath his and stepped back.

"Riana," he managed to say.

She shook her head, then turned and bolted from the lab.

Creed watched her go and wanted to shout.

He settled for slamming his hands against the bars and literally rattling his own cage. When that didn't satisfy him, he spun toward the cell's back wall and brought his fists down against the cold, smooth stones.

Pain flared through his fingers and wrists. His breath caught in his chest, and he swore until he felt better. Most of him. His cock would probably never recover. But it was more than that. Yeah, he wanted her. He wanted to be inside her right that very second, but he wanted to be holding her, too. He needed to be the one she turned to right now. The thought of her in her room or upstairs, upset and alone, it ripped him up inside.

She doesn't need you, idiot.

Of course she didn't. Besides, her triad clearly didn't like the idea of them together in any way, not to mention the Sibyls he had met at the park.

If you still call it meeting people, when you're a demon and they're trying to stick a bunch of steel in your heart.

What had he been thinking?

Why in God's name would Riana want to be in *his* arms?

His mind flipped to earlier years, to his grandmother, the

only woman he had ever really loved. She was dead now, partly because of him.

Riana was smart. She was following her good instincts, and more power to her.

"You have the right of it, honey," he said aloud, barely resisting the urge to break his hands against the stones. "Stay away from me."

For a long time, Creed just stood there, his arms braced against the back of his cell and his head down. When he thought he could handle himself, he sat on the cot, then leaned against the wall and tried to think about work. Work always got his mind off everything. Crimes were like complex puzzles. It never hurt to spend time moving the pieces around in his head. Sometimes that's when he made them all fit together.

For a minute or two at least, he was successful. He decided that with all they had learned in the last couple of days, he and Andy should go back over the transcripts of all the initial interviews on the Latch case. That assistant Frith Something-or-other, Senator Latch, Raven Latch, Corey James, and Alisa James, too—though her transcript wasn't too coherent. If Sal Freeman, the captain in charge of OCU, wanted them on the case but off the grid, fine. But they'd get a little more "on" come Monday morning. And Creed wanted to talk to Riana's friend himself, see what his gut told him about the earth Sibyl who had been arrested for slaughtering a child. That would probably be trickier, with lawyers involved and all the press coverage. That, and if the interview transcript was any indication, she might not have too much to say. Creed even wondered if her defense team might question her capacity to stand trial.

Something rustled and clanked just outside his cell.

Creed sat up in a hurry to find Riana standing in the open cell door, dressed in a white silk bathrobe that barely reached her knees. Her hair was damp and hung against her face and neck in dark ringlets. The way that robe clung to her, she might as well have been naked, and he wanted to run his mouth over every silk-clad inch of her.

Her fingers wrapped around the bars of the door on one side and the bars of the cell on the other. Her beautiful eyes were wide, and she was still breathing like a hunted bird. Her lips parted.

A warning?

An invitation?

She let go of the bars and tossed the keys into the cell. They landed on the cot beside Creed. He wanted to say something, but he didn't dare speak and break whatever spell she had fallen under.

Maybe she's putting the spell on me.

Do I care?

This time, when Riana turned and walked away from him, her meaning was clear enough.

Now or never, big man.

Creed got up without the sheet and moved faster than he ever remembered moving. Respecting her tense silence, he followed Riana out of her lab.

(15)

Dear Goddess, what am I doing?

With every step, Riana's heart pounded harder.

Cynda and Merilee would probably be back soon. They would *not* be okay with this. But her body was on fire. Her nipples throbbed as they rubbed against her silk robe, and she was so aroused she was sure Creed would catch the scent each time she moved her legs.

She had tried to go to her room and lie down. She had tried showering, then relieving herself in the shower. It didn't help. With every passing minute, she had just grown more miserable.

Riana actually ached for Creed. She needed him in a way she didn't think she had ever needed any man, and she didn't know why, or why him.

At the moment, she didn't even want to figure it out.

She just wanted him in her life, in her room, inside her head, inside her body.

Now.

She pushed open the door to her bedroom, sensing him behind her, barely holding herself together until she heard the door shut behind them.

All the candles in her room flickered from the breeze.

A faint *click* told her Creed had turned the door's lock.

She saw herself in the mirror on the wall by the foot of her bed, almost naked, nipples jutting against the thin fabric of her robe. Her expression was half-hungry, half-desperate.

Creed moved behind her, a hulking dark shadow, rough where she was smooth, huge where she was delicate. He looked like a mountain, a powerhouse. He could snap her in half, but she knew he wouldn't. In the reflection, she saw his hands grip her waist even as she felt a jolt of pleasure from his touch. His head lowered, and she felt his hot breath on her neck, then the press of his lips and the sensual bite that made her moan with need. He moved against her, naked, his erection already tight and hot against the small of her back. He would take her hard, make her crazy, make her scream, and oh, damn, she wanted to scream.

Pleasure washed over her just from being so close to him, from letting him take control of her and give her what she wanted so much. She couldn't close her eyes because the scene in the mirror transfixed her. Creed kissed her neck, her ear. She felt it. She saw it. His big hands took hold of the sash on her robe and pulled it free.

Her robe fell open, baring her breasts and the dark triangle of hair below for her view and his, and he was looking even as he kissed her shoulder.

"Incredible," he said against her ear, keeping his eyes on her reflection. "I want to memorize every curve."

His hand passed over the bruise on her side, gently, carefully, and he kissed her ear again. "You take a lot of chances, honey."

Don't I know it.

At least the healing had begun, and she wasn't sore anymore.

Riana wanted to tell Creed how delicious it felt to have his hands on her, but she couldn't speak. She could only watch those hands move up, up, until he cupped her bare breasts, thrusting her hard, tight nipples forward.

Riana gasped, barely able to stand the anticipation building like a force of nature inside her.

"I knew your nipples would be dark," he said, his voice so low and deep she could feel it right between her legs.

Then he pinched her nipples and she almost lost her mind. She sagged back against him, finally closing her eyes, submerging in the delicious shocks of ecstasy. Each time he rolled the sensitive nubs between his thumb and forefinger, she almost came. Chills broke out across her body, and her damp hair and the excitement made her shiver.

He turned her around, slid her robe over her shoulders, and let it drop. She felt the silk whisper over her ass, and then his hands were there, squeezing her, pulling her tight against him as he found her mouth with his.

Riana moaned into the kiss, wishing she could somehow get closer. She had never tasted anything better than the heady tang of Creed's mouth. His tongue met hers with a rumble of desire. She smelled the lavender rinse from her shower mingled with Creed's cedar and mandarin musk, and she wanted to cry from relief. Joined. Together. This was how it was supposed to be, her body mingling with his. No division. No place where she stopped and he began. Her sensitive nipples rubbed against the hard muscle of his chest, and her right hand found the scar on his arm and traced it to his elbow.

Battle scars. Wounds from combat. He had seen his share of battles, this man. She just knew it. The warrior part of him excited her even more. When she pulled back from their kiss, he bit her bottom lip just as he had done the first time he kissed her. Upstairs on the table, just before she jerked off his ring and nearly blew up the whole world.

Riana shivered harder.

Unfinished business. I should have done what I wanted to then, right in front of the Goddess and anybody else who wanted to watch.

She wrapped her fingers around the velvet iron of Creed's cock just as she had done upstairs, only this time, she didn't let go. She stroked him from balls to tip and back again, at the same time guiding his cock downward and pushing herself up on her toes, rubbing her whole body against him.

He groaned. "Damn. Do you know what you do to me?"

Unfinished business.

She sank to her knees, still holding on to him, and licked her lips at the sight of his erection.

Yes, it was her turn. She hadn't gotten to taste him back at the cell. But she'd taste him now, and make sure he never forgot it.

Gazing up at him, keeping her eyes fixed on his, Riana took Creed's cock in her mouth.

His head snapped back, and he said her name over and over, and she loved hearing it. She adored the uncontrolled sound of his voice.

His skin was so hot, and he tasted salty and light at the same time. Good. Too good. She gripped him at the base and pulled his pulsing shaft deeper into her mouth, farther back, half swallowing him until her lips met her own hand.

"Riana," he said again, more a gasp than a real word. She hummed against the sensitive skin, and his cock bucked in her mouth. He grabbed her hair in both fists and pulled, forcing her face down until he caught hold of himself and relaxed his grip. His hips seemed to move against his will, pumping, showing her how he'd take her, with long, smooth strokes. Every inch of her vibrated at the thought, and from the feel of his cock pushing into her mouth over and over. She swallowed him deep again, and he jolted to a stop.

"Honey, I can't take much more of that. Just looking at you is about to get me there."

Riana eased up on his cock and let him slip out of her mouth just enough to think he was escaping. Then she ran her tongue along the soft underside, tracing the vein until he tugged her away.

The strained look on his face let her know she had tortured him—and that he had never felt anything better.

She smiled at him and started to get up, but he grabbed her by both arms and almost yanked her to her feet and into a kiss. His palms pressed against her arms as he pushed his tongue into her mouth, and she more than welcomed him as he rubbed his damp cock against her belly.

"I want you inside me," she said against his mouth, kissing him again, and then pulled back. "Don't make me wait any longer."

Creed's growl of assent sent ripples of heat from her neck to that throbbing spot between her legs. She let go of his cock, put her hands against his chest, and pushed him backward toward her bed. She felt hollow, needy, waiting to be filled up and finally, finally satisfied.

In the dim reaches of her mind, Riana realized Creed was speaking, asking her something.

"Have something . . . some protection?"

"I'm a Sibyl," she said breathlessly. "I know how to keep myself from getting pregnant—and I know how to kill diseases if you have any. Which you better not."

He answered her by sweeping her into his arms and cradling her against his chest. She kissed him, hungry, ravenous, shaking with excitement as he placed her tenderly on the bed and immediately stretched himself over her, bracing himself just above her with his powerful arms. His lips crushed hers as he pushed her legs apart. So ready. So open for him. She felt the tip of his cock rubbing against her slick, swollen folds and almost came again.

"Now," she whispered into the kiss. "Please!"

The look he gave her was utterly feral and possessive. *Once I take you, I'll never let you go.*

She couldn't breathe. Didn't know if she still needed air.

Creed held her still with the force of his gaze as he thrust deep inside her channel in one smooth, mind-blowing stroke.

Goddess! She drew a long, ecstatic breath. Her walls stretched to hold him, and she lifted her hips to meet the perfect sensation. So good. So right. She moaned and wrapped her arms around his neck, then clamped her legs against his thighs.

"You feel perfect," he said, his voice ragged.

"Perfect," she echoed, then moaned again.

His arms rubbed against hers as he kissed her and rocked her, moving his cock in and out of her aching center, slow at first, almost gentle, then picking up speed.

Riana couldn't stop making noise. The sounds wound out of her chest, from somewhere deep in her soul. Her mind unraveled, and her eyes pasted themselves shut. He was taking her someplace new, someplace unique and wonderful and all their own.

"Open your eyes," Creed demanded. "Let me see how much you want me."

Riana didn't think she could do it, but her eyes sprang open as if her body wanted to obey him. He pushed himself deeper inside her channel, moving her in the bed with each thrust. His eyes seemed to pin her to the bed beneath him, claiming her, marking her. He really was memorizing her. He really did want to know every line, every expression, every inch. Riana clenched around him, loving the sensation, wanting Creed to stay a part of her body forever.

"Deeper." She barely got the word out, but she forced her eyes to stay open. "I want you deeper."

Creed's dark eyes blazed as he thrust harder, faster, deeper. Her nipples scrubbed against his chest, doubling her bliss and driving her closer to the edge. Chills gave way to burning heat and then sweat. She could hear their skin sliding together, smell the musk of their sex thick in the air. When Creed kissed her, she held him even tighter. When he let her breathe, she couldn't stop the moans rippling out of her throat.

"Yeah, honey," he murmured, riding her, stretching her, bringing her to that unbearable blend of pleasure and pain. "Scream for me. I like you crazy. I *love* you crazy."

Riana's ears rang. She gasped for breath against his next kiss. Her vision started to swim, and she tingled all over. Goddess, the mother of all orgasms. Now. Right now!

And she did scream, loud and long and endlessly, letting

every bit of feeling and emotion drain out of her. She couldn't stop moving, couldn't stop lifting her hips to meet his strokes. She dug her nails into his back, holding on, clinging tight, and still he rocked her, rocked her, and didn't stop. He stretched out her sensation, kept it going forever, until she thought she might come apart from the over-whelming flood of emotions.

He wanted her crazy.

He got his wish.

As Creed came, groaning but still pinning her with those dark, dark eyes, Riana heard herself hit a new note of de-light as she writhed beneath him.

So perfect. Goddess, had she ever felt anything so per-fect, so good?

And it stayed perfect, too, until somebody hammered on her bedroom door, then kicked the thing right off its hinges. Wood splintered and sprayed as the door fell heavily to the floor and Cynda and Merilee spilled into the room, weapons at the ready.

Creed froze on top of her.

His stricken expression told her he didn't know whether to pull out, keep her covered with his body, or prepare to die.

The third option seemed probable, for both of them.

"Oh, for Chrissake," said Andy from somewhere in the hallway. "I *told* you he wasn't hurting her. I so don't need to see this. I'm hiding my eyes. Shit, shit, shit!"

Riana felt herself turning nine shades of red as she twisted her head to get a better look at her triad sisters.

"Going to put your clothes in the jail cell, Creed," Andy said loudly. "Like you'll need clothes."

Creed rolled off Riana gently, letting his cock slip free and somehow managing to pull part of the bedspread over both of them. He propped himself beside her, draped his arm over her half-covered belly, and bravely faced the fir-ing squad—or the sword-and-arrow-squad—with her.

Merilee actually looked amused, almost pleased to find

Riana okay and getting a little relief from the horrible weight of the previous night.

Cynda did not look amused. Anything but. The fire Sibyl was red-faced, furious, and her eyes communicated disgust and betrayal.

"You owe me money," Merilee said. "I said they'd do the deed before the week was out. Fifty bucks. Pay me now."

"Shut the fuck up," Cynda snarled.

Andy came back toward the bedroom singing at full volume, something Springsteen. "Ooooohhh, I'm on fiiii-iiiire." Hands over her eyes, she marched past the door, heading for the steps.

Cynda cranked up, ranting about Riana having no sense of reality, no respect for the dead, and putting everything in the world before her duty as a Sibyl.

Riana didn't fight back, and she kept a hand on Creed's arm, hoping he wouldn't defend her. His fingers dug into the bed, but he didn't say anything. Maybe he knew it wouldn't have done any good, not when Cynda's sword and bodysuit were already smoking. Riana could tell her triad sister was tired to the point of exhaustion, sad, rattled, and a little bit—maybe a lot—right, anyway.

Finally, as Andy's off-key warbling reached the earsplitting stage from upstairs, Merilee shouldered her bow. "Come on," she said to Cynda. "Put away the big pocketknife and let's go upstairs. I'm hungry, and we need some sleep."

"You've got to be kidding." Cynda sheathed her smoldering sword and turned on Merilee. "How can you possibly think about food right now?"

"Uh, because my stomach is empty?" Merilee tried to hold her sarcastic expression, but ruined it with a big yawn. "Come *on*. I feel like I'm at a peep show."

She stretched and left the bedroom.

Cynda turned back toward Riana, and Riana braced for another barrage of accusations and admonitions.

Instead, Cynda gave Riana a miserable, distressed look, hung her head, and left without saying another word.

Riana swallowed hard.

She wished Cynda had slapped her or threatened her with the sword. Anything but look at her like she had just lost her best friend.

Creed tensed behind her.

Riana started to turn over and try to be bright and cheerful, started to say that Cynda would be okay, that she'd get over whatever she was feeling, but Creed was out of the bed in a heartbeat.

Just as fast, he jumped over the destroyed bedroom door and took off toward the lab.

All Riana could do was blink at the splintered doorframe. Then she glanced at the ceiling, thinking about upstairs, where Cynda, Merilee, and Andy were no doubt discussing her in great detail. She flopped back against her pillow, lay there for about a minute, then felt that wash of loneliness and need that had driven her to fetch Creed from his jail cell in the first place.

It wasn't long before she was up, putting on her robe, and heading down the hall to the lab. She figured he left so quickly to keep her from having any more trouble with her triad, but that horse was so totally out of the barn. Screw it for now. She wanted to curl up next to him and feel his arms around her while she slept. She wanted to wake up next to him and see his sexy eyes gazing at her, see that grin and revel in the tender way he looked at her, even if it was just a onetime indulgence.

She pushed open the door to the lab and immediately saw the cell keys on the floor. Confused, she stooped and picked them up. When she stood, she saw Creed in the cell. He had put on jeans and a T-shirt, and he was sitting on the cot with his fists pressed into his eyes.

"Are you okay?" she asked, unfamiliar anxiety and doubt spreading through her chest like a cold chill. She walked toward the cell, intending to open the door and go in to him if he wouldn't come out to her.

"Stay away from me," he growled—only it wasn't totally his voice.

Riana stopped abruptly and tightened her fingers around the keys. She narrowed her eyes. He looked normal enough, but she was starting to recognize that rock-hard tightness in his muscles, that agonized expression, and the half-hateful way he spoke when he was battling the *other*.

"What made it come forward?" she asked, keeping her voice low and quiet. "Cynda and Merilee bursting into the bedroom? The things they said?"

Creed offered no response.

"Did they make you angry?" She fidgeted with the keys, hating how worried and jumpy she felt. "What set the *other* off?"

Creed jerked his fists away from his eyes. He glowered at her, or the *other* did, then Creed seemed to regain control. His expression softened to one of apology, then regret.

"You did, honey." He sounded as unhappy as he looked, and the voice was all his again. "I'm sorry. I don't know why, but the *other* goes crazy every time I touch you."

It was Riana's turn to be silent. She gazed at Creed, wanting to reject the enormity of what he'd just said. And the fact that this didn't seem new to him. He wasn't the least bit surprised, was he?

"I thought—when I got back here, it went dead inside me. I didn't think it would be a problem." He opened his hands in a pleading gesture. "Give me some time. I'll figure it out. But right now I need to be alone."

Riana nodded, increasingly numb. She backed out of the lab and closed the door behind her. All the energy seemed to drain out of her body as she forced herself down the hallway. From upstairs, she heard Andy, Merilee, and Cynda talking, then laughing. All of a sudden, it seemed like they were on a different planet from her, off-limits, unavailable. She didn't think she'd be welcome if she went up there, and she couldn't talk to them about what Creed had just said. They'd tell her they knew it was a bad idea. They'd tell her she was stupid to have taken such huge chances, and even more stupid because she had trusted him. Because she still did trust him, and still wanted him with her so badly she felt it like a fist around her heart.

Taking care to avoid the bigger chunks of wood, Riana eased into her bedroom. She picked up her broken door and propped it against the doorframe as best she could. Then she blew out all the candles, crept into her bed, wrapped her arms around herself, and cried herself to sleep.

(16)

Creed did everything he could to force his thoughts away from Riana for the rest of the weekend, and the ten days following that, too, when he was out of the cell during the day and on the job. Work was boring as hell, and frustrating. Captain Freemen denied his requests to interview Alisa James, and bitched about Creed and Andy wanting to question Senator Latch and his wife, and even their assistant, Frith Gregory.

Interviewing James would be useless. Something's wrong with her, I'm telling you . . .

Talking to Latch or his wife would not be under the radar, Lowell. We're bringing them in end of the week for follow-up with the Special Victims cops actually assigned to this investigation. Read the transcripts and make do . . .

Yes, we need to resolve the occult elements in this murder, and they might be important, but you can't start a media frenzy . . .

Don't make me use these stripes against you, Lowell . . .

Life at the brownstone was exciting by comparison—and that wasn't saying much. As Creed knew, no Asmodai had caused any trouble since the attack in the park, and the Sibyls never went out to deal with anything else. They rarely came downstairs, either. Creed had to rely on Andy, who brought him food—and she spent way too much time enjoying the fact that he had spent the better part of two weeks hanging out in a jail cell, when he wasn't imprisoned by work.

Can't believe you let a woman lock you up and do experiments on you, Lowell . . .

Daaay-umm, she must be good in bed . . .

Hey, sweet cheeks, she must have the keys to your heart. Oh, wait. Look here. She loaned them to me . . .

Andy's ribbing aside, Creed slept some, ate a lot, and talked case strategy with Andy every time she came into the lab. And every time Andy took him for a walk downstairs, he felt Riana's absence like an ache in his gut. Riana had apparently moved out of her room, turning it over to Andy for the duration. When Creed asked Andy what was going on, Andy said Riana was sleeping upstairs on the couch.

Upstairs. Definitely away from me.

That hurt, but Creed understood. She probably didn't want to see him after realizing the *other*'s reaction to her. Even if she wanted to see him, she didn't need to.

Still, whenever he went into her room to use her bathroom, he smelled her.

He smelled them, together, even though the sheets had been changed.

The broken door had been tossed to one side of the rumpled bed, and Andy had left her clothes lying everywhere, but even that didn't stop Creed from remembering how it felt to see the need on Riana's normally composed face. He couldn't stop thinking about the wet heat of her excitement as he drove into her, the fire of her nails on his back, or the sweet sound of her screams as she came. He wanted to make love to her again. He wanted to hold her all night and kiss her awake the next morning.

Creed wanted to make Riana scream again.

No real chance of that, with her living upstairs now.

Finally, early Thursday morning, Riana came into the lab to get the pistol-thing she had been working to adjust. Creed was wide awake, doing push-ups, waiting for Andy to finish her shower and let him out. They usually hit the station early, and he still had to go by his place to pick up some clean work clothes.

Maybe it was a faint whiff of lavender or rain, or maybe

it was the whisper of fine cloth over soft skin, but he sensed her before he saw her. It took him two seconds to get to his feet and mop his face with his sheets. When he turned around, she was holding her pistol and watching him, her green eyes wide and misty.

He put his hands on the bars and started to speak, but couldn't find any words to say. She was just too damned beautiful.

She had her hair brushed over one shoulder of her tailored black jacket, which flowed seamlessly over her form-fitting black skirt. Underneath the jacket, a white silk shirt was open at the neck, just enough to give him a glimpse of her crescent moon pendant—and a hint of cleavage beneath it. His body responded to her so immediately he was grateful for his loose-fitting warm-ups.

She broke the silence with, "I hope you haven't been too uncomfortable down here."

"Not uncomfortable." He stared at her, caressed her with his eyes, and enjoyed the flush of color spreading across her cheeks and neck. "Just lonely."

She moved, not much, but definitely toward him. "I—I couldn't. Be down here with you, I mean. With Bette's death, I couldn't abandon Cynda and Merilee. I had to—"

He stopped her by raising one hand. "I understand. And I think you made the right decision."

She blinked. Actually looked disappointed. "Yes, well." The way her lips parted when she took a breath nearly made him groan. "I suppose I should get back upstairs."

"Stay." He gripped the bars harder. "Let me look at you."

Riana swallowed hard and started breathing too fast . . . but she didn't leave. Her fingers traveled over her pistol in that way that made Creed want to grab her and kiss her until she couldn't breathe.

"I realize you didn't have to come back here once you left Monday before last," she said, "but I appreciate your co-operation. I'd advise you to keep spending your nights with us, or at least another triad. Asmodai can find you if they're targeted to you, even if you go to another city."

The thought of not returning to Riana, even if he couldn't be in the same room with her, actually caused Creed physical pain. He shook his head. "I'm staying because I want to. When I'm here, I keep myself in this cell because it's safer for you."

Riana stroked the pistol a little faster. "Look, if you're planning—I mean, hoping to have another chance to—you know. Don't."

"Damn straight I'm planning. As soon as I can, I'm going to make you scream again, maybe louder this time." He winked at her and watched her turn a deeper shade of red. "I'm coming back because of that, yeah, but also because of your friends and the woman who got slaughtered at the park. And the women who tried to kill me. I'm coming back for Andy and the dead kid, and the Sibyl who probably shouldn't be in jail."

She walked toward him again, and he held her gaze.

"I don't fully understand this battle," he admitted, "but I'm in it now. I never walk away from a fight, honey."

"I don't suppose you would." She stopped a few inches from the cell bars and held her pistol in front of her like a shield.

He willed her to stay away and come closer at the same time. As long as he was in the cage, the *other* barely stirred—but could he guarantee that? Did he know for sure that it would be safe to touch her as long as he was behind the treated bars?

"I want to kiss you," he said.

Riana drew another shaky breath.

She leaned forward, then seemed to dredge up the strength to hold herself in check. "Bad idea," she murmured. "I'm not up for interruptions."

As if taking a cue, Andy burst into the lab yelling, "You ready to roll, because we're gonna be late."

Riana jumped so badly she nearly dropped her pistol and had to jerk it to her chest with both hands. She whirled toward Andy, who pointed to the contraption and said, "If that silver thing is some kind of freak-ass sex toy, I don't even want to know."

"Andy." Creed let go of the bars.

"Don't tell me!" She put both hands over her ears. "I can live my whole life without knowing what it is—and I sure as hell don't want to know what it does."

Riana waited until Andy lowered her hands. "It's a portable spectrograph."

Creed vaguely remembered the term from college.

Andy frowned and stared at the silver barrels. "Spectrograph. Is that a kinky medical thing?"

Riana laughed, and Creed felt like the whole lab brightened at the sound. "It's a device to measure and give photographic images of the light spectrum."

Now Creed remembered, but the machines he saw in chemistry and physics were ten times the size of the instrument Riana held in her hands. He said so, and Riana agreed with him.

"They can be huge, but I don't need huge for what I'm trying to see." She ran her fingers over the metal barrels. "Last year, I determined that all three types of Asmodai leave traces of gas behind, especially the fire demons. I'm looking for a filter that will isolate trails of sulfur dioxide. Footprints, if you will."

"Okaaay. Whatever." Andy fished the cell keys out of her pocket. "Sulfur. That shit reeks." She headed across the lab to release Creed. "Why don't you take your—uh, the stink-a-scope and move to the other side of the room. We need the *other* to play nice, because we have to get on the road."

Riana looked down at her newly christened stink-a-scope, looked back up at Creed, and smiled at him. The sight of her beautiful, amused face warmed him up inside.

If wishes melted bars, he would have had her in his arms at that moment, Andy be damned.

But Andy, of course, wouldn't be damned. She got the cell door open, dropped the keys on the cot, grabbed Creed's arm, and more or less dragged him out of the lab.

Creed ignored the mess Andy had made of his apartment the times she retrieved clothes for him. She kept apologizing as he sorted his way through slacks, coats, socks, and T-shirts. Good thing he didn't wear underwear, or she likely would have plastered it to his window. And that was before she started cleaning because something stank in the kitchen. Pretty soon she had emptied the kitchen trash, the living-room trash, and tossed out a bottle from the television table.

Creed dressed in his usual jeans and blazer, pissed that his best leather jacket had gotten torched at Riana's. His old brown leather bomber jacket seemed beat-up and shabby next to the jacket he lost, but it would have to do.

He looked up and realized Andy was absently pitching out unmatched socks he had left on his dresser the last time he did laundry.

"Knock it off," he told her before she started junking his unfolded gym shorts. "Just—give it a rest."

At the sound of his voice, Andy went pale. The trash bag trembled in her tight grip.

Creed took the bag out of her hands and tied it.

Andy watched him like he was performing some sort of miracle, then seemed to come back to earth.

"We've got to get to the house by oh-nine-hundred for the interview Freeman finally approved with Corey James." She rubbed her hand over her eyes and took a deep breath. "I want to see what we can dig out of him about his wife's activities as a Sibyl. I bet there's a lot more that Alisa hasn't told anyone, because she doesn't think she can. That jacket looks good, by the way. I like it better than the black one."

Creed glanced down at the worn leather. "Thanks. Listen, Andy, we'll find our way through this."

Andy didn't look like she believed him, but her color was slowly coming back. "I didn't transfer to the OCU for shits and giggles, I guess. I just never really thought—I never really believed . . ."

He nodded. "I know. Yet all along, your partner was an alien and you never knew it."

They started out of the apartment and actually made it part of the way down the hall before Andy said, "You're not *really* an alien, right?"

Creed got them to the station house in record time. OCU was headquartered on West Thirtieth, in the old Fourteenth Precinct station. The refurbished building served as headquarters for the Traffic Task Force. As the powers-that-be hoped, nobody paid much attention to the back corner of the top floor, where the double doors read simply, POLICE ANNEX. Six desks, one office, a storeroom, and two all-purpose rooms were crammed into a space not much larger than an elementary school library, but it was enough to do the job. They even had two "cover cops," regular detectives not officially assigned to OCU, who could investigate and interrogate without raising too many eyebrows. As for the old Fourteenth, the building's stone entrance looked like a castle with four turrets, giving way to smoother facing and polished windows. It had a modern Gothic charm that Creed couldn't help but appreciate. It seemed right to put the OCU—"Freak Squad" to the officers who knew about them—in a modern, half-creepy castle.

Suspects and persons of interest brought in for questioning thought the OCU was only there to take the overflow for Midtown South, and no one told them any differently. *Police Annex* was generic enough not to raise many questions. The minute Creed and Andy got off the elevator, though, they could tell something was out of the ordinary.

A bunch of guys in dark glasses and suits hovered in the hallway between the elevator and the main door.

"Feds?" Creed murmured.

Andy sighed. "No. Hired protection, I guess. Bodyguards."

"For a Senate challenger?" Creed shook his head as they pushed into the office. "Never thought of that being so high-risk."

Captain Freeman was standing in the door of his office scowling at a clipboard, his dark eyebrows pulled together in a sharp, telltale V-shape. Another cluster of guys in suits crowded in the hallway leading to the all-purpose rooms.

"I think we have special company other than Corey James." Andy nodded to Creed's desk, where a beige blazer, the very expensive kind with leather *and* lace, draped over his chair. "Unless Mr. James is a cross-dresser."

Creed noticed the blazer's scent drifting seductively through the station house. Something classic and musky, the kind older women preferred. Older women with boatloads of money. Right about then he remembered what Captain Freeman had said about a follow-up with Senator Latch and his wife toward the end of the week.

Was this Raven Latch's blazer?

Could he and Andy wangle a few minutes with the senator and Ms. Latch before they hit the streets again?

"Your guy's in Two," Freeman barked. "Keep it clean and quick."

Andy paused to grab a pen, pad, and a tape recorder, then the two of them plunged into the sea of suits clogging the main hall. They passed up the first door, at which point the clot of well-dressed guys with earpieces thinned considerably. Creed glanced back toward One, wondering what VIP had stopped in to ruin Captain Freeman's morning. He didn't have time to give it much thought, though, because Andy opened the door to Two and marched in to greet Corey James.

The man appeared to be in his early forties, with brown eyes and close-trimmed brown hair, dressed in a standard blue business suit and tie. Creed knew from Andy's notes that the guy was retired Army, and he looked the part in build and bearing, and in the way he kept his gaze level and straightforward, ready to meet any challenge. He didn't have any bodyguards, and to Creed's surprise, no team of attorneys or press agents or spinmeisters flanked his chair. He was sitting in a wooden chair at the room's small conference table, absolutely alone. Morning sunlight streaming through the screened window provided the only light. The guy had no trained pets, no props. Nothing but a cup of coffee in front of him. No cream. Probably no sugar, either.

Pretty basic. Creed studied him, knowing that Corey James had married a Sibyl, apparently with full knowledge of who and what she was. Straight A's in high school, toward the top of his class at the Citadel, eight years in the Marines, then business and politics. A little to the left with his environmental policies and social consciousness, but the guy was no idiot, that was for sure. He looked the type to make his decisions deliberately and carefully.

What would make him take on a political liability like a Sibyl?

An image of Riana floated through his mind, and Creed clenched one fist. He guessed he knew the answer to that question, didn't he?

When Creed and Andy sat down, Andy put her pad, pen, and recorder on the black oak table in front of her. She gestured to the recorder, and James nodded his permission for her to turn it on. Clearly, he'd been through his share of interrogations already.

Andy pushed RECORD, and Corey James opened the conversation with, "You've made a terrible mistake, arresting my wife."

Creed didn't correct him about which division and officers arrested Alisa James, and neither did Andy. They just asked him to explain.

Corey James leaned forward and gripped his coffee cup with both hands. "She would never harm a child. She protects the weak and innocent."

Andy gave the man a smile, tuning up for the role she'd play in this questioning. Creed didn't have to work at looking sympathetic, either. He felt for the guy, assuming he wasn't a psychopathic bastard who made demons in his spare time.

"Maybe you can tell me again why your wife was at the Latch house the night Jacob Latch was murdered?" Andy kept up her sweet smile, but Creed saw James sizing it up for what it was: a sugar-coated snarl.

James looked down at his coffee. "She was taking care of the boy, like she told you. She often watched him when his parents went out—Raven Latch is one of Alisa's best friends, and she doesn't—didn't—trust too many people with the boy."

He looks down when he doesn't tell the whole truth, Creed noted to himself. *Not a guy accustomed to lying, even for his wife's benefit. What the hell is he doing in politics?*

"How does that work, her being friends with the man you're running against?"

"Alisa and Raven met through their work on the Children's Council five years ago, and they hit it off right away. As for Davin, he and I do fine. Our rivalry is political, not personal."

"He's pretty far to the right of your positions." Andy tapped her pen on her pad. "That's got to piss you off every now and then."

James shook his head and let out a breath. "On paper, Davin's aligned with his party. He's not that stiff interpersonally."

When they gave him matching quizzical expressions,

James added, "He's been a mentor to me, tried to sway me more to the center. We're not enemies, Detectives. There's no mudslinging going on, no vindictive bullshit. We're just two guys slugging it out in the polls."

Andy put down her pen and leaned back in her chair. "May the best man win?"

"Exactly." James killed the rest of his coffee. "Look, you know I was across town from Raven and Davin when this horrible thing happened. At a fund-raiser—hundreds of people saw me, so I know I'm not a suspect."

"Killers can be hired," Andy said, beginning to really unleash her inner bitch.

James put down his empty cup and stared at her.

Andy stared right back at him.

Game on.

Creed felt completely relaxed for the first time in days. He was in his element, playing off Andy's lead. Thoughts of Riana, the *other*, and the outside world faded away as he watched his partner spend the next fifteen minutes doing what she did best: pissing people off. She absolutely infuriated Corey James, asking leading questions about his campaign finances, bank accounts, timings of withdrawals and transfers, and ultimately whether or not he screwed around on his wife or had a thing for little kids.

James held it together longer than most people, Creed had to give him credit, but he finally lost it over the infidelity question. James turned red in the face as he banged the table and pushed back his chair. He stood and pointed his finger at Andy. "I don't know what you're trying to do, and I don't give a damn. I came here to help my wife. Have you seen her? They—those people—*did* something to Alisa. You don't understand. You have no idea!"

"We have a better idea than you think," Creed said as Andy settled back in her chair, satisfied she had him rattled and off his guard. He reached in front of her, turned off the tape recorder, and landed the next blow. "We know your wife's a Sibyl, Mr. James. An earth Sibyl, trained at Motherhouse Russia. We know that her triad got caught in a shit-storm at Van Cortlandt Park this weekend, and that her friend Bette got killed by man-made demons known as Asmodai."

The expression on Corey James's face defied description. His muscles went slack, and he sank back into his chair, gaping at both of them. For a long time, he couldn't say anything. When he did speak, he said, "I heard about Bette, and about Camille going—uh, home. It's going to kill Alisa. She'll blame herself for Bette's death."

Creed nodded, and his gut ached when he saw the torture in Corey James's eyes. By the time he asked his next question, he already knew the answer. "Are you a member of the Legion, Mr. James?"

James shook his head, staring at his hands. "I know a little about them, but just what Alisa's shared. I never thought it would get like this, so bad. What are they doing?"

"We don't know," Andy admitted. "Killing kids for one thing."

James's head came up. "So you know Alisa's innocent, right?"

"*We* do," Creed clarified. "But I'm afraid we don't matter much in the grand scheme of things. We need proof, Mr. James. Tell us where to find it."

Once more, the look of pain on the man's face punched Creed in the gut. James opened his hands. "I don't *know*. Raven and Davin were afraid, though. I think they've run into these bastards before."

Andy kept her expression steady. Creed hoped he did as well. She didn't turn the tape player back on, but instead picked up her pen. "Go on. Please."

James eyed the pen and pad.

"This isn't official, Mr. James," Creed assured him. "You won't be quoted. Just give us something. Anything."

James frowned and lowered his head. "You know Jacob

was a late-in-life baby, right? That Raven called him her little miracle, since she was almost forty-two years old when
he was born."

Creed and Andy both nodded. That was in the main file,
front and center.

"Their first baby was stillborn, back when Raven Latch
was just twenty," Andy said.

Corey James looked down at the table, which put Creed
on the alert. "Tell us, Mr. James. Your wife's freedom may
depend on it."

"I can't prove anything, you understand." James lifted
his head with that torn, tortured expression. He felt like he
was giving away his wife's secrets, betraying his friends.
That much was obvious. Still, he wanted Alisa out and
back with him, and Creed couldn't blame the man a bit.

"We understand," Andy said quietly. She put down her
pen to make him more at ease.

James hesitated, then seemed to decide. "From some
things Alisa said before all this happened, I'm not sure their
first son was born dead. I think something . . . weird . . .
happened to him, and Davin's people covered it up. I
think—I think the Legion killed that baby."

This time, Andy didn't hide her stunned expression.

"I know it's far-fetched, but Alisa said something about
Raven and Davin being targeted, though she didn't know
why." James scrubbed one cheek with his hand and made
himself continue. "She said the death of their first baby was
a bloody tragedy. That's why Raven Latch was so protective of Jacob, and why Alisa and her triad saw to the boy
when Raven and Davin had to be away."

Creed and Andy kept up their strategic silence, but all
James had to add was, "Regular bodyguards don't make
much difference with Asmodai."

"Yeah." Andy ditched her bitch routine and frowned, actually showing a trace of sympathy. "That we know."

After a few minutes of cooldown, Creed and Andy

thanked Corey James for talking to them. James stood and straightened his clothes, but the guy looked like they had gut-punched him about six times.

At the door, Creed stopped and extended his hand, looked the man straight in the eye, and said what he needed to say. "I'll do what I can to get your wife home to you."

Corey James shook his hand with a firm grip. "Thank you, Detective. I hope you're as good as your word."

Andy opened the door to Two, and Corey James quickly lost himself in the now-moving crush of men in suits.

Creed and Andy followed him into the hall. Creed elbowed his way past Captain Freeman's office and a still-jumpy-looking Captain Freeman, who was heading toward his desk. The crowd of bodyguards closed around Creed and cut him off from Andy. Then the men in suits stepped aside as a woman's voice said, "That's okay, boys. I think he's one of the good guys."

Seconds later, Creed found himself facing a tall, thin woman who might have been a fashion model in her younger years. She had pale, perfect skin, high cheekbones, and almost translucent blue eyes. Her blond hair, streaked with ash and darker highlights, was drawn up in an elegant sweep, and her beige skirt matched the jacket she was retrieving from Creed's chair.

"Mrs. Latch," Creed said, recognizing her photo from the case file.

To his surprise, he felt something he had never felt on the job before—the *other*, stirring in his gut, beginning to growl.

Raven Latch folded her blazer over her arm with a graceful flick of the wrist and appraised him the way a buyer might size up a stallion for a stud fee. He didn't think she approved of his jeans, and she didn't seem to think much of his pressed blue shirt, either—but the jacket, the old piece of junk Andy had complimented, drew a smile.

Raven Latch reached out and brushed a hair off his sleeve.

Creed flinched at the contact because the *other* let out a howl inside his mind. Not just any howl, either. A scared, wary keening. He had never heard the thing make that noise before.

The woman's nails, expertly done in a glossy French style, raked across the leather, leaving faint marks as the *other* pulled back from her inside Creed. He had to fight not to shake as waves of the creature's fear washed through him.

"Now we're talking," Raven Latch said, and Creed couldn't help thinking she sounded a little like Lauren Bacall in old movies—before she got hoarse from smoking. "Why aren't you working my son's murder, Detective? You look like a man who gets the job done."

Creed cleared his throat and took a step back from her. He clenched his jaw to keep control of himself. There was no reading the woman's face, but her eyes were rimmed with red and her makeup was streaked from crying. Emotional, at least, though she seemed to have a core of well-frozen ice.

"I'll do what I can to assist, ma'am," he forced himself to say, feeling Captain Freeman's gaze like hammers on the back of his neck.

"Start by getting my best friend out of jail, would you?" Raven Latch patted his arm, making his gut roil. "She's no more a murderer than I am."

"We're looking into it," he assured her, giving her the most noncommittal assurance he could muster and using all his strength to stand his ground.

A distinguished-looking older man with salt-and-pepper hair broke through the ring of guards then and took Raven Latch by the arm. Creed had only a few moments to size up Davin Latch. He looked polished in his new-style Armani silk suit, but also serious and worn, as if the death of his son sat on his shoulders like a gruesome weight. Senator Latch spoke gently to his wife and started to lead her away, but she held on to the sleeve of Creed's leather jacket. At a wail from the *other* and a reserved but pleading glance from Senator Latch, Creed reached up to gently pry loose her fingers.

Raven Latch's eyes fell on his signet ring, and her gaze snapped to Creed's face.

Shit. She's going to start yelling that I'm one of the Legion like Riana and crew.

But Raven Latch did no such thing. She just stared at Creed as if she was memorizing each line, hair, and detail on his face. Her husband gave her arm a tug, and she moved away from him, still staring, and she never stopped, not until the crowd of bodyguards blotted her from his view.

The minute he couldn't see her any longer, the *other* went quiet and seemed to drop into oblivion. The next thing Creed heard was Captain Freeman clearing his throat, followed by Andy's sarcastic snort from beside him.

"Well, well, loverboy." Andy laughed. "You certainly made a friend."

17

Riana helped place the last mirror, then stood back with Cynda, the South Manhattan triad, and the North Queens triad to survey the repairs. Everything looked right, in place, and ready to go. Thank the Goddess the Mothers kept a ready supply of treated glass.

"Listen to this from the *Times*," Merilee said from the couch, where she was eating chips and going over the day's newspapers with highlighters and taking notes. *"Latch Proclaims Friend Innocent."*

Bela Argos came out of the kitchen, her triad in tow. She was wearing a tool belt complete with hammer and bag full of nails. Her pestle had hold of a circular saw, and her broom was dusting sawdust off leather gloves.

"Door's fixed," Bela said, eyeing Riana. "Though I still can't figure out how the big blast you described did *that* damage, too."

Cynda, who was standing on the big oak table and turning to check the position of all the mirrors, coughed loudly.

Riana didn't offer explanations, choosing instead to thank Bela and all the Sibyls who had pitched in to restore her brownstone. They even had chimes again, balanced, tuned, and ready to transmit as needed.

Creed and Andy would be surprised when they returned tonight.

If they come back. If he comes back. When am I going to stop worrying about that? They've been coming back every night. They'll be here.

Riana's chest ached, and she caught herself tugging at her crescent pendant. She forced herself to put down her hand

and see her guests to the door, making sure to lavish them with as much praise and gratitude as she could muster.

Bela tried to ask a few more questions about the bedroom door, but Riana saw the twinkle in the woman's unusual black eyes as she took her triad and departed. She was teasing, a rare thing for Bela Argos. Probably trying to help Riana feel better, and herself, too. The loss of Bette and the North Bronx triad had rattled them all.

The Mothers had ordered one of the ranger groups to move up from Hempstead and Jamaica Bay to cover the North Bronx region. They were sending a newer triad to get started in Nassau County and the surrounding area. At least the east rangers had experience, since they were often pulled north and west to lend a hand in Brooklyn and Staten Island. Riana liked their mortar, too. A same-year graduate. Still, she could feel the absence of Alisa like a worrisome thorn, poking her, poking her. It felt unnatural. Wrong.

Something to be rectified.

She got herself a late lunch of apples, nuts, and soft cheese, and sat down on the couch beside Merilee. Cynda couldn't be bothered to eat or talk. She was up on the oak table, barefoot and dancing, absorbed with playing with her new mirrors and chimes.

The set over the door rang, and Riana picked out Cynda's message.

I can sing again.

She had to smile. It must have been killing Cynda, to be so cut off and quiet. Now she could ring the chimes all over the world if she wanted. And she probably would.

"I don't like Davin Latch," Merilee announced, tossing her copy of *The New York Times* on the floor. She crammed her hand into the chip bag and munched loudly before adding, "He's too composed. Too slick."

"He's been a politician for what, twenty years?" Riana paused to eat a piece of red apple, enjoying the cool, sweet taste. "He probably acts like he's on camera twenty-four/seven."

Merilee tucked her highlighter behind her ear, marking a yellow streak across her cheek as she went. She snatched the next paper out of her lap, the *Daily News* by the look of it. "We are deeply saddened by our loss," she read, talking through her nose and mimicking a terrible highbrow accent. "We'll live under the shadow of this tragedy forever."

"Give the man a break." Riana downed a bite of cheese, then went after a sliver of toasted pecan before continuing. "His kid died a week ago. What's he supposed to say? My son was a heinous little brat and we're thrilled to pieces somebody murdered him?"

Merilee pulled the highlighter from behind her ear, marked something, and put it back. "I wonder if he was a brat? Some kind of burden to Mr. I-Want-to-Be-President-Next-Term. That might be an angle."

"If Jacob Latch had been trouble, I bet the press would have blabbed that by now."

"If they knew." Merilee put down the paper and her chip bag. "This guy, I swear, Ri, he's Teflon. I searched back to his high school days in every database I've got, and couldn't find even a hint of scandal or wrongdoing."

"Maybe because he's just what he seems?" Riana shrugged. "Maybe he's an honest man."

The chimes above her head rang, old code this time. Merilee spelled it out. "G-E-T R-E-A-L." She grinned and looked at Cynda, and gave the redhead a thumbs-up. "No shit. Get real, honey. You don't survive this long with the sharks without getting bitten."

"Or biting a few asses of your own." Cynda got down from the oak table, came over to where Riana was sitting, and snitched some nuts off her plate. "Maybe we should look for who Latch has bitten," she said with her mouth full.

Then, after chewing and swallowing and plopping down on a chair arm, "Maybe this was all about vengeance."

Merilee rolled her eyes. "Only a pussy kills somebody's kid to get even."

"A pussy or a psychotic bastard without mercy," Cynda corrected. "The Russian mob is like that, right?"

Riana sighed. "The Russian mob doesn't use Asmodai."

As usual, Cynda didn't seem fazed by simple logic. "Maybe they hired somebody who does."

"Let's make a list of possibilities, and go over it with Andy and Creed tonight," Riana suggested, mostly so she could finish her lunch in peace.

At the mention of Creed's name, Merilee and Cynda got very still.

Riana choked down her bite of apple, felt herself blush, and hated it. "Look, I know you're not comfortable with him. With me being with him."

"We're not," Cynda agreed. She snatched a bite of cheese. "You haven't even told the Mothers about him— and I'm betting, now that I can reach them again, you don't want me to tell them, either."

Heat rose up Riana's neck, and her muscles tensed.

Telling the Mothers would likely mean losing Creed. No doubt they would demand that she send him to one of the Motherhouses for containment and evaluation.

And I should, shouldn't I?

No. He's more useful here. He's no real threat, and he's cooperating.

"Uh-huh," Cynda said, responding to Riana's silence. "I thought as much. So again, no, we're not comfortable with demon-man."

"But we could be," Merilee said brightly. "If you let us do what we need to do."

Riana eyed the broom of her triad and handed her plate of food to Cynda. Her appetite was fading fast. The thought of sending him away to the Mothers made her physically ill. "We already tried to question him—and you saw how that went. I'm running my advanced analyses, but they aren't finished yet. What else do you have in mind?"

When Merilee didn't answer, Riana looked at Cynda, who got off the chair arm and actually sat down in the chair's seat. "Either tell the Mothers and let them take Creed, or let us investigate him. Thoroughly, like we should."

Merilee nodded. "Even Andy doesn't know much about his past, you know? Just the same stuff he told us, about his mother and grandmother, and his missing brother. Oh, and he told her he was born here, and he went to Columbia. He's never even told her his major."

"That should be easy enough to hack." Cynda polished off the cheese and put the plate on the floor.

Riana glared at her.

"It's just punching keys on a keyboard," Cynda said. "Don't get all protective of your boyfriend."

"He's not my boyfriend," Riana blurted. He's—"

He's what?

The question stopped her cold and made her chest ache again, but it didn't stop Cynda.

Cynda twirled her index finger in a circle, like *Come on, chick, let's go.* "What do you want to call him then? Boy toy? Fuck-buddy? Look, Riana, he's in our house and in your bed, and we don't even know what he is, for the sake of the Goddess."

"I'm working on that!" Riana wrapped her arms around herself and scooted back on the couch. "I've got an advanced genetic analysis running as we speak."

"Then let us work, too." Merilee leaned toward her and put her hand on Riana's wrist. No false brightness now. Her expression was earnest and concerned. "If you're not going to turn him over to the Mothers, let us use our tools to find out all we can."

Riana's insides twisted. She wanted to yell at her triad

sisters and tell them no, to stay away from Creed and stay out of her business—but it didn't work that way, did it? They were in this together, and if they pulled in different directions . . .

The image of Bette's burned body flared in Riana's mind.

She took a breath to steady herself. Then she nodded. "Okay, all right. I don't want to send him to the Mothers, but I don't want disasters, either. Do whatever you think you have to."

"Good, good. Thank you." Merilee's relieved smile seemed like a reward. "Now, we can't help it if one of the other triads rats you out, but they'll probably figure we've kept the Mothers informed. And there's no saying we'll find out anything dark or bad about him."

"Yeah." Cynda managed a smile, too.

So much for loyalty. Riana gazed at her triad sisters, and seeing Cynda and Merilee with happier looks on their faces made the dread and worry feel farther away. *Sorry, Creed. I was loyal to them before I ever knew you.*

18

Creed didn't miss the delicious aroma of fresh bread, fruit, spices, and roasted meat when he and Andy walked through the front door of the brownstone. He also didn't miss the sexy maroon skirt and blouse Riana was wearing, or her bare feet. He was grateful the *other* stayed quiet, because for some reason, seeing Riana dressed casually turned him on more than seeing her in one of her body-hugging suits or those mind-blowing leathers they wore to go out hunting. She looked softer, and so much more vulnerable. He almost couldn't stand it, and couldn't help thinking how it would be to come home to her after a day's work and be able to take her in his arms.

Then there would be those nights the chimes rang and she took off dressed like Catwoman, armed and dangerous, ready to fight God-knows-what. And what about the night she didn't come back? What about the night he became like that poor bastard Corey James, lying in his empty bed, wondering if his wife was okay, if he'd ever be able to touch her again?

Creed shook his head. *You're a little bit ahead of yourself, buddy. You've known her, what, a couple of weeks?*

Maybe a lot ahead of himself, or so said the look on Riana's face when he and Andy walked through her front door. Her expression was a mix of relief, excitement, and something else. Fear, maybe. Or worse—dread.

Great. I barely stop thinking about her all day, and she's spent her time dreading my return.

He had a duffel and a garment bag full of more clothes, and Andy had three more suitcases plus an attitude about having to board her cat at the vet's for another week be-cause Merilee was allergic. Andy brushed past everyone to take their gear downstairs, and Creed just let her go.

"Place looks amazing," he said as he sat down in one of the chairs facing the huge oak table. He scanned the re-paired living room and tried to ignore the food, clothes, and trash all over the floor. Merilee, who was sitting in an-other one of the chairs working on some arrow fletching, gave him a dazzling smile before she scrubbed the fletching against her jeans to straighten it, put down the arrow, and got up from her seat. He almost moved aside, expecting her to hurl something straight at his heart. She didn't, though. She just said something about getting drinks for everyone, and headed for the kitchen.

Cynda, who was dressed in a pair of green warm-ups, was setting out dinner on the big oak table—basted salmon, herb-crusted potatoes, peas, cranberry sauce, and a big bas-ket of rolls. She didn't speak to him, but didn't glare at him either.

Something was definitely wrong in the universe.

The scent of cinnamon wound around the tantalizing smells of olive oil, spices, cranberries, hot bread, and but-ter, and Creed's stomach growled. He didn't know which one of the Sibyls knew how to cook, or if they all did, and he wasn't about to ask. He kept his mouth shut as the women chatted back and forth, and gratefully accepted the plate and silverware Cynda offered him, along with one of the bottles of water.

Riana came into view and fixed herself a plate, and Creed found himself watching every move she made. Did she try to be so graceful? Did she know what she did to him with every move?

Apparently not.

Riana settled into one of the remaining chairs and crossed her sexy legs, showing just enough calf to make Creed miserable even as he ate. Cynda took a spot on the floor on the far side of the table, and Andy took the near side when she got back—sans cat-titude, thank God.

The Sibyls went first, giving a report of their home repairs and letting Creed and Andy know the Mothers were reporting increased Asmodai activity all across the globe. "The bastards seem to be getting more organized, targeting whole groups of Sibyls directly. We don't know why aside from the obvious fact we kick their demon-asses every time we get near them—but more important, we don't know why *now*. Sibyls have been locking horns with the Legion for a hundred years, and they've never paid much attention to us before."

"Maybe you're a bigger threat now," Andy said, waving a roll and dropping more crumbs to add to the mess on the floor.

"Nothing's changed on our side," Riana said, the low timbre of her voice bringing an instant response from Creed's body. She seemed to sense his thoughts, his immediate arousal, and turned to face him. "Something's changed on their side. Like I've told you, the Legion is patient. I think they're just moving to the next phase of pursuing their long-term goals. We're just in the way. All the Sibyls. Everywhere."

Damnit. Those eyes. Not to mention that every time she spoke, every time she moved, he imagined her on her back, eyes misty with desire, lips parted, moaning from the pleasure he gave her. He couldn't survive if his cock stayed on this level of alert whenever he was around her. He had to get her out of his system—but he could only think of one way, and he wasn't sure sex three or four times a night for the next ten years would do the trick.

"Creed told me something about what the Legion wants," Andy said from the floor, rescuing Creed temporarily from the need to say anything. "To-do list for the assholes. Let's see. That would be endless wealth and power, world domination, and us pathetic lesser life-forms in perpetual servitude to our proper lords and masters."

"That's about it," Cynda said. "So what's their next phase?"

Creed cleared his throat. "Corey James doesn't know. He seemed like a straight-up guy in his interview."

"Of course he's a straight-up guy." Merilee looked at him like he was an idiot. "Alisa married him, didn't she?" She stabbed her fork into a piece of potato. "Sibyls aren't psychic, Creed, but we have pretty good instincts." Her gaze flicked to Riana, and her eyes narrowed. "Most of us do, anyway."

"For example," Cynda cut in, "Merilee thinks Davin Latch is bent, but she couldn't find any proof."

Merilee swallowed a huge mouthful of cranberry sauce and salmon. "No way the guy has stayed in D.C. that long with no skeletons in his closet."

"We might know of one." Andy raised what was left of her roll.

Everyone fell silent as Andy explained what she and Creed had learned from Alisa's husband. The silence continued when she finished, too, until Riana put her plate down on the oak table in front of her and folded her hands in her lap.

"Well, that makes no sense whatsoever." Riana's gaze traveled around the room. "What could the Legion have against the Latch bloodline?"

"Do you think the senator used to belong?" Merilee leaned forward and put her plate down on the table, too. "I mean, if he did, and he backed out on them, maybe they want to control him by threatening his family."

Andy scooted across the floor to the table. "If they wanted to control him, they would have swiped the kid, not killed him." She didn't put her plate down because she was too busy piling it with second helpings.

"Not necessarily," Cynda said as she took another serving of potatoes. "Asmodai aren't perfect machines. They can be confused and distracted, or the maker could fail to give clear enough instructions."

"Somebody told the demon how to carve that boy up," Creed observed. "It's hard to imagine one of those monsters being so precise."

This brought another long silence, during which the Sibyls looked from one to another. It was Merilee who put their thoughts into words. "So, what if the Asmodai was just there to serve as a protector for the real killer?"

"Which brings us back to Alisa James," Creed said, then added quickly, "according to the evidence, that is. Her, or one of her triad." He glanced from Riana to Cynda and then to Merilee. "They *were* there, Bette and Camille. I'd be willing to bet the partials found at the Latch house would be a match for them."

He fixed his gaze on Riana, who lowered her head.

That's okay, honey, he wanted to say, thinking about the *other*'s response to Raven Latch earlier in the day. *We both keep our secrets, don't we?*

Instead, he said, "You knew that, didn't you? All three of you knew it."

"What, you wanted us to hand you two more Sibyls for suspects?" Cynda lost interest in her plate and put it on the floor beside her. "Fat chance."

"Bette's beyond our justice now." Andy didn't lose interest in her plate, despite the topic of conversation. She did shift on the floor to make better eye contact with Cynda, though. "Odd that she was the only one who died in Van Cortlandt Park, though. Do you think the big pack of demons was just a cover to take out one of the only other witnesses to this crime? Think before you answer, all of you, because either Alisa's a nut-job psycho who might move against Camille, or both Camille and Alisa are at risk."

"Are you interrogating us?" Riana asked, and Creed

imagined he could see ice forming in the air between her and Andy.

As usual, Andy wasn't fazed. "No. I'm warning you and asking you to think—to look beyond your basic belief in the goodness of all Sibyls. Who are the potential victims here?"

"I say we bring Raven and Davin Latch over here to question them." Cynda ground both fists against the table's edge. "No offense to NYPD, but we don't have some of the limits you guys have to observe."

Creed glanced at her. "Yeah. No shit. Are all your prisoners naked when they confess?"

Cynda's green warm-ups started to smoke, and Creed's shoelaces caught on fire.

"I think we've had enough for tonight," Riana said as Creed used his hands to smother the flames. "Let's get some rest and try this again tomorr—"

The chimes by the front door started to ring.

At the same time, all three Sibyls grabbed their tattoos.

Andy fumbled with her plate, spilled some potatoes on the floor, and looked around the table at her friends. "What's up? More Asmodai?"

"Sssshhhhh." Cynda put her finger to her lips, staring at the chimes.

Riana and Merilee were already up. They abandoned the food and dishes, dashed over to a closet and started jerking out leather bodysuits, daggers, a sword, and the bow and arrows. Creed got to his feet, as did Andy, hand on her sidearm. She swore quietly about not having the right bullets yet and being useless. Creed felt the same way.

Cynda shook her head and groaned. "It's not Asmodai. It's Herbert again. Bela says he's screwing up the power grid around Trinity Church, and she can't figure out how he's doing it or where he is. They need our help to trap him."

"Who is Herbert?" Andy and Creed asked at the same time.

"He's a dickhead," Merilee snarled. "For this I'm going to get to bed late?"

"He's a dickhead with latent talent." Riana walked back in from the kitchen and, as if Creed and Andy weren't standing there, started taking off her clothes. "We can't ignore him."

"What's latent talent?" Andy stepped in front of Riana, now naked except for a pair of lacy bikini panties—maroon, too, Creed noted—and a thin red tank top. "What's a Herbert?"

"A *houngan,*" Cynda said, stripping off her clothes and reaching for a bodysuit. "A priest who practices Vodoun rituals. Herbert wants to be a *houngan* really, really bad. Problem is, the shithead has just enough latent talent— untrained affinity with the elements—to cause problems now and then."

"So this guy does voodoo?" Creed rubbed his hand through his hair and tried not to watch Riana zip herself into form-fitting black leather. "Is he from the islands?"

"Hardly." Merilee's laugh was harsh. She had on her black suit and gloves now, but she was holding the face mask like she didn't want to pull it over her head. "The sawed-off bastard's a redheaded white boy from TriBeCa, raised by a Haitian nanny who taught him too much for his own good."

"He probably learned from watching her work rituals to stick pins in his ass," Cynda added as she pulled on her face mask.

"He likes to kill chickens and make a bloody mess," Riana explained as she finished suiting up. "Freaks people out, bilks money from tourists and superstitious people to remove curses. That kind of stuff. But sometimes he actually puts out a little dangerous energy."

"When he's smoked too much weed," Merilee said, still hesitating about her face mask. "Then we have to shut him down for the night."

"Put the mask on, Merilee," Riana instructed, belting on her daggers. "This won't take long."

Creed looked at the heavily armed women, amazed by the transformation. He knew the bodysuits didn't give them any special powers, but the change was palpable, almost like a crackle of electricity in the air above their heads.

It's like the planet suddenly knows they're here, and nature's standing ready to give them a hand.

And his next thought was, *So this is what it feels like to be Corey James.*

It was alien to him, to stand by and watch other people go out to do the fighting. He had never been so frustrated, or felt so powerless. He wanted to step forward, be the big man, and tell the women he'd take care of it, only he had no idea what to do.

Shit. No wonder the OCU hasn't ever found real psychic activity. The Sibyls always get there first.

Riana herded her triad toward the door, then paused and looked back over her shoulder.

Wonder Woman, Creed thought. *Wonder Woman in tight leather instead of an American flag and a push-up bra.*

"I know this isn't pleasant for you," Riana said, and Creed thought she was speaking mostly to him. He imagined her bright green eyes shining through the eye slits in her face mask. "But please, this time, stay out of it and let us do our job."

Andy kicked at the floor, but she nodded. "No worries. I'm not making the same mistake twice."

Cynda opened the door, and Merilee followed her out. Riana remained still and seemed to be waiting for something. When Creed didn't give it to her, she said, "You're a man of your word. Tell me you'll stay here and keep Andy safe. Use the cell if you have to."

Creed ground his teeth. *Maybe Corey James is a better man than me. I don't know if I'm strong enough to let her walk out the door.* But he kept looking at her, at her daggers, at the lean line of her fit body and the way she almost leaned toward the door, as if she longed to play her assigned part in the world.

Finally, he sucked in his doubts and pride and said, "Yeah. Okay. Go do what you do."

The door slammed behind her before the last word left his lips.

For a long time, Creed just stood there, staring at the spot where Riana had been only moments before.

"Not bad," Andy murmured, the sound of her voice reattaching him to the real world, at least a little bit. "I didn't think you could do it."

"Do what?" Creed asked, more than a little irritable.

Andy patted his arm. "Let her be who she is. I'm impressed. If you can tame that beast inside you, you just might have a chance with Riana after all, partner."

19

Riana let Cynda drive the Jeep. She was too distracted by her emotions to pay close attention to the road.

Creed had wanted to come with her. She sensed his frustration so powerfully she imagined it was following them down Broadway. Yet he put his feelings aside and gave his word not to interfere. This time, she knew he would keep it.

Her heart fluttered. She didn't think she had ever known a man strong enough to let *her* be strong, too.

Is this what Alisa felt with Corey? Is that why she petitioned to marry? Other Sibyls had married before, of course. A lot, in fact. Riana never understood that, never believed a man could give her the freedom she needed. She hadn't had much luck with boyfriends. In fact, she'd never felt relaxed enough to explain who or what she was to any of the men she had dated. Plenty of Sibyls had active social lives outside the sisterhood, but Riana had never been too comfortable with that. Too much risk, too little benefit, and too little time.

Until now.

Cynda and Merilee chatted nonstop, discussing strategies for preserving Herbert's balls once they caught him and took them for trophies. She had to agree that if Herbert didn't stop soon, or if he figured out how to tap into his abilities any better, they would need to put him in irons and send him to the Mothers. Probably Motherhouse Ireland. Herbert liked to play with fire.

Merilee circled around the Financial District and parked the Jeep out of the flow of traffic on Wall Street—or rather, on a Wall Street sidewalk, far enough from the church to keep the vehicle safe if something exploded or stones fell from the walls. Unfortunately, that was a likelihood with Herbert sometimes.

When Riana got out, she took a deep breath of crisp fall air, catching a hint of cloves, cinnamon, and pepper from the restaurants of nearby Chinatown. There was something else in the air, too—a bitter, unnatural tang, and not just exhaust from the cars, cabs, and buses streaming past between her and the churchyard.

"Fire," Cynda muttered. "I smell accelerant, but earth, too. Somebody's put it out, I think."

The South Manhattan triad, led by Dani Petrov who graduated Motherhouse Russia a few years after Riana, met them across the road, on the sidewalk in front of the preternaturally darkened church. Riana could sense the massive stone building with its peaceful, heavy energy of rock and mortar, looming ahead of her. City lights not affected by Herbert's asinine shenanigans blazed from all directions, outlining Trinity in eerie blues and grays. The neo-Gothic spire, which reached a height of almost three hundred feet, probably wasn't visible to anyone without the keen vision of a Sibyl.

"I can't find the cockroach." Dani gripped the hilt of her scimitar, and Riana imagined her dark-haired friend glaring into the pitch-black windows of the church. "I sent Maura and Shell to scout, but no luck. The lights have been off and on about ten times, and we've put out two fires in the churchyard. He lit one on Alexander Hamilton's marble pyramid—with fire paste, the little shit. I'm surprised cops aren't crawling all over the place."

Riana settled her mind and reached into the nearby earth, letting her awareness run along the natural veins of the ground. Even beneath asphalt, even torn and split by subways and utilities, she could feel patterns in the dirt, find lines, and follow them along until she sensed life energies. All earth Sibyls had some terrasentience, or the ability to sense what was in or on nearby earth, but Riana's senses were sharper than most.

She quickly found one human entity, then two, but recognized the unmistakable energy signatures of a fire Sibyl and an earth Sibyl. Dani's triad sisters were returning to her empty-handed. They were moving through the Trinity Churchyard Cemetery now.

Riana carefully circled around the cemetery in their wake, not wishing to disturb any graves or spirits that might be lingering. She tasted the aberrant sourness of accelerant on her tongue as she passed the Hamilton monument, then she moved on to other vaults and finally back outside the fence again.

Nothing.

No dead chickens, even. No feathers, no blood, no shoddily constructed *vévé* made as if to summon a Loa—one of the god-figures from the astral plane who responded to true practitioners of Vodoun.

The absence of Herbert's usual trademarks made Riana's muscles tight. She didn't like it when patterns changed. Assholes like Herbert changing their patterns—that was rarely a good sign.

Yet . . . wait.

There, somewhere near the Livingston vault, where engineer Robert Fulton was laid to rest . . . a disturbance. She couldn't quite get a fix on it, but there was an energy that didn't seem to belong. And another patch of bitter-tasting ground, this one not burned, right around the cenotaph bearing Robert Fulton's name.

"Herbert's hiding in the graveyard somehow." She closed her eyes and shook her head, drawing her awareness out of the earth as Maura and Shell joined them outside the fence. "He might actually be underground, but for some reason I'm not getting a clear reading. Something's interfering with his energy signature."

Maura sheathed her intimidating African *shotel,* but not

before Riana caught the gleam of fire running along its wicked sicklelike curve. Her leathers gave off smoke at both shoulders. A classmate of Cynda's, Maura shared much with her in the way of personality. "We've been through that churchyard a dozen times now," she said. "What the hell is going on?"

"He must have learned to use more of his abilities." Shell, the air Sibyl in Dani's triad, palmed the two tiny throwing knives—darts, in proper terminology, with orange-gold tassels that made them look like deadly goldfish—she had been keeping at the ready. The air Sibyl slid her stealth weapons back into one of the black bandoliers she wore on the insides of her forearms. "We need to catch him now and send him to the Mothers."

"Agreed," Cynda said, and Merilee nodded.

For a moment, the six of them stood quietly in front of the church, staring through the bars of the metal fence separating them from the cemetery. Riana kept her eyes on the churchyard. In the low, strange backlight, the old grave markers looked like people kneeling, heads bowed, over the graves of their loved ones.

"If he can block himself from us," she said, "we don't have much choice. Let's move in again and surround the Livingston vault. Whatever's happening, it's centered on that spot."

As if to confirm her statement, a small fire broke out on the grass very near the brownstone slab covering the Livingston vault.

Dani tensed, and Riana sensed earth energy moving as her South Manhattan counterpart prepared to douse the flames. She reached out and touched Dani's arm, interrupting the other woman's concentration.

"Don't." Riana nodded toward the fire. "I think he wants us to come to the flames, not put them out. The sooner we get into his game, the sooner we can get out of it."

Merilee shook her head. "What if it's some sort of trap?"

Riana's heart skipped at the thought of Merilee or Cynda getting injured by one of Herbert's nutcase schemes and tricks. She sucked in a breath and blew it out, frustrated with the limits of her terrasentience. "I didn't sense any explosives. He doesn't have the ground wired, at least. I don't know what else to look for."

"I didn't pick up anything, either," Merilee said, sounding far more tense than she usually did. "But you know my wind-sensing isn't that sharp. Did you pick up anything, Shell?"

Shell, who was one of the most talented ventsentients in Sibyl history, said, "No. Just a hint of something . . . wrong. Too pungent. But it's hard to tell with the fire and accelerants, and Chinatown nearby—and so many other restaurants still open. I can't tell where it's coming from." She turned to her mortar. "Dani, I think one of us needs to stay back, just in case."

"Keep a position outside this fence," Dani instructed. "Stay in throwing range. Watch our backs, okay?"

Riana patted Merilee on the shoulder. "You've got the longest-range weapons. Find yourself a vantage point, and if we make a mess, clean it up."

Merilee was running away into the darkness before Riana drew her next breath.

Dani glanced in her direction, eyes hidden behind the leather of her face mask. "Left or right?"

Riana gestured to the right, and she and Cynda moved out, down along the line of the fence. She noticed Cynda was walking as slowly as she was, wary, hands on her weapons. Something about this setup felt wrong to Cynda, too, but what choice did they have? It was go in, or wait all night for Herbert to tip his hand. By then, any number of passersby might be involved, not to mention the NYPD.

Cynda went first, gripping the black metal fence, putting her foot on the top railing, and vaulting over the spiked fence caps. She dropped to the cemetery's grass almost without a sound. Riana followed, careful to clear the sharp metal points. Her heartbeat accelerated the moment she touched the ground. Cynda drew her sword. On instinct, Riana unsheathed her daggers. At the other end of the cemetery, Dani and Maura approached the flames near the Livingston vault with caution.

Riana tried to keep her senses open and her body alert, but the fatigue of the last couple of weeks weighted her, slowed her. She crept beside Cynda, both of them in a half crouch, ready to bolt, spring, or attack. Cool air made her eyes water, and her breath came too fast, too short.

"Something's wrong," Cynda murmured. "I feel it in my blood. I just don't *see* it."

The four Sibyls kept up their slow advance.

The dark churchyard seemed bizarrely empty and removed from the rest of the city, set apart in time. So many of the graves were very old, well kept, but with definitely weathered and worn markers. Even the slightest creak or crunch made the hair on Riana's neck stand up.

Five feet away now, and still nothing.

Where the hell was Herbert?

What the hell was he up to?

Riana picked her way between headstones, staying to the left of Cynda so Cynda could swing a sword with her dominant hand if needed. The more nervous she got, the madder she got. It would almost be a pleasure to dispatch this wannabe shit to the Mothers, even though that punishment was harsh indeed. She felt the cool, steady pressure of her crescent pendant pressing between her breasts, and imagined what Mother Yana would do to the likes of Herbert—including, but not limited to, feeding him to one of her gigantic pet wolves if he didn't do as he was told.

Three feet.

Two feet.

Riana, Cynda, Dani, and Maura encircled the flames.

Still, nothing happened.

With a wave of her hand, Riana summoned enough earth energy to douse the flames.

The ground all around them trembled—and burst open.

Dank graveyard dirt rained all over Riana and her companions.

Like corpses rising from the dead, six Asmodai exploded from the torn earth, cutting off all escape routes.

Six huge Asmodai.

Ambush!

And they were surrounded.

"Earth!" Riana shouted out the proper locking element. The demons had to be made of earth, or they couldn't have hidden from her awareness.

One of the Asmodai had Herbert under its right arm.

Herbert's red hair was matted. He was stark naked, and he was laughing.

"Got me some new friends!" His quavery, dramatic voice made Riana's skin crawl as she locked her dagger blades with earth energy. "Bet you bitches won't be bothering *me* again, *oui*?"

"Idiot," Cynda yelled as she lunged forward and lopped off the head of the Asmodai holding Herbert. Before it even decayed, she kicked Herbert in the crotch and left him doubled over in the growing pile of Asmodai dirt. Herbert tried once to take his hands off his wounded genitals and then passed out.

The Asmodai on either side of the crumbling demon and the fallen Herbert turned on Cynda with their filthy, shifting hands stretched out to grab her. Riana had to hope Dani and Maura could handle the other three. She turned her back on them and rushed the Asmodai on the right, slashing with both blades.

It noticed her when she hacked off its arm.

Cynda engaged the other Asmodai, stepping over Herbert's inert form to do it. The sound of her sword whistling through the air comforted Riana as she gave ground to the towering earth-demon charging her.

Too big. Too friggin' big.

Its shape shifted from a walking black mountain to a burly priest to rugged biker to Wall Street businessman, then lost coherent form as it opened its mouth and roared.

Riana dodged the fetid stream of air and rocks blowing out of the thing's mouth. The ground rumbled beneath Riana's feet. She cried out and pitched forward, almost dropping her daggers as she shoulder-rolled rather than falling on her face.

She barely got to her feet before the Asmodai hurled a dirt-boulder straight at her midsection. Riana swung sideways. The huge clod smashed into a headstone and knocked it flat.

Before the Asmodai could form another ball of dirt, she hurled a surge of her own earth energy at the grass below the thing's feet.

A section of sod jerked sideways like a yanked tablecloth, and the beast crashed down, half catching itself with its only arm. Riana ran forward, kicked its arm from beneath it, and plunged both daggers into its chest as it fell on its back.

Missed!

She straddled the thing, hating the writhing feel of its body between her thighs. With all her strength, she yanked one dagger free, but the other stayed trapped. She tried for it again, but the Asmodai's arm swung up and buffeted her shoulder.

She fell sideways and rolled into a headstone, her back taking the brunt of the blow. Air rushed out of her lungs, and pain crushed her chest. She fought to move, to breathe, but couldn't even roll to the side as the Asmodai lumbered toward her.

Here's where I die.

She clenched her teeth. Sweat broke out across her face as she tried to gather the breath to yell.

No sound came out. She couldn't make a squeak.

Like a troll from some fairy story, the Asmodai raised its clublike fist and swung down.

Riana braced for the fatal blow.

Dirt landed on her head.

Rocks scratched Riana's face and filthy mud clogged her nose, mouth, and eyes. But her head was still in one piece, still on her shoulders. She clawed the junk out of her mouth as her ability to breathe and move returned. The minute she got her eyes wiped, she saw the arrow dead center in the pile of dead Asmodai dirt.

Merilee. Thank the Goddess.

And Cynda's foul mouth was at full bore, so she was okay, too, for now.

Riana struggled to her feet, retrieved her second dagger, and plunged back into the fray. Three Asmodai were still standing.

Dani crippled her Asmodai by cutting off its leg, then ducked to allow a dart to bury itself in the demon's head. It fell to dirt, clothes and all, and she joined Maura, who was scorching the shirt off an Asmodai. The thing was missing both ears and a hand. Riana ran to Cynda, who dropped to her knees, swung her sword, and clipped off her Asmodai's foot.

"Down!" Riana yelled.

Cynda dropped face-first on the ground.

Heart hammering, jaw clenched, Riana jumped over Cynda and planted her daggers dead on target, one in the thing's chest, the other between its eyes. On her way back to the ground, she ripped off a piece of its shirt, hoping the piece of cloth would stay intact. No such luck. She had dirt in her hand by the time her feet touched the ground.

For a few seconds, she just stood there panting and aching, let the foul-smelling earth trickle between her fingers.

"I got one," Cynda wheezed as she got up. "And you got two."

Riana twisted her neck to stretch out some of the growing stiffness. "Just one," she corrected as Dani and Maura finished off the sixth monster. "Merilee shot one right before it almost killed me."

"What the hell was *this* all about?" Maura kicked a pile of Asmodai dirt as she walked toward them, Dani following close behind. The right sleeve of her leather jumpsuit had been burned away. "Asmodai joining forces with dickweeds like Herbert? Give me a break!"

Cynda's shoulders were bare from her own smoldering emotions. She shook her head as she dusted dirt off her face and chest. "Got me. I'm gonna enjoy opening the channels for his skinny ass. I think he should go to Motherhouse Russia. He's about the size of a good wolf bone."

As Shell came jogging across the cemetery, Riana and Dani began repairing damage to the grass and resetting headstones. Riana used a directed burst of her earth energy to reposition the carpet of grass and sod she had moved during the attack. From the corner of her eye, she saw Merilee clear the fence around the cemetery and start across the graveyard toward them. In a few moments, she had forced one of Herbert's arms around her neck, and she was helping Cynda lift him.

Harsh blasts of gunfire tore through the night.

Pain slammed into Riana's left arm and right side. She dropped to her knees, gasping, grabbing for the throbbing wounds as more bullets sang past her ears. She fell forward and lifted her good arm over her head.

Her mind spun out of control. She felt the earth moving, then willed herself to stop it. Then she felt herself moving, heard yelling. Dragging. Somebody dragging her. Dirt in her face. Up, high in the air. Then down. Her feet stumbling across pavement.

"Move, move, move!" Cynda was screaming, from somewhere. Beside her? Behind her? Who was pulling her arms?

She couldn't get a whole breath. The air was so cold. She

was cold. But Cynda and Merilee were pushing her, pulling her, shoving her down into the graveyard dirt, then jerking her up again. Riana tried to focus on making her feet move.

More shots rang out. Bullets struck stone with loud cracks. Dirt exploded just in front of Riana and her triad. Cynda spun away from Riana and fell, cursing. Merilee pushed Riana from behind and she moved forward. Her arm and side hurt so bad she couldn't see straight. Instinct made her concentrate on the lodged bullets and give the metal a strong yank with her earth energy.

Goddess! That hurt worse!

Riana screamed from the pain.

More shots. More bullets.

Where were they coming from? North? West?

The road. Yes. Somewhere on the street in front of the graveyard.

"There!" Riana tried to point as another burst of gunfire made her duck.

Shell fell backward, holding her leg.

Riana heard Dani shouting to Shell and Maura, then a long wall of fire flared just outside the graveyard fence.

Smoke stung Riana's eyes. Tires squealed. Cars honked. People started to shout.

Dani and Maura made the fence and scaled it in almost one motion. The fire would keep them out of view of traffic and the shooters, but only for a few seconds.

"Get to the Jeep!" Merilee shouted as she turned back to help Cynda. Riana stumbled, slammed into the fence, grabbed it, and tried to pull herself up.

She felt like her body was tearing into pieces at the sites of her bullet wounds.

Cynda was up again, limping, using Merilee for a crutch. The two of them charged toward Riana and the metal fence separating them from the sidewalk, Wall Street, and the Jeep.

Merilee used a burst of wind to lift her over the fence in

one giant leap. Riana felt her triad sister's wind gather beneath her and push her up, up, as she pulled as hard as she could, yelling from the blistering, pulsing ache in her arm and side. Cynda pushed from behind her, and Riana managed to get over the fence tips without impaling herself. Cynda came next, bolstered by Shell, who followed in a wind-supported leap.

Riana lurched toward the fire.

It vanished before she scorched herself.

Bystanders had gathered along the opposite sidewalk, and people started shouting when the fire disappeared. Merilee and Shell made a wind-screen to force the gawkers to look away and blur their images. The wind pounded against the people on the street, driving them back, back, as the Sibyls ran, limped, and staggered past.

Bile washed up Riana's throat as she gripped her bleeding side.

The Jeep. Not far now. Not far. She could see it. See Merilee yanking open the doors and swinging her arm to say, *Come on. Come on.*

Almost there.

Five steps.

Three. Cynda grabbed her hand and they managed the last few feet together. Maura and Dani were pulling Shell in through the hatch.

Riana said a little prayer of thanks that she bought the bigger model, two seats in the front, three in the center, and a hatch, too. Perfect for great escapes.

Then she was in the Jeep, her face pressed against the familiar, comfortable leather.

And then she just . . . wasn't.

20

Creed knew something was wrong the minute the door opened.

He had tried to go downstairs, but ended up cleaning the living room and kitchen instead. Then he paced the brownstone's living room until Andy threatened to shoot him in the kneecaps. She was dead asleep on the overstuffed couch when the wind chimes starting ringing, but she popped awake when the front door banged like gunfire against its stop.

The first thing through the front door was a naked guy, all pale and white and freckly with dark red hair. He was awake and staggering, hobbled by a rope tying his ankles together. His hands were tied, too, in front, firmly covering his dick. By the way he was limping and grimacing, that dick had taken some serious recent damage.

Next came three women Creed didn't recognize. The first had dark hair and delicate curves like a movie star, an effect marred only by a big bruise along her left cheekbone and the friggin' gigantic scimitar belted at her waist. Another was a brunette with a scary-looking African sickle dangling from her waist, a bunch of scratches on her face, and part of her bodysuit burned away. The third woman was big-boned and tanned. She had a bloody bandage tied around her left thigh, what looked like two dozen tiny knives in bandoliers along the inside of her arms, and purple hair cut in a short jumble.

"I'm Shell," said purple-hair as she brushed past him. "The two in front of me are Dani and Maura. Excuse 'em for being rude." She turned back and winked at him. "You're the demon-cop, right? Good. Stay out of the way."

Before Creed could even get his wits about him to speak, Shell had turned her attention back to their prisoner. "Herbert! Don't even think about sitting on the floor. Get on that big round table like I told you."

When Herbert didn't move toward the table fast enough, a gust of wind shoved him forward into the waiting and unfriendly arms of Dani and Maura, with their evil-looking swords.

"Fuck me," Andy said sleepily, eyes fixed on the door. "Did you guys run through a buzz saw?"

Creed wheeled back to the door, mouth dry, fists clenched. Cynda limped in next. The lower left leg of her bodysuit had been cut away. Blood streaked down the visible part of her thigh and knee, and she was bandaged, too. Merilee, who didn't seem to have a bandage, helped Riana through the door.

The world stopped for Creed.

Riana was pale and barely walking on her own. One of her sleeves had been cut off to allow for a bandage on her arm. She was missing another piece of her bodysuit on her side, with a bloody bandage peeking out between the dark pieces of leather.

He strode to her, took over from Merilee, and lifted Riana into his arms. "What the hell happened?" He gazed into her pain-stricken eyes and felt the way she was breathing, shallow and harsh, as if she might pass out any second. "You're going to the hospital right now. Andy, get your keys."

"Somebody shot at us," Merilee said as she closed the door behind Creed and Riana. "And no hospitals. They have to report gunshots and stabbings, and I really don't want to be making up yet another set of we-got-mugged stories."

Fury raced through Creed, and the *other* snarled like a roused lion. He fought to master it, and steadied himself enough to say, "Who shot you? Why?"

"No idea," Cynda yelled from across the room as smoke seemed quite literally to come out of her ears. "Never happened before. But we're gonna find out in a minute." She opened the closet and hurled her face mask inside. "We got ambushed by friggin' Asmodai in a friggin' graveyard, thanks to this piece of shit." She turned and tossed her sheathed sword at the big oak table, where the naked guy was huddled. He flinched when the weapon struck the wood and bounced onto the floor.

"Hospital," Creed said again, blood pounding in his temples. His chest ached at the thought of Riana injured so badly, that she'd been shot. He hadn't been there with her, damnit. Why'd he let her leave alone? "And I'm calling the NYPD to go after the shooters."

"Flesh wounds," Riana managed, though her voice sounded weak. "The bullets are out, and we've started the healing. A day or two, and you'll never know I got hurt. The NYPD can't do anything, Creed. Whoever fired on us is long gone."

Creed realized that Cynda and purple-hair—Shell, she said her name was—they had been shot, too, and they were moving fairly well. "How did you get all the bullets out?"

Riana blinked at him, and he thought she might be trying to smile. "They're metal, aren't they? Dani and I are earth Sibyls. We work with rock, dirt, and metals."

"I want you to get real medical attention." He held her gaze. "What if you get an infection?"

"Like I said, I'm a Sibyl." She reached up one long-fingered hand and touched his cheek. "We know how to kill infections before they even start."

The silk of her fingertips made him want to growl at everyone in the room and chase them all away. He would have squeezed her tighter, but he didn't want to hurt her. And he didn't know what to say to convince her to get help.

But . . . the color was coming back to her cheeks, and her

breathing had slowed to normal. She trailed her fingers down his cheek again, and this time, she was able to smile.

How fast do *they heal?*

He was clearly in uncharted territory here, and his mind ticked back over Cynda's ass wound and other minor bumps and bruises he'd seen the triad take in the short time he'd known them. The smaller injuries had become non-issues pretty quickly.

But bullets?

Riana's musical voice was lower when she spoke, more sexy, more alluring. Her expression said, *Take me downstairs. Now.* Out loud, however, she said, "Please take me to one of the chairs. We've got to question Herbert before we send him away."

Creed didn't know whether to shake Riana or refuse to put her down until morning. He finally had to give in and carry her to the nearest chair, settling her gently between the padded arms. Then he pressed his lips against her ear and whispered, "Next time the shooting starts, I'll be with you."

Riana gazed up at him, and he knew she wanted him to kiss her. The sadness in her eyes told him she also knew that wasn't a good idea with this audience, and with the *other* creating menace every time their passions flared. He tried to get a breath, felt furious and suffocated, but didn't frown at her. He wouldn't take out his rage at the *other*'s interference on her. In fact, he never wanted to frown at her again, for any reason.

I almost lost you tonight, didn't I, honey?

How did Corey James handle this?

Andy yawned, way too loud as usual. She was sitting up on the couch now, eyeing the ugly naked man on the big oak table. Dani and Maura were standing on the table with the man, one in front, one in back. They had their fearsome swords drawn inches from his back and chest. Shell, the big purple-haired woman, stood to the side. She had adjusted the bonds on his hands, lifted his arms over his head, and she was finishing tying him to the same ceiling beam that Riana and her triad had used to immobilize Creed.

"So if you earthy-types snatch out the bullets," Andy asked in her slow, sarcastic drawl, "who does the stitches?"

Cynda was busy changing clothes in the corner, discarding her black leathers in favor of a long green skirt and loose blouse. "We do," she said. "Fire Sibyls are hell on infectious processes. We know how to bring the heat. And Motherhouse Ireland prides itself on fine sewing."

Creed had a sudden image of a bunch of sword-toting grandmas, flannel nightgowns smoking at the fringes, sitting in a circle swapping curse words and needlework patterns.

"I want to go home," whined Herbert as his captors left him standing on the table tied to the ceiling beam.

"Shut up," all the Sibyls said at once.

"You may not want to watch this," Riana said to Creed.

"I'm watching," Andy said. "We're watching. You're not going to kill him, right? We can't let you kill him, even if he is a sniveling weasel-fucker."

"Nah, we won't kill him." Cynda picked up her sword and pointed the tip toward Herbert's shriveled little manhood. "We'll just neuter him unless he spills what he knows."

Herbert glared at her and flushed a deep red all over his body.

"If you're going to watch, then step back." Riana dug her fingers into the arms of her chair and pushed herself to her feet. "Stay over by the couch, and don't interfere for any reason. His safety depends on our concentration."

Creed wanted to protest, but as he watched, amazed, she pulled off her bandages, balled them up, and tossed them in the general direction of the room's only trash can. The bullet wounds beneath the gauze were neatly stitched and barely red around the edges. The stitches looked to be the modern, dissolvable kind.

Does one of them drive an ambulance? He shook his head. *They're probably as good or better than military medics at first aid. Guess they'd have to be.*

It did bother him, though, seeing how pathetic Herbert Whatever-his-name-was looked, naked on that table, arms stretched above his head, at the mercy of six pissed-off Sibyls. Creed rubbed his hand across the stubble on his chin.

"So they did that to you, huh, partner?" Andy grinned at him. "At least you have a bigger package." She squinted at Herbert. "Lots bigger."

Creed wished he had a spare sock to stuff in Andy's mouth, but he didn't have to worry. Riana silenced Andy with a ferocious look over her shoulder. Then she turned back to the table, positioned herself on the floor in front of Herbert, and stood very still. Four of the other five Sibyls dimmed the lights in the room, lit a few candles, and took up spots on the floor a few paces away from each other. Merilee left briefly, went to the closet, took out a bag, then stepped into the kitchen. She returned from the kitchen with a sterling silver pitcher. First, she put the pitcher down and opened the bag. Creed watched as she poured what looked like dark brown dirt into the lead-lined trench carved into the oak table's edge. When she finished walking around the circle, she put the bag down, picked up the pitcher, and made another lap around the table, pouring water into the trench. Not much, but Creed figured it was enough to count.

No sooner had Merilee taken her place in the circle than flames broke out atop the trench. They danced in a light breeze now traversing the room.

Earth, water, fire, air, Creed's brain catalogued. *Let's hope the elements lock Herbert on that table better than they locked me.*

The Sibyls didn't seem worried. In fact, they all appeared to be relaxing into some sort of meditative state.

The atmosphere in the room shifted. Creed felt pressure against his ears, heat on his cheeks, and hypnotic breezes blowing back and forth across his skin. It got harder to take a breath. Andy sat heavily on the couch, a sudden look of intense exhaustion on her face. Creed shared her exhaustion, and found himself sinking down beside her and leaning back.

The *other* grumbled and moved around inside him, a distant thrum against the hum that seemed to fill Riana's brownstone. His inner beast was distant enough, but now wary. Creed didn't remember much about his initial interrogation by the Sibyls, but the *other* apparently remembered plenty.

Time passed, but Creed wasn't sure how much. Misty images flickered in the mirrors hanging all around the big table. He thought he saw women in robes, and odd runic symbols, and occasionally, weird Gothic-looking buildings looming in the dark glass. Chimes rang softly, softly, keeping a beat not unlike a human heartbeat, only at different pitches. The smell of smoke and wet earth filled Creed's senses. Reality bent around him, and he wasn't certain of anything except the *other* inside him, Andy next to him, and Riana in front of him, right across the room.

"State your name," Riana commanded.

Creed heard Andy mumble, and he almost said his own name aloud. He had to shake his head, pinch himself, then pinch Andy's shoulder to get his senses back under control. It helped when Andy popped him upside the head for pinching her.

"Herbert Delwiggin," the naked guy said. His head drooped toward his chest and he sagged against the ropes holding his wrists above his head. "You don't want to mess with me. I've got friends."

The chimes pulsed. As if someone had choreographed the movement, the Sibyls shifted around the table so that Cynda now stood on the floor in front of their prisoner.

The flames along the lip of the table burned brighter, and Creed caught a bigger whiff of smoke.

"How did you find those friends?" Cynda asked.

"I didn't find them." Herbert's speech was slurred. "They found me. Not the demons, get me, but the guy who made them."

Creed saw all six Sibyls grow tense. He felt tense, too, as if they might be on the verge of something. The *other* grew more present, pressing forward enough to cause Creed some pain in his gut, but he knew he wasn't losing control. If things got bad, he'd go downstairs and put himself in the cell.

Chimes rang, and the women around Herbert shifted again. The wind picked up, and Merilee asked the next question. "What was that guy's name?"

"He called himself Smith. Mr. Smith."

Creed closed his eyes and opened them as he once more felt a stronger pressure against his eardrums. Chimes. The Sibyls moved. Dani, the other earth Sibyl, spoke in low, clear tones. "Describe Mr. Smith."

"Tall." Herbert's ropes shifted and Creed saw that he was trying to make the gesture for way over his head. "Older guy. Mustache. White hair brushed back. Nice threads." He coughed. "Karloff in *The Climax,* you know?"

Karloff. Old movies? Creed made a mental note to look up the flick online and find some stills. Andy twitched beside him, and he figured she had come to the same conclusion.

The chimes rang and the Sibyls shifted. "How did Mr. Smith first contact you?" Maura asked over the intensified flames and pale smoke.

Herbert stood in his stupor for a few seconds, then laughed. Definitely a cracked, on-the-edge laugh. "Sent me a lawyer. Helped me last time you bitches got me arrested. Mr. Smith drove me home."

More chimes, another shift of the circle, and more wind circling slowly about the room. Shell inquired about the ways Mr. Smith stayed in touch. They asked about phone numbers, addresses, the make and model of the car Herbert had seen, and got nothing much. Finally, when it was Riana's turn, she asked what Smith wanted.

Once again, Herbert hesitated. When he answered, the word seemed to ripple around the room like a mild electric shock. "Alliance."

The little man grinned, looking just as cracked as he sounded. "Smith trusted me for names of other people like me, with abilities and stuff. Gave him what I could."

The Sibyls paused in their questioning, just long enough for Creed to realize how badly this information had shaken them. It lodged in his gut, too. The *other* writhed around, making halfhearted growls in his head. Bothered, but not too threatened. It seemed clear on the fact that this interrogation was happening to some other poor bastard.

These Legion freaks, they're building allies, carving out territory like some fancy, well-dressed street gang.

Gangs always do that when they're planning to go to war.

With the next set of questions, the Sibyls made Herbert give them as many names as he had given his mysterious Mr. Smith. Andy had retrieved a pad from the floor and found a pencil, and she scribbled furiously as he spoke.

Over and over, the Sibyls tried questions relating to Smith's larger purpose, but Herbert didn't seem to know. Whenever they asked about what Mr. Smith hoped to accomplish, all Herbert would say was, "He's gonna make things right."

Yeah. Right for who—or what?

As the night wore on, Herbert wore down. It became more and more apparent to Creed that the man had blabbed all the useful knowledge he possessed. A few moments later, the Sibyls seemed to come to the same decision. As one, all but Cynda broke away from the table.

Instantly, the odd pressure in the room dissipated. The chimes stopped their rhythmic pulse, and some of the mirrors went dark and still.

Cynda picked up her sword, unsheathed it, and climbed onto the table. The fire in the trench parted to let her pass. As she took a position directly in front of Herbert, Creed's nuts actually contracted.

Goddamn, is she really going to neuter him?

She raised the sword, and in one powerful stroke, cut through the rope holding Herbert's hands aloft. His arms dropped, and Herbert dropped, too, collapsing on the table's broad surface. He didn't move, but he was breathing regularly, so Creed figured the guy had passed out.

Cynda tossed the sword to the floor and started to dance around Herbert's unconscious body.

Creed swallowed. He wasn't certain he had ever seen anything so bizarre. Yet Cynda moved deliberately, with purpose, and Creed sensed another change in the room. More tension. A brightness. A sense of something big about to happen.

The other five Sibyls stood in a straight line, holding hands. They seemed to be supporting Cynda somehow, concentrating their formidable energies and lending them to her. The flames ringing the table flared higher, and the chimes started a different sort of ring. Creed could swear the sound was dancing along with Cynda, from pipe to pipe and set to set, circling, circling, just as the fire Sibyl was circling.

After a few minutes and a growing swell of chime-song, Cynda shifted to dance in front of the oldest, darkest, most ornate mirror. The way Creed and Andy were sitting, they were facing it with her. Creed kept his eyes on the glass.

His gut clenched when fog appeared in the mirror. It brightened, as if someone had trained a light on the mirror's center. Then it started to swirl.

Every hair on his body came to attention as a wild energy buzzed around the room.

Something's happening. Right now.

"What the fuck?" Andy whispered. She stood slowly, letting the pad and pencil drop to the couch behind her.

The *other* shouted in Creed's mind, and he stood beside his partner. If he'd been wearing his sidearm, he might have put his hand over the grip like Andy. He couldn't take his mind off that mirror, or the image forming inside the glass.

A woman came into clear view, dark-haired like Riana but much younger, dressed in flowing brown robes. She was standing in a stone chamber, and huge sets of chimes hung all around her. The big pipes swayed and hopped on their strings, and Creed knew they were ringing, too.

On the table, Cynda started to whirl in a circle, arms over her head.

The woman in the mirror bowed, then paid rapt attention. Every so often, she nodded. Creed had a sense that Cynda was telling the younger woman everything that had happened recently, along with what they had learned from Herbert.

A lot like giving a report. Just . . . more complicated.

Cynda's dancing slowed, and the woman in the mirror danced for a few moments. Her gestures were more clumsy, less polished, but she got through whatever she wanted to communicate.

Cynda picked up speed again. Her arms moved up and down, and she circled around Herbert three times.

The other woman in the mirror nodded, then receded from view. She returned maybe a minute later, leading a bent, stooped figure dressed in heavy, hooded robes. The robes were brown like the ones the young girl wore, but with ornate green embroidery. Creed saw that the elderly woman—for the figure did appear to be an aged female—walked with a staff that had blue, green, red, and sparkling white jewels inlaid along its carved crown.

When the old woman was fully before the mirror, she straightened and pushed back her hood.

The *other* let out a shriek of anguish and terror, slammed through Creed's chest, then dropped away like a rush of physical discomfort. It happened so fast that Creed didn't have a chance to fall. He swayed and Andy steadied him, giving him a look that said, *What?*

He shook his head and made himself look back at the mirror.

She had long white hair pulled back and braided into a single thick cord that reached to her waist. The angles of her face were sharp and abrupt, and her dark skin was deeply lined around her bright green eyes and wide mouth. Her lips were parted, showing white teeth, and her expression seemed openly hungry, almost carnivorous. The fingers gripping the staff were knobbed and bent, but somehow her hands looked too powerful and firm for a woman of her age.

A Mother?

The moment Creed asked himself the question, he knew she had to be one of the Motherhouse elders Riana had described. And the *other* was terrified of this decrepit-looking being.

Amazing.

The Mother handed her staff to the younger girl, who then moved away.

Without comment, the Mother began to dance in a circle like Cynda. At first she moved slowly, stiffly, then faster than Creed thought possible, around, around.

The room crackled with a strange, undeniable power. Creed felt wide-eyed and completely awake, but like someone had pitched him headfirst into a dream or some alternate reality.

As he watched, not quite trusting his own mind, a tangible link seemed to form between the Sibyls' big oak table and the mirror showing the image of the old woman as she danced.

Herbert started to wake up. He twitched. Then he moaned. Finally, he screamed.

From seemingly a thousand miles away, the *other* screamed with him.

Creed jerked from the rush of terror that didn't belong to him.

Before the sensation completely died away, Herbert was gone.

He didn't lift up or float or vanish in a shimmer of sparks. He was simply on that table at Cynda's feet one second, then gone the next.

Creed gaped at the mirror.

Herbert was in the image now, lying at the feet of the strange old Mother. A pair of gigantic wolves entered the picture and paced toward the fallen man. Cynda slowed her dance, then gradually reversed her direction. The Mother did the same, and seconds later, the image clouded, then faded completely away.

"Fuuuuu-uuuuuck meeeeeeee," Andy said, staring at the empty place where Herbert had been not two minutes before. "What did you *do*?"

Cynda stopped dancing and tossed Andy a look. "We didn't kill him. Happy now?"

Riana folded her arms and sighed. Her back was still to Creed as she said, "I hate doing that."

"No choice," Dani said. "Did they have any suggestions?"

Cynda shook her head. "Shit's happening everywhere. Mass Asmodai attacks, people going missing, and yeah—alliances between the Legion and other fringe groups. Thank the Goddess a lot of them are pip-squeaks and weirdos like Herbert, or we might have a full-scale war on our hands."

"Don't we?" Andy muttered. Creed had to agree. He studied Riana's trim lines. Her shoulders were tense. Even though she wasn't looking at him, he knew she was worried. Hell, he was worried, and he didn't understand half of what was happening.

"We're to keep up patrols as usual, but make every effort to capture and question members of the Legion, or anyone who has even *seen* a Legion member in person." Her gaze snapped toward Creed and Andy. "If the cops don't release Alisa by eighteen-hundred Friday night two weeks from now, we're to go get her and send her back to Motherhouse Russia."

Creed realized what Cynda meant, and he saw the stoic way the other Sibyls took this bit of news. Apparently, the prospect of assaulting Rikers Island, the largest penal colony in the United States, didn't distress them one bit. Merilee and the earth Sibyl Dani actually looked relieved.

"Just talk like we aren't in the room," Andy said brightly. "We don't mind."

No one answered her. No one even looked at her.

We're inconsequential as far as the Sibyls are concerned, Creed realized. *Inconsequential to this battle.*

Hell no, they weren't! But what could he and Andy do to stop an Asmodai—short of risking everything by taking off his signet ring? What could they do against the Legion?

He'd think of something.

He gazed at Riana, determined to find a way to fight beside her. One way or another, he damn well *would* make a difference. His gaze dropped to the cut places in her bodysuit, to the wounds she suffered when she went out to save the world without him.

And that shit stops tonight. The next time she draws those daggers on some freak-ass monster, I'll be next to her.

(21)

Riana felt relieved that her bullet wounds weren't throbbing anymore, and grateful for the superior healing rates of Sibyls. Flesh wounds weren't much of a problem, if they got proper tending. She was tired, though, and jumpy way down inside. Everything was happening too fast, and she felt like she was losing control of her life and her little corner of the world.

Bullets. She rubbed her side. *Somebody shot at us*.

She was deliberately not turning around to look at Creed, who was far too sexy in his jeans and white shirt. That man could fill out his clothes in the most perfect way. If she saw him, if he was looking at her with that same intensity and concern, she would just melt into his arms. That wouldn't be wise, given Cynda and Merilee's doubts about him. Dani and crew would probably think poorly of her judgment, too. Unless—no, *until*—the Mothers gave approval for the risky, unusual relationship, all the Sibyls who knew Creed would worry that Riana's feelings were blinding her to the dangers his *other* posed.

Also, Riana felt a bit guilty for questioning Creed the way they had questioned Herbert. No doubt he realized what his fate might have been had he not won her interest and trust. The sight of Mother Yana's wolves made Riana nervous in a whole new way.

What if the Mothers one day demanded that Creed be sent to Ireland, Greece, or Russia? Could she do it? And what would happen to him if the Mothers claimed him?

Better that than the order to kill him. I know I couldn't obey that instruction.

Dani was saying something about warped times calling for warped measures. She jerked her face mask out of her belt and jammed it over her head. "It's been fun, but we need to roll. I need at least a little sleep before making morning rounds."

Shell and Maura said their goodbyes, too, and Riana saw the South Manhattan triad to the door. Once she got the door closed and locked, she turned to her own pestle and broom. "Cynda, are you okay?"

Cynda glanced down at her leg and pulled off her bandage. She didn't bother trying to throw it away. She just dropped it on the floor. "Looks okay. It's stopped hurting, so that's a good sign."

Merilee patted down her leathers. "I still don't think I got hit anywhere. If I did, I just got nicked."

Riana closed the distance between them and, keeping her eyes studiously away from Creed and Andy, she took Cynda's hands into her own.

Cynda looked at her steadily, her eyes asking, *What, boss?*

"Thank you for pulling me out of that cemetery." She hugged Cynda, then Merilee. "I don't know how you got me over that fence."

"Muscle and air," Merilee said as she let go of Riana. She laughed. "Maybe you should dial back a notch on the bagels and cream cheese at breakfast, though."

"Pick, pick, pick," Cynda grumbled. "Next you'll be calling her a fat-ass, too."

Riana held back a groan. "We all need to sleep. Let's hit this again in the morning. By then the Mothers will have taken their turn with Herbert, and we might have some new information."

She bit her lip, took a breath, then made herself turn around. "The molds I needed came in. I should have the first round of bullets cooled, hardened, and ready for you in two days. A week or so, and I'll have a fairly good supply. We'll see what comes of it, but my expectations aren't high that they'll bring down an Asmodai."

Andy nodded. "Thanks. I'll take my chances, because I don't do well on the sidelines. This whole Legion invasion thing is starting to suck. If the bullets work, we can get the rest of the OCU involved and have a lot more dead demons."

Riana tried to pay attention to Andy, but her face was heating up. Creed's eyes never left her, and she couldn't stop looking at him. She felt his dark eyes moving over her skin like a touch, and dear Goddess, she wanted his hands on her body instead. Her nipples tightened just at the thought, and her heart fluttered. Tonight of all nights, she could use the release of the pleasure he gave her, not to mention the safety she found in his arms.

Until that thing inside him pops out and eats me. Yeah. That's real safe.

She rubbed one eye and tried to keep her composure, but he needed to stop looking at her that way.

He didn't.

She had to force herself to turn around and say good night to Cyndá and Merilee, and put up with their knowing looks before she escaped to the kitchen. The glass of ice water she drank didn't cool her down at all. She'd just have to hope she fell asleep fast after she went downstairs for her shower. She and Andy had traded spaces again, with Andy taking the living room. Riana wanted the comfort of her own bed, now that the door was fixed. A solid barrier between her and Creed. That should be enough to keep her in her right mind, yes?

One could hope.

She just hoped that her shower would do the trick, relax her, and put her in a better frame of mind.

Unfortunately, the shower turned out to be its own torture. The warm water soothed her scrapes, bruises, and healing wounds, but it did nothing to decrease her arousal.

Neither did touching herself, or bringing herself to orgasm. Riana toweled off, frustrated beyond words.

Steam floated around her bathroom like the smoke from one of Cynda's temper tantrums. She took a deep breath, letting the warm, moist air ease the catch in her throat and chest. When she looked down at the towel on her body, at her hands, she felt different. She couldn't find the right words to describe the sensation, but she imagined how Creed might see her. What did he think of this curve, of that freckle? Did he like her smile? Her skin?

She didn't feel insecure about her looks, just about his re-action to her. She hadn't had enough time with him to have a real sense of his emotions, or the truthfulness of his compliments.

Maybe he could come to my room tonight and just hold me. Maybe we could talk.

Riana dried off her face, rubbed the towel over her silver chain and crescent pendant, and remembered how Creed's *other* had crushed an Asmodai's head with its bare hands.

"Yes. Don't forget that part. Honey, could you just hold me tonight—and try not to smear my brains all over the pillows. Dry-cleaning bills are just throooough the roof these days."

She tossed the towel over her shower bar and put on her robe. When she opened her bedroom door, her heart sank because Creed wasn't in her bedroom. She knew he wouldn't take chances with her safety, but she had hoped . . . well, no sense hoping for much in a hopeless situation. Her genetic analyses would be completed soon, and they'd have some real answers. It was probably best that they keep their distance until they had facts in hand.

She hugged herself and tried to make herself get in bed.

Tried, but failed.

Riana ended up standing in the middle of her own floor, wanting to cry over a man she knew she shouldn't want, and couldn't have.

No denying what she felt now, the strength of it, or the intensity. She wanted Creed, and nothing else would do. And she didn't just want to touch him.

Well, there was that, definitely.

But she wanted to talk to him and hear the deep rumble of his voice when he talked to her. She wanted to look in his eyes and see what he really thought, what he really felt about the Legion and the Asmodai, his job, life, his god or the Goddess, and even more important, her. Them.

Us.

I'm on the edge of a cliff, and I'm about to fall.

Her heart thumped as she imagined his lips pressed against hers. She could almost feel his electric, demanding touch.

"Never going to sleep like this." She glanced to her right, at the closed, locked door. The barrier. Yeah. On impulse, she decided to open it. At least she could feel a little closer to him that way, even if he was down the hall in the back of the lab, behind locked bars.

Andy would lock him in, right? She wouldn't have to endure that temptation and torture. Riana clenched her teeth and opened the door. The hallway to the lab was dark and empty, and once more her heart sank because she didn't catch him on his way to the lab for the night. A glow spilled into the hall from beneath the lab door, just enough to light the way—but she knew she couldn't go to the lab.

I'm pathetic. I want to see him, but I don't. Just shut up and go to bed.

She turned away from the dark hallway, blew out her candles, pulled back her sheet and blanket, and got into bed. Her mind immediately wandered to Motherhouse Russia, to the teachers and Mothers who had raised her with so much love. How many nights did they tuck her in and calm her fears?

Everything will be fine, little one.

Trust your mind. Trust your instincts.

You can lead a triad. You can handle what life brings you, even if life brings you monsters.

She reached up and gripped the crescent pendant Mother Yana had given her. Why did the old woman believe in her so much? She had failed at unifying groups in training so many times. Riana just couldn't seem to *get* what other women needed, emotionally. Yet Mother Yana singled her out and gave her the pendant, and insisted she was meant for greatness.

A few weeks ago, *hadn't* she been learning to trust her mind and instincts without question? Riana chewed the inside of her lip. Back then, she had slept easily and well, and didn't even have any dreams. A few weeks ago, she thought she finally knew what to do in any situation.

Then came Creed . . . and all the old doubts came rushing back.

The upstairs door opened, and she heard someone coming down the steps. Her heart started beating double time, and her hopes soared that this time, she wouldn't be disappointed. It wouldn't be Andy on the stairs, or Cynda or Merilee. In a few seconds, she'd see Creed, just for a moment, but it might be enough to sustain her.

When his muscular profile passed by her open door, she had to hold her breath to keep from calling out to him.

Yet he seemed to sense her watching him, and he stopped walking.

Oh, Goddess.

Creed came back to her door slowly, and her heart pounded harder with each step he took. When he stopped in the doorway, he hitched his shoulder against the doorframe. With the gift of her keen vision, Riana could see the look of concern and longing on his handsome face, and it nearly killed her inside. She could tell he wanted to stride across the room and hold her, maybe just to know she was alive.

I'm alive. I'm so alive.

He probably couldn't see her, and she had a wicked urge to touch herself while she could see him. Now *that* orgasm would probably give her a little relief, at least enough to sleep.

She refrained. Barely.

He cleared his throat, and Riana realized he was trying to figure out if she was awake. She hardly trusted her voice not to give away the desire storming through her.

"Do you need something?" she asked, trying her best to sound calm and a little sleepy.

His intake of breath made her body ache.

"I need a lot, honey," he said in that low bass that made her want to crawl to him on her hands and knees and beg for attention. "But for now, I'd settle for you locking me into my cage."

Riana let loose a stream of curses in her mind. She'd never get through this. Never. Not without doing something stupid. She should tell him the keys were on the cot, that he could lock himself inside the cell and toss the keys on a nearby counter.

Instead, she slipped out of her bed, tightened her robe, and walked straight to him.

He didn't move until she was a step from him. Then he caught her and pulled her to him in one smooth movement. His body felt like molded steel against hers, and his rough jeans scrubbed her thighs through her robe. He smelled so good. Fresh and strong and ready to give her what she needed—and he was hard as a rock. She could feel his erection pressing into her belly, straining the fabric that held it in check. Creed's grip had such power, but when he stroked her face with both hands before twining his fingers in her hair, he touched her with such careful restraint.

Then his lips found hers, and she couldn't think anymore.

All Riana could do was kiss him back, and give herself completely to the task. His mouth felt so warm, and the way he held her face and claimed her lips made her melt. He kissed her again and again, tracing her tongue with his, answering her soft moans with quiet rumbles of pleasure.

When he finally pulled back and pressed his lips to her forehead, Riana imagined he might be able to hear her heart beating in the absolutely silent space. Cynda, Merilee, Andy, the Legion, New York, and the entire world were just . . . gone. On some other planet. Tonight, there was only Creed, and the way he made her heart pound.

Creed tucked her head under his chin and held her in that embrace she had so wanted. She molded her body to his and pressed her face into his chest.

Yes, yes. Please. Never let me go.

"I don't know if I can let you walk out of here alone again." His words vibrated against her ear and face. "I know it's what you do, and I never want to take anything away from you. But I can't turn my back while you walk into that kind of danger."

Riana heard the honest, raw emotion in his voice, and didn't feel offended or threatened. Only held tighter, closer, in a whole different way. She nodded to let him know she understood. She didn't want to get shot again, either, and she was tired of fighting an enemy she couldn't predict or control. Maybe Creed and Andy could help, if she could get the bullets made tomorrow. It would be nice to have more backup. They needed all the help they could get.

How could she let him go, lock him in that cell and walk away from him? She wished she could just stand there in his arms all night. Things felt simpler in his arms, more basic, and much more clear.

"You better give me those keys," he murmured, and kissed the top of her head. "This is headed where it shouldn't go in one big hurry."

Her chest tightened. He was already pulling away from her, and she wanted to hold on tight and wail for him to stay.

"They're in the cell," she finally whispered, running her

hands over his shirt, loving the feel of his muscles through the fabric. "I'll lock you in."

He put a finger under her chin and tilted her face up until she was looking directly into those blazing black eyes. Even in the minimal light, they captured her completely.

"That's a bad idea," he said, his voice hoarse. "I'll lock myself up and toss the keys out."

Riana's heart dropped to her toes. Her head drooped against his fingers, but he tilted it back up toward his.

"You have to know how much I want you." He brushed his lips across hers, sending more waves of need crashing through her body. "Tell me you know."

Riana answered him by stretching up on her toes and joining her mouth to his. He welcomed her, kissed her back just as passionately, then separated from her with a reluctant groan.

"If I could, I'd hold you all night, honey."

Riana squeezed herself against him as she had done before, pushing her face into his chest.

"The last thing I want to do is let you go." He kissed the top of her head one more time. "But I can't—I won't—put you at risk. It's all I can do to hold the thing back right now."

The anguish in his voice finally pierced Riana's steaming passion. She heard his misery and worry, and the reality of his last statement. The *other* was trying to burst out even now to attack her, and Creed hated that as much as she did.

He had to go.

She had to let him go.

"I'm sorry." She pressed her lips against his neck and turned him loose. It was all she could do to turn her back on him.

"Me, too, honey. You have no idea how sorry."

Riana stood still in the silence, heart aching as she heard him walking away down the hall.

It was going to be one hell of a long night.

22

Almost two weeks after the Trinity Church disaster, Creed sat in the captain's office contemplating murder.

"You're tying our hands." He clenched his fists against the chair arms, but didn't bash the top of Freeman's desk like he wanted to. Creed knew where the line was, and he knew he had his toes right on the edge.

"Don't take that tone with me, Lowell." Captain Freeman narrowed his eyes. "OCU cannot—*will* not—have any official involvement in the Latch case. We're taking a big risk even assisting on the occult elements."

The captain's cluttered little office smelled like sweat and cologne. It felt too small, and Creed wanted to kick the shit out of four or five of the towering stacks of paper. He didn't get the chance, though, because Andy shifted in the chair next to Creed's, bumped one of the piles, and spilled two or three folders on the floor.

"Why can't we interview Davin or Raven Latch, or the assistant, for God's sake?" Creed relaxed his fists and scrubbed his hands against his knees. "You let us talk to Corey James."

"James isn't spending all his time creating headlines to fuck the department." Freeman whirled in his chair and grabbed a newspaper off one of his stacks. He slapped the *New York Post* on the desk in front of Creed and jabbed his finger at the headline.

LATCH WIFE BLASTS NYPD
"Find my baby's *real* killer!"

Creed pushed the paper back toward Freeman. *James keeps quiet to protect the woman he loves,* he thought. *Alisa doesn't need any more attention focused on her—on the Sibyls.*

Aloud, Creed said, "Raven Latch has got a point."

"Shit," Andy whispered from beside him.

Freeman's face turned a light shade of red. "We have a suspect arraigned and awaiting trial. Did you forget that?"

"Come on!" Creed couldn't help standing up this time. "You know it's not that simple. There's no way Alisa James carved up that kid—did you read her interviews? Something's gone way wrong with her mind. She can't even recite the alphabet. And even if she did kill the boy, do you think she did it alone?"

"What I think doesn't matter, does it?" Freeman's voice was dangerously quiet.

Taking the cue, Creed dropped back into his chair and turned his furious gaze on the floor. One of the files scattered beside his feet bore the name of Frith Gregory, the assistant employed by Senator Latch and his wife. Creed had to force himself to look away from it.

Sal Freeman leaned forward in his high-backed chair, his black eyebrows pulled together in that shut-the-fuck-up way only he could accomplish. His muscular arms flexed beneath his rolled-up sleeves. "No more interviews. We have several very competent interrogations already transcribed and on your desk, Lowell. Make it work. This case is too hot to go any further. Every move you make, fifty reporters will be right up your ass."

Creed battled the rush of heat and rage threatening to unhinge his mouth and likely earn him a demotion or jail time for punching his captain. He sat back in his chair and swallowed a string of curses that would have made his missing brother proud. Andy remained silent in the chair beside his. Her lips were pressed tight, and her jaw was set.

Creed couldn't tell if she was mad at Freeman or mad at him for pushing Freeman. Andy hadn't been herself since the bullshit at Trinity Church, and since the triad wouldn't let them report what really happened and get the OCU involved. Andy thought she and Creed were dancing close to putting their badges on the line—and they were getting nowhere with the investigation of the murder, the Legion, and who shot at the Sibyls. The best they had been able to do was look up stills of Karloff in old movies like *The Climax*, which had been useless. None of their principals looked like Boris Karloff, at least not that he could tell.

Creed was surprised Andy didn't say anything when he used his foot to open the Frith Gregory file. She still cared about her job, even if he didn't. He knew he was being a bastard to Captain Freeman, but he didn't have any choice. He hadn't had a decent night's sleep since Riana got shot. Not to mention the fact that it was only four days before the Sibyls would raid Rikers Island.

From what Creed could understand, they would treat it like a military rescue operation, pulling in as many triads as they could. Most would hold the perimeter while the Bronx and Manhattan groups penetrated the Singer Center, where female detainees were held. They'd get Alisa James out, killing as few people as possible, and send her to Russia. The Bronx and Manhattan triads would be pulled home for a time and replaced with new groups, then reassigned elsewhere in the world.

In four days, Riana would be dead, in jail, or gone to some other country, beyond his reach forever.

No way. Not happening.

Not even if he had to bully Captain Freeman every minute of every hour until he got what he wanted.

Which apparently wouldn't be today.

He wound up to try again, but Andy stopped him with a sharp kick to the shins. He turned to glare at her, then sighed and bent down to pick up the spilled folders. The desk blocked Freeman's view when Creed tore the face sheet out of Gregory's and folded it double in two quick motions.

Andy noticed, but only her eyes flickered. She kept a grim, resigned look on her face. After Creed sat back up and slipped the face sheet into his pocket, she cleared her throat and said, "We hear you, Captain. For now, how about we get back to work on the dozen or so reports we got about that unnatural wall of fire around Trinity Church?"

Freeman's eyebrows lifted.

The man had an entire language of his own, communicated by the hair over his eyes.

This look said, *Good, good, but what the hell are you up to?*

When Andy didn't elaborate, Freeman's eyebrows leveled off to *Okay, whatever. Just don't piss me off or sink this unit.*

Andy got up. So did Creed. She didn't speak to him as they left Freeman's office, or on the elevator down to the ground floor. It wasn't until they pushed through the doors at the stone entrance of the old Fourteenth that she asked, "What are you going to do?"

Creed let the cool outside air chill his temper a few degrees before he shrugged. "I have no idea. But I'm going to do something."

Andy elbowed two passersby as she pulled back her red hair and fastened it with a holder she had been wearing around her wrist. "Does that include facing reality?"

Creed didn't answer that out loud. Hell, no, he wasn't facing reality. Reality didn't include a fighting chance for them to stop the Legion and those Asmodai, or for him to have a real shot at serious time with Riana. Reality sucked.

They reached the Crown Vic in silence. Instead of going around to the driver's door, Andy leaned against the curb side of her car, folded her arms, and looked at him. Traffic whizzed by, stopped. Whizzed by, stopped. Another cool breeze traveled down the street, carrying the scent of pretzels and burgers. Creed's stomach growled. He was hungry enough to buy out the nearest cart, but he knew better than to rush Andy when she had a mind to tell him off. Besides, this went way beyond a passing argument over methods of investigation. He knew he was putting his career at risk, and if she went along with him, hers, too. That was too much to ask, even from a loyal partner.

Finally, Andy lowered her head and decided to speak to him. "Is this about Riana or the crime?"

He shoved his hands in the pockets of his blue slacks. Tough question. And the answer changed every few minutes. "Both," he said, giving her the most honest answer he could find. "And the Asmodai and the Legion, and whatever they're planning."

She looked up at him. "If we play by the rules, we'll never solve this case, and come Friday, Riana, Cynda, and Merilee will be gone."

"Yeah, I know." Creed's stomach stopped growling. "Why do you think I pushed Freeman so hard?"

"Pushing Freeman isn't going to get us shit. Once he's made up his mind, he's iron." Andy frowned. "But you're right. It shouldn't end there. If we don't act fast, we'll be stuck with new Sibyls we don't even know, who might or might not work with us. I think we'll be on our own."

She fell silent again, then shook her head and looked at the sky.

It was Creed's turn to fold his arms and study Andy. She was dressed in a black pantsuit that reminded him of Riana and her triad, lots better than his work slacks and blue jacket. All Andy needed was a face mask. Only, with her hair pulled back, she looked a little like a Catholic-school teacher, or one of those women who talked so sternly about STD risks on television. It was the look in her eyes, though, that bothered him the most. She was sad now. Distant. Like she was grieving something—but what?

Dread mounted in his gut, pushing away all thoughts of hunger. "What are *you* going to do, Andy?"

"If I smoked, I'd light one up right about now." She looked away from him and blinked. A tear slipped down her cheek.

Creed felt a stab of guilt. He started to ask her if she wanted him to leave, or maybe turn in his badge and take her off the hook, but she spoke before he could open his mouth.

"Since I don't smoke, I guess I'll just go for it." Andy turned back toward him and leveled her misty gaze at him. "At Van Cortlandt Park, when I saw—really *saw*—something supernatural for the first time, everything changed for me. We're out of our league with the Legion. The OCU, the NYPD, the whole city—humans in general. Without the Sibyls, I think we're screwed."

When she paused, Creed said, "Following you so far, and I agree."

"My gut tells me that without you, the Sibyls might be screwed."

That surprised him. "I don't know how you're figuring that," he allowed, "but okay."

She picked up speed and volume as she went. "I sure as hell don't want to be left on the sidelines when this war with the Legion explodes." She pulled out her badge and looked at it, then locked eyes with Creed again. "The way I see it, we've got to choose sides, all or nothing. We have to let the Sibyls know that we're with them, *and* that we're worth something in this fight."

Creed stared at Andy. He knew how he felt and why, but he hadn't realized that Andy felt the same way, and so strongly. It occurred to him that he might have a habit of underestimating people, or assuming that he was all alone in the world, especially since Dominic went AWOL. "Fuckin'-A," he muttered.

"As much as I like being a cop, some things are more important. I'm ready to chuck the rules and stop these bastards." Andy tucked her badge back into her waistband, leaned forward, jammed her hand into Creed's pocket, and yanked out the papers he had lifted from Captain Freeman's office. She pulled open the folded information.

Creed watched as she ran her finger across the typed lines at the top.

"Let's get 'em, one at a time if we have to, all the principals, and take them to the Sibyls for interrogation. Starting with him, even if he does have an alibi." She turned the paper around and showed him the neatly typed face sheet from the file of Frith Gregory. Her finger rested on the home address. "You know they can get more out of this asshole than we can. We'll probably get charged with assault, false arrest, kidnapping, and God only knows what else. So, partner, I've only got one question. You want to drive, or me?"

Frith Gregory lived in a flat in Little Italy. From what they had read in the newspaper and dug up by badgering the "cover cops," the guy was on paid leave from the Latches' employ until the murder investigation into Jacob Latch's death was resolved. Hopefully he'd be at home. If not, they'd wait.

As Creed guided the Crown Vic into a paid lot, the smells of garlic, basil, and fresh, hot pasta made him remember exactly how hungry he was. Two minutes later, he pulled Andy into the nearest restaurant and crammed down a meatball sub, then made a side trip into La Bella Ferrara and ate his fill of chocolate-covered cannoli. Andy ate her share, too, and topped it off with a chocolate-dipped gelato dessert. It wasn't every day that two good cops threw their careers down the drain. Creed figured they might as well commemorate the occasion.

By the time Creed and Andy flashed their badges at the bored-looking guard at the door of Gregory's building, Creed was actually yawning from the sugar-and-carb over-load. His mind snapped awake as they got off the elevator, though.

Gregory lived in a nice place, with clean white walls, pol-ished oak banisters, and shiny stone floors. The whole place smelled like clean, new furniture, with a faint odor of fresh paint. They caught a break, and the hallway leading to Gregory's door was empty. With any luck, they might get in and out without causing much of a stir. He and Andy had discussed how to play this, and it wouldn't be gentle. The fewer people who saw and heard, the better.

Creed drew his SIG. Andy drew hers, too.

He reached across the doorframe and banged on Frith Gregory's apartment door. "Police!" he boomed as loud as he could, hoping the guy would imagine a furious, well-shielded SWAT team about to break through the door.

Nobody answered.

Andy looked at Creed.

Creed nodded.

He spun out from the side of the door and delivered a hard kick to the door. It groaned, but didn't give. Damn New York heavy doors and eight thousand locks. He kicked it again, feeling the shock up his ankle and knee, all the way to his teeth. The door *still* didn't give.

Somebody started yelling in the apartment.

Creed got out of the way in a hurry. "Police!" he bel-lowed again.

The sound of turning locks started immediately, along with a lot of grumbling and swearing. "I was in the shower!" a male voice announced. "Give me a moment."

Another nod from Andy, and Creed got ready.

As the door opened, Creed waited just long enough to be sure the guy matched the photos he had seen, then threw his shoulder against the door and rushed inside. Andy was right behind him. She slammed the door and screeched, "Get on the floor! Get on the floor!"

Most perps acted like Andy was nine feet tall with big muscles and fangs, and this guy was no exception. Dripping wet, wearing nothing but gold-rimmed glasses, a black tank, and a pair of black silk jogging shorts, he dropped to his knees and lay facedown, hands over his head.

"What is this about, Officers?" Gregory had to turn his head to talk. His glasses had come off one ear, but he sounded a little too calm to suit Creed. He had expected the guy to be nervous, as fast as he got on the floor. "I've given my alibi, and answered every question I could."

Scrawny bastard, Creed thought. The guy talked like a Harvard graduate, but he looked like a reject from the still-lives-with-Mommy club. Frith Gregory was sandy-haired and pale, not an ounce of fat on him anywhere. Tattoo on his back, and a big one, but the tank hid most of it. He wasn't shaking. Cooperative, but not terrified. His apartment smelled a little like rotten eggs, and Creed wondered if he needed to clean out his fridge.

As Gregory stared at him, Creed's ring started to hum against his finger.

What the hell?

"This feels wrong," Andy said. "Let's bag this freak and go."

Creed moved on instinct, holstering his sidearm. He straddled Gregory and ordered him to put his hands behind his back. Once more, Gregory complied, but he said, "Please give me an explanation."

Creed glanced at Andy, who shrugged to say, *Shit. Do I have to do everything? Make something up!*

"Frith Gregory," Creed said as he locked the cuffs, "you're under arrest for . . . uh . . . interfering with a police investigation and conspiracy to commit murder."

Gregory stiffened in Creed's grip, but the cuffs were already fastened. Creed recited Gregory's rights just to make it sound official. Then he started to sweat like he had run six miles.

What the hell? It's not that hot in here.

"You'll regret this." Gregory sounded confident and still way too calm. "I'm completely innocent in this matter, and I have dozens of people, tickets, and receipts to back up my alibi. I wasn't in New York City when Jacob died. Your associates have already verified all this information."

Creed wiped the sweat off his face, got up, and pulled the guy to his feet, then pushed Gregory's glasses up on his nose for him. "Yeah. We'll check all that back at the house," Creed said. "Come on."

Andy, who was sweating too, enough to stain her blouse under her neck, holstered her weapon and turned to get the door. "Must be hot in here. Jesus. I'm wet as a rag." As she took her first step, her knees wobbled, and she dropped to the floor on all fours.

"I'm—I'm thirsty," she wheezed.

Creed's mouth went dry. His ring jumped and started a painful, electric buzz against his skin. At the same instant, he almost doubled over to manage a sudden charge from the *other*.

His gut felt like it was splitting in two, and his head buzzed. He let go of Gregory before he accidentally shoved the cuffed guy to the floor face-first.

Andy lurched forward. "My head. Christ! Creed, I think my brain's exploding."

Creed couldn't see. The room seemed suddenly dark and misty. He felt pressure on his temples. It hurt so bad his teeth clamped together.

"My head," Andy rasped like she had been in the desert for a week. "My fucking head!"

The *other* roared inside Creed. He heard waves crashing. The beast inside him shoved against something.

Something . . . that shouldn't be there?

Creed had a sense of the creature shredding things with its wicked claws. The loud buzz in his mind stopped as if something had crushed it. A second later, the pressure ended with an almost audible *pop,* and Creed could see again. His mouth was drier than a petrified sponge, but by God he could see.

Frith Gregory was standing next to Andy, handcuffs on the floor at his feet, holding Andy's gun. His glasses glinted in the afternoon sunlight coming through the windows of his spacious apartment. He didn't seem to realize Creed had recovered his senses, because he had the gun pointed straight at the floor.

". . . Irregular," he was saying. "Something's fishy here, and I'm afraid I can't—"

Creed launched himself at Gregory, no longer caring what kind of damage he did to the guy. He had him by at least sixty pounds, with surprise on his side. The guy squealed as Creed hit him, dropping the gun and crumpling beneath Creed's bulk.

Blood pounding, anger at max, Creed was feeling no pain. He grabbed the guy's tank, jerked him off the floor, and hit him so hard he thought he heard Gregory's jaw break.

Gregory's head snapped back and his glasses flew off. His eyes fluttered, and he was down for the count.

"Scoot over" came Andy's hoarse croak from over Creed's shoulder. "I got my gun back. Let me shoot him. Please?"

Creed did get out of her way, but not to let her murder the unconscious guy. She staggered off while he flipped Gregory over, pulled his skinny arms back, and cuffed him again. This time, he fastened the bracelets a lot tighter than he normally would, wondering how the hell Gregory got out of them in the first place.

"I thought I was having a stroke," Andy mumbled, coming back from the kitchen with two cups of water. She drank both cups, looked at Creed, and apologized. Back to the kitchen she went, and this time, she gave him one of the cool, full drinks.

He guzzled it.

They drank three more cups apiece, then Andy worried that the guy might have some disease dishwashers wouldn't kill. Creed assured her that probably wasn't possible.

"I think that was his fault," Andy muttered, taking Creed's cup and putting both of them in her bag, so they wouldn't leave any more evidence than necessary. She also bent over and picked up Gregory's glasses, and stowed those as well. "What did he do to us?"

"No clue. Let's get him the hell out of here before he wakes up." Creed bent down, grabbed Gregory, and positioned him on the nearest floor rug. A few seconds later, he had the guy rolled up tight. Son of a bitch was heavier than he looked, too, when Creed picked him up commando-style.

"Head out in the hall and flash that badge," he told Andy. "We need to move."

23

Afternoon sunlight glinted off polished chimes and mirrors as Riana sat in her living room on the edge of the big oak table, beside her newly calibrated portable spectroscope. The metallic barrels gleamed, and she couldn't help thinking that the device looked like some futuristic ray gun. She was ready to test it, but Merilee had come downstairs with her initial report on Creed. Riana stared at the folder Merilee had compiled on Creed. It was sparse, for sure. A lot slighter than most of the dossiers she put together. She didn't want to open it, but Merilee and Cynda weren't going to let her have the luxury of ignorance.

"Born in NYC, but not in a hospital." Merilee bounced her fingers against the knee of her black jeans, impatient as usual. "His birth certificate was signed by a doc who retired three days later, over on the East Side. He's dead now. Mother's name was Grace, grandmother's name was Delilah, twin brother Dominic, just like he told us. Year of birth is consistent with his age, but no father listed."

Cynda, who was sitting in the chair beside Merilee's, said, "His mother's dead or vanished like his brother. We couldn't find a record of what happened, but his grandmother signed all the official documents we located. The grandmother died when he was sixteen."

"Maybe his mother died giving birth," Riana murmured, gazing at the grade cards and handful of medical records they had been able to hunt, hack, or pay to retrieve from Internet databases.

"Maybe giving birth to half-demon kids is dangerous," Cynda shot back.

Riana ignored her. She rested the transcripts against her khaki slacks and fiddled with the edges of her white blouse as she read the printout. Bachelor of Arts in Criminal Justice from CUNY—City University of New York. Straight A's. Impressive.

"There's no missing-persons report on Dominic, but his records are even more scarce than Creed's," Merilee added. "Last report of income on Dominic Lowell's Social was a little over five years ago. He was a cop, too."

Riana looked up at her triad. "So Creed is checking out so far?"

A tiny plume of smoke rose from the elbow of Cynda's loose white tunic. "If you don't count the fact that everyone he's ever been close to is dead or missing, sure. He's checking out."

Merilee tossed Cynda a withering glare, then nodded to Riana. "This info's consistent with what we've been told, but we're hitting his apartment next. Probably tonight, after he's down in the cell."

Riana barely heard her. She had grabbed her jury-rigged spectroscope at the first sign of Cynda playing with fire and looked through the lens opening. A second or two later, she had the main lens trained on Cynda's arm.

Not quite.

She tweaked the knob to reduce the input from sunlight, and this time, she saw what she was looking for. A faint red glow, just outside what a normal human eye might be able to perceive. Well, all of Cynda seemed to have a reddish outline, but her elbow was definitely a dark maroon, almost black hot spot.

"This'll work better at night, for sure." She turned the knob a bit more, getting an idea how clear the images would be at twilight, or later in the night.

Cynda leaned down to stare directly into the filtered lens of the spectroscope. "May I ask what the hell you're doing, Dr. Demented?"

Riana eased the device from her eye and laid it gently on the table. "Nothing much. Just outstripping human science with leftover junk in my lab." She patted the spectroscope. "I think we might be able to track Asmodai with this, or at least see where they've been. If it works, I might be able to make us all filtered glasses to approximate the same results."

"Approximate the same results," Merilee mimicked. She took Creed's folder back from Riana. "You sound like that Vulcan from the old *Star Trek* shows."

Cynda stared at her elbow. "Do I want to know what my elbow has to do with Asmodai?"

"Your elbow? Nothing." Riana watched as the smoke around Cynda subsided. "Your fire—everything. Whenever you make it, the energy conversion produces a by-product of sulfur dioxide. I'm pretty sure fire Asmodai do, too. All Asmodai, actually, though the earth and air demons will have smaller traces. Merilee and I make tiny amounts whenever we tap the elements . . ."

Riana trailed off.

Cynda and Merilee were looking at her without saying anything, but she read their meaning clearly.

English, please.

"Demons give off gas traces that last six to ten days." She picked up the spectroscope. "I can see the traces with this."

"Now that's pretty amazing." Cynda reached out and touched the spectroscope's top metal tube. "But we're still searching your boyfriend's crib tonight, okay?"

Riana's mind slowly processed what Cynda said, and what Merilee had told her earlier, about hitting Creed's apartment. "Wait a minute. I'm not sure how I feel about that."

"We know how you feel about it," Merilee said. "That's why we're telling you and not asking you."

"Creed's been completely cooperative with us." Riana

stood. "Everything in your folder checks out—and I need you guys with me tonight, to try out the scope. I wanted to take it by the museum, and maybe past the Latch house. It's likely all the traces will be gone, but still I think it's worth a shot."

"You just don't want us in Creed's apartment." Cynda got up. More smoke seeped from her back jeans pocket. "You're afraid of what we'll find."

Riana clenched her hands together. "I am not. I just—"

"Did you make those bullets?" Merilee interrupted, scooting forward in her chair as if to separate Riana and Cynda.

"Yes. Several batches." Riana gestured toward the basement. "I have about a hundred rounds for each of them. They could go with us tonight, and if something happens, we'll get our trial."

Cynda got up, all the better to glare at Riana over Merilee's back. "I think this is irresponsible, involving humans in our fight." She walked around the chair until she was face-to-face with Riana. "I think it's irresponsible not to tell the Mothers about Creed—and I think it's insane to let Creed and Andy face down demons with nothing but a gun and untried bullets."

Riana felt each word like a blow, and Cynda's mistrustful, angry expression hurt her more than anything. She dug deep and tried to find her calm center, and considered explaining her line of thinking again. The more she looked at Cynda, though, the more she knew it would be useless.

How am I supposed to do this? I suck at being a leader. To hell with it.

She swallowed hard. "You're right. On all counts."

Cynda's mouth came open. "Oh. Um, yeah."

"I should tell the Mothers, but I'm scared to death they'll take him." Riana looked down at her clenched hands. "I'm not ready for that yet. I don't know—I don't know how I'd stand it."

Silence claimed the room. *Heavy* wasn't quite the word to describe it. More like shocked, and no one more than Riana, over what she had just admitted.

They'll give up on me now. And why shouldn't they? Clearly I'm not using a Sibyl's good judgment. Her fingers flew to her crescent moon pendant. *Mother Yana was wrong about me. I'm no mortar. How can I trust myself when I'm still that pathetic little girl who just wants other people to help her feel safe?*

Merilee broke the stillness by sucking air. "You've got it this bad for Creed Lowell? Ri. You haven't even known him a month."

"I don't know how bad I've got it." Riana turned away from both of them. "I just know—I want—I need . . ." She rubbed both hands over her face. "I need a little more time."

Silence took over again. She thought about offering to take herself back to Russia and send them a new mortar, but the thought of losing Cynda and Merilee tore at her. The thought of leaving Creed behind tore at her in a whole different way. She knew Friday and the raid on Rikers was coming, but that was still a few days off. It wasn't now. She didn't have to face leaving him just yet, did she?

Arms slipped around her waist, and she smelled a hint of smoke and fire as Cynda hugged her from behind. A second later, Merilee hugged them both from the side. They stood quietly for a few moments, then Cynda said, "Okay. I'm sorry. I hate it when I hurt your feelings."

"I'm okay," Riana said automatically, then knew it was a lie.

Cynda let Riana go and moved around to look Riana in the eyes. "Ri, do you really think those bullets will work? Or are we just going to get Creed and Andy killed?"

Riana rubbed her face again. "They'll shoot, if that's what you mean. But work against Asmodai?" She turned up one palm. "Your guess is as good as mine."

"Why don't we test the bullets before we put Andy and Creed in harm's way?" Cynda asked.

Riana smiled at her. "Do *you* know how to shoot a gun?"

Cynda's frown turned thunderous. "No. Just how to disarm and destroy one." She turned to Merilee. "What about you? Don't air Sibyls know how to handle any weapon that moves freely through the air?"

Merilee shook her head. "Not bullets and guns. Mechanical weapons are unreliable around supernatural phenomena. Disarm, destroy. That's all I know, too."

"They truly don't need to be in this fight." Riana walked slowly back to the table and sat down next to her spectroscope. "Even with his *other,* Creed's more human than anything else. Andy's braver than a charging rhino, but she'd never even seen something outside her understanding until we showed it to her. Still, the Asmodai *did* target them."

Merilee sat down again, too, curling her legs underneath her. "I think the Legion only targeted them with Asmodai because of their association with us. If they faded back from this situation, went back to work, and got away from us and the Latch case, I don't think they'd have more trouble."

Cynda paced by the end of the table, arms folded. "You can't say that for sure, though. They could be in even *more* danger without us. Creed's ring—he's got some connection to the Legion, even if he doesn't know what it is. Or so he says."

"To be totally practical, they're in the way." Merilee sighed. "If the bullets work, that's one thing. If not?" She shook her head. "They're more a liability than an aid. When Ri's ready, we should get them out of Dodge, maybe to Greece or Ireland for a while, then let them come back to New York when the heat's off."

The chimes over the front door started to ring.

Riana, Merilee, and Cynda startled.

"What the hell?" Cynda walked away from the table and chairs toward the door, listening. "It's the middle of the day."

Merilee got up. She looked from Riana to the closet where their gear was stowed.

"It's a general alert," Cynda said. "But no one's sending it."

"That's not possible." Riana got up and walked over to join her, facing the door. The chime message was simple enough for her to follow, but garbled—almost faint, as if the sender didn't know she—or he—was transmitting.

33. Code 33 . . .

927 . . .

5150 . . .

Incoming . . .

"Incoming?" Riana shook her head. "Just a bunch of numbers and that one word." She looked at Cynda, who had gone unnaturally still beside her.

33, said the chimes. *5150.*

Louder, this time.

The color drained out of Cynda's face. "It's police code, I think. I don't know much of it, but I recognize the first number. An emergency—or all units stand by. Maybe both? And I think 5150 is a mental case, or something."

Merilee came up beside them holding their weapons. Cynda took her sword without comment, and Riana palmed her daggers. Her heart had started an uncomfortable thumping in her throat.

"Police code," she said, though her voice was no more than a whisper.

Merilee whistled as the chimes blared the same numbers over and over. "So who's ringing our bell, Andy or Creed?" She nocked an arrow. "Or some other shitwad trying to trick us?"

"Trace it," Cynda demanded. She strode over to the chimes, reached her hand up, and silenced the pipes, which were beginning to sound discordant.

Riana watched as Merilee lowered her bow and arrow, closed her eyes and concentrated on the breeze striking the pipes. She imagined the air Sibyl slipping her awareness into the breeze, using her ventsentience to become aware of direction, force, and any sensory information associated with the erratic little wind.

"Close," she said. "Half a block? Coming closer."

Riana's heart rate jumped. She readied both daggers.

"Human, I think. Masculine. He smells a lot like cedar—but something else, too. Something that stinks." Merilee's eyes flew open. "Sulfur, only more faint than an Asmodai."

Cynda stepped back from the chimes and raised her sword.

The doorknob rattled. Someone put a key in the lock and turned it.

The door swung open.

Andy stood at the threshold, outlined by bright afternoon sun. Her eyes traveled from Merilee's bow and arrow to Riana's daggers to Cynda's sword. "Nice to see you, too," she said. "Now move. We've got a present for you."

Riana lowered her weapons, as did the other Sibyls. Cynda didn't sheath her blade, though, because Creed walked in next. He was wearing navy slacks, a blue shirt open at the collar, and a navy blazer that highlighted his broad, powerful shoulders. And he was using one of those shoulders to carry a big rug.

Riana's heart clutched at seeing Creed, but she didn't have time to enjoy the way he filled out his slacks and shirt, because the rug started to move. Actually, it started to swear in a slurred voice and threaten to take Creed's badge and "telephone the authorities this instant."

"Don't make me break your jaw for real this time," Creed said to the rug in a cold, matter-of-fact voice.

The rug tried to buck off Creed's shoulder, but Andy grabbed the end of it and held tight.

"Why are you just standing there?" Andy called to Cynda. "Shut the damned door and help us before he makes us thirsty again!"

Cynda didn't seem able to move for a second. The chimes above her head danced crazily, but they weren't making any sense at all now.

Creed yanked the rug off his shoulder and dropped it heavily to the floor.

The chimes stopped ringing.

With Andy's help, he reached down and pushed the rug. It flipped over once, twice, and then a third time to reveal a very thin, very pale blond man dressed in black shorts and a black tank. He had a massive bruise on his left jaw, he was barefoot, and he was squinting as if he couldn't see three feet in front of his face. Creed helped him stand, but only to take hold of his cuffs and the back of his neck.

"Just what we needed," said Cynda in her sweetest voice. "A blind toothpick with bad gym clothes and absolutely no ass. Thank you so much."

Creed shot her a look. "This is Frith Gregory. He works for Senator Latch and his wife. We brought him to you for questioning, but I think he did something to us at his apartment. Something, uh, unnatural."

Riana felt her eyebrows lift. Merilee started to ask the first in what was no doubt a long line of crude questions about what Gregory might have done to—or with—Creed and Andy.

Cynda grinned. Just as fast, she stopped smiling. Sweat broke out on her face. Riana felt it, too, a sudden heat—or rather, a sudden knee-weakening dryness spreading through her entire body. Immediately, she used her earth energy to shield her body's water and gradually draw it back from the air, much as soil takes in mist and rain.

"He's working with water," Riana said. "Taking ours."

"Shit." Merilee blew out a breath and raised her bow and arrow. This time, she aimed the tip right between Frith Gregory's squinting eyes. "You better knock that off, asshole, or I'm gonna make a much bigger mess of your face."

Andy was swallowing over and over, clearly thirsty, but doing her best to keep her senses. She rummaged in her purse, drew out a pair of glasses, staggered over to Gregory, and put the glasses on his face at a weird angle.

She pointed to Merilee. "See? She means it."

Gregory frowned, but Riana felt instant dissipation in the energy disrupting her fluid balance.

"I'm getting some water." Andy walked off, heading for the kitchen. "I'll bring you some, too, Creed."

"I'm okay," he said. He pressed harder against Gregory's neck, bending his head forward. "I was ready for him this time."

Cynda stalked across the room, sword in front of her. She marched straight up to Gregory and rested the tip at the neckline of his tank top. "Oh no you did *not* just try to dehydrate me."

Flames broke out along the lines of her body, just above her clothes, licking against the thin man's chest.

Gregory made a little noise and tried to lean away from her, but Creed wouldn't let him. When Gregory's shirt caught fire, Cynda hooked it with her sword tip and ripped it right off his body.

"Put him on the table, Creed," Riana instructed as she stretched her hand over the burning shirt and put out the flames with a small wave of earth energy.

Creed turned Gregory toward the big oak platform, but stopped mid-stride.

Riana saw what froze Creed in his tracks, and she stopped breathing.

Cynda gaped, lowered her sword, then raised it again in a hurry.

Merilee craned her neck to see and let out a little cry.

Tattooed across Frith Gregory's back in vivid red-brown, like a magnified version of Creed's signet ring, was the image of a coiled serpent.

(24)

The air in the brownstone crackled with wild energy. Afternoon sunlight danced off the mirrors and played against the metal edges of the big oak table.

Creed could only stand there with Frith Gregory at arm's length, halfway between the women and the oak table, facing that bizarre collection of mirrors and the red serpent etched into Gregory's skin. Creed's signet ring vibrated against his finger as he stared at the tattoo. A nasty chill twisted through his gut. He knew he should shove the guy forward and put him on the table like Riana had asked him to do, but he found himself unable to move. Unable to think straight. The sight of that serpent rattled him in ways he hadn't thought possible.

He wanted to spin the guy around and break his head just for having the tattoo, but that made no sense. The *other* wanted to eat Gregory whole, but the beast stayed back, snarling from a distance.

Is it afraid of him like it was afraid of Raven Latch?
What the hell?

Andy walked back into the living room, her arms loaded with water bottles. She dropped them all when she spied the serpent on Gregory's back. "Creed, that tattoo looks just like your ring."

Frith Gregory wrenched around in Creed's grasp until he was face-to-face with Creed. The skinny man's blue eyes flared. He looked shocked and curious all at once.

Creed felt a weird pressure against his eyes, his ears. Almost in his head, but not quite.

Then the bastard started to smile.

"Curson," Gregory said so quietly only Creed could hear him. The man had to struggle to speak because of his bruised, damaged jaw. "You won't hurt me. I know your true parents."

Creed's mouth went dry. His throat contracted.

The *other* charged forward, but didn't try to take over. The beast sat in his consciousness like a companion, watching, listening—eager, yet wary. Creed had never felt so joined with the creature inside him, and the sensation almost made him ill.

Gregory's eyebrows twitched. Air moved in and out of the skinny man's nose and mouth. Time sped up. Creed heard heartbeats, smelled distinct odors from every person in the room, yet everyone seemed to vanish save for Gregory.

True parents?

Curson?

What does that mean?

Does he think I'm falling for that shit?

Creed kept one hand firm on Gregory's biceps and jammed his right forearm under Gregory's chin. "Think I won't hurt you?" He forced his arm into Gregory's throat until the smaller man choked. "Try me."

Gregory twisted out of Creed's grasp enough to paw at the arm under his chin.

"Creed!" Riana's sharp voice penetrated Creed's fog and brought him back to normal speed and awareness—just in time to realize Gregory had wrapped his bony fingers around Creed's signet ring.

Once more smiling, Gregory gave the ring a firm tug.

Creed roared. The *other*'s strength combined with his own as he brought his arm up hard against Gregory's chin. The man's glasses jiggled. His eyes widened as his teeth slammed together.

The water bottles on the floor at Andy's feet exploded, firing their caps like tiny plastic bullets. Andy dropped to the floor. She swore and grabbed her ankle. The spilled water from the bottles rose into the air and crashed into her face in a circular stream.

The Sibyls all jumped at once, so fast Creed barely perceived them as individuals.

Cynda dived toward Andy, dragged her away from the water, and evaporated the swirling stream with a huge burst of fire.

Riana lunged forward and yanked Gregory out of Creed's grasp. She knocked off Gregory's glasses, forced the skinny man's mouth open, and slid her dagger between his parted lips.

All the pressure left Creed's mind, and his senses cleared completely.

The room went quiet.

Checkmate.

Riana won that round.

Habit made Creed bend down and swipe Gregory's glasses off the floor. He stuck them in his jacket pocket, reminding himself Gregory wasn't at the station being interrogated.

Gregory stood very still for a moment, trembling in his gym shorts. Then he opened his mouth wide around Riana's knife blade and tried to pull back. Creed caught him from behind again, wrapped his arms around the guy's stick of a waist, and grabbed his cuffed wrists. No way was Gregory moving. If Riana planned to stab him in the throat, Creed supposed she had her reasons. So what if Gregory really did know something about his heritage, his bloodline? Bastard could eat that dagger and leave Creed wondering.

I'm a big boy. I can handle it.

He took a breath.

Shit. What if he turns into a werewolf or something?

Merilee snapped an arrow over her knee, then broke one of the pieces of the shaft in half. She tossed the pieces to Cynda.

Gregory narrowed his eyes and grunted when Cynda approached him, and clamped his teeth on the blade of the dagger. Riana wiggled her knife, making him open his lips or get cut. Then she removed the dagger smoothly as Cynda rammed the heel of her hand between his lips.

Smoke rose from her arm.

With a shout of pain, Gregory shoved backward against Creed and parted his lips.

Creed held him stone-still a few feet from the table as Cynda crammed the two thick pieces of arrow into Gregory's open mouth. She wedged the wood between his teeth so the man couldn't close his lips or bite down.

"I'm fine, by the way." Andy struggled to her feet, drew her SIG, and trained it at Gregory's head. "You want me to put him down? Just say the word."

Riana glanced at the gun. "No guns. He'll try something so you *will* kill him."

Cynda whirled away from them and jumped onto the big oak table. Without comment or hesitation, she tossed that double-telescope—the spectroscope—that Riana had been fiddling with for so many days into the seat of one of the nearby chairs. Then she started to dance in wide, fast circles.

Gregory tried to struggle, but Creed only gripped his prisoner tighter, pulling the man's wrists hard into his belly.

Chimes rang.

Shadows rolled inside the mirrors.

Cynda danced faster, faster.

Creed didn't know what the fire Sibyl was saying, but she was saying it loudly, and in one big hurry.

Riana moved to the side of Gregory, dagger drawn and positioned to slide back into his mouth should he dislodge the wooden props. Creed noticed how soft she looked in her khaki slacks and white blouse, but that core of pure steel was showing through. God, he loved that. Watching her in action only made him want her more, even when the world kept handing them weird shit on a silver platter.

Merilee nocked an arrow and leveled it at Gregory's crotch. "Don't get any ideas about playing with water again, assface. I can think of *so* many things worse than death."

Creed glanced at Riana over Gregory's shoulder, at her dagger, then back to her pretty face again, letting his eyes ask the question.

"Cyanide," she said, her voice low and tense. "The only suspected Legion members ever captured by Sibyls managed to poison themselves." Her dark eyes blazed with determination and anger. "A hidden capsule, maybe in a tooth? But this one's getting to the Mothers alive."

Creed doubled the force of his grip on Gregory's cuffed wrists. He had known it, with what Gregory said about his true parents, and now Riana had confirmed it.

Gregory is a member of the Legion.

Christ.

I'm lucky I didn't get Andy killed—and get my stupid ass blown away, too. I'm not giving him the chance to hurt Riana.

From the corner of his eye, Creed saw Andy holster her pistol, bend down, and rub her right ankle. Trickles of blood smeared across her fingers. "I can't believe he shot me with water bottle lids." She stood and wiped her fingers on her slacks. "Cut me up! I wish *you* would interrogate him, Riana. I'd totally enjoy watching that. And I'd get to shoot him in the kneecaps if he misbehaved."

Riana didn't respond to Andy. She kept her gaze on Gregory and her dagger poised. The tight lines of her face made Creed's teeth clench. She had a bad feeling about this, he could tell.

He had a bad feeling about this, too, but somehow, he'd help her get this bastard to a Motherhouse where he belonged.

Curson, his mind whispered, as if to tease him. The *other* actually whimpered at the sound of that word. *Curson.*

What the hell does that mean?

Andy stood to the side, looking angry but a little clueless. Merilee looked just as grim as Riana, and Cynda seemed to take no pleasure in her dancing. Riana reminded Creed of a sleek, beautiful cat just before a fatal pounce. She was incredible, even in a dangerous situation.

Especially in a dangerous situation.

I will *take care of her. I'll protect her from this dirtbag, and I'll protect her from me, too, if I have to.*

Despite his mounting concern, Creed sensed that odd change in the room that told him Cynda's bizarre phone calls were being answered. The air hummed with new life, and the lights in the mirrors got a little brighter. There was no fire this afternoon in the table's lead-lined trench, but Creed imagined the flames leaping to respond to Cynda's frenetic movements. Just as they had the night the Sibyls sent Herbert to Motherhouse Russia, the sound of the chimes began to keep rhythm with the dance.

This time, all three of the largest, oldest-looking mirrors brightened. Fog swirled through the lighted spots. Pictures formed, then grew more distinct. Three stone rooms. Women in blue robes on the left. Women in green robes on the right. Women in brown robes dead center. This time, no one had to leave to summon a Mother. Several ancient-looking women occupied each mirror.

Creed's skin crawled at the sight of them.

Gregory made an unintelligible noise and jerked against Creed's grasp. He pushed backward with his feet. Creed wrestled with him for a second.

"Move, Riana," he warned, and she did.

Creed whirled Gregory around and hit him with a roundhouse, right in the jaw that didn't have a bruise.

Just the way he did back at his apartment, Gregory went out like a light.

Creed caught him as he fell and threw him over his shoulder. The wooden props in his mouth shot out and bounced across the floor, but Creed didn't figure they needed to be replaced. He strode forward and stopped at the table's edge, and found himself facing Cynda, with Merilee to the side. In the mirrors, the Mothers watched with an unnerving intensity.

Suddenly, the last place Creed wanted to be on planet Earth was in that room, facing those women. Green eyes, brown eyes, black eyes, and worst of all, the icy gray eyes of the oldest Russian Mother seemed to stare directly into his essence. Beside her, her wolves stared at him with those same gray eyes.

Every hair on his body stood up.

The *other* gave an anguished snarl and pushed around in his mind, making his head throb.

Yeah, dickhead, no shit, he thought. *If I could find a way out of my own skin and away from those women in the mirrors, I'd go with you.*

Instead, he yanked Gregory off his shoulder and laid him on the table at Cynda's feet.

"Here," he forced himself to say in a light, almost careless tone. "Have fun."

Cynda nodded. Her red hair was pasted against her face from the effort of her fast, powerful dance. She raised her arms and moved around Gregory's unconscious form, ringing the chimes once more.

Creed stepped away from the table and stopped beside Riana. Despite the serious look on her beautiful face, she winked at him.

He almost smiled.

When he turned back to face the Mothers, he set his jaw and stared down any of the Motherhouse women who looked in his direction.

The *other* didn't seem quite so comfortable. The beast stirred in odd ways, vigilant, almost anxious, though Creed had never experienced that exact emotion from the creature before. His vision and hearing sharpened, and the sound of Cynda's feet on the table seemed to double, triple, as he became aware, too, of wind and the subtle groaning of the earth. Not in the brownstone, no. Coming through the mirrors. Coming from the Motherhouses.

The music of the chimes seemed to have a logic. He couldn't say why, but he knew Gregory was going to the Motherhouse in Russia. Fire against his water. Motherhouse Ireland could control his rogue energy better. They wondered who Creed was, the Mothers. They seemed to know Andy.

A lot of excitement over this capture.

Discussion of how best to help Cynda with transport and shield against unexpected energy or protections.

Protections. That word bounced around Creed's mind, and he knew the *other* was causing the reaction.

More pain in his head, and pain in his finger, too, from his ring. It was hot.

It had never gotten that hot before.

His vision blurred as he watched Cynda dance, as he saw the Mothers begin their dance, with the Irish women taking the lead.

Protections.

Protections.

Time speeded up—and jumped.

Creed blinked.

The room lay in ruin, burned and broken.

The mirrors were cracked and black.

He saw parts of Cynda. Andy dead on the floor. Merilee, bruised, her arm hanging at an awful angle, crawling to sob over—over—bile rose in his throat.

Over Riana's burned body.

No!

The *other* screeched. Creed's mind screeched, too.

Protections!

The scene shifted back to a normal room, to Cynda,

whole and dancing. Andy watching from a few feet away.
Merilee unhurt. Riana alive beside him.

Thank God.

Creed's enhanced perceptions picked up a smoky image
rising off Gregory's back.

The serpent. Growing. Uncoiling to strike at the mirrors.

Something awful was about to happen.

Creed lunged forward.

The strength of the *other* blended with his own again.

He reached the table in one leap, grabbed Cynda and
took her down to the smooth wooden surface. At the same
time, he planted both feet in Gregory's skinny ass and
kicked him off the table. Gregory flopped on the floor like
a bag of sand, flipped over once, and twitched.

Thunder rattled the room and knocked one mirror off
the wall. It shattered near Gregory, who seemed to be wak-
ing. Creed saw Riana and Merilee kneel on his back. Riana
pressed her dagger to his skin just behind his heart, while
Merilee rested the tip of her nocked arrow against his neck.

His breathing slowed, and the power of the *other* receded. He slowly became aware of something elbowing
him in the gut. Something that was swearing a lot, and
with great volume.

Creed's jacket and pants caught on fire.

"Get off me, numbnuts," Cynda growled.

Creed rolled off the fire Sibyl very fast, coming to rest on
his back, but still on the table beside Cynda.

At the feet of three ancient Mothers, one in a blue robe,
one in a green robe, and one in a brown robe.

They weren't in the mirrors anymore.

His worst nightmares were right there in the room with
him, standing on the table, surrounding him. From his vantage point, they looked about twenty feet tall, and just as fit
as any cop he'd sparred with in hand-to-hand.

The Mother in the blue robe had two small Greek *falcata*

swords—the kind sharp enough to shear off helmets in battle—ready to hurl into Creed's chest. The Mother in the green robe had an Irish hand-and-a-half sword raised to swing down on his neck.

It was the Mother in the brown robe, though, who made Creed's blood turn to ice. The one with the cold wolf-eyes, who had two Russian hunting daggers drawn and poised to pierce him right where it would hurt the most. She glared at him as if daring him to so much as twitch.

Creed didn't move at all.

He didn't even breathe.

Somewhere inside him, the *other* actually cowered.

Oh, fuck.

25

If Riana hadn't had to guard Gregory, she might have
fallen on one of her daggers.

What the hell was Creed thinking, to grab hold of Cynda
in the middle of a transport? To throw her down in front of
the Mothers?

She was surprised they hadn't killed him instantly.

And now the oldest of the old, including Mother Yana,
were right here in her living room, standing on the big oak
table. The room seemed too still, too quiet. Smells from her
childhood washed over her—fresh, clean cotton, snow,
wolf fur, and pungent, ritual herbs.

From the other side of the table, the glare on Merilee's
face spoke her thoughts plainly enough, and echoed Riana's own whispers of doubt.

Creed didn't want Gregory transported.

He thought he could stop us from taking him.

That was stupid. Why would Creed bring Gregory to the
brownstone in the first place if he didn't want the Legion
member turned over to the Mothers?

Why would Creed help her contain him and get him on
the table?

But Riana knew what Cynda would say to that.

*Who knows what kind of twisted games your boyfriend
is playing?*

Cynda would say maybe the Legion was researching
the Sibyls. Maybe Creed was the bait in one big, giant
trap.

Riana risked a glance in Creed's direction.

Was he playing a game?

Other than possum on the table, of course, to keep the Mothers from rendering him into so much wolf chow.

Was it possible that he would betray her and all the Sibyls in some vicious, final way?

She couldn't believe that. She wouldn't. But why the hell had he stopped the transport? Riana felt like her insides were tearing into pieces.

Cynda scooted off the table, kicked Gregory on the floor to make sure he was still out, then walked straight toward Andy, who had her SIG drawn and pointed at the nearest Mother.

"Don't." She gestured for Andy to put away the gun.

"I'll put mine down when they put theirs down," Andy said stubbornly, even though her voice was shaking. "I'm not letting them hurt Creed."

"Creed stands or falls on his own merit with the Mothers, Andy." Cynda's voice was much more gentle than usual. "Don't make me hurt you. I like you, okay?"

Andy still didn't surrender the gun—until the grips turned red-hot and she had to drop it.

Cynda caught it before it bounced on the floor. "Probably wouldn't have worked anyway. You don't have the right bullets yet, so don't bother drawing the backup piece."

Andy rubbed her hands together. "Bitch," she whispered loud enough for people next door to hear her. She scowled from Cynda to Creed, who still hadn't moved. "You better not let them cut him."

Mother Yana turned her stern gaze on Riana, and Riana wanted to fold up into a tiny speck and disappear. She felt five years old, in from the snow, sobbing because the wolves had frightened her and the other adepts still didn't like her.

Chin up, moya smelaya. *The world is not kind to little girls who flee their own destiny.* Mother Yana had given her a loving but firm look. *How can you lead them if you fear them?*

She had let Mother Yana down so many times during her training.

And wasn't she letting her triad down now, too? Wasn't she taking risks and breeding disharmony?

She wasn't ready for a reckoning over Creed.

And yes, damnit, she was afraid.

She was scared of Gregory and what they didn't know about him.

She was scared about the Legion and all the changes in their tactics.

And she was terrified at the thought of losing Creed.

"Vill you speak for him?" Mother Yana asked in heavily accented English. "Or do you vish us to take him, too?"

Riana swallowed hard. She glanced at Merilee and Cynda.

"Let him go," Merilee whispered.

Cynda looked relieved at the thought of the Mothers taking Creed, yet troubled, too. Uncertain.

Definitely not a normal state of mind for Cynda.

Riana wasn't uncertain at all.

It made her heart ache to wound her triad, but she said, "I'll speak for him, and ask you to let him speak for himself."

Merilee closed her eyes in utter frustration.

Cynda rolled hers.

Mother Yana nodded and turned her attention to Creed. "Give a reason for vhat you did, and use few vords."

Creed remained very still on the table. Only his lips moved as he spoke. "I saw something," he said in quiet, yet powerful tones. The sound of his rich, deep voice made Riana's back straighten. Each note and rumble touched her like his fingers, and she couldn't help feeling proud of him. He was strong without being reckless . . . well, that whole tackling-Cynda-on-the-table thing aside.

"His tattoo gave off some sort of—of image." Creed moved enough to turn his head toward Gregory. "It was a moving serpent, and it was about to strike at the mirrors. I thought that would be dangerous."

Cynda seemed to come to attention. She turned her back on Andy and stared openly at Creed as he spoke.

Riana and Merilee looked down at the red serpent tattoo on Gregory's back. The skinny man moaned and twitched, as if sensing their scrutiny.

Another minute or two, and he'll be awake. What kind of problems will we have then?

Mother Yana lowered her hunting daggers, sheathed them, and stepped off the table. Cynda got there quickly to give her a hand down. Despite her advanced age, Mother Yana moved with a supple grace and authority. Riana moved aside as she approached, and avoided her piercing gray eyes.

With Cynda attending, Mother Yana knelt beside Frith Gregory and held her fingers over his serpent tattoo. After a few seconds, she used a Russian word that Riana didn't know, then followed it with English.

"Henna." She lowered her fingers closer to the serpent, but didn't touch it. "And badger's blood mixed into the dye. It is locked by the elements, and these designs on the serpent's skin strengthen the vork. Strong job. Powerful job. Definitely powerful enough to turn our energies against us—a protection against all evils."

Merilee blinked.

So did Riana. "But Mother . . . we're not evil."

"My child." Mother Yana cupped Riana's cheek with one knotted hand, and her blue eyes blazed with wicked humor. "Ve are quite evil in *his* eyes, I am sure."

"So, if we had tried to transport him—" Cynda began.

Mother Yana cut her off with a shrug as she stood. "Ve vould have died. Most of us."

Merilee's mouth fell open.

Andy muttered something in a sarcastic tone, but thankfully out of earshot.

On the table, Creed let out a breath.

The Irish Mother and the Greek Mother put away their weapons and immediately began to discuss the safest way to get Frith Gregory to Motherhouse Ireland. They settled on an additional elemental-locking procedure that Mother Yana directed Riana, Cynda, and Merilee to perform. They used water, too, given Gregory's water-working skills.

Creed got off the table, dusted the sleeves of his charred jacket, and quietly went to stand beside Andy.

Riana glanced at him, hoping her eyes conveyed what she wanted to say.

Thank the Goddess you're okay.

And thank the Goddess twice you know when to be quiet.

He nodded to her. He didn't look angry, or even irritated. Just calm and understanding, and as if he wanted to touch her, right here, right now.

Despite the total chaos in her living room and the presence of the Mothers, Riana wanted to throw her arms around Creed's neck and kiss him all night. Maybe tomorrow, too.

Instead, she asked Andy to get some water from the kitchen and turned away from Creed.

Riana worked with her triad sisters to finish stripping Gregory and coat him from his bruised head to his pencil-shaped toes in all four elements. They all used their energy to lock the earth, air, and fire into place, then combined efforts to lock the water—which Andy happily poured all over Gregory's face, chest, private area, and legs when they asked her to splash him.

Gregory woke to full awareness just as they finished the process.

Riana considered jamming his mouth open again, but decided against it. If he'd had easy access to cyanide, he would have used it by now—or Creed would have ruptured it, punching the guy in the face.

She and Cynda stood Gregory up and bound his hands behind his back with a piece of rope Mother Yana produced from the pocket of her robe. Meanwhile, Andy got right in his face and said, "Ooooh. Nice bruises. Both sides! At least you match now."

He glared at her, then squinted as Riana and Cynda marched him to the table where the Mothers were waiting. He tried to resist, but they shoved him onto the wood, and the Mothers closed around him like a trio of hungry crows.

"May I have my glasses at least?" he begged, his speech labored and slurred from his injuries. "A little decency, if it's not beyond you?"

Mother Yana looked at Riana, who in turn looked at Creed. She thought she remembered him picking up the glasses from the floor, and she couldn't see the harm in giving Gregory that kindness. He might be a Legion bastard, but he was a human being.

Or at least he appeared to be.

Creed pulled the man's glasses out of his jacket, walked over to Riana, and handed them to her. Riana quickly locked them with earth energy, and Cynda and Merilee took care of fire and wind. Andy splashed a little more water over the lenses.

She took the treated glasses over to the table and held out her hand to give them to Mother Yana.

At the last second before Mother Yana took them from her hand, Creed jumped forward and snatched them away.

"Wait a minute," he said, and brought the glasses to his nose.

Riana watched, having that wishing-she-could-fold-up feeling again, as Creed sniffed the frames and earpieces.

He looked up at Gregory. "Nice try, you son of a bitch." To Riana, he said, "Here's your cyanide."

Creed held out the glasses to her.

Riana took them, surprise and embarrassment heating

her face and chest. No sooner did she bring them close than she smelled it.

A faint hint of almonds.

Why hadn't she noticed it before?

Where is my head?

She lifted the glasses to her nose and sniffed at the earpieces and rims.

The entire pair had been treated with cyanide. If they had given the glasses back to Gregory, he could have killed himself easily, at his convenience, just by the simple nervous act of chewing on his glasses.

Riana motioned for Cynda, and passed the glasses to her. Cynda would dispose of them in a controlled burn, somewhere where she wouldn't have to smell the fumes. Fire Sibyls were good at destroying things.

All three Mothers gazed at Creed with their wise, sharp eyes.

Mother Yana pointed one crooked finger at him. "Some power in you, yes, to have seen vhat Sibyls did not see and smelled vhat Sibyls did not smell."

Riana tried to breathe, but found it very, very hard. Once more, she felt the blazing gazes of Cynda and Merilee, urging her to do the right thing, the safe thing, the sane thing. Spill it to the Mothers now, about Creed and his *other,* ask their guidance and help.

Obviously, they weren't ready to trust him yet, even though he had just brought them a live Legion member—a feat no Sibyl had yet accomplished—and saved their lives on top of that.

You know why. He isn't safe, not with the other *threatening to take control. You know you should tell them. Tell them now!*

She opened her mouth, looked at him, and said, "He has some latent abilities, yes. But he uses them for the greater good."

Mother Yana nodded. "Ve vill speak of this later, vhen time permits, yes?"

After a deep breath, Riana forced a smile and nodded back. "Yes, Mother. Of course we will." She almost substituted *v*'s for her *w*'s, just because she was so nervous.

Cynda looked like she might say something, but Merilee warned her off with a glare and a blast of wind to her right ear.

The Irish and Greek Mothers noticed this, but didn't speak.

Mother Yana forced Gregory to his knees, then with an ungentle tap from a dagger hilt, laid him out on the table.

The three Mothers raised their hands.

Riana moved back with Cynda and Merilee, and gestured for Creed and Andy to get out of the way, too. The two of them walked away quickly, and came to stand behind Riana and her triad sisters.

As Mother Yana and the other two Mothers began their dance to open the channels, Riana felt the pressure of Creed's hands on her waist. She sensed him behind her, and she could almost feel the firm, warm embrace he would give her if she leaned back. Goddess, she wanted to do that, but she couldn't. Merilee and Cynda looked angry enough to skin cats with their eyes as it was. They'd have a lot to say to her when the Mothers were gone. She was lucky they hadn't spilled the beans.

One more chance, at least. I have one more chance to get myself ready and do what I know I should have done tonight. She let one of her arms brush Creed's fingertips. Electric pleasure traveled across her shoulders, and she imagined his lips on her neck. *Tomorrow, maybe. Or the next day. Before the raid to save Alisa, for sure.*

She didn't even want to think about the raid, or the inevitable reassignment to protect them from the legal consequences of breaking human society's laws. That was too much right now. One day at a time. One hour at a time.

Riana felt the room's energy shift, pouring itself into the infinitely commanding call of the Mothers. The projective mirrors of Motherhouse Ireland, Motherhouse Greece, and Motherhouse Russia brightened. Blurry images formed and cleared, revealing troops of concerned adepts and several worried-looking Mothers.

Their faces took on looks of avid concentration after they assessed the situation, and the Mothers in the mirrors began to dance, adding to the energy for transport.

The Mothers on the table began to walk in a circle.

When the Mother in the green robes walked in front of the mirror for Motherhouse Ireland, she vanished into the channels, Frith Gregory along with her. Immense relief almost made Riana sink back into Creed's waiting arms. He gave her waist a soft squeeze, as if reading her desire in the lines of her body.

Riana watched as the adepts at Motherhouse Russia bound Gregory hand and foot, and carried him away. Soon, they might have valuable information from him— the only real intel they had ever been able to retrieve, thanks to Creed.

Motherhouse Greece reclaimed the Mother in the blue robes as she passed by the proper mirror. The glass winked out quickly, leaving only Mother Yana.

Before she stepped into the channel that would transport her home, she glanced back at Riana. Her gray eyes held a measure of worry, as a real mother might bestow upon a wayward child.

Does she know something? Riana swallowed and found her throat dry. *She always did sense when I was up to no good. Of course she knows something. Who am I kidding?*

Then Mother Yana was gone, back home to her wolves, back home to the cold winter woods outside of Volgograd.

Riana pulled away from Creed's touch on her waist, even though she didn't want to do it. She knew she had to face

Cynda and Merilee and make the right promises, but when she saw their expressions, she had no idea what to say.

Merilee looked hurt and scared and confused. She glanced from Creed to Riana, and cleared her throat. "Um, thanks. For, uh, bringing us Gregory. And stopping the transport before it was too late."

Creed nodded. "Sure."

Andy groaned. "Why don't you gloat, Lowell? At least a little bit?" She glared from Riana to Merilee to Cynda. "Well? See? We *can* be useful, bullets or not, right?"

Cynda's shoulder twitched. "Yeah, of course. And thanks. You are useful. I knew that. Plenty useful, when you aren't almost getting yourselves killed. I wouldn't recommend going after Legion members without us again."

"Like we knew that?" Andy put a hand on her hip. "We just wanted to solve the case before Friday, so you guys don't have to bust out Alisa and get sent back to God-knows-where."

She seemed to realize what she had said, and knocked off the smart-ass pose. "Not that we'd miss you or anything," she added. "We just don't think your replacements would take us seriously or keep us in the loop—and we have to be in the loop now. We've come too far to go back."

"You put your jobs on the line for us." Riana tried not to look at Creed and fall into his dark, gorgeous eyes, but she couldn't stop herself. He looked too good in that casual suit.

He gazed back at her. "We didn't just do it for you, honey. We did it for us, too, and all the people in New York." He rubbed his hand over his black hair. "We can't play this game by the normal rules. That's obvious."

"Riana made you a lot of bullets," Merilee blurted, then looked at the floor. "At least load up with the right tools, so maybe you'll both stay alive."

She looked at Riana, and Riana could tell she wanted to say something about the Mothers and how Riana should have been honest, no matter what the consequences. Merilee was pretty sure Andy and maybe Creed, too, were going to end up dead if they didn't turn Creed over—and soon.

Riana's stomach twisted.

Don't let her be right. I could never live with that.

Cynda's stare was equally intense, but like Merilee, she held her peace.

In the end, they both headed for their rooms instead of chewing out Riana, which bothered her more than all the yelling she expected. She watched them go, then stood for a time, awkward and quiet, not sure what to say to Creed or Andy.

Andy finally broke the silence with, "Got those bullets?"

Riana gestured absently toward the kitchen. "Yes. I'm sorry. They're on the table."

Andy nodded and pushed through the kitchen door.

Before the door even stopped swinging, Creed grabbed Riana and turned her around to face him.

She melted into his fierce hug, then into his deep, passionate kiss. His lips pushed against hers hungrily, mirroring her own unbridled need. Her nipples swelled against her shirt, and she felt the crush of his muscled chest against her hands as she answered him, ounce for ounce, with every bit of heat she possessed. He smelled so good, so male, and he tasted even better. The warmth of his mouth felt like a balm on her heart.

He slipped his hands into her hair and held her there, kissing her, kissing her, until she wanted to scream with need, with relief, with sheer, raging want.

He made her feel so adored, and so very safe.

How could she have mistrusted him?

How can you trust him, knowing that part of him wants to kill you?

But that part was nowhere evident in his gaze when he pulled back and murmured, "I'm sorry I put you at risk. I had no idea that bastard was so dangerous."

Riana thought about telling him not to take any more chances, that the Latch case was literally a nest of serpents, and they couldn't be sure of anyone involved in it. She also thought about telling him that come Friday, she would have to hand him over to those Mothers who almost ran him through back on the big oak table.

She couldn't get her mind or her body to cooperate with reason, though.

She was way past reason now. Her lips tingled from his kiss, and her body tingled from wanting his mouth, his hands. She wanted him inside her, and she didn't want to think about anything else.

"Take me downstairs," she whispered. "Now."

26

Creed followed Riana through the kitchen, pausing only to lay his sidearm on the table for Andy to load with the elementally treated lead bullets. Andy said something about condoms and chastity as he shut the door at the top of the stairs and headed down, keeping Riana in view.

He liked keeping her in view.

Everything about the woman was perfect.

The way she filled out her khaki slacks made his cock throb in time with her movements. Her dark hair bounced against her soft white blouse as she descended the stairs, and Creed imagined unfastening that shirt and kissing the skin beneath each button. Part of his mind insisted that this was crazy after all that had happened, that he had lost his mind somewhere between Gregory's apartment and nearly getting de-balled by a bunch of scary crones with big knives, but he ignored that voice of reason.

He wanted Riana.

He had to have her.

The *other* seemed completely detached, and for one of the first times in Creed's life, he felt almost vacant, like he was inside his skin all by himself. That didn't fool him, however. He knew the beast could challenge him at any second, but there had to be some way to keep Riana safe.

Hell. I should go upstairs and get one of those guns with the special bullets. If I get out of hand, she can just shoot me. At that second, getting shot seemed like a small price to pay to see her lose control, to hear her scream from the pleasure he gave her.

Riana didn't stop at her bedroom as he expected. Instead,

she went straight down the hall to the lab, opened the door, and marched inside. Creed followed and closed the door behind him. If he could have figured out how to lock it, he would have done it.

"Turn off all the lights but the left switch," she said, her voice low and edgy.

Creed complied, loving that she sounded so excited.

The lab went dark except for a bulb in the far corner, which bathed the end of the room, including his cell, in a soft yellow glow.

Riana opened the cell door, went inside, and pulled the mattress off the cot. Before Creed could get to her, she dragged the cot's frame outside. He helped her prop it against the wall. Then he helped her straighten the mattress on the cell floor and spread out the sheets.

Inside the cell, as always, the *other* seemed a million miles away.

Yes.

Maybe this was possible, being with her safely. He could make love to her in this cell every night—every day—for the rest of his life. That would be just fine by him.

Riana stood on the mattress and faced him, her back to the cell's gray stone wall. The hungry, heavy-lidded look she gave him made his cock strain against his slacks.

"I have the keys," she said in that voice that drove him wild, holding up the ring to prove it. He breathed in her light fragrance of rain and lavender, and wanted to bury his face in the wet heat between her legs. "If anything happens, I'll get out and lock the door behind me. This is the best we can do for our safety, and I can't stand this anymore. Don't say no."

Creed couldn't take his eyes off her. "I'm not saying no."

He reached for her, but she held up a hand to stop him. "My way tonight. You can have your way tomorrow night."

Creed felt a fierce rush of inner fire at knowing she wanted him more than once.

"You're mine," he said aloud, unable to hold the words back. "Tell me the truth. You *are* mine."

She blinked at him, and her lips parted. Her dark eyes went misty, and he could tell she was breathing faster at his words.

"Yes," she whispered at last. "I'm yours, for as long as we can have each other."

As Creed watched, blood rushing in his ears, she set the keys on the floor beside the mattress, stood, and began to unbutton her blouse. He leaned back against the cell bars and watched her graceful fingers move from button to button, exposing a little more and a little more of the silky white undershirt he wanted to tear off with his teeth.

"Any word from the *other*?" she murmured as she let her blouse fall to the floor.

Creed was temporarily unable to speak. He shook his head and devoured her with his eyes. Her breasts made beautiful swells against the silk undershirt, and her hard, waiting nipples stood outlined against the thin fabric. If his cock got any harder, he didn't know if he could hold himself back. As it was, he clenched his fists and jaw and tried to stand still.

Riana kicked off her heels next. They clattered on the stone floor beside the cell door. Her feet were bare. No hose. Now those were feet made to rub and pamper.

Would she laugh if he kissed her toes? He made a mental note to find out.

He wanted to know everything about her body. Everything about her. The good, the bad, the secrets, the lies, the fantasies—all of it. By the flush in her cheeks, making love in a jail cell with a dangerous, shady man just might be on that fantasy list.

I'll make your dreams come true, honey.

"I'm not standing still much longer," he warned. His voice sounded like he had swallowed sandpaper.

Riana's eyebrows arched.

A little smile played at her sensual lips, and she unfastened her slacks. It took her only seconds to slide them down her long, sexy legs and toss them on top of her shoes. She had on panties, the same silky white as her undershirt, and he could already see a dark, moist spot spreading on the fabric between her thighs.

Rip . . . them . . . off . . . with . . . my . . . teeth . . .

She paused long enough to gauge his reaction, and he knew she must be pleased with what she saw. He was ready to tear off her clothes and his, too, right now. But she wasn't finished torturing him yet.

Riana pulled off her undershirt, exposing her breasts. Her dark nipples puckered at the ends, and his mouth watered.

So he wasn't going to have to shred her shirt. That was probably a plus.

"You're killing me," he said. He was dying and living more than he had ever lived, all at the same time. "You can have your way for five more seconds, maybe ten. Then I've got to touch you."

Without taking her eyes away from his, Riana slid her fingers into her panties and slipped them down over her hips. His eyes fixed on the dark patch of hair between her legs, and he imagined he could smell the musk of her desire. He wanted to taste her. He had to taste her.

She stepped out of her panties and tossed them toward the rest of her clothes.

Now she was totally naked, and totally his.

"I'm not like you," she whispered. "I don't have hidden aspects or powerful secrets. What you see is what you get. I'm no more or less than most women."

Creed started to point out the dozens of incredible ways she represented her gender, but she silenced him with a shake of her head and a soft, "No." Then, "You want my body just like I want yours."

"Of course I do." Creed couldn't think of anything past showing her just how much truth he was telling.

She gazed at him with wide, worried eyes. "But do you want *me*?"

"Yes," he said with no hesitation at all, wanting to kiss her until she knew that for sure, until she knew it forever.

Riana's dark eyes misted, and her voice grew even softer. "You have to be aware of what you're facing if you make love to me—what we're both facing. The *other*. My triad. The Sibyls. The Mothers—and the whole Legion on top of that." She closed her eyes, seemed to gain her composure, and opened them again. "No one will be on our side, except maybe Andy, and you never know with Andy. Can you tell me, honestly, knowing what will be aligned against us, that you still want me?"

This time Creed answered her by striding forward, taking her in his arms, and claiming her mouth with his. He was vaguely aware of moving her backward as his tongue thrust across her lips and tangled with hers. He was even less aware of stopping when they hit the gray stone wall at the back of the cell.

Everything about Riana was smaller and softer than him. He loved the difference. The difference was perfection.

Riana moaned into his mouth and wrapped her arms around his neck. He ran his hands over the satin of her skin, tracing the outline of her shoulders, her sides, her hips, her ass, pulling her against him, loving the dampness soaking through his slacks as he pressed his thigh between her legs and rubbed. He ran his lips across her cheek to her ear, then to her neck, and tasted her skin with a sharp bite.

She moaned again, and he stopped long enough to whisper, "Nobody bites you but me." He kissed her again, then, and again, and again, until she sagged into him and rubbed her hands against the sides of his face.

"Nobody kisses you but me," he murmured.

She didn't argue.

When he braced his hands on either side of her head, bent down, and took a nipple in his mouth, she tangled her fingers in his hair and pulled. "Yes," she whispered as he sucked and bit the beautiful, dark tip. "Yes. Like that."

Creed used his tongue on the rough surface, flicking it back and forth until her head rocked against the stone wall. Then he moved to the other nipple and bit the sensitive end again. Riana gasped and thrust her breast farther into his mouth. He sucked hard, pulling the pebbled flesh through his teeth until she nearly ripped the hair right off his head.

He went back to her lips then, tasting her warm, wet mouth over and over until he pulled back and studied her face. She was breathing hard, and her eyes were closed. The color on her cheeks spoke of need and pleasure and raw want.

"Nobody sucks your nipples but me," he said, and once more, he got no argument. One kiss at a time, one bite at a time, one inch at a time, he was taking her, and he wanted to be sure she never forgot each moment—or what he said.

"You're mine, Riana. I'm keeping you."

She molded to him as he lifted her off her feet, then released him without struggling as he laid her gently on the mattress. For a moment, he just sat on his knees beside her, staring at the treasure who had given herself to him so freely, so openly.

Riana opened her green eyes. They blazed as they met his, and she whispered, "Nobody looks at me like this but you."

A surge of possessive passion made him bend down and kiss her, rough and demanding, and she answered him completely. Creed stretched himself beside her, held her, kept kissing her, acutely aware of each naked inch of her pressed against his clothing. He ran his hands over her skin, over her breasts and the nipples still damp from his mouth. Each time he touched her, she made a soft, ecstatic sound, and he wanted to hear it again and again, all night, tomorrow, for always.

He traced a pattern down her silky belly until his hand

trailed into her wet thatch of dark, curly hair. Her body tensed, but he worked his fingers carefully, stroking across the top but never quite inside her swollen lower lips. Riana arched her hips, begging for his touch, but he kissed her and teased and made her wait.

When he ran his tongue across her parted lips, her eyelids fluttered, but she didn't seem able to open them.

He liked that.

Turn loose. Let me take you where you need to go.

He wanted tonight to take forever, and he definitely wanted to leave her limp and spent. She gripped his shoulder and tugged against his shirt, asking without begging, pleading without a sound other than those quiet, delicious moans.

Creed ran one finger right along the moist divide, and she bit his bottom lip. This time when he gazed down at her gorgeous face, those green eyes were open and on fire. Creed pressed his finger into the folds, into her hot juices, and drew his hand up until he brushed across her clit.

Riana's head rocked against the mattress as she raised her hips to meet his touch.

"Please," she said so softly, "touch me again."

He brought his finger back down and swirled it in lazy circles, massaging the sensitive bud just enough to drive her out of her mind. "I know you want more," he told her. "I'll give it to you—when I'm ready."

He didn't think he could wait much longer to be inside Riana. Every time he stroked her clit, she spread her legs and moved against his fingers and hand. He had to have a little sample. Just a little. Then he planned to make her nuts a little longer.

Creed made sure to capture her lips with his before he slid two fingers deep inside her velvet walls. He felt her clench against his skin, and heard more of those eager, throaty moans.

She rocked her hips, taking his fingers deeper, and he

moved them in and out with a slow rhythm. "I like the way you move, honey. Let me see you."

He slid a third finger into her folds and let her arch to take it inside her channel. Then he brought his thumb and pinkie together and used them to press against her clit as he pumped his hand up and back, up and back, making her twist on the mattress. Her nipples had turned to hot stone, and her breathing grew more ragged and desperate with each thrust.

Creed had never been so hard, so in pain, yet he couldn't stop touching Riana, couldn't stop kissing her or staring at her. His cock pulsed every time she moved, every time he caught the scent of her musk. The way she shuddered when he touched her took him someplace sweet and perfect. He felt like a man granted the perfect blessing, and all he wanted to do was show his gratitude.

Riana's body tensed. Her juices flowed over his palm, and her nipples pressed against his chest. He could feel them through his shirt like hot magnets, drawing his mouth down, down, until he caught one in his mouth. She cried out and pushed her breast farther into his mouth, demanding his attention, keeping him completely in her spell. He sucked on the straining flesh, rewarded by the volume of her moans.

She was saying something, gasping it, whispering it. Creed ran his tongue over her nipple and caught the words.

"I *am* yours. I *am* yours . . ."

His fingers curled inside Riana as he bit her nipple, and this time her body arched off the mattress, shoving against his as she let out a tight, deep cry. Her walls squeezed his fingers even as her thighs crushed into his hand. The way she shook felt like another reward. Each jerk, each tremor was a prize.

Creed released her breast and gazed at her.

So much for making her wait. Delayed gratification sucks anyway.

And could he ever make himself wait to see her like this?

The flush of color in her cheeks, the blush spreading from her face to her neck to her breasts, the quiver of her muscles each time he moved his fingers . . .

Nah, probably not.

She moved her hands off his shoulders and quickly found the zipper on his pants. Her eyelids fluttered open again, and this time the dark depths sparked with intensity and a new kind of need and desire.

"I want your cock," she said, and Creed wondered if it could rip straight through the fabric.

Damn thing comes when she calls it.

Before he could answer her, she had his pants unfastened and her hand around his throbbing erection.

"I want you, Creed." Riana's fingers tightened around his hard-on, and he thought he might die all over again. A soft, slow stroke from balls to tip almost made him explode.

"Ease up, honey," he managed before he lost the ability to speak again. "If you don't play nice, we might not get that far."

He smiled at her, but the look on her face was vulnerable and serious. Her eyes got that misty look that tore at his heart, and in a low, quiet invitation, she said, "I want to hear you say it when you take me. Nobody but you. Please, don't make me wait for that."

Creed's mind hummed, then buzzed, like something was shorting out. Blood thundered in his ears, and his cock bucked and jumped like he was a teenager about to get his first shot at a woman. His chest squeezed as he pressed Riana back into the mattress and kissed her until he got his pants down far enough to free his cock.

Then he was between her legs, pressing against her wet entrance, ready to take her—and he still couldn't tear his eyes away from her face. He had to grip his erection at the base to hold himself back from her body long enough to make his voice work.

"You're so beautiful, Riana." He stroked her moist folds

with the tip of his cock and positioned himself to plunge inside her. "Tell me you know I want *you,* and everything that comes with you."

Her lips slipped apart, and he wanted to groan from the sight of her, legs wide, waiting, welcoming him in that open, guileless way that rattled him so deeply. Her eyes blazed so bright and hot he wondered if he might get burned.

I want you, her expression said. *I want everything you have to give.*

"You want me," she whispered.

He stroked her clit with his cock, drawing a gasp.

"Damn right." He stroked her again. "Don't forget it. *Ever.*"

She kept her eyes fixed on his, mouth parted, hands gripping his arms and pulling like she was trying to pull him straight into her heart.

"Nobody makes love to you but me," he growled, and thrust into her as the words squeezed out of his throat. "You're mine."

27

Riana almost came from the rough, dominant sound of Creed's voice and the forceful way he moved against her.

As it was, she let out a moan that had no end.

He felt so good inside her, so perfect and full and strong and right. Creed's cock stretched her side to side, back to front as he pumped into her, deeper each time. He drove into her until she lost track of where her body ended and his flesh began. She felt like he was everywhere—in her depths, in her mind, in her heart, and, oh, yes, Goddess, in her mouth as he kissed her. She loved the possessive way he kissed her, especially with his cock buried to the hilt.

His clothes scrubbed against her naked skin, and it felt delicious to have him take her while he was still dressed.

Wanton.

Hot.

Everything about him was hot. Everything about the way he touched her was perfect.

Riana could barely catch a breath between kisses, but when she did, the air smelled like man and metal, sex and stone, and everything wild and primal.

Creed rocked her world in every conceivable way, and she loved surrendering to that sensation, just for tonight, or a few nights. However long she could keep the feeling. There was no tomorrow or yesterday, only now, and Creed making love to her, and the feeling that no one could make her feel this way but him.

Nobody bites you but me . . .
Nobody kisses you but me . . .
Nobody makes love to you but me . . .

"Yes," she said against his mouth, and the word came out like a shout. "I need you deeper. Yes!"

She wanted to scream that she was his. She wanted to *be* his, and not just for tonight. There was something magical between them. She didn't understand it, but she couldn't deny it.

The stubble on his face made her cheeks tingle. The rasp of his shirt and pants against her tender nipples and thighs made her mind expand.

With a body-warming rumble, Creed pounded into her. His muscles tightened with every thrust, and he found that hidden sweet spot that made her gasp each time he moved. She wrapped her legs around his rock-hard thighs and took him as deep as she could, wishing she could melt into his skin. She loved the solid feel of his muscles beneath his clothes, and the way he seemed to adore everything about her.

Her mind started to spin off on its own, and for a moment, she imagined she was floating high above, still experiencing every delectable second of his lovemaking. She imagined she could look down and see them, joined together on the mattress in the cell, riding each other like some incredible wave.

Creed was amazing. So strong and handsome and determined. The darkness battling his soul couldn't touch them in that space, that special place. The rock encasing the cell seemed to lend its force and gravity to Riana's body, and she took every bit of power Creed offered her, squeezing her legs against him over and over, milking each drop of sensation.

Creed kept up his devastating rhythm, pushing her higher, harder, faster. Riana couldn't even scream anymore. Her mouth hung open and she clung to him, holding back as long as she could. She never wanted him to finish. She never wanted him to stop loving her like this.

Without further warning, her body exploded. The cell

exploded with her, shattering into jagged sparkles of gray and black and bright yellow crystals, and what was left of Riana flowed into the throbbing, twinkling lights. Her essence pulsed each time Creed's cock rocked inside her channel, and she heard someone—her?—letting out a long, soul-deep cry of absolute pleasure.

"Riana," Creed bellowed as his cock jerked inside her.

She opened her eyes just in time to meet his as they peaked together, gasping, panting, clawing for breath and closeness, somehow more closeness. She just couldn't get close enough to this man.

To Riana's sex-sated mind, they seemed to float there together, outside of reality, for minutes, hours, days. She had never had an orgasm like that one, and it wouldn't turn her loose. Tears formed in her eyes and spilled down her cheeks.

Her eyes slammed shut, and she lost all track of the world beyond Creed's body pressed against her own and the aftershocks he created each time he slid his cock forward inside her. Murmuring that she was beautiful, whispering that she wasn't like anyone he had ever known, he drew out her orgasm until she didn't know if she could ever put herself back together again.

Total satisfaction.

Total release.

Then, some centuries later, he was holding her, letting her cry as he kissed her head and face and cheeks, and he left his cock sheathed in her channel. Right where he belonged. She didn't plan to let him out unless he begged.

The tiny rational fragment still functioning in her brain was impressed. Most men didn't know what to do when women cried after perfect sex.

But Creed was not most men.

She had already determined that much.

Gradually, her tears subsided, leaving her in a state of boneless exhaustion. Creed rolled her to her side and gently slipped out of her, and Riana felt the immediate ache of his absence. She opened her eyes as he stroked her face, and his expression was so focused and intense that she felt a flicker of nervousness.

"That was incredible," he said quietly, letting his dark eyes caress her as he took off his clothes. "You're incredible. Nothing in my life will ever be the same again. You know that, don't you?"

Riana tried to speak, but just started crying again.

Once more, Creed held her. He massaged her arms and shoulders, stroked her back, and kissed her face until she was ready to try again.

"I—I—" she gazed at him, tracing the scar on his left arm, lost in those eyes. "Yes."

Creed brushed his lips against hers. "Everything changes from here, Riana. I'm not playing around with this—with you. I want you. Do you understand?"

She swallowed hard and nodded, trying to keep her mind away from things like Cynda burning him to ashes, Merilee ramming an arrow into his skull, or the Mothers using his teeth to make a necklace.

How could she be more worried about her own triad and fellow Sibyls than the *other* or the Legion?

That was ridiculous. She really had lost it, and she didn't think she'd ever find it again, either.

"I know you're worried about what the Sibyls will do to me." He kissed her, unnerving her by reading her expression so easily. "Look at me."

She looked at him. Goddess, how could she look anywhere else?

His black eyes burned into hers. "I'm not worried. We'll find a way."

Riana snuggled into him and let his protective embrace drive back her worries.

Maybe he was right. Maybe there was a way to make this work. They'd find it if they searched together, right?

Like a cosmic answer to her question, somebody pounded on the lab door.

Creed gave her a wry, oh-well smile.

Seconds later, over Creed's shoulder, Riana watched Andy, Cynda, and Merilee spill through the door. Merilee was carrying Riana's double-barreled silver ray-gun—the spectroscope, she called it. Somebody flicked on all the lights.

Riana braced herself for the flood of Andy-remarks about screwing demons in jail cells, for Cynda to breathe fire like a medieval dragon, and for Merilee to break everything in the lab with a mini-tornado or throw the spectroscope against the bars as she yelled about Riana taking stupid chances with her life.

When none of that happened, Riana actually got worried.

The three women approached the cell with their eyes averted just enough to be respectful. Cynda waved a hand, and Riana noticed that her knuckles were smoking.

Bad.

Very bad.

Cynda's knuckles only smoked when something *really* scared her to death.

Riana pushed back from Creed, got to her feet, and headed for her clothes as he got up to stand behind her. "What happened? Tell me. You're making me nervous."

"I'm—uh—sorry." Cynda, who was unnaturally pale, looked at the lab's stone floor as she gestured toward Merilee and the spectroscope. "We wouldn't have—I mean—it's important."

Merilee held up the spectroscope. "This doomaflitchit sees Cynda's fire, right? It's supposed to be, like, black-colored when we look through the lens?"

Riana struggled into her damp panties as she nodded. "Yes and no. I've calibrated the spectroscope to be sensitive to the sulfur from her fire. I thought we could use it to track sulfur output from Asmodai—like trails or foot-prints."

"Do a lot of things make sulfur footprints, or just As-modai?" Cynda, who was getting impossibly paler, came over and helped Riana shrug into her blouse.

"No." Riana grabbed her slacks off the floor. "I mean, of course there's some sulfur floating around in a city like this, but I'm counting on the Asmodai prints to be more concentrated and deliberate, not wispy and easily dispersed like exhaust fumes or chemical waste."

"Then according to your stink-o-scope or whatever it is, we've got big problems," Andy said. She beckoned to Creed, who had finished fastening his pants. "Come on. You guys have to see this."

Riana finished dressing as fast as she could, and she and Creed hurried upstairs behind the obviously shaken Cynda, Merilee, and Andy. When they passed the kitchen table, Andy stopped long enough to hand Creed his pistol and a bandolier she had loaded with the elementally treated bullets.

The women then led them into the living room and straight to the front door. Merilee jerked the door open. Above her head, the chimes rang softly in the mournful light of a New York sunset, communicating Cynda's unbridled agitation.

Merilee handed Riana the spectroscope. "Look around and tell me this is some sort of fluke, please?"

Riana put the spectroscope to her eye and started scanning the sidewalk in front of the brownstone.

Her throat went dry, and her stomach clenched.

"What the hell?" She looked out to the road, at the other sidewalk—there were sulfur "footprints" everywhere!

The pattern was unmistakable.

Asmodai must have been walking up and down in front of the brownstone, on both sides of the street, for days.

The trails crisscrossed so often she couldn't even pick out individual paths.

"It's bad, isn't it?" Cynda asked, sounding tired and frightened. "They've been on us for Goddess only knows how long."

Riana was about to say they had to go, to leave, that they weren't safe in the brownstone any longer, when she caught a particularly dark flare of sulfur.

"There's an Asmodai at the mouth of the alley to our right," she muttered.

Twilight faded into darkness.

More dark spots came into view, moving through Central Park in their direction.

Three, then five, then ten.

Even more dark spots came rushing into view from the north and south, on both sides of the road.

Riana jerked the spectroscope away from her eye and made sure she wasn't seeing things.

"Sweet Goddess," she whispered as she visually confirmed at least a dozen of the demons elbowing their way toward the brownstone.

She handed the spectroscope to Creed, who looked through it for only a second before his head snapped back. He lowered his free hand to his weapon and glanced at her.

"How many?"

"I didn't count."

"Shit," Andy said. "Here? Now?"

Riana backed up and Creed helped her push everyone inside. He slammed the door behind them, drew his pistol, kept the spectroscope in his other hand, and took a stance at the door to shoot anything that came through. Andy took the other side of the door. She was shaking.

"Ring the chimes, Cynda." Riana couldn't take her eyes off the closed door. It was locked in every conceivable way, but she knew it couldn't withstand the force arrayed against it outside. Her Sibyl's instincts flared, jarring her with truth after terrible truth. "Tell them to get out. All the Sibyls. Everywhere. Tell them to get to a Motherhouse or a safe house!"

Cynda was on the table and dancing before Riana finished her instructions.

To Merilee she said, "Grab your gear and Cynda's. We're going out the back."

For once, Merilee froze. Her eyes jerked to the stairs. "But . . . my records. All my books. My research! I have to—"

The chimes started a loud, rhythmic ringing in response to Cynda's hurried, desperate warning dance.

Flee . . .

Flee . . .

Attack under way . . .

Flee . . .

Flee . . .

Riana's heart was pounding so hard she could barely think. She grabbed Merilee by the shoulders and shook her. "Don't you get it? The change in the Legion's tactics. The attacks all over the world, the child-murders—the Legion's making itself more powerful. They're through studying us, and they've decided what to do. We're going to be slaughtered!"

Creed jerked his head toward her.

So did Andy.

Then they looked at each other.

"Slaughtered?" Andy said. "Well, fuck that."

She nodded to Creed, who raised the spectroscope to his eye and yanked the door open.

As Riana dragged Merilee toward the closet where they kept their suits and weapons, Creed and Andy started yelling for people to get on the ground.

Then the deafening crack of gunfire blotted out all other sound.

(28)

The first kill was easy.

Bastard was right on the stoop when Creed opened the door. He had Riana's spectroscope pressed to his eye, and the thing lit up like a dark solar flare.

Creed didn't stop to think.

The *other* snarled inside him as he jerked the spectroscope from his eye, verified target, aimed, and fired at the same time Andy did.

The Asmodai's head exploded, and it fell into a pile of dirt, leaves, and rock.

It's helping me. I swear to God the other *is helping me.*

"Bullets work," Andy shouted over the screams, running people, and squealing tires. The tang of gunpowder and sulfur made Creed's eyes water. His heart hammered as he yanked the spectroscope up again and focused on the freak standing on the sidewalk below the steps to the brownstone. The vibration in his ring almost made his hand jump, but he held it steady.

"Noon and below," he told Andy, and they blew the head off the next demon.

A blast of wind roared up the brownstone steps.

"Save ammo now," Creed yelled over the roar of the air. "Don't know when we'll get more."

Andy nodded.

Creed experimented with asking the *other* to let him handle the situation, and felt a profound shock when the beast seemed to recede. Some of the tension left his muscles, and it got easier to aim and fire.

Most of the people on the street had cleared out, or were

scrambling away in one big hurry. Streetlights illuminated what looked like an army of advancing Asmodai.

Creed swallowed.

They couldn't possibly shoot all those demons.

They didn't have enough bullets.

Riana . . .

He bit back his concern. "Tell us when you're ready to go," he shouted to Riana and her triad. "Out through the alley's our only hope."

They needed backup. They needed to bring the OCU into this fight, get more officers, get them properly armed—more firepower. But the Sibyls would never trust the NYPD because of Alisa James's arrest.

Creed targeted the next demon, ambling down the sidewalk in what looked like a red silk Armani suit.

It's on fire.

"Three o'clock, in red," he told Andy.

She took the Asmodai out with a single shot to the chest. It burst into flames.

Creed had to dodge behind the door to avoid the fireball it created when it fell apart.

Before he could target the next monster, another fireball slammed past him and whistled through the brownstone. Creed heard the crack as it hit the back wall and shattered a mirror. Then he heard Riana's curse, and felt the prickle on the back of his neck that told him she used her earth energy to put the fire out.

"Shit!" Andy jumped back out of the doorway and flattened against the wall to dodge another fireball hurled by an Asmodai.

Cynda caught the flaming missile and lobbed it back out the door.

It struck one of the Asmodai full in the face, and Creed shot the thing as it staggered in a drunken circle, burning from top to bottom.

The demon fell apart. Air whistled from the spot where

it stood, slammed through the door, and propelled hard clumps of earth and more fireballs.

Lines of Asmodai surged forward faster than Creed could dodge their wads of earth, balls of fire, and roaring blasts of air. He couldn't pick them all off. They looked like rows of movie extras, all different heights, dressed in all different outfits. Some looked male. Some looked female.

None of them looked normal, or completely human.

He started shooting anything weird—and anything running toward them instead of away from the gunfire.

So did Andy.

Howling wind flattened his skin against his face. Dirt and sticks and rocks pelted him as he tried to raise the spectroscope again. Fire blasted past him on both sides.

Andy shouted.

Somebody in the brownstone shouted back.

Creed fired until he emptied his magazine, then fell backward under a big blast of wind and rocks. He landed on his ass and just as fast scrambled back to his feet, ready to shoot.

Somebody slammed the door.

"Come on, come on!" Riana was jerking him up even as Cynda and Merilee picked up Andy, who looked like she had been in a fight with a really pissed-off porcupine. Trickles of blood covered her face and hands. Creed felt smears of blood on his own cheeks, and about a thousand bruises on his chest and arms.

Holding Riana's spectroscope tightly, Creed half walked, half fell through the brownstone behind Andy and the three Sibyls. The triad had pulled on their leathers, face masks and all, and they were carrying or wearing what looked like every weapon they owned.

Creed could tell them apart now by their height and how they moved.

Merilee's shoulders shook as she cried.

Cynda's eyes blazed from the slits in her mask, furious and terrified.

Riana's gaze was unreadable as she helped Creed through the kitchen. He stopped long enough to pocket the few special bullets Andy hadn't managed to load into the bandoliers. When they headed out the back door, he tucked the spectroscope under one arm, popped out his magazine, and topped it off with the extra lead slugs.

No way was he going to be helpless now that they had a way to fight the Asmodai.

No way was he leaving Riana with no backup.

"Garage is two blocks over," Riana said as she slammed the back door. "The Crown Vic's out front, right?"

"Yeah." Andy glanced toward the mouth of the alley. "In the middle of all the demons. We'll have to run for it—no cab will touch us with all these swords and knives and guns."

"Keep your hand on my shoulder," Riana told Creed. "Andy, hold on to Cynda. Sibyls see well in the dark."

Creed wished he could fasten the spectroscope to his head so he could look through the lens constantly. Instead, he thrust it into the waistband of his slacks, gripped Riana's shoulder with one hand, and kept his SIG ready to fire in the other.

They ran down the alley.

Creed felt like his ring was going to vibrate right off his finger. He charged forward, holding on to Riana, hoping they weren't running straight to their doom. At least he trusted Riana not to let him fall or slam into any walls. It was never totally dark in New York anyway, and his eyes adjusted to the low gray light of the alley soon enough. The safety lights must have been burned out—or destroyed on purpose.

They banged past a bunch of dumpsters and a fire escape, and forward, toward the blur of taillights and headlights and streetlights marking Sixty-sixth Street.

A figure stepped into the mouth of the alley.

Then another, and another.

The *other* roused inside Creed, enhancing his senses and letting him see what lay in wait for them.

Hulking Asmodai blotted out the light at the end of the alley, outlined in the faint glow of the road lights behind them.

Creed felt his lungs pinch shut as the crowd grew.

Merilee's bow twanged.

A split second later, a demon dropped, releasing a screaming flow of wind up the alley. A clatter told Creed that Merilee's second arrow had blown wild in the unnatural gust.

Riana stopped running and pulled Creed behind a dumpster. Cynda pushed Merilee behind the metal barrier with him.

"Do what you can to cover our backs," Riana told Creed as she backed away from him and turned toward the demons. "Just don't shoot the three of us."

That fast, she and Cynda were gone, running directly toward Merilee and the monsters.

"Stay to the center!" Riana called to her triad.

Merilee fired another arrow that went wide in the growing wind. Cynda drew her sword. Fire licked along the blade, lighting a path to the Asmodai.

Creed didn't bother using the spectroscope.

He and Andy aimed to either side of the Sibyls as best they could, squeezed off shots, then ducked to avoid the howling wind and spewing earth the demons released as they fell apart. The demons still standing—there had to be fifteen or more—hurled fireballs at the advancing Sibyls.

Creed's chest clenched as Riana took the lead, swinging daggers at an Asmodai who charged her.

Damnit, he couldn't stay back even if it gave him a better shot. The *other* seemed to hang inside his body, sharing power, giving power, as he elbowed past Andy, ran into the alley, aimed his SIG, and blew the head off a second demon trying to attack Riana from the left.

Andy fell in beside him as he charged toward Riana and the triad, firing whenever he had a clear shot. Andy didn't shoot and yelled at him to save ammo for a sure target.

Asmodai ringed Riana, Cynda, and Merilee.

Bursts of fire lit up the alley. Creed didn't know if it was coming from Cynda or the demons.

Riana hit the pavement.

No!

Creed ran faster, trying to reach the mouth of the alley and get to Riana before a demon did.

Merilee screamed and went down hard. Riana rolled to her feet, leaped past Cynda, and rammed her daggers into two Asmodai at once.

Creed reached the fight just in time and shot a third monster trying to grab her. It spun around, but didn't fall apart.

Missed. But the fucker knows I shot it.

He didn't miss with his second shot.

Andy reached the Asmodai at the same time he did, raised her SIG, shoved it against the nearest demon-head, and fired.

Dirt blew all over Creed, blinding him.

A blast of fire knocked his SIG out of his hand. He dropped to the asphalt, eyes pinched shut against the heat. His hands felt the stone of the alleyway as his clothes caught fire.

Instantly, a wave of cool energy put out the flames.

"I told you to stay back!" Riana yelled.

Creed blinked against the dirt in his eyes, spied his gun, and grabbed it. Thing was hotter than hell, but cooling off fast. He rolled to his back and took out a demon just as it fell toward him, intending to burn him to death with a fiery embrace.

He got up in a hurry and stood shoulder to shoulder with Riana, firing at demons she hadn't stabbed with daggers.

He was vaguely aware of Andy beside Riana, shooting at beasts Cynda hadn't already engaged. The *other* was present, but for once, it didn't distract him. It still seemed to be helping him.

Wind hit him again and again, and what felt like waves of rocks and sticks buried in sour dirt. He tried not to look into the dull, shifting faces of the Asmodai—especially the fire Asmodai, with those sickening, burning sockets where their eyes should have been.

In a matter of minutes, the demons had fallen into dust, eddies, and bits of burning cloth, covering the stones marking the mouth of the alley. Cynda, Andy, Riana, and Creed were still on their feet, but Merilee lay in a heap against the alley wall, her bow broken beside her.

Creed dropped to his knees and checked her pulse. Still strong. He hated to move her since he didn't know the extent of her injuries, but if they stayed in the alley, they were toast. He holstered his SIG, grabbed Merilee, swept her off the pavement, and called to Andy to pick up her bow.

Riana's eyes, glistening in the light from a nearby streetlamp outside the alley, swept over Merilee's unconscious form. Riana's breath came in a sharp, agonized gasp, and Creed wished he could hold her, or at least think of something soothing to say.

Cynda grabbed Riana's shoulder and turned her back toward the road. "No time. Come on!"

They ran out of the alley, dodging traffic as cabs and cars slammed on brakes and drivers shouted out of their windows. Andy followed. Creed checked over his shoulder in time to see another group of Asmodai plodding down the alley behind them.

He gripped Merilee tighter, relieved to feel the steady rhythm of her breathing, and hurried across the road, keeping Riana firmly in view.

Sirens wailed, and Creed knew the NYPD was responding to shots fired. He didn't have any illusions about him and Andy flashing shields and slipping through the ranks. The uniforms would shoot first and sort the dead later. He, Andy, and the triad had to get the hell away from here, and fast.

Behind them, he heard the dull thump of an explosion and felt a blast of heat on his neck. Horns blared. People shouted. The night got a little brighter, and Creed had the sick feeling Riana's brownstone was burning. He didn't look back.

Neither did she.

Merilee stirred in his arms, moaned, then fell still.

They pounded up Fifth Avenue, staying in the shadows as much as possible, plowed across Sixty-seventh, and charged into the garage where Riana leased a parking space. Cynda set the guard arm on fire as they ran past. No need for an exit card now.

Alarms rang.

Sprinklers turned on, dousing them as they hurried up the concrete ramp.

Cynda jerked a remote out of her weapons belt and used it to unlock the Jeep, yanked open the driver's door, and jumped behind the wheel. Andy got in on the passenger side. Creed opened the hatch and laid Merilee carefully on the carpet. Riana crawled in beside her, and Creed secured the hatch before jerking open a back door and climbing across the three center seats.

He laid the spectroscope on the floorboard, but he didn't even get a chance to fasten his seat belt before Cynda revved the Jeep, swung the big vehicle out of its parking space, and barreled down the ramp toward the still-burning guard arm. Sprinkler water splashed against the front windshield, and wood bounced as she slammed through the remnants of the wooden arm. Creed held on to the back of the seat with both hands, teeth clamped firmly together, and managed not to pitch headfirst through the side windows as they careened out of the garage.

Fireballs slammed against the Jeep. Flames licked across the windows, and dirt smashed into the glass near Creed's head. He ducked as wind whistled, so strong it rocked the whole vehicle as they exploded out of the garage.

The Jeep thudded into solid objects. Cynda swerved, but kept driving, as if running down Asmodai and jamming into traffic was the most normal thing in the world. Smoke was literally coming out of her ears. For some insane reason, Creed found that comforting.

"Thank the Goddess those bullets worked," Cynda said as she straightened the Jeep and made it into the flow of traffic. "You were great, Andy. You took down what— three or four Asmodai? And more than that before we got out. You should keep a tally. We do."

"Merilee's hurt badly," Riana murmured, her voice too quiet for anyone but Creed to hear. He turned and looked over the back of the seat.

Riana had her face mask off, and Merilee's, too. One of Riana's hands gripped the back of the seat, and the other rested on the singed edges of Merilee's bodysuit. Merilee's chest was totally bare, burned and blistering, and Creed thought he saw the dark etchings of wicked bruises beginning to emerge as well. "She's put herself in a healing trance, but I think her ribs are broken, and maybe her sternum, too." Riana's voice sounded choked. "She took a huge fireball in the chest while she had her bowstring drawn."

Creed imagined how vulnerable Merilee would have been, with one arm extended and the other pulled back.

"I should have left her back with you two." Riana took a shaky breath. "She's a distance fighter. What was I thinking?"

"The same thing we were," Creed told her as he reached over the seat to stroke her arm. "Kill demons and get the hell out of that alley alive. We made it, honey. That's saying something."

"My pants didn't make it," Andy griped from the front of the Jeep. "Christ. The legs burned. I look like I'm wearing Bermuda shorts."

Cynda cut the wheel, slinging them all to the right, and stepped on the gas. "How is Merilee, Ri?"

"She's out, but I think she's doing okay." Riana gave Creed a miserable glance that warned him not to say anything to Cynda while she was driving.

No worries there. He didn't plan to die tonight.

Cynda turned off on a cross street, and the lights and commotion of Fifth Avenue faded into the rearview mirrors. Gradually, the sound of sirens died away, much to Creed's relief.

"So, where are we going, ladies?" Andy's bright tone was forced, but welcome. "I have a discount card for Econo Lodge."

"We have a safe house on Staten Island." Riana gazed steadily at Creed, and he picked up the meaning.

This is beyond bad. I'm about to take you into a hive of warriors who might eat you for breakfast.

"The New Jersey ranger group uses it as a base, but it's huge. Big enough to accommodate the New York triads— if it hasn't been compromised."

Creed didn't know whether to hope it was still standing, or to suggest Econo Lodge might be a better bet. He was having a hard time thinking, because Riana's face reflected an agony that dug straight into his gut.

Every time she looked at Merilee, it got worse. She stroked the air Sibyl's blond hair so tenderly, and she seemed on the verge of breaking into pieces. If that happened, Creed knew a part of him would die inside. He couldn't take seeing her in so much pain.

He reached out again, this time brushing his fingers against her cheek.

Her look said *don't* and *don't stop* all at once.

Creed ran his fingers from Riana's cheek to her neck. He

knew he would do anything to save her from hurting. He would die to protect her. Hell, he would damn near die just to make her smile. He realized without much shock that he was in love with her.

Now he just had to figure out how to make it through a safe house full of Sibyls, spring Alisa James from Rikers before Friday, slay the *other*, and defeat the Legion so he could have her.

29

Riana couldn't handle how Creed was looking at her, like he might suddenly scoop her up in his arms and kiss her until she forgot her own name.

Goddess, how she wanted him to, even though he was covered with soot and ash and blood. He and Andy had worked miracles with their sidearms, fighting Asmodai in ways she knew no human—or almost human—had ever accomplished before tonight. Riana had no doubt that she and her triad wouldn't have made it out of that brownstone alive without their help.

She wished Creed could work miracles of healing, too, and bring Merilee back from the edge of shock and stupor. Battling a flood of emotions, Riana used her earth energy to shore up Merilee's healing trance. Air Sibyls didn't have much use for earth-grounding, but Riana gave her triad sister what she thought she could tolerate. Merilee's breathing was shallow, and her pulse thready. Now and then, her eyelids fluttered, but she never came to full awareness, which was probably a blessing, since they had nothing to offer her for pain.

The Staten Island safe house would have that much, at least—and some Sibyls were doctors, nurses, and surgeons. If enough of them survived.

Riana bit her lip.

If the Sibyl ranks were too decimated to see to their wounded, or if the safe house had been compromised, they would have to think up some story and show up at the local hospital.

She closed her eyes. Why hadn't she told Merilee to stay

back, to fight in the cleanup position the way she always did? Because Creed and Andy were there with their guns and lead bullets?

Merilee was her backup, not two well-meaning NYPD refugees, no matter how well they were shooting.

Had she been distracted by new players in this deadly game and gotten her precious friend and the broom of her triad killed in the process?

I'm so sorry, Merilee. What have I done to you?

"She's holding her own," Creed said, his voice low and comforting. "Take a deep breath and stay with us, Riana."

Riana opened her eyes. She obeyed and took a deep breath, and she tried to ignore the stench of burned leather and singed hair seasoned with the coppery tang of fresh blood. Her hand shook when she stroked Merilee's hair again. "She was devastated over leaving her books behind. Archives and records—that's all that grounds air Sibyls."

"We'll get what we can tomorrow." Creed's loving look almost made Riana break down. "I'll rent a truck if I have to. Merilee's tough like the rest of you. I know she'll pull through."

"Damn well better," Cynda said as she sped east over the Brooklyn Bridge, before turning south to head for the Verrazano-Narrows Bridge connecting Brooklyn to Staten Island. "I'm not dealing with friggin' Bela Argos and those South Bronx bitches by myself."

Riana could tell from Cynda's tone that she thought Merilee was awake enough to hear her. That made her chest ache all over again. She realized her heart was still pounding, and she was sweating so hard that her crescent pendant was stuck to her chest inside her bodysuit. All of a sudden, she wanted to roll down all the windows and gasp for air. She was so tired she hurt down in her bones, and she felt like she had a hundred holes in her skin from the Asmodai attacks.

Attack. No. That was a military operation. An invasion of endless, renewable soldiers.

"So the Legion's gone on offense." Cynda let out a loud sigh. "I wonder how many Sibyls died tonight."

Riana's stomach churned at the thought, and Cynda voiced her next question before Riana could even ask herself.

"What the hell are we supposed to do now?"

"Regroup," Riana said as she pressed her palm against Merilee's clammy cheek. "Rest. Plan."

"Improvise, adapt, overcome," Andy added immediately. When Creed and Riana stared at her, she shrugged. "Sorry. Four years' active duty in the Marines warps the mind forever."

"The safe house will have projective mirrors, at least, and rudimentary supplies." Cynda rolled her hands against the steering wheel until they made a squeaking noise. "They have a decent archive, and a basic lab, too, I think."

Lab. No. No! Riana looked at Creed.

The initial analysis of his genetic profile would be ready tomorrow. Or it would have been, if it hadn't blown up in the brownstone.

Still, the lab was downstairs, encased in stone and metal. The Asmodai might ransack it searching for their biological targets, but who knew what they would destroy or leave intact?

She would have to go and check to see if the analysis was spared, but in the light of day, if she could leave Merilee by then. She didn't plan to go too far from her triad sister until she was certain Merilee didn't need her. Nothing in the world was more important than that for now.

Priorities.

Riana glanced at Creed one more time, and the affection in his dark eyes rattled her yet again.

I've got to keep my priorities straight.

The harsh lights of the toll plaza at the Verrazano-Narrows Bridge seemed to pound into the Jeep. Riana had moved by then to cradle Merilee's head in her lap, and Cynda obviously had gotten profoundly nervous at Merilee's continued silence. Smoke drifted freely through the Jeep, carrying the exact heat and frenetic energy of Cynda's worry.

"Don't set the tollgates on fire or blow up any of the cars in front of us," Riana cautioned as they slowed to get in line. "We can't afford that kind of attention."

She heard Cynda's hands squeak against the steering wheel, and it made her skin crawl. At least she made her point about the gates and cars, though. That was important.

The Jeep crept forward, stopping and starting, stopping and starting.

Andy and Creed were discussing how to handle checking in with the station, acting like they had been out of the city all night. The little matter of Andy's Crown Vic in front of the brownstone where all the shooting and the explosion occurred—well, they would play that by ear, if their captain brought it up. If no one had caught on to Frith Gregory's disappearance, they were planning a few more impromptu interviews, too.

"Do you think we could speak with Camille—the Sibyl who was in the Latch house that night?" Creed turned his intense gaze on Riana. "Captain Freeman's blocking us every time we try to interview Alisa James, and—"

"No," Cynda shouted from the front seat. The haze of smoke in the Jeep got a little thicker, and Riana imagined her leather seats singeing dark black under Cynda's ass. "The NYPD doesn't even know she's no longer in town, and it needs to stay that way. She can't handle anything else right now."

"We could go to her," Andy suggested. "You could, you know, zap us through the mirrors and let us talk to her in—where is she? Ireland?"

"The Mothers would kill Creed if he came through the channels," Riana said at the same time Cynda said, "No way Creed's getting into a Motherhouse."

Creed looked annoyed, then angry. "Shit. What's it going

to take to prove myself to the Sibyls? Do I have to get my legs burned off by a demon?"

Riana didn't know what to say, and Cynda, for once, kept her mouth shut. She rolled down the Jeep window, handed money to the tollbooth operator, and rolled the window up. Thank the Goddess a little of the smoke cleared—though Riana didn't enjoy the more detailed look at Creed's expression.

Her heart felt heavy.

She hadn't realized that Creed thought he could earn the trust of the Sibyls as a whole, that he could earn the trust of the Mothers. That would never happen, not with the *other* inside him.

Outside the windows of the Jeep, the ink-black waters of New York Bay stretched beneath them. They drove quickly and steadily across the bridge that was once the world's longest suspension span.

Damn, but he would be disappointed—and pissed— when he realized the truth. That he was busting his ass to fight for a bunch of women who would never admit him into the ranks of the trusted.

It didn't matter how much she wanted that for him, or how much she wanted him. It didn't matter that Sibyls rarely selected the wrong friends or mates.

Creed was not completely human, and he had no real understanding of the supernatural force inside him.

Creed was, without question, dangerous.

Riana held Merilee's head close against her belly and stared at the man, hoping the darkness hid her eyes. Praying to the Goddess that her feelings weren't etched on her face.

He's dangerous, and I think I'm falling in love with him. Goddess help me. What am I going to do?

They didn't have to scout the safe house to see if it had been compromised. The Todt Hill mansion that served as an emergency fallback for Sibyls working in the eastern reaches of the State of New York blazed with life as they approached. Every light in the gigantic three-winged, three-story house burned brightly. They had to get in line to pull through the gates of the compound, which always reminded Riana of the Corleone estate from the *Godfather* movies, except that the house and yard were bigger. In the daytime, the view from the house nestled into the eastern slope of the small mountain ridge was breathtaking. At night, the lights of New York's other boroughs twinkled steadily in the dark distance.

Riana eased Merilee's head from her lap and climbed out of the hatch, immediately shivering in the cold night air. The exhausted ache in her muscles doubled in the chill, and her breath issued in frosty puffs as she watched other triads disembark. A lot were limping or cradling injured arms.

Riana's throat tightened.

"Dear Goddess," she said aloud as she caught sight of a huddled, sobbing figure pressed against the side of a black SUV. "There's Maura from the South Manhattan triad. And she's alone."

Maura, the fire Sibyl from the group Riana worked most closely with, stood beside her vehicle, looking utterly lost and broken.

Riana felt twice as icy in the cold night. She wasn't sure she could breathe, and when she did, her sides ached as if her whole body was about to explode.

Creed and Andy came up behind Riana and stopped, staring at the crowd of wounded women making their way into the safe house. Cynda moved up beside Riana, pale, shaking, and smoking from all her curves and edges. Her voice trembled when she said, "Jesus, Ri. A lot of these triads aren't whole." Then she turned and saw Merilee lying in the back of the Jeep, and Riana had to catch Cynda when she staggered backward.

"She's—she's—why didn't you tell me? I would have driven faster. I would have—"

Riana grabbed her triad sister and held her tightly even though Cynda was hot enough to burn her. "You were driving," she whispered into Cynda's ear as Cynda let out a jagged sob. "I didn't want us all to die."

"I'm taking her inside," Cynda said as she pushed back.

"No. Let me." Riana pointed to Maura. "I don't think Dani and Shell got out alive. We can't just leave Maura standing there like that. She looks like she's on another planet."

When Cynda hesitated, Riana cupped her face and made her focus. "Merilee's alive. We still have her—and I think she'll come through this. Dani and Shell didn't."

Cynda hesitated, then bit her lip and nodded. "Can you carry Merilee by yourself?"

"Creed can," Riana told her. "Now go."

Cynda didn't move. "You can't be serious. There's no way you're taking him into a Sibyl safe house. Riana, I know you care about him and I know he helped us, but with that monster inside him, he's a big risk."

Riana let go of Cynda's face. Her gaze jumped to Creed against her will. She saw that same pain and anger on his face she'd seen in the Jeep, and she wanted to collapse from the weight of it.

Andy looked pissed, too, as she gaped at Riana. "What, we're good enough to cover your ass when you're in a jam, but we can't enter your precious witch-mansion?"

Riana held up her hands. "We'll figure something out. Creed, please take Merilee inside. Cynda, in the name of the Goddess, go help Maura before she completely falls apart."

Cynda folded her arms and glared for a few seconds. Then shook her head as if to clear her thoughts, and hurried off toward Maura.

Creed, his cut, bruised face a mask of frustration, picked

up Merilee without comment and started toward the safe house's main door. Riana followed, with Andy by her side. The lights of the house and the safety lights ringing the compound made it almost as bright as day outside, though the corners of the huge lawn seemed dark and menacing. Riana's teeth were actually chattering from the cold, and she wanted nothing more than a long, hot bath.

At the door, the New Jersey ranger group—three tall dark-headed women Riana recognized as Ann, Shay, and Perry—held up swords, daggers, and throwing axes to stop them.

The crowd of Sibyls milling outside the front door fell silent as Ann, the triad's earth Sibyl, said, "He isn't a Sibyl. He doesn't go inside."

She nodded to Shay and Perry, who took Merilee out of Creed's arms. Creed didn't resist giving her up, and Riana didn't argue, either. She wanted Merilee treated as soon as possible. Over Ann's square shoulders and the tip of her broadsword, she saw Shay and Perry carry Merilee to a section of cots where Sibyls trained as medical profession-als were examining the injured, stitching wounds, and hooking up intravenous fluids.

Creed stepped away from the door, off to the right, and stood beside Andy, who looked like a thunderhead about to rain all over the Sibyl safe house.

After a minute, and as Shay and Perry returned, Riana gestured to her friends. "Creed and Andy are NYPD offi-cers with the Occult Crimes Unit. Using modified lead bul-lets, they helped us shoot our way out of Manhattan tonight. My triad would be dead if it weren't for their help."

A wave of mutters and exclamations ran through the small crowd outside the front door. Riana picked out a few she knew well, like the North Queens group, and, as Cynda had dubbed them, Bela Argos and her South Bronx bitches.

Perry, the air Sibyl in the ranger triad, palmed two

throwing axes. Shay, the fire Sibyl, kept her hand on the hilts of her swords. Ann kept her broadsword raised. Her dark eyes narrowed as she studied Creed. "I think I heard about you."

Bela Argos elbowed to the front of the crowd, and Riana's chest started to ache.

This is bad.

"If you've heard about him," Bela said to Ann in her typical icy, sarcastic tone, "then you've heard he kills Asmodai."

Ann blinked.

So did Riana.

She heard someone from the crowd say, "Well, shit," and recognized Cynda's voice.

Creed stood very still with no expression on his face. Andy had plenty of expression, most of it confused.

"He crushed a demon's head to save his partner in Van Cortlandt Park," Bela continued. "And he's beat all to hell from helping take out a bunch more tonight. So what's the problem?"

A lot of arguing erupted then, from Sibyls who had seen or heard about Creed's dramatic shift into the *other*. Opinions ranged from giving him his own suite in the safe house to beheading him and tossing his remains into New York Bay.

Andy drew her SIG, waved it in the air, and screeched, "Will you people just shut up? I *will* shoot!"

Her voice was louder than any gunshot, and Riana saw the same worry on everyone's face. If Andy discharged her weapon, every denizen in Todt Hill would telephone the NYPD in one big hurry.

All arguments died away almost instantly.

In the shocked silence that followed her outburst, Andy said, "Look, I'm tired. I'm filthy. I'm cut in like a hundred places, and half my *best* pants got burned off by a freaking fire demon. I want a bath, some clothes, a meal, and a bed—in that order—so I'm going inside. If you don't like it, kill me in my fucking sleep."

With that, she stalked toward the door, gun still clenched tightly in one fist.

Ann and her triad almost fell over themselves getting out of her way.

Andy stopped at the door, looked back over her shoulder, and raised her eyebrows at Creed. "You coming?"

Riana held her breath.

Some of the Sibyls looked amused. Others looked wary, or even furious.

Creed glanced from Andy to the crowd to Riana, then shook his head. "I'm taking first watch—and I'll sleep in the Jeep, thanks. Just send me out some dinner."

Andy gave him a you-pussy glare, shrugged, and went inside.

Ann nodded to Creed, relief stamped on her aquiline features.

Riana felt relief first, and gratitude at his compromise, then misery that she wouldn't have him beside her. She wanted to stay outside with him, but she had to be with Merilee. And she and Cynda had to help Maura until the sad task of sending lone Sibyls back to their Motherhouses could be undertaken—not to mention participate in planning for defense and counterattack.

That feeling of being torn into two pieces overcame her, and she clenched her fists as Creed moved farther off to the side of the crowd to let the women pass. Sibyls flowed around him and jostled past Riana, too, into the safe house. Cynda came last, holding Maura's hand. She spoke gently to the bereft fire Sibyl, then sent her inside and came back to give Riana a hug.

"I'm glad you're okay," Cynda said quietly. She kissed the top of Riana's head, then looked at her eye to eye. "But you know you've *got* to tell the Mothers about Creed now, tonight or first thing in the morning, or somebody else will."

Riana opened her mouth, but couldn't say anything. She dug her fingers into the leather of Cynda's jumpsuit.

Cynda frowned. "Ri, in two days, we're raiding Rikers Island, springing Alisa, and getting reassigned anyway. We can't just leave Creed for the next triad to deal with—and we can't take him with us."

It took most of the energy she had left, but Riana nodded.

Cynda gave her another quick kiss on the cheek, then handed her the keys to the Jeep. Her expression as she pulled away said, *Good. Thank the Goddess. This has to be, and you know it.*

Riana waited until Cynda was all the way inside before she approached Creed.

He had folded his arms across his chest, and he looked as exhausted as she felt, but still so unbelievably handsome. Riana wanted to take his hand and lead him to that hot bath she had let herself imagine. She would wash away the dirt and blood and tend his bruises, and she knew he would do the same for her. She could almost feel the warmth of the water, and the deep satisfaction of pressing herself into his hard, powerful body.

As it was, she stopped in front of him and fought to keep from throwing her arms around his neck. Instead, she handed him the keys to the Jeep.

"Are you sure about this?" she asked, trying not to let her voice shake.

Creed gave her a knee-melting grin and a wink. "It's the best thing for both of us tonight, but I hope they'll let me shower in the morning."

"They have to," Riana said. "Or Cynda and I will take you by your apartment." She swallowed. "I'm sorry the other Sibyls don't know you. I'm so sorry you're having to do this. I want you with me. I'd stay out here with you, but Cynda and Merilee need me, and we have so much to do—"

Creed held up a hand. "I know that. You don't have to explain. Besides, if you don't keep an eye on Andy, she might shoot somebody before morning—and those bullets will work."

Riana made herself slow her breathing when she looked at Creed's bruised, cut face. The cold night air stung her eyes. He gripped his own biceps, and she realized he wanted to hold her, that he was keeping himself in check because of the audience in the safe house behind them. The door was still open, and no doubt Ann and her triad were still standing watch.

"I'll do whatever it takes to make this work," Creed said, his deep voice wrapping around her like a sweet caress. "Sleeping in a Jeep is a small price." His dark eyes burned so brightly she thought her heart might melt on the spot. "I love you, Riana."

Riana's mouth dropped open.

She stared at him, too stunned to move or speak.

Had she heard him correctly?

She couldn't have . . . but the heat in his gaze and his tender, caring expression pushed away her disbelief.

Oh, this was too soon. She hadn't known him long enough. There was no way she could accept that, much less return it. No way at all.

Her heart beat so fast she thought it might march right out of her chest, and the cold stopped bothering her all of a sudden, as if someone had snuggled her into a warm, soft blanket.

Was she blushing?

Goddess.

She lifted both hands to her cheeks, touching the hot spots that had to be as red as ripe strawberries. The feel of her own skin brought her back to earth enough to realize she needed to say something, to set this man straight before her life got completely and entirely out of hand.

"I love you, too," she whispered before she could stop herself. The words just flew out, as if they had been trapped inside her for years. "I love you, Creed."

He smiled, and Riana wondered if she could fly. She felt like she could walk off a rooftop and sail away on strong, steady wings.

"Now don't look at me like that, honey," he said in that devastating, sexy bass. "I'll kiss you if you do, and Cynda will blow her stack, and every harpy in that house will come screaming out here to pitch my corpse into New York Bay."

Riana smiled back at him.

He loved her.

He loves me.

Creed gave her a look as deep and passionate as any kiss, then turned and strode away, toward the Jeep.

Riana went inside, shaking all over, torn up and put back together in ways she hadn't even thought possible.

Fire Sibyls had gathered at the far end of the main room, and most were dancing, sending information and receiving it through the safe house's projective mirrors. Wind chimes rang out solemn reports as yet more bleak news poured through the foggy glass.

The Asmodai attacks had been worldwide, just as Riana feared when she saw the demons bearing down on her brownstone. The Legion had gone to war with the Sibyls, and their first attack had been devastating. Many dead. Even more wounded.

Only the Motherhouses and safe houses were spared, probably because triads didn't consistently use those locations to launch operations against the Legion. Maybe the locations were still unknown to their enemies. Maybe not. They had to be on their guard at all times. Motherhouse Russia hadn't yet gained much useful information from their Legion captive Frith Gregory, other than the fact that the Legion was highly decentralized.

Riana tried to shut it all out as she made her way to Merilee's bedside. She couldn't take any more. Not now. Not tonight.

She was much relieved to find that Merilee wasn't on the

critical-care side of the makeshift medical ward in the safe house's gigantic living room. As she sat down on the edge of Merilee's cot, everything swirled together, from the loss of her home to the near loss of her triad. Goddess. Too much loss! The way of life she had known since birth. Her friends and fellow warriors—and soon, the man she loved, too. The Mothers would take him, or she'd be yanked away from New York City after Friday night.

Riana put her hand on Merilee's cheek and sobbed out loud.

She covered her own mouth, but she couldn't stop, and soon Cynda and Andy and Maura were standing around her, hands on her head and shoulders.

One of the Sibyls from the Jamaica Bay ranger group, a doctor, came over to explain about Merilee's broken ribs and cracked sternum, and to reassure Riana that Merilee would probably make a full recovery. She couldn't concentrate on what the doctor was saying, but she did snap to attention when Merilee opened her pretty blue eyes.

"Gross," Merilee said in drugged, slurred tones. "Don't get snot on my sheets."

Cynda and Andy cracked up.

Riana laughed in the middle of all her crying. "I'll try not to," she said. Then she proceeded to do just that.

30

Creed got his shower the next morning—Wednesday—
with an honor guard of six heavily armed Sibyls, who at
least didn't insist on hanging out in the bathroom with
him. He barely got to see Riana, but she hadn't shot down
his initial proposal that the Sibyls reveal themselves to the
OCU and involve the NYPD in the war against the Legion
in a much more direct way. If the Sibyls could make enough
bullets, a handful of well-trained police officers might go a
long way in a fight.

The hungry way Riana had looked at Creed when he left
gave him enough energy to face the day, and then some. He
needed it. He had cricks in his neck and spine from sleeping in the Jeep, and he hadn't gotten much uninterrupted
shut-eye because of the groups of Sibyls arriving at inter-
vals all night long. Apparently, every triad within two hundred miles of the safe house—which covered a fair number
of territories and a lot of sizable cities—called the Staten Island mansion their own.

Andy's crankiness, however, far overshadowed Creed's
own. She was wearing a black pantsuit a few sizes too large
for her, and she bitched about the outfit being leather as
they drove across the long suspension bridge back into
Brooklyn. Still, she refused to get any clothes when they
stopped and bought Creed a few pairs of jeans, several
shirts, and a couple of jackets.

Nothing here will fit me right, Andy had insisted. *My ass
is too big.*

After freaking out a few salespeople and changing in the
store dressing room, Creed threw away the torn, burned,

blood-streaked clothes he had taken off, got back in the Jeep, and stowed his extra outfits in the hatch. Andy started talking about Senator Latch immediately. Latch was their target for the morning, despite Captain Freeman's threats against their jobs if they went near the man. Creed had checked in with the station that morning, and Freeman had repeated his standard cautions.

Work on the sidelines and behind the scenes.

Stay away from the principals. Stay away from the press. Don't be visible, or I'll fire you both, damnit.

No one seemed the wiser about Gregory yet, and apparently the investigating officers hadn't finished running the plates on cars spotted near the shootings and explosion. Captain Freeman didn't even mention the brownstone debacle when they spoke. He just groused about Creed and Andy being unavailable, and failing to produce tangible results on any of the minor cases they were ignoring.

The clock was ticking, though. Even if Freeman didn't start finding out about their transgressions soon, Creed and Andy would tip their hand in less than an hour. They were going to shake things up for Senator Latch and his wife, for Alisa James's prosecution team—and for the OCU, too.

"I say we just barge into the bastard's house, snatch him up by the short hairs, and haul his ass to that Sibyl-den on Staten Island to find out why he was employing a Legion member—and what else he's hiding," Andy announced as she drove Riana's big Jeep up the Brooklyn-Queens Expressway. "I mean, seriously. Will the world really suffer if one politician disappears?"

"Guy's got, what, twenty bodyguards?" Creed watched the city stream by the Jeep window. "That might be a problem."

"We've got good bullets," Andy grumbled. "It would warm my heart to shoot something today. Too much estrogen in that house last night, I swear." She squeezed the steering wheel, reminding Creed of Cynda. If Andy had been a Sibyl, she would have been a fire Sibyl, definitely.

Despite their situation, the entire world felt brighter to Creed, just because he knew Riana was in it. He grinned at his partner. He couldn't help himself, even though he knew it would set her off. Maybe *because* it would set her off.

She cut him a wicked glare. "You're chipper this morning, Mr. Man. Do you thrive on near-death experiences?"

He shrugged. "Something like that. We're probably about to have another one, right?"

"Uh-huh." Andy eyed him with great suspicion. "I'm missing something, and you're not going to tell me what it is."

Creed couldn't help another grin.

"I probably don't want to know anyway." Andy took the first exit that would take them over into Manhattan. "Not before I break a bunch of laws with you for my backup."

Senator Davin Latch and his wife, Raven, lived in a townhouse on the Upper East Side, north of Riana's brownstone, just above the Reservoir in Central Park. Parking was either private or taken, and without their police placards, they had to resort to a pay lot on Ninety-fifth and Third. Andy set a brisk pace as they covered the two blocks to their destination.

When they reached it, they both stood outside the gates for a time, simply staring at the five-story Federal-style brick building with its fence, white-columned entrance, and American eagle emblazoned in bronze across the stones directly over the door. He noted a rooftop terrace that stretched the length and width of the building, and terraces off three of the fourth-floor rooms, too. The place probably had a full basement and all the amenities—gardens, back terraces, elevators, intercoms—everything. Not too many people in New York enjoyed that much living space. On the open market, the place would probably go for twenty million, easy. And he bet he'd underestimated how nice it was inside.

Two men in dark suits and sunglasses staffed the main gate. They stood with arms folded behind their backs. Andy elbowed Creed, and they approached the armed guards with their best police-business faces in place.

At first, the men looked bored and sarcastic as they examined Andy's shield and then Creed's. When they spotted Creed's name, though, they both stood straighter. One of them touched his earpiece and spoke quietly, then nodded to the other to admit Andy and Creed.

The man who let them through the gate said, "Senator Latch will see you in the library on the fourth floor. One of our people will meet you at the front door and escort you to him."

"Thank you." Creed closed the gate behind him, and the guard promptly locked it. As Creed and Andy mounted one side of the dual set of white flared steps leading to the front door, he glanced at her. "Is it me, or was that too easy?"

Andy's expression had gone from sleepy and grouchy to tight and wary. She was climbing the steps with her arms loose and her right hand near the concealed holster of her SIG.

"Too easy," she confirmed.

They reached the columned entrance.

When the door swung open, the *other* gave a loud howl. Creed startled and damn near pitched backward down the steps. Andy grabbed his arm, asking *what the hell* with the lift of her eyebrows.

Creed shook his head and brushed off his new jacket and jeans. He didn't fight with the *other*, not after the last few days of its eerie cooperation. Instead, he sent a big *chill out* message, which seemed to work. For the moment, at least, the *other* went still again.

The armed guard who had opened the door beckoned for

Creed and Andy to come inside. He walked them across the polished herringbone hardwood floors to the cage-style elevator, and rode with them to the fourth floor. Creed and Andy stepped out and headed down a hallway, a high-end blue carpet now cushioning their feet. Creed glanced at bedrooms and bathrooms, all decorated in dark, expensive antiques and lace. He didn't notice so much as a speck of dust or a fingerprint on the furniture or paneling, or a wrinkle in the linen. The house smelled faintly of fresh paint, fabric softener, and lemon. Clean. Fresh. Almost antiseptic. Fans stirred the air just enough to create a cool breeze and prevent the hallway from being stuffy.

Their guide took them toward a door at the end of the hall.

A few steps from the door, Creed's signet ring started to vibrate.

Oh, fuck.

The *other* rattled its cage in Creed's mind, and he closed one eye, trying to stave off a headache.

They reached the door, and the guard rapped one knuckle against the heavy oak.

"Come in," instructed a resonant, practiced voice that reminded Creed of guys who used to take theater classes.

At the sound of that voice, the *other* gave another long, unhappy howl. Creed was ready for it this time, and managed not to fall over his own feet as the guard opened the door and admitted them to a paneled room with hardwood floors, fancy area rugs, polished tables, and endless shelves of books. The scent of fresh paint gave way to old paper and leather. In the back was a small office area with a desk, three chairs, and Davin Latch, standing in front of a set of doors curtained with gauzy fabric. Through the fabric, Creed could see one of the terraces he had noticed from street level.

The senator wore a green velvet smoking jacket on top of black slacks, and the man actually had a wine-colored ascot with a matching hankie in the jacket's front pocket. On anybody else, that getup would have looked effeminate, or at best, stuffy and pretentious. Instead, Davin Latch managed to look relaxed, sophisticated, and to-the-bone wealthy and privileged.

Like an old movie star.

Creed tensed as he walked.

Jesus, could this be the guy that houngan *freak told us about? Did Davin Latch send Asmodai against the Sibyls at Trinity Church—and hire those shooters?*

The *other* snarled, then seemed to be trying to charge backward out of Creed's body. The pain made his eyes water, but he steeled himself and held it together.

Give this time. We have to find out. We have to be sure.

When the guard left, the quiet thump of the door settling into place sent the creature into long, rumbling growls.

Creed ground his teeth.

The senator greeted them with the smooth warmness Creed expected from a seasoned politician, and invited them to sit down in his office chairs. He sat behind the ornate desk, rested his elbows on the polished oak, and turned up both palms. With the morning light through the doors behind him, he looked like a religious icon getting ready to bless his followers.

"I must say I'm relieved to see you, Detectives." He smiled, and the expression seemed genuine enough. Creed didn't much like how the guy was staring at him, though. He instinctively covered his still-vibrating signet ring by clenching his fist on his thigh.

Neither Creed nor Andy spoke in the silence that followed. They hadn't expected this sort of welcome, and both were trained to let suspects talk if they seemed in a chatty mood.

Senator Latch was definitely chatty. "My wife has been beside herself since the arrest of her friend." He rested his forearms on the desk and clasped his hands. "The OCU officers we've dealt with thus far don't seem to take the supernatural aspects of my son's murder seriously enough. After meeting you in the station, however briefly, my wife believes that you two might feel otherwise."

My son. My wife. The way he commands the room from behind that desk—hell, this guy owns it all, doesn't he? Creed gave the senator a calculated smile.

Andy was doing the same thing.

Creed did his best to look respectful and attentive despite the fact that his head and spinal column felt like they were about to split open and discharge a demon onto Latch's dust-free hardwood floor. That, and he was hating Latch more by the second.

Go on, Andy's wide eyes said. *We're listening.*

"You realize Alisa James did not murder my child, correct?" Senator Latch's next smile sparkled almost as much as the floor and the top of his desk.

Andy made a noncommittal noise and leaned forward in her seat, making eye contact with the senator. "My partner and I are open to other explanations, yes. That's why we're here."

"Excellent." He leaned back, and Creed wondered if he was aware of his body language, moving away from Andy like that. "Do you have new information? Something to share with me?"

Creed tried to say something, but the *other* intruded and cut off the air to his throat.

Andy stepped in with, "No, sir. I'm sorry, but we don't. We were hoping to ask you a few questions, if it wouldn't be too hard on you considering your recent loss."

"I'm accustomed to adversity." The senator was answering Andy, but looking at Creed. Another smile played at his thin lips, which seemed increasingly out of place for the situation and topic. "I'll give you whatever answers I can. Detective . . . uh . . . it's Lowell, isn't it?" he said to Creed. "Detective Lowell, might I call for some water for you? You look pale."

Creed's face went hot. He managed to speak enough to politely decline, then got heavy-handed with the *other*, driving it back from his consciousness as much as he could.

Andy threw a soft pitch first. "You have a lot of bodyguards, Senator. More than I'm accustomed to seeing. Do you have a history of receiving threats against yourself or your family?"

Latch caught the ball easily. "No, Detective Myles. I normally keep five private guards on staff because I have considerable assets." He folded his hands. "Since the murder of my son, I've tripled that. Even though I've received no threats, I'm concerned for my wife's safety, and for my own."

Creed rubbed his throat and took the next toss. Definitely a harder pitch. "Senator Latch, have you ever heard of an organization called the Legion?"

Latch didn't smile, but he didn't frown, either. His sharp brown eyes studied Creed with a new energy. "I have, Detective Lowell, and I see my wife's faith in you was not misplaced." His gaze shifted downward toward Creed's still-hidden ring. "My wife and I encountered the Legion some years back, just out of college. Well-educated intellectuals, deeply into ancient mysticism and the supremacy of the enlightened mind." His smile broke through, and Creed sat back, more than bothered by the man's weird expression.

Andy kept her forward position as she slammed home her fastball. "Senator, we have reason to believe you may have lost a child to the Legion already. A son, over twenty years ago. Is that true?"

For the first time since Creed and Andy entered the library, Senator Latch's relaxed demeanor faltered. Creed saw a flash of something—was it anger? No. More like . . . wounded pride. The older man composed himself, and once more, his steady gaze never left Creed's face.

"My first son was stillborn," he replied a little too quietly. "That's in the record, is it not? I gave the information in my first interview, and I'm sure my wife and my longtime assistant Frith Gregory said the same thing." He paused, but before Creed could speak, Latch said, "Detective Lowell, have you questioned Mr. Gregory?"

Once more, Creed started to answer, but Latch cut him off again.

"I wonder, Detective, because Mr. Gregory hasn't reported to work today." Latch stood, his cheeks gaining a faint red tinge at the edges. "And when I checked his apartment, I caught the distinct stench of the NYPD—and foul play."

31

Riana stood on the sidewalk in front of her brownstone, wearing a blue pantsuit she had borrowed from Anna and holding the keys to the SUV she borrowed from Bela Argos. If Cynda hadn't disappeared with Maura before sunrise, she would have been just as shocked as Riana at what Riana was seeing. Merilee, who had been energetic enough to antagonize the Sibyls trying to nurse her, would have been thrilled.

Riana's home—her triad's home—was crisscrossed with yellow crime-scene tape, and a uniformed officer stood on her steps, but the brownstone was still whole and probably habitable. A huge char-mark covered the face of the building, and Riana realized the Asmodai had tried to use some combined elemental force to blow it to bits. The bindings and protections long used by Sibyls to guard their dwellings from such attacks had repelled the explosion. A few windows were broken, but the damage didn't seem more extensive than that.

The Asmodai came down both ends of the alley after us. Maybe they didn't even go inside, since they sensed their targets weren't there.

Feeling almost buoyant, Riana marched up to the young police officer, presented her identification, and made a huge show of being distressed by whatever had happened to her beloved brownstone while—of course—she was away for the night, visiting a friend in Staten Island.

The police officer radioed his station house, and verified her ownership of the brownstone. He told her how sorry he was, that apparently there had been some gang activity on her street last night. Witnesses thought somebody had been shooting out of her front door, but it could have been gang members using her stoop as cover and a vantage point as they attacked some rival down on the street.

"Lots of gunfire out front and in the alley, and one of them must have tossed some kind of homemade incendiary." The young man shook his head and looked beyond annoyed at the thought of the punks who had shot up her street. "The FDNY has already been out and inspected, though, and there was no damage to the structure itself beyond the windows."

Riana put her hand on her chest. "Oh, thank the— I mean, thank God."

The young man grinned. "I'm happy to report that the house is safe, ma'am, and your insurance probably will cover the cleanup on the stones. If they don't, a victim relief fund may pick it up. Do you have someplace to stay until we can clear the scene and turn it back over to you?"

"I can't stay here?" Riana asked, pumping as much wide-eyed innocence and shock into her voice as she could manage.

"No, ma'am. Not until we're sure it's safe, and until we've finished our initial investigation. You can probably have it back tomorrow. Friday at the latest." He used the radio on his shoulder again, and his station house confirmed that they could release the brownstone to her control tomorrow. They also gave him two hotels where she could stay. He told Riana she would have to give a statement, and perhaps information pertaining to the friend she had stayed with last night, but that was just a formality.

Riana gave Ann's full name, since the Todt Hill safe house, the address, and the landline number were listed in Ann's name. The officer's eyebrows lifted when he heard where the house was, and he got a little more nervous when he realized Riana might be a somebody. No doubt he was thinking that somebodies usually had connections that could get his ass chewed out if he took a wrong step.

Riana thanked him for his help and concern and said she would return to her friend's house for the night, then asked if she could get some clothes. The young officer hesitated only briefly, then nodded and stepped aside to let her unlock the door. It probably wasn't strictly protocol, but the Todt Hill address had him rattled. She felt a little guilty, and told the young man he could feel free to inspect anything she brought out.

He flushed and told her that wouldn't be necessary.

She slipped inside and closed the door behind her.

Goddess. Unbelievable. Her house was still standing. Other than a couple of shattered windows and the mirror broken by an Asmodai fireball, everything was just as they left it. She couldn't believe she was in the living room, looking at her things, at Cynda's things, and Merilee's, too. They would be able to retrieve their belongings and send them ahead to wherever they were reassigned on Friday—and when it was safe, the triad who replaced them could have the brownstone.

Riana's stomach clenched at that thought, but she held her emotions in check. What had to be, had to be. At least something had been preserved after last night, and she and her triad wouldn't be starting over completely when they got to their new home.

Riana ran to the kitchen and got some trash bags and duct tape. Then she hurried upstairs and taped the plastic over the broken windows to offer the house a little protection in case it rained. To make Merilee feel better, she grabbed her some clothes and a few books from her archive, including the most current stack of notebooks pertaining to the Latch case.

When she returned to ground level, she rummaged through one of the closets until she found a big enough suitcase, and packed Merilee's things inside along with a few extra outfits for Cynda and Cynda's cleaning gear for her sword. The fire Sibyl hated not having a perfectly polished sword, and the gear would be as much comfort to her as Merilee's research notebooks would be to Merilee. Then Riana went downstairs, picked out a few outfits for herself, and piled them on the steps.

When she finished, she knew she didn't have anything else to do except check the lab and read the results of the advanced analysis she had run on Creed's DNA. Her legs felt too heavy to walk down the hallway, and the brownstone suddenly felt too chilly and dark.

Riana folded her arms.

She could always pitch the sample and tell the Sibyls it went bad, maybe destroyed by shock waves from the explosive Asmodai attack.

Like anyone would believe me.

She shook her head.

"I know Creed," she said aloud. "Whatever he is, we'll manage. He needs to know." She made herself start walking down the hallway toward the lab. "I need to know."

She reached the door and opened it, then stepped inside and turned on the lights. Her attention immediately fixed on the cell, on the mattress and jumbled blankets she and Creed had left behind after their incredible sex. Riana walked to her private jail and put her hands on the bars as she gazed at the mattress.

Her whole body responded to the memory of Creed making love to her. Her arms and breasts tingled, and she got wet just thinking about how it felt to have the man inside her, to have him all to herself.

Goddess, but she wanted him again, and right now.

Her chest started to ache, and her throat tightened.

When would she get to have Creed like that again?

Would she?

"Stop it." She let go of the bars and pressed her hands against her eyes to blot out the sight of the cell, then made herself turn away, toward the main work area.

Once she walked to the first workbench, the feel and smell of the room captured her, and she went on autopilot. First, she flicked on the terminal the Sibyls used for genetic comparisons. It was online with a powerful mainframe located in one of the Motherhouses. For a moment, Riana worried that the mainframe wouldn't be operational because of the Legion attacks, but the familiar emblem—mortar, pestle, and broom against the dark crescent moon—blazed to life almost as fast as the terminal booted up.

Riana made herself activate the connection between the terminal and the computer storing the results of the genetic analysis. She selected the file marked *Lowell, Creed,* and holding her breath, she started the data transfer.

Seconds later, the mainframe acknowledged receipt. Names of databases scrolled by at lightning speed, followed by streams of numbers as the advanced technology did its job. Riana caught her breath as matches flashed up on the right side of the terminal screen. One, then two, then three, then four, then five.

Her heart flipped against her chest, and she wanted to scream.

Riana realized she had been hoping there wouldn't be any definitive genetic matches, that Creed's origins and makeup would just stay a mystery. Mysteries, they could live with.

But realities?

Three minutes later, the terminal display informed her that the match process was complete.

Heart pounding, mouth dry, Riana stared at the machine. Her hand itched to touch the screen and select the hard-copy option, but . . .

After a few more seconds, she forced her muscles to move, punched the correct touch-sensitive key, then waited for her high-speed printer to spit out the full results. She grabbed each page as it whistled out of the machine.

Sibling match. Jacob Latch.
Parent match. Davin Latch.
Parent match. Raven Latch.

Riana stared at the first three pages, not believing what she saw despite the intricate proofs and graphs supporting each statement. The Sibyl mainframe had pulled three matches out of the NYPD database—all related to the Latch murder.

"Creed shares DNA with the Latch family," Riana said, listening to the hollow, unreal sound of the words.

How could that be?

How could Creed be related to that poor, dead child—to those people?

And if he was related to them, how could he not *know* that? What were all those records Merilee had found on his mother and grandmother?

She squinted at the papers, one at a time. Each data sheet warned of anomalies, or extraneous strands of DNA that didn't match known human genetic codes, or codes from any known supernatural species.

Still a mystery, then—but there were two more pages to go.

The fourth and fifth pages were marked as partial experimental matches, meaning that Creed's genetic anomalies were consistent with theoretical models developed by Sibyls dedicated to DNA research.

Riana really, really didn't want to look at those sheets, but she knew she had to. The lab seemed so quiet, so uncannily still. Her breath echoed in her ears.

Stomach churning, she read the first page.

It was a study out of the Russian Motherhouse, positing what combination of codes Asmodai DNA would have to contain, given the appearance and abilities of the demons.

"Asmodai," Riana mumbled. Her lips felt numb. "He can't be Asmodai. That's not possible."

The data agreed with her to some extent, noting only a partial match to the profile.

At best, Creed was only half Asmodai.

Riana didn't know whether to be relieved or hysterical. Her hands trembled, and the papers crinkled in her fingers.

The answer had to be in the second study, the sheet she hadn't read, but how could she stand to look at it?

Half Asmodai . . . and half . . . what?

She squeezed the pages until the Asmodai study tore at one edge.

"I told him I loved him."

Why did she feel so disloyal?

"He loves me. He *loves* me."

Riana shivered as if fingers of ice were resting on her neck. She had to close her eyes, count to twenty, and imagine the landscape around Motherhouse Russia before she relaxed enough to brave that second page.

She started with the header, announcing that the experimental match came from a Greek Motherhouse think-tank study positing how DNA from a Curson would look, if such a being could be created in modern times.

Oh, Goddess. Oh, no.

Riana couldn't read any further. She crumpled the papers in her hand.

A Curson.

She had studied those in her own training. They had been common in ancient days, but fallen out of use as society became more enlightened and aware.

Cursons were half-human, half-demon.

Asmodai were made with blood and the elements, but only a small amount of blood, and a few drops from any adult would do the trick.

Cursons were a completely different story.

Fighting a wave of nausea, Riana sat on the lab floor. She cradled the papers in her arms and rocked slowly, back and forth, back and forth.

To make a Curson, only the blood of a child with elemental talent—all of the blood in that child's body—would do.

But so few children had untapped elemental talents today.

How did Creed's creators find a child with abilities strong enough to warrant sacrifice?

Riana kept rocking. The answer skirted the back of her mind, but she couldn't grasp it, or maybe she just didn't want to. Not yet.

In ancient days, dark priests had taken concubines to breed children from their own bloodline, to ensure elemental gifts. Those children were sacrificed by ritual. Part of their blood formed the protective circles and elemental regulations necessary to create Asmodai, while the rest of the blood was mingled with pure traces of earth, air, fire, and water. The mixture was locked onto a talisman, and implanted in donor wombs as newly created fetuses.

The births were always twinned, and the donor womb, the birth mother, always died. No human female could survive giving birth to two Cursons.

So, Creed was both created and born—and so was his missing twin brother.

Their mother must have been a Latch employee or a Legion follower. And Creed's grandmother. Did she know what her daughter had agreed to bring into the world? The poor woman. No human caregiver could survive the puberty of one Curson, much less two of them.

Riana's mind spun in slow, sick circles.

Her thoughts fixed on the talisman, the object around which Creed's demon essence had been entwined while his doomed host carried him to term.

The signet ring.

It's always been mine.

Isn't that what Creed and the *other* told her when she asked where he got the ring?

And he'd been telling the truth. Creed likely came out of his surrogate mother's womb with the ring attached to his body in some fashion. His twin brother must have a token, too, perhaps a different one. If they took off the talismans and held them in their own hands long enough to complete their transformations . . .

If no one else held the talismans to control the demons when they appeared, the demons inside Creed and his brother would ultimately return to their makers.

They would return to Senator Latch and his wife.

Riana felt like a massive, ghostly fist had punched her right in the gut. "Creed doesn't just look like a demon when the *other* comes. He *is* a demon. Half, at least. I'm in love with a half demon."

She bent forward and barely kept from vomiting, then threw the papers away from her like they were on fire. She wanted to go stomp the words into the stone floor, but what good would that do? Truth was truth, wasn't it?

And minutes from now, hours at the most, one of the Motherhouse adepts or one of the Mothers themselves would review the transmission log and realize that Riana had found a Curson.

Maybe if she went straight back to the safe house and had the fire Sibyls send her to Mother Yana, she could—

"I could what?" She hugged herself and shivered, staring at the floor. "Explain how I've been sleeping with a Curson? But they should give him a break because he doesn't even know what he is—or what kind of psychos created him?"

Raven Latch and Davin Latch had to be members of the Legion, and a lot higher up the food chain than their employee, Frith Gregory.

Council members? She shook her head. Probably.

All this concern about Alisa's arrest. It was a show. A smoke screen to keep the Sibyls pacified until the Legion finalized its plans to destroy them.

And she couldn't forget the political capital Latch had earned from the outpouring of public sympathy.

The bastard.

Riana couldn't stop shaking.

Raven and Davin Latch had used Alisa and her triad, arranged the museum break-in to get the dagger and perhaps a mortar or other objects of power they needed for the ritual, then set Alisa up to take the fall when they sacrificed their own son to achieve—what?

"Goddess. They didn't just have a child with elemental talents to sacrifice. They had objects of power."

What did they use those stolen artifacts and that child's blood to spawn?

No doubt they made something, just like they made Creed. Maybe worse.

And what if Creed had taken off his ring before he met Riana, and returned to the Latch house the night the boy died? What if Creed or his brother were the demons who attacked and killed Jacob Latch?

She had to talk to Alisa. Not Friday. Now.

But first . . .

Riana knew she had to go back to the safe house and spill all this to her triad and to the Mothers. She would rather die, but she had no choice. She wasn't dealing with unknowns and possibilities anymore. This was reality, and reality didn't bend to suit her will.

The floor beneath her feet shook, and Riana had to sit still for a few minutes to collect herself and get her energy under control. When she stopped trembling enough to move, she crawled to the printed sheets, picked them up, smoothed them out, folded them, and slipped them into the pocket of her slacks.

She got to her feet slowly, fighting a wave of dizziness and despair. More than anything, she wanted to run out of the lab and down the hallway, throw herself into her bed, and not get up for a week, or until the Legion sent more Asmodai to kill her.

The image of the young police officer flickered through her consciousness, and she became aware of how long she had been in the brownstone. Whether or not she thought she could survive it, she had to get her clothes, pack them in the suitcase, and leave.

Right that second, Riana never wanted to return to her lab or her house. She sure didn't want to go to the safe house on Staten Island. She reached in her shirt, grabbed hold of her crescent pendant, and for the first time in all the years it had rested around her neck, she thought about tearing it off and throwing it across the room.

Damn the pendant. Damn the tattoo on her arm. Damn what it stood for—all of it!

Sometimes we have to do things we haven't the courage to face, moya smelaya. Mother Yana's voice rang through Riana's mind, as clearly as if the oldest Russian Mother had materialized right beside Riana, to urge her once more to find the reservoir of her own courage. *Sometimes we have to lose people. Such is the way of our world.*

"Our world sucks," Riana whispered.

She dropped the pendant back into place and left the lab without closing the door or turning off the lights.

32

Andy sat back, shying away from Senator Latch's implied accusation that they had been in Frith Gregory's apartment.

She was *definitely* giving the wrong message with her body posture. Practically screaming, *Okay, yeah, we made the little weasel disappear!*

Creed tried to right the ship by forcing himself forward in his chair, despite the *other*'s panic at the aggressive move. "Frith Gregory was a member of the Legion, Senator. Did you know that?"

"*Was* a member?" Latch smiled again, and this time the expression was barely civil. "Don't you people usually pounce when suspects speak about victims in the past tense?"

The library door burst open.

Creed nearly jumped out of his skin at the sound, and Andy let out a squeak. They both turned to see Raven Latch striding across the room.

At the sight of her, the *other* went into barely suppressed fits. Creed had to fight every muscle in his body not to jump from his chair and walk straight out of the Latch house. He couldn't even stand up when she came into the room, even though years of habit demanded that he do just that.

Damn, he hoped he wasn't glowing.

The *other* didn't want to be here in the worst way, and Creed was starting to agree. So was Andy, judging by the fixed, anxious look on her face.

Who are the suspects here? Shit.

Raven Latch still looked every bit the aging fashion

model, even in pink silk warm-ups with her streaked blond hair pulled back in a ponytail. Her blue eyes flashed at her husband as she approached his desk, and her smile wasn't at all warm. "If I hadn't heard from one of the guards that we had visitors, I wouldn't have known," she said in a waspish voice. "Honestly, Davin, can't you function at all when Frith isn't at work?"

Senator Latch didn't stand, and he barely looked at his wife. "I was just discussing Frith Gregory's absence with the detectives." He studied Creed again. "Perhaps these two are taking their affiliation with the Sibyls a bit too seriously. Damned inconvenient, Alisa's arrest. Squelched our best source of information and inflamed the bunch of them. Almost forced our hand before we were ready."

"We agreed not to be confrontational." Raven Latch's admonishment was sharp as she stopped at her husband's desk. "Van Cortlandt Park, Trinity Church—confrontational just doesn't work well unless we have overwhelming force on our side."

Her words slammed into Creed's shocked mind.

Andy's face changed at the same instant. *Bastards,* her expression said. *Guilty bastards!*

Before either of them could react, Raven Latch turned around. Instantly, her attention fixed on Creed, and his urge to get the hell out of the townhouse doubled.

"They were asking about the Legion and our son." Senator Latch pressed the tips of his fingers together and once more leaned forward on his desk.

Andy twitched like she might jump over the back of her chair. Creed gripped the arms of his seat. He felt disoriented and half-terrified. Not normal feelings. Not himself.

"Our first son," Senator Latch added. "They've heard a rumor that our baby wasn't stillborn—that the Legion might have killed him."

Raven Latch's chilly blue eyes widened. She looked at Creed with a mixture of pity and something like affection.

His skin crawled.

"My sweet, confused Curson," she said as Latch got up and circled around behind her, blocking the path to the library door. "If only your birth mother hadn't been such a cowardly, backstabbing bitch, your questions would have had answers years ago."

Andy stood.

So did Creed.

He wasn't sure he was hearing right. And if he heard the woman right, he wasn't sure she was sane.

Curson.

That word again.

Frith Gregory had called him that, and now Raven Latch, too.

Creed's throat went dry. The *other* rampaged back and forth, so active Creed was sure the beast was crushing his bones to dust. He started to ask what the hell a Curson was, but a wave of dizziness made him clamp his mouth shut.

The next wave almost forced him to sit back down—and he felt pressure against his brain. Definite. Forceful.

Just like he felt when Frith Gregory had tried to zap all the water out of his body—only much worse, and somehow dirty. Tainted.

Totally wrong.

Creed tried to shake off the feeling. He even let the *other* come forward a fraction, but the sensation remained and got even stronger. Imaginary hands groped him everywhere at once, and pawed through his thoughts, his memories, his very being.

He shook his head.

The forced intimacy repelled him, revolted him. He battled to stop it, resist it, but he couldn't.

Andy gripped the desk to steady herself, and Creed knew something was happening to her, too.

Damnit. I have to help her.

But he couldn't. All he could do was try to push away the oily fingers picking and prodding at his insides.

Raven Latch's smile was arctic, even though Creed's instinct told him she was trying to show him concern. He staggered back a step.

"Don't you know what happened to our precious firstborn?" Raven Latch moved toward him, making him back up again. Andy lurched to the far end of the desk and looked like she wanted to vomit.

"You're him, Creed." Raven Latch reached for him, but Creed leaned away from her touch. "You and your brother are both made from our baby. You're Cursons. We created you, my husband and I, with help from one of our devoted employees who volunteered to be the donor womb, until she lost faith in our plan and kidnapped you. Stupid bitch thought she might live through the birth with her mother's help."

"To be technical about it," Senator Latch added from behind Creed and Andy, "you and Dominic carry the blood of our firstborn. You're our special twins, half-Asmodai and half-human, born from a servant womb. That's my ring you're wearing on your finger. Your brother has the chain."

Raven Latch's awful smile went on and on. "Dominic found his way back to us, but he refused to retrieve you. He told us he was in contact with you via e-mail, that you were sympathetic to the Legion's cause, but he said your return would have more meaning if you followed your own path. I must admit he was correct. Your connections with the NYPD will be quite valuable."

"Dominic and you aren't what we hoped, of course." Senator Latch sounded every bit the disappointed father. Creed couldn't stand to listen to the bastard, but between the force pushing on his mind and the rabid struggling of the *other*, he couldn't move at all. "Cursons were failures for our purposes. Long-lasting, durable—but too costly to create for the benefit, and too independent. Still, you're ours, and we will find a place for you, just as we did for Dominic."

Raven Latch opened her arms. "Welcome to your true home, Creed." She lowered her arms and glanced at Andy. "Let's take care of her and discuss your future."

When Creed didn't respond, Raven Latch said, "Kill her."

Who is she talking to—me? The other?

Andy made a choking sound.

Creed figured she was finally puking. He wanted to barf, too, but he still couldn't move too well. His brain felt like a roiling stew.

Dominic. They talked about him like they see him every day.

Is he here?

No. He's in a cult.

Is this the cult? The fucking Legion?

And Gregory. What had Frith Gregory said back at the brownstone?

Curson. You won't hurt me. I know your true parents.

"I thought he was kidding." Creed heard his own voice in echoes. The *other* roared and pushed back at the power desecrating the most private parts of Creed's mind, but it couldn't throw off the attack. He felt like he was being stripped naked, beaten, taken against his will in ways that turned his gut inside out.

"You—you're both full of shit." He fought to keep himself from yelling and hitting anything close to him. "You're fucking insane."

Raven Latch moved to her husband's side. "Come here, Creed," she said in a harsh, commanding voice. "If you don't walk on your own, I'll have you carried."

Andy's choking got louder. Creed finally managed to turn his head—and realized his partner was clawing at her throat and turning gray-white.

She really was choking—no. Something or some force he couldn't see was squeezing the life right out of her.

The ring on Creed's finger throbbed and pulsed. The *other* rushed forward, as if to obey Raven Latch's order to go to her, but Creed kept his attention on Andy.

He had to get her out of this alive.

He could see the terror in her eyes, the horror at the mental violation they were both enduring.

Even if they got out of the library, how would they get downstairs? Out the door? One word from Latch, and those guards would open fire.

He and Andy would be full of holes before they ever made it to the street.

He reached for Andy and caught the gleam of his signet ring.

The *other* turned, confused and panicked. The beast seemed pulled between Raven Latch's command and Creed's will. It was terrified. Furious about the force intruding on his—*their*—mind.

Andy pitched forward against the desk. Her eyes seemed huge, and her face was swelling.

Dying. Right in front of me!

Creed let out a long, low shout. He shoved against the force binding his mind with all his might, and the *other* joined him.

The power wavered, then turned him loose.

Senator Latch swore and slapped his hands to the sides of his head.

Creed lunged toward Andy and struck something soft and human-feeling before he got there. He shook his head. Nothing.

Nothing but Andy.

He jumped toward her again, and at the same time, he ripped off his ring.

Just as he had at Van Cortlandt Park, he crammed the

ring into Andy's flailing hand and closed her fingers around it. She grabbed hold of his arm with her other hand and held tighter than a drowning victim. Pain erupted from every joint and muscle in his body. Creed yelled in agony but made himself keep moving.

Raven Latch rushed toward them.

Creed ignored her as he swept Andy into his arms.

As the *other* literally exploded through his skin, Creed plowed into Raven Latch like a football tackle and knocked her right on her ass. He slammed past the desk without looking back at her, then crashed through the curtained doors behind Senator Latch's desk in a shower of wood and glass.

The world started to turn black as the *other* took full control.

With a last burst of strength and self-will, Creed threw himself and Andy across the terrace and over the railing.

The last thing he saw was the fence and sidewalk rushing to meet them—from four stories below.

For Riana, the drive back to Staten Island went by too fast. The minute Riana pulled into the Todt Hill compound, things got even worse. It was obvious that something had changed.

The Sibyls working out in the yard stopped all activity to stare at her as she parked Bela's SUV—even the group using her spectroscope to scout for any sign of Asmodai activity nearby. They kept staring as she lugged her big suitcase up the sidewalk toward the mansion's front door. Groups ahead of her whispered, and when she passed them, everyone stopped talking.

Riana looked right and left, but no one met her gaze.

Goddess. Has something happened to Merilee?

Hot panic drove her forward, and she rushed up the steps and burst into the mansion.

Just the same as outside, everyone inside fell quiet and stared at her.

Riana couldn't get a full breath. She spun toward the infirmary cots.

Merilee's bed was empty.

A scream built in Riana's chest, but broke into nothing when she saw Merilee standing beside the neatly made cot, dressed in white medical scrubs that looked about three sizes too big for her. Riana ran forward, dropped the suitcase beside Merilee's bed, grabbed her triad sister, and hugged her with all her strength.

"I'm so glad you're okay, Merilee. I was scared to death!"

"Ow-ow-ow." Merilee groaned and pushed against Riana's shoulders. "You're cracking my cracked bones."

Riana let her go with a sympathetic grimace "Sorry. I thought—the way everyone's acting, I thought something might have happened to you." Her panic came flooding back. "Where's Cynda? She was gone when I got up this morning—"

"Cynda's fine." Merilee raised both hands. Her blue eyes turned misty. "She's in the conference room. Riana, I'm so sorry. I didn't do it."

Riana felt a lead weight settle on her heart all over again. She rubbed the waistband of her slacks and felt the folded papers she had brought back from the lab. "Whatever Cynda's mad about, it'll have to wait. I need to talk to the Mothers right now."

Merilee let out a breath. Tears slipped down both cheeks. "Good. Because they're waiting in the conference room with Cynda."

A slap wouldn't have shocked Riana so badly.

All the staring, silent Sibyls made perfect sense now. People were always quiet when they watched a condemned prisoner approach an execution squad. Or the new widow facing the messenger with the We-regret-to-inform-you letter in his hand.

Her voice sounded strange to her own ears as she asked, "Why . . . are the Mothers here already? What happened?"

More tears from Merilee. "When Cynda and Maura got back from Creed's apartment at noon, they went straight back to the conference room and opened the channels. The Mothers have been waiting to see you for over an hour."

"Cynda and Maura went to Creed's apartment?" A buzzing started in Riana's ears, and she had to center herself to keep the earth from rattling. "Why?"

Merilee eased herself down to sit on the edge of her cot. She looked completely miserable. "Cynda and I were planning to go before that whole Frith Gregory thing, and then the Asmodai attack put us off again. Don't you remember us talking about that?"

Riana rubbed the bridge of her nose. "No—yes, wait, I do. That conversation seems a million miles away."

"I'm so sorry," Merilee said again. "But you better not keep them waiting any longer."

Numbly, Riana nodded. She started to walk away, then turned back and gestured to the suitcase. "The house is intact. I brought your most recent research notebooks." When she swallowed, the growing lump in her throat almost choked her. "I thought—I thought you might need them."

Merilee gripped the side of her cot, hung her head, and cried harder.

Great. I thought I was finally doing something right.

Riana turned back toward the far side of the living room, walked out of the infirmary area, and stepped through an archway into the hall. To her left lay the kitchens, a full bath, a half bath, and breakfast room, and a formal dining room/banquet hall. To her right was a study, the library they used for an archives room. At the far end of the hall, past the row of impressive oil paintings illuminated by individual portrait spotlights, lay the large conference room.

The room's carved cherry door was closed.

Riana sucked in air and tried to muster her courage. The air seemed too still, and the house smelled of spices and perfumes and sweat, and faintly of antiseptic and bandages. Riana wondered what fear smelled like, and desperation.

Something like this, probably.

What had Cynda found at Creed's apartment that made her summon the Mothers?

She touched the papers in her waistband.

Could it be any worse than what I found?

She wasn't sure she wanted to know, but she didn't have much choice.

After a few seconds of centering herself, she reached under her shirt, removed the two daggers she was carrying, and placed them on a nearby table that held a sickle and a bunch of swords. With a silent prayer to the Goddess, Riana started down the hall, only to be stopped by Merilee's desperate cry for her to wait.

The air Sibyl came hobbling into the hallway, carrying two of her notebooks. Her face looked pale and strained from the effort of moving, but before Riana could send her back to her bed, Merilee said, "You're not going in there alone."

"Cynda's in there." Riana reached out and took Merilee's notebooks for her. "You should rest."

"You're not going in there alone," Merilee repeated. Her voice shook, but her gaze was determined.

Riana's heart sank as she read the meaning in Merilee's statement. She fumbled for her crescent pendant and felt the warm metal pressed into her fingers.

Cynda . . . Cynda wasn't in that room as her friend, as her chosen sister?

No . . .

But there it was, etched across Merilee's sad, tired face.
My triad has fractured.

She stared at Merilee, then at the door, already feeling
the loss like the death of part of her soul. Then she looked
down at the pendant in her hand.

Mother Yana was waiting for her.

Mother Yana would expect Riana to walk in and face the
results of her choices. She would expect Riana to show
courage and at least honor her teachings.

That much, Riana knew she had to do.

She let go of the pendant, tucked Merilee's notebooks
under one arm, and gave her other arm to Merilee to help
her down the hall. When they reached the door, Riana
didn't hesitate or give in to her desire to run away and
never come back. She turned the handle, pulled the door
open, and walked straight into the conference room, with
Merilee right beside her.

Sunlight streamed into the room from a wall of floor-to-
ceiling windows with the blinds wide open. The wood paneling looked dusty, and the hardwood floors needed a little
buff and shine. A long polished maple table commanded
the room, and in the padded leather chairs surrounding it,
six women were seated. The three nearest were the most
disconcerting. Closest to Riana on the right was Mother
Yana, wearing her brown robes and looking as much like
ancient paintings of the Russian crone Baba Yaga as she always did. On Riana's left sat the oldest Irish Mother, who
reminded Riana of Yoda from *Star Wars*, only with bright
green robes and longer hair. Beside Yoda-ette was the oldest Greek Mother, a complete contrast to her Irish counterpart with her long legs and arms, her form-fitting blue
robe, her sweeping mane of white curls, and her bright,
mischievous blue eyes. Though she was wrinkled from the
years now, rumor had it that the Greek Mother was once as
beautiful—and as dangerous—as Helen of Troy.

Behind the mothers sat Camille from Alisa James's North

Bronx triad, Maura from the destroyed South Manhattan triad, and farthest away, with her head turned toward the windows, Cynda. All three fire Sibyls were in traditional leathers, but as was tradition in a formal conference, they had left their weapons outside the room on the hall table.

Thank the Goddess for small favors.

Riana couldn't read Cynda's posture, or sense her emotions. Nothing was burning. Nothing was smoking. Cynda looked deflated somehow, as if she had no spark or flame left inside her. Riana would have preferred seeing Cynda furious and smoldering. Anything but this. Her heart ached from the wish to go to Cynda and hold her and apologize for not listening to her advice, for making her feel left out, for making her feel insecure—anything and everything she might have done wrong as the mortar of her triad.

Instead, she pulled out the chair nearest the door and helped Merilee sit down before she fell down. Riana took the chair beside Merilee's, placed Merilee's notebooks on the table, then pulled out the papers she had brought from her lab and placed them on the table, too. Merilee opened the top notebook and turned some pages, and Riana recognized the section she had read about Creed's history before Creed and Andy brought Frith Gregory to the brownstone.

Merilee pushed the notebook to Riana, and Riana slipped it under Creed's DNA analysis.

Reaching deep for the courage that always tried to elude her, Riana forced herself to meet Mother Yana's fierce, steady gaze and slide the notebook and analysis printouts across the table for her scrutiny.

To anyone else, the Russian Mother's face would have looked impassive, but Riana saw the minute quirk of the lips and brows that told her Mother Yana at least approved of the way she came into the room and handed over her findings without blinking or flinching. Everything was a test with the old woman, and Riana never knew quite when—or if—she passed.

Maura had a stack of papers in front of her. She shoved them toward Riana. "We took these e-mails off Creed Lowell's computer. You need to read them. Now."

Riana accepted the papers, but she didn't rush. It made her feel dirty and wrong to look at Creed's private things without his invitation. Her hand hovered over Merilee's notebook and the lab papers, and she let out a breath.

DNA profiles.

How much more private did things get?

And she was about to share them.

Before she could second-guess herself, she slid Merilee's notebook and her findings toward Mother Yana, who picked up the top paper without comment and began to read.

Riana glanced down at the e-mails.

They were from dominic297@tempmail.com. Creed's brother Dominic. She thumbed through the stack. All from Dominic to Creed. All within the last year.

The first one, dated almost eleven months before Riana met Creed, read,

Finally happy.
You need to join me, brother. We have big things ahead of us.
Yours in enlightenment,
Nick

"Yours in enlightenment," Riana murmured aloud, shocked.

The signature line of the Legion.

Creed's twin, the other Curson, has already rejoined his parents.

The e-mails were spaced two to three weeks apart, and each spoke glowingly about Dominic's new "ministry," and how he desperately needed Creed's help. Each post had a phone number affixed to the bottom of it. The number was always different.

Had Creed ever dialed those numbers?

Cold dread began to weigh Riana's fingers as she turned the pages.

"Read the last one," Cynda said.

Her quiet, flat voice slammed into Riana like a sledge-hammer. When she raised her head, she saw that Cynda was still turned away from her. Cynda had her hands clenched so tightly Riana wondered if the fire Sibyl's nails were cutting into her palms.

Hardly able to concentrate, Riana returned her attention to the e-mails. She paged to the last message, and read,

> *Time is running out, brother.*
> *Change is coming. Be a part of it, or be swept away by it.*
> *Think.*
> *This is a chance to atone for the deaths that stain our souls. We can make up for those killings. We can set things right if you'll only join me.*
> *Nick*

Riana barely saw the phone number affixed below Nick's name. The other words jumped out at her like shouts con-firming her worst nightmares.

Deaths.

Killings.

Atonement.

"Creed and his brother are murderers." Maura leaned forward and put her hands on the table. "The Mothers have to take him. Tonight."

Despite the evidence in her hands, Riana wanted to argue, to insist that Creed be given a chance to explain himself.

Camille spoke before she could say anything, in a voice so weak and soft Riana had to strain to hear the words. "I've seen him. Not Creed. The other one, Nick—at the Latch house. Two or three times at least. His hair is longer." She touched her neck. "And he has a gold chain."

A few things clicked into place for Riana. "Alisa knew the truth about the Latches, didn't she?"

Camille nodded, keeping her eyes cast down. "They thought they were watching us, but we were watching them. Alisa suspected Raven Latch the moment she met her, and she knew Jacob was in terrible danger." The girl swallowed. "We just never thought—never considered that his own parents—for the sake of the Goddess. They did something to Alisa's mind that night while Bette and I were taking the outside watch—and they butchered their own child. I'm sure of it."

Cynda leaned over and put her hands over Camille's. The younger fire Sibyl seemed ready to crack at the seams, but Cynda's touch apparently reassured her enough to face Riana and ask, "Have you gone to see Alisa?"

Riana shook her head. "I didn't know I could visit her at Rikers."

Camille shivered. "When she came out of that house, something was wrong with her. She won't look me in the eye, and she doesn't say more than two words. The Latches hurt her mind, Riana. I don't know how, but it's like they opened her head and left her empty."

Riana looked at the Irish Mother and the Greek Mother, then at Mother Yana. "Why weren't we told about this?"

The Irish Mother frowned at her. "We considered it need-to-know, especially with you."

Mother Yana snorted and shoved Merilee's notebook and Riana's lab findings sideways, almost forcing them into Yoda-ette's lap. "I told you she vould be taking steps. She already knows vat he is—she has proved it the only right way. Vith science. Creed Lowell is a Curson, as I said he vould be."

The Irish Mother glared from Riana to Mother Yana, then looked down at the papers.

"She still should have told us," said the beautiful Greek

Mother. "The day she met him. Certainly after she saw him change."

Mother Yana shrugged one shoulder and gave the woman a wolflike curl of the lip. "Vat do you know? Air Sibyls." She touched her temple. "You take chances only in the mind. Fire Sibyls risk the body, yes." Mother Yana pinched at her elbow and made a rude sound of disgust. "Earth Sibyls, ve trust our instincts. Ve take real chances." She pounded her fist against her chest. "Vith our *hearts*."

The Mothers started yelling in three different languages before Riana even had a chance to process that Mother Yana was defending her. Protecting her, even.

The old woman was still her champion, after all these years, and all the disappointments Riana had laid at her knobby feet.

Cynda was finally looking at Riana, too.

Riana met Cynda's eyes as the Mothers bickered.

"Before you say anything, I asked to be reassigned." Cynda's lips trembled. "You don't have to bother. I did it for you."

Merilee blew out a noisy breath, and Riana stared at Cynda, confused. "What? Why would I ask to have you reassigned?"

"Because I'm against your boyfriend." Cynda gestured to the Mothers. "And I summoned them and told them everything. I knew you'd hate me, but it had to be done."

Despite all her pain and befuddlement, Riana wanted to hug Cynda, then maybe shake her and slap her a few times. She became aware of the weight of the crescent pendant hanging between her breasts, of the waxing moon, rising to its power, that Mother Yana had given her so many years ago. Riana realized she understood the symbol in a whole new way—how the moon was ever-changing, and even at its darkest, at its weakest, it was always cycling back toward its full, bright state.

Trust myself. Trust my instincts.

Even if part of me thinks I'm crazy . . .

"Cynda, you did the right thing." Riana leaned forward to make sure Cynda could hear her over the ranting Mothers, who had degenerated into ethnic slurs involving Russian wolves, Irish cows, and Greek asses, with and without olives inserted. "It hurts, but I totally understand. You're my triad sister and I love you. I would never send you away for doing what you thought was best. I would never send you away for being who you are."

Cynda's lips parted. She knotted her hands together, and tears rimmed her eyes. For a moment, Riana imagined that Cynda looked just the way she must have at the age of six, when her terrified and slightly singed family abandoned her at the gates of Motherhouse Ireland and fled. Color came back to her cheeks, and smoke rose slowly from her elbows and shoulders.

Merilee made a sniffling sound, and when Riana looked at her, she was grinning and crying all at the same time.

Riana had the distinct sensation of her broom and pestle settling firmly back into the mortar's stone bowl.

There. That's better. That's where they belong.

She reached past her mortification and grief over the e-mails, and she smiled at Cynda.

Cynda's return smile was nervous, but wide.

"We're losing focus here," Maura shouted over the din. Flames erupted across the center of the table, separating the three Mothers and ending their debate.

Maura tucked a shock of brown hair behind her ear and closed her eyes as she pulled back her fire energy. The flames on the table sputtered and went out, and Maura turned her focus to Riana.

"Where did Creed and his partner go today?"

Riana had to scramble through the events of the last day to remember the first step in Creed and Andy's plan. Her eyes widened, and breathing got hard all over again.

"They went to interview Davin Latch." She pushed back from the table. "Goddess. He walked right into the lion's den."

The Irish Mother stood and put her hand on Camille's shoulder. "Or he went home, child. To his parents and his twin brother."

"This safe house has been compromised," the Greek Mother said as she got to her feet. "We must withdraw all of you, back to the Motherhouses immediately. New York City will have to fight or fall on its own."

Merilee held up a hand. It took her forever to stand. "Wait a minute. We have no idea what Creed and Andy are doing—and we can't just abandon them!"

Riana's mind raced as she looked to Mother Yana for guidance.

From somewhere in the safe house, chimes started to ring.

Seconds later, shouts rang out from the yard of the compound, then from the living room area.

Riana groped for daggers she didn't have. She saw Cynda, Maura, Camille, and the Mothers doing the same.

The door to the conference room sprang open. Andy staggered inside, doing her best to help support Creed's weight.

Riana let out a little cry at the sight of him. He was dressed in what looked like jeans just off the rack, a new blue shirt, and a new blue jacket. The shirt and jacket weren't torn, but they were already stained with blood. A lot of it. His eyes were closed, and he had his hand pressed over his left side. His face was as pale as death itself.

"Latch and his wife are dirty," Andy gasped. Her expression told Riana they had been through something horrible, something soul-damaging. Andy's red curls hung in matted rings around her dirty face. Her too-big black leather jumpsuit was torn along one side. She had a blazing patch of road rash showing through the torn edges, and her throat was bruised as if a giant pair of hands had almost choked her. "Legion. Brain-raping bastards—they're Legion! We had to jump off their terrace. Fourth floor." She held up the tatters of her shirt, then gestured to her road rash and to Creed's injury. "Creed landed on their front fence. I would have brought him sooner, but he wouldn't come until I helped him put on more clothes—even though he's bleeding right through that jacket."

Riana sensed rather than saw the Mothers move as Andy spoke, forming a circle around Creed and Andy, with Maura and Camille taking up defensive positions on either side of the room.

"Ve vill take him vith us." Mother Yana gestured to Creed's side. "See to his vounds."

Riana gasped. *No. Don't take him. Don't touch him!*

Creed's eyes snapped open. He looked at Riana, the Mothers, and then at the table. She realized he could see the e-mails Cynda had printed, and the papers from her lab.

It took him only a second to add up what was happening in the conference room, and the meaning of Mother Yana's not-so-subtle invitation. He looked at Riana, then, and she wanted to tear out her own heart when she saw the crushing pain in his eyes.

You let them do this, he said with that horrible expression. *I trusted you with my life, with my love. I thought you trusted me.*

"Creed." Riana started toward him, but he shrank back, almost yanking Andy off her feet.

"Stay away from me," he said through clenched teeth, his voice hoarse and labored.

His words hit Riana like a slap. Her head snapped back, and she grabbed her chest out of reflex.

Creed let go of Andy and stood on his own. She knew he saw her pain, but his eyes offered no comfort.

Before Riana could say anything else, Andy lunged forward, grabbed Mother Yana, and jammed her SIG against the Mother's temple.

"Oh, Goddess." Riana couldn't believe what she was seeing. She felt like her entire world was catching fire, only she didn't have the power to put out the flames.

Riana had never seen Andy look so serious, or so angry. Andy glared directly at Riana and said, "If any of you so much as spark my ass, I'll take her out. Don't try me. Not after this morning."

To show she didn't intend to challenge Andy, Riana slowly held up her hands.

Andy glanced at Creed. "What's happening here?"

"We aren't welcome." Creed pressed both hands against his side, and Riana saw blood run across his fingers. "It's time to go."

Sibyls were gathering in the doorway. Sibyls with weapons at the ready. Angry Sibyls. Merilee had her face on the table with her arms covering her head as best she could with all her injuries. Maura and Camille moved slightly, just enough to block Creed's path to the door.

Riana was caught between misery at Creed's expression and words, and shock that Mother Yana hadn't broken both of Andy's wrists.

Maybe Mother Yana sensed the same thing Riana did, that Andy wasn't herself, that she'd been hurt today in ways it might take her years to heal.

Creed met Riana's gaze. His dark, sad eyes let her know the depths of her betrayal.

"I'm sorry, honey," he said, anger laced through every syllable. "I guess this is goodbye."

With that, he yanked off his ring.

Cynda shouted as Andy shoved Mother Yana to the floor, caught the ring Creed threw to her, and yelled, "Go now!" to the golden, muscled *other* ripping its way out of Creed's human form.

The *other* snatched Andy off her feet, barreled straight at the wall of windows, and crashed through the glass.

Riana dropped to her knees as a curtain of arrows, daggers, knives, and jagged metal stars went flying out the broken window after them.

Cynda blasted the weapons out of the air with a massive jet of flames.

When the Irish Mother whirled on her, Cynda said, "They might have hit Andy!"

Cynda looked at Riana then, and her split-second wink said it all.

Heart hammering with fear and relief, Riana watched the *other* run faster than any known creature could run.

Go. Don't stop. Keep going!

The *other* took Andy straight to Riana's Jeep, put Andy in the passenger seat, temporarily shielding her from the Sibyls charging toward him, blades drawn, then thundered around to the driver's side and got behind the wheel.

Before the attacking Sibyls could reach the Jeep, it spun around and shot down the compound driveway, smashing through the closed metal gates like they didn't even exist.

Everyone started talking at once, but as soon as Riana saw that Creed and Andy had gotten away clean, she crawled over to Mother Yana and helped the Russian Mother pull herself to a sitting position on the floor.

"Are you hurt?" Riana touched Mother Yana's arms, checking her wrists and fingers gently.

"No." She beamed at Riana. "Fine. No vorries." She tapped Riana's blouse, her finger pushing against the concealed crescent pendant. "You pulled your triad back together, *moyo chudo*. I am proud."

Moyo chudo. My wonder. That was a nice change from *moya smelaya,* my courageous one—Mother Yana's perpetual encouragement for Riana to buck up and face her fears about being a leader, to finally learn to trust herself and her own instincts.

Riana smiled back at her, then narrowed her eyes. "I trained with you, Mother. You could have gotten away from Andy with no effort at all."

Mother Yana's eyes twinkled. She winked at Riana and gave her cheek a quick pinch. All she said was, "I know."

33

Creed hung up Andy's cell as Andy drove Riana's Jeep through Queens.

"What did he say?" Andy asked without taking her eyes off the road.

"Corey James is calling Alisa's lawyers. They'll make the arrangements and meet us at Rikers, if we don't get arrested first." He rubbed the spot where his fence-wound had been before he let the *other* out at the safe house. He was still cold as hell, and weak from blood loss, but becoming the *other* had almost totally healed the gash in his side.

Too bad shifting in and out of demon-form didn't heal everything—but at least they had bought enough clothing to keep him from going naked between transformations.

They drove in silence for a long time.

Creed missed Andy's chatter and banter, but all that seemed dead inside her right now. He alternated between worrying about her, wondering whether or not Corey James and Alisa's defense team would beat them to Rikers, and trying to force all thoughts and images of Riana Dumain out of his head.

Riana let the Sibyls raid my apartment, my computer. My private mail, for God's sake. How was I supposed to know Dominic's cult was the Legion? If it is. If those assholes weren't just screwing with my mind.

As for Riana, when Creed had looked into her eyes, he had seen her intentions. She would have let the Mothers take him. She was ready to hand him over to those crones.

Guess I know where I stand with her, and it's sure as hell not where I thought.

Creed caught his scowl in the side mirror and scrubbed his finger against his chin. He had cut himself twice with that stupid disposable razor. When they had gotten back into Brooklyn from Staten Island, he and Andy had gotten her some clothes and used a fast-food bathroom to clean up and comb their hair. The Sibyls could report the Jeep stolen at any time, or just come after them. Then there was the Legion, Senator Latch and his harpy wife, the department—hell, half the world might be hunting for them by now.

It made perfect sense to go to Rikers Island. If one group or the other caught up with them, it would be a short trip to the cells with their names emblazoned over the doors.

Creed knew he ought to tell the Mothers, Riana, and all the Sibyls to get fucked, but that wouldn't change anything about the Legion, or the very real danger to Alisa James. The wrongly accused Sibyl was a captive target of no further use to the Legion. Now that Creed and Andy had experienced a taste of the mental invasion Alisa no doubt endured at the hands of the Latch duo and the Legion, they knew why her husband was so distraught. Why her interviews were so flat and her defense team was thinking about an insanity plea. The Legion hurt the woman's mind, maybe broke it like they almost broke Andy's.

"Nobody was there to save Alisa from those bastards," Andy muttered as she piloted them into Long Island City. "I thought I would go insane if that . . . attack . . . didn't stop." Her hands shook on the steering wheel. "And if it's any consolation, I'd like to slap the shit out of Riana, too."

Creed's jaw clenched against his will, and he made himself take a breath. "I don't want to talk about her. Any of them. This—what we're doing now—has nothing to do with Riana or the Sibyls."

Andy nodded. She didn't say anything or even change her position until they fell in behind the 2:10 Q101 bus carrying visitors across the Rikers Island Bridge. Once they were over the water, she glanced left at the stony bank of the East River, and Creed saw her blink at the blaze of the afternoon sun on the no doubt frigid gray water. Creed wondered what was going on in his partner's head. Andy had been too quiet and too distant since they left the Latch house. For a second back on Todt Hill, he had been worried that Andy really *would* shoot that Russian crone.

Andy's hurt with no bruises to show for it—and now she doesn't even have her friends to help her, except for me. A demon-thing. A Curson. How does she feel about that?

Creed felt a new wave of anger toward Riana and the Sibyls. He thought about losing the woman he loved, about finding out his brother might be in the Legion, and the whole Latch true-parent bullshit.

Everything was just . . . broken.

The cool air over the river wafted through the Jeep vents. Andy slowed behind the Q101 as they approached the entrance checkpoint. "If Latch called the department, our shields might get us detained. What if the lawyers can't get permission to see Alisa?"

"Then we'll go in without permission," Creed said.

Exhaust from the bus rolled across the Jeep's windshield.

Andy gave Creed a look, but she didn't argue.

Corey James looked much as Creed remembered him from their interview two weeks earlier—two weeks? Shit. It felt like two months. James's brown hair had grown out a little from its military cut. The man looked wrecked from worrying about his wife after Creed's phone call, and Creed understood that in ways he didn't want to think about.

James met them in the Rikers Island parking lot with a cadre of four lawyers, all with similar pressed black suits and expensive briefcases. James had told Creed on the telephone that the men were retired Army, like James, and they knew him from the old days. They also knew what was really going on, and they were ready to play their part in this charade. Impressive, considering the possible consequences. Creed knew then that Corey James had to be a man who inspired loyalty.

The lawyers didn't ask any questions. They just pulled out their Unified Court System passes, signed the logbook, got Corey James a day-pass, and gave the necessary info about Alisa's book and case number. Creed and Andy presented their shields, and Creed felt a wash of relief when nobody started yelling or pulling out handcuffs.

After Creed and Andy locked up their weapons in a security office, the lawyers walked them straight through the metal detectors and out of the Control Building, two on either side. Corey James led the way. As they entered the Rose M. Singer Center, Creed figured that to anyone paying attention, they looked like detectives going to question an arraigned suspect, with her lawyers present.

The attorneys secured them a visually monitored conference room that smelled like pine cleanser and bleach, and assured them that by law and policy, without their permission, audio-monitoring couldn't be used during attorney visits. Then the lawyers positioned themselves at the scarred, gum-infested conference table a few seats away from Creed and Corey James. Andy sat down on the side of the table farthest from the door.

The setup looked authentic enough. At least Creed hoped it did. And he hoped Andy held up for this. Her eyes kept darting right and left, and now and then, her hands started shaking again. She finally put them in her lap.

A few minutes later, two female guards opened the conference room door and brought in Alisa James.

Creed had to work not to suck in his breath as he stood in deference to the lady entering the room. Corey James was on his feet, too, as were the lawyers.

The woman looked a little like Riana, but her posture was stooped and her head was down. Her dark hair hung limp against the shoulders of her prison-issue shirt, and her green eyes seemed dull and distant. As the guards took off her cuffs, Creed realized Alisa James probably hadn't eaten a real meal in weeks. She was so thin she looked like she might be seriously ill. When she looked up, her gaze fixed on Creed, and a look of horror spread over her pale face.

Creed glanced at Andy, confused, and this time, he did suck in his breath.

Andy was crying.

She stood up from her chair, wiped her face, and walked around the table to greet Alisa James as the guards withdrew from the room and closed the door. The afternoon sunlight through the barred window cast long shadows on the two women as Andy spoke to Alisa in low tones.

Corey James looked at Creed, who murmured, "I don't know."

He had no idea what Andy was saying. Something worked, however.

Alisa raised her head and seemed to focus in on Andy, then on Creed, her husband, and her lawyers. Her body relaxed a fraction. She nodded, and let Andy lead her to the table. After Alisa acknowledged her husband with a weak smile, Andy pulled out the chair between Creed and Corey James for her, then returned to her own chair on the far side of the table as James helped his wife get seated.

Alisa turned immediately to Creed. "I'm sorry. I thought you were your brother. I've met Dominic at the Latch house."

The confirmation that his twin really had been at the Latch residence hit Creed hard. He swallowed, fished for something to say, and came up empty.

Alisa filled the silence with her quiet dignity. She steadied herself with a deep breath, kept eye contact with Creed, and said, "So you know what they are. Raven Latch and her husband. You know what they did to Jacob . . . and me."

Those few words were more than Alisa James had spoken in a row in any of her interviews. Creed did his best to honor that by clearing his throat and responding with, "We do know." He felt sharp stabs of sympathy for Corey James, who took his wife's hand with a pained expression on his face.

Alisa seemed to relax a little more. "They're going to kill me." She shook her head. "I was so damned stupid, to think they didn't realize I knew they were Legion. I should have taken Jacob out of that house as soon as I was sure about his parents. I got him killed, and I as much as got Bette killed, too."

Andy cut her off with, "Oh, no way. I'm not listening to you blame yourself for what those sociopaths chose to do." She wiped her cheeks again. "After being in that house, after being—after what happened to Creed and me there— the bastards have the power to go after whatever they want, whenever they want it."

Alisa folded her hands on the table in front of her. Her gaze drifted from her husband to her lawyers. "They'll wipe out anyone who knows me, anyone who might know about them. Camille's only alive because the Mothers took her."

"We have to get you out of New York, too," Creed said. "The Sibyls are coming for you on Friday, but that won't be soon enough."

Alisa's thin shoulders shook when she took a breath. She glanced at her husband. "Corey, your career. I'm so sorry! You'll never be able to—"

Corey James leaned forward and would have kissed his wife if one of the lawyers hadn't smacked a hand on the table, cut his eyes to the video monitors, and shook his head. James sat back.

"I don't care about my life in New York anymore," he said. "It's not worth anything without you. The Sibyls will relocate us." He smiled. "I don't mind being a house-husband for a while. Later, who knows." He turned his profile to her. "A new nose, a little hair dye, new identity papers—maybe I'll become an English lord, or something."

Alisa's lips trembled. Tears formed in her red-rimmed eyes. "Are you sure?"

"Positive, babe." He winked at her. "No question at all."

Alisa glanced at Creed, then Andy. "So what happens from here?"

Creed avoided looking at Corey James, since he and Andy hadn't shared this part of their plan beyond, *Andy and I have a foolproof way to get you both off Rikers Island— just have a boat waiting downstream at Hell Gate Bridge.*

"I have some abilities." Creed raised his right hand, careful to keep the Legion insignia on his ring turned away from Alisa and Corey James. "When I take off this ring and give it to Andy, I—uh—won't be myself, but she'll be able to control me. I'm strong enough to take the three of us through the walls of this building and off the island. I'll get us to the boat your husband has waiting."

He hoped.

"What about the lawyers?" Alisa glanced down the table to her defense team.

The attorney closest to her smiled. "We'll make valiant attempts to stop you, but fail. Probably get lots of press coverage, better name recognition, and a slew of new referrals."

Alisa lowered her head and closed her eyes, and seemed to be steeling herself. Creed watched Andy do much the same thing, and his desire to rip off Davin Latch's head and feed his evil wife to a Russian wolf increased tenfold.

And that's just two of them. How many of the Legion are running around New York?

When Andy raised her head, Creed asked, "Are you ready?"

She gave an almost imperceptible nod.

Corey James tensed.

Creed was about to ask Alisa if she was good to go when

the atmosphere in the conference room changed. It was subtle at first, but definite. A feeling of wrongness. A taste, a smell, a breeze—something that shouldn't have been there.

The hairs on the back of Creed's neck stood up.

Expensive perfume?

The *other* shifted and growled in his mind.

Where's that smell coming from?

Creed turned back toward the door, which was still closed.

His ring started to vibrate, and he got to his feet in a hurry.

Andy pushed her chair back so hard and so fast she almost fell as she stood. Alisa got up, too, followed by Corey James and the lawyers. They all looked at Creed.

"What's happening?" James asked, pulling his wife to him.

"I don't know." Creed walked to the conference room entrance, looked out of the small barred window in the door—and saw Raven Latch, still dressed in pink warmups, ice-blond hair loose and wild, sweeping through the Rose M. Singer Center. Fury radiated from every line of her thin, angular face, and she scattered guards and inmates like so many broken bugs each time she gestured with her skinny, colorless arm.

The *other* let out a roar, and Creed had to use all his strength to stand still. He had time to wonder if Raven Latch was using wind to blast the people trying to stop her, then the sounds of small explosions, splintering wood, and shattering glass blotted out his other thoughts. Alarms rang. Women screamed.

"She's coming!" Alisa James cried above the mounting chaos. "Oh, Goddess. I can feel her. I can smell her!"

Andy made a terrified gurgle and literally climbed over the table to grab Creed's arm. "Give me the ring! Give me the ring! Get us the hell out of here!"

Creed whirled around, grabbed the ring on his finger to pull it off—and the conference room door ripped off its hinges and smashed upright into his back.

Pain exploded across Creed's head and shoulders. The impact threw him forward and he slammed Andy to the floor with him. Her head bounced off the tile with a sickening crack, and her eyelids fluttered and closed.

Dazed, Creed reached back and shoved the door off his back, then rolled off Andy and tried to get up. The *other* howled in his mind, kicking and pushing against his skin. He was sure it would tear him open this time, but it never got the chance.

The toe of Raven Latch's sneaker caught him under the chin. His teeth slammed together so hard the room seemed to rattle. Bolts of agony shot down both jaws as he pitched backward onto his ass, sitting and coughing and gasping. His fucking throat felt paralyzed. His vision swam.

Strong, earthy energy swept across the room.

Creed saw Alisa James step away from her husband and raise her arms as she focused her Sibyl's power on Raven Latch.

The ground started to shake.

Splits and cracks shot along the concrete floor.

Corey James tried to throw a chair at Latch, but he stumbled.

As Alisa broke open the floor, bringing up the earth to swallow Raven Latch, the lawyers hurled their briefcases at the woman in pink.

Raven Latch stood very still. Nothing struck her. The briefcases veered off as if somebody had knocked them out of the air. Then the lawyers went flying, two at time, against the conference room walls.

Andy stirred on the floor, moaned, and tried to sit up.

Before the lawyers hit the floor, Alisa jerked. The ground stopped shaking. Her arms came down and she clawed at the air in front of her.

Corey James lunged toward his wife, seemed to hit a solid wall in midair, and crashed down on the table, his head at an odd angle. James rolled sideways, collapsed to the floor like a cloth doll, and didn't move. Creed tried to get up, but he wasn't fast enough. He thought he saw something in front of Alisa, but it was gone as quickly as it came. Creed tried to force his muscles to cooperate and managed to stand—just as Alisa's head wrenched to the side.

Bone snapped.

Creed felt sick as Alisa crumpled where she stood, her neck obviously broken. Her arm flopped out, coming to rest on Corey James's chest. The man's eyes were as wide and still as his wife's.

Raven Latch wheeled on Creed. "I'm giving you one more chance. Come with me. I can teach you things you can't begin to imagine."

Creed doubled his fists and started forward to take her down and hold her until help came, but someone— *something*—grabbed him by both arms and held him in place. He looked at his arms, didn't see anything—but he felt hands holding him.

Was this some sort of power Raven Latch could wield? Was she tricking his mind into thinking two big guys had hold of him?

"Leave him," Raven Latch commanded.

Creed felt a shove in the small of his back and whatever had hold of him let him go. He lurched forward, got his balance, and spun around just as the far wall of the conference room exploded outward. Raven Latch shoved the conference table out of her way, strode to the wall, and stepped out through the jagged hole into the bright afternoon. Ignoring the riot team charging toward the Singer Center and the helicopters pounding toward the island, she walked across the Rikers compound. Nothing seemed able to get near her.

A second later, she vanished from view.

Following instinct, Creed ran to Andy, dropped to his knees beside her, and checked her pulse. Strong and steady.

Thank God.

The lawyers were stirring and groaning, but there was nothing he could do for Corey or Alisa James. They were dead on the floor together, Alisa's arm still draped across her husband's chest.

Creed cut his eyes to the hole in the wall. Raven Latch was out there somewhere. She and whatever force she commanded could attack the Sibyls at the Todt Hill safe house, and how could they stop her?

Andy groaned again, and this time, she did manage to sit without sliding back to the floor. Her eyes were cloudy, and she looked absolutely addled.

"Creed?" she mumbled like he wasn't even there.

Creed looked from her to his signet ring. Riana had told them that if an Asmodai took off its talisman and held the talisman in its hand, it would return to its maker.

If he took off his own ring and held it, would that lead him to Raven or Davin Latch?

Andy shook her head. She looked so out of it as she called for Creed again and again.

Shouts rang through the decimated building as the riot squad forced its way through the rubble and the groaning crowd of injured prisoners and guards.

"You stay here," Creed said, gripping his ring. "I've got to go."

Andy's mouth came open as she pushed up on her elbows.

Creed tugged the signet ring off his finger, stuffed it into his palm, and gripped it with all his strength.

A split second later, all his muscles seemed to catch fire. The *other* came blasting out of him, taking over with a rabid rush of triumph.

The remnants of Creed's awareness saw Andy's eyes

clear, saw her take in the death and devastation around her, then look back at the *other* in horror.

As the *other* turned away from her and charged forward holding the ring, the last thing Creed heard was Andy yelling, "Creed. Oh, my God, Creed! What did you do?"

34

Riana dug her nails into the leather seat of Bela Argos's SUV and held on for dear life. Bela steered the mammoth vehicle into the Rikers lot and stomped the brakes, barely missing a pickup truck careening out of its space. Riana's whole body slammed against her seat belt as the SUV rocked to a stop. The pickup truck's driver didn't even glance in their direction. The guy just burned rubber out of the parking lot.

With a loud curse, Bela yanked the wheel of the SUV and hit the gas, almost tagged a speeding Toyota, and slid into the empty space left by the pickup. Riana had to bite her lip to keep from yelling. If she pissed off Bela, the temperamental Sibyl might make Riana walk back to the safe house.

People wove in and out of the rows of cars. Some were running. Some were screaming. All of them looked panicked.

Bela's dark eyes gleamed with worry and suspicion as she gazed toward the people, then at the buildings ahead of them. "What the hell was that explosion we heard as we came off the bridge?"

Riana shook her head. "No idea."

"Is that a helicopter? A boat?" Bela turned off the SUV and grabbed the door handle. "Fuck. There's a riot squad and paramedics coming out of that building. I knew I should have brought my triad."

Riana threw open her door, bracing against the chilly blast of fall air. Her leathers shielded her from the worst of it, but her cheeks tingled from the temperature change. "If you'd brought yours, mine would have insisted on coming. Merilee's not ready to fight yet."

"What makes you so sure Creed and Andy came here anyway?" Bela called from the other side of the SUV as even more vehicles left the parking lot.

"It's what I'd do," Riana said. "And Creed's been trying to get his captain to approve an interview with Alisa."

"No way they'd get in."

"You don't know Creed and Andy." Riana rubbed her hands together for warmth. She didn't have on her gloves yet because they couldn't dress for battle and expect to get into a prison for visitation. "Creed and Andy will find a way—and so will we."

Alarms and Klaxons blared all at once, seemingly from all over Rikers Island. More sirens joined in, probably fire, police, and ambulances approaching across the Rikers Island Bridge.

Bela responded with a new flood of curses as people surged out of the Reception Center—with Andy leading the way.

Andy came staggering across the parking lot, followed by a Rikers guard, a woman in a nurse's uniform, and a couple of FDNY paramedics, who kept trying to grab Andy's arms. Every time somebody touched Andy, she snarled, "Get away from me." Her breaths came out in great puffs visible in the cool air, making her look like a redheaded dragon.

Riana wasn't sure where Andy was headed, and from the way Andy was weaving and swearing, Andy didn't seem sure, either. She had on different clothes than she'd been wearing earlier—khaki slacks and a white blouse. The blouse seemed to be streaked with blood and dirt, and Andy had visible cuts and bruises on her face. When she spotted Riana and Bela, she changed course and lurched straight toward them.

After what happened at the safe house, Riana half

expected Andy to shoot her. Bela's hand dropped to her hip, reaching for the sword she had left in the SUV, but Andy didn't draw her firearm. The Rikers guard succeeded in grabbing Andy's elbow. She stomped his foot and jammed her elbow into his ribs. The man dropped to the pavement like a bag of flour. Andy kept moving as the woman in the nurse's uniform knelt to see to the wounded guard.

As she got close enough for Riana to catch her when she stumbled, Andy's wide eyes took on an even more desperate, crazy gleam. Her teeth clenched. She was so pale she looked ready to faint, but she grabbed Riana's outstretched hands and started talking instead.

"I didn't see—but when I woke up, the *other*—I think he's a killer, Ri." Tears spilled down Andy's ghost-white cheeks. She squeezed Riana's wrists in her clammy palms, and Riana could tell Andy was close to going into shock. "Creed took off his ring. The *other* followed Raven Latch out of here."

Riana stared at Andy, uncomprehending.

Andy tightened her grip on Riana's wrists. "Br-broke their necks. Creed, I think. Oh, God. I think Creed did it. Alisa's dead. Corey and some guards, too." Andy's knees wobbled, and Riana barely held her upright.

Riana opened her mouth but couldn't speak. Her heart seemed to beat slower and slower until it stopped altogether, squeezing all the air from her lungs. The madhouse around them escalated. More people. More screaming. More sirens.

"Alisa's dead?" Bela's voice sounded uncharacteristically weak. Riana felt Bela's fingers digging into her shoulder. "Corey . . . oh, Goddess help us."

The real world peeled back from Riana, escaping her in fits and starts. Time passed, but she had no idea how much. Her mind kept repeating the same two phrases as grief weighed like hot rocks in her belly.

Alisa's dead. She's dead.

Riana could see the parking lot, see the paramedics and nurse and limping guard taking hold of Andy, but none of the actions made any sense. Everything seemed to be happening miles away instead of right beside her.

Andy let go of Riana's wrists as her captors wrestled her away, then forced her onto a stretcher.

Where did the stretcher come from?

Oh.

The ambulance backed up to the sidewalk. Flashing lights struck Riana's face like a physical force, and she blinked.

Alisa's dead. Corey's dead. Riana watched as paramedics lifted a crumpling Andy into the ambulance to examine her.

Andy said Creed killed people. That he broke Alisa's neck, and Corey's, too.

No. She couldn't believe that. She absolutely wouldn't.

Bela was crying and repeating, "I'll kill the bastard. I'll tear him apart."

Riana turned slowly and faced Bela. The other woman's jaw was set. No doubt if Creed walked into view, Bela would lunge at him and tear out his eyes.

"Andy's confused," Riana said, surprised by the force in her voice. "Creed wouldn't murder anyone."

Bela looked stunned. "Weren't you listening? Riana, how stupid and blind can you be?" Bela raised her hand and pointed to her fourth finger. "He took off his ring. He turned into that demon-thing and *he killed Alisa and Corey!*"

Each word made Riana's heart ache. She shook her head again, then put out her hand, palm up. "Give me your keys."

"You're fucking crazy." Bela lowered her arms and hugged herself, guarding her pockets. "No way."

Riana stared at her friend, then realized she had pulled her fingers into a fist.

I'm losing it.

"Don't make me take the keys away from you, Bela." Her tone sounded flat and insane, the way she felt. "I'll shake this whole island into the river, piece by piece."

Bela studied her, incredulous—but Riana saw the worry in her friend's eyes. Worry, and resignation. Without further comment, Bela relaxed her stance, stuffed her hand in her pocket, and produced the keys.

Riana took them and ran for the SUV.

She barely made it off Rikers before they shut the whole island down.

Numb, barely paying attention to the road, Riana drove straight to the Latch house. The sun hung low in the sky now, blinding her around curves and making her squint when she reluctantly braked for lights.

Creed is not a murderer.

But if Andy was right and he took off his ring, if he kept it, he's probably in serious trouble.

Poor Andy was so addled and confused, she could have seen anything. Or nothing at all. Raven Latch had come to Rikers to kill Alisa James. That much was clear. Andy had been injured badly enough to disrupt her perceptions—but if Creed or the *other* did murder Alisa and Corey, Riana would kill him herself.

She would.

She would have to.

He didn't kill anybody. I won't believe that. I can't.

Raven and Davin Latch might not even be in New York anymore, but Riana didn't know where else to start. She had to go to their house. She had to find Creed.

The Upper East Side seemed alien to her even though she had traveled each road dozens of times on patrol. She raced along the outer boundary of Central Park, feeling a loneliness and emptiness more profound than any she had known.

Creed thought she had betrayed him.

And hadn't she?

She let Cynda and Merilee dig through his apartment, his private information. And she hadn't opposed the Mothers outright when they sought to take him.

Now, Riana had left Andy and Bela no doubt thinking she was an idiot, that she was chasing insanely after a Sibyl-murderer. Riana didn't have her triad, either. If she didn't come back whole from this, Cynda and Merilee probably would believe the worst about her judgment and her love for her triad sisters.

The thought of leaving no legacy but condemnation and doubt nearly choked Riana with frustration and grief.

Maybe love blinded her. Maybe love tainted her instincts. But it was past time for her to trust her judgment.

Creed was *not* a murderer.

She trusted that judgment enough to stake her life on it.

Riana shook her head to clear her thoughts. She was close now. Traffic was heavy and cumbersome, but she wove through the cabs, buses, and increasingly upscale cars like a professional stock-car driver.

A few seconds later, Riana slammed the SUV to a halt half a block from the five-story monstrosity the Latch family called home. From her vantage point, she could see that one of the house's three upper terraces had a smashed railing. Debris lay inside the fence and gates, which had been opened to admit the tail end and ramp of a huge yellow moving van. A dozen or so armed men in black suits and dark sunglasses were traversing the ramp bridge between the front steps and the van, loading boxes, rugs, exercise machines, and small pieces of furniture. A handful stood along the fence, facing forward, hands on their weapons.

Feds? Bodyguards?

She didn't really care.

Traffic streamed past the house, oblivious to all the evil inside, and the fact that the bastards were trying to make their great escape.

The Latch family was obviously closing up shop, and she needed the guards and their guns out of the way. Without taking her eyes off her potential enemies, she pulled on her face mask and hand-checked her daggers.

Set.

Ready.

Except for the crushing ache in her chest, and the fact her body had turned to lead.

Get a grip.

For Creed. For Alisa. For your triad and all the Sibyls.

You can do this.

Jaw set, refusing to give in to her urge to run, Riana climbed out of the SUV and walked along the curb with the flow of traffic, letting a big bus hide her approach to the Latch house.

At the same moment, she unleashed a powerful burst of earth energy. The ground rippled, throwing up pavement, concrete, and stones all the way to the moving van. Cars swerved right and left to avoid the sudden tear in the road.

The bus shielding her from view hit the gas.

Damnit!

As it roared out of the way, Riana could see the yellow moving van rocking and pitching. Furniture fell out and shattered on the steps. The men in black suits ran and shouted. Some stumbled backward and dropped their weapons. Cars skidded past the fence, barely staying on the street.

Riana gripped the hilts of her daggers. She intensified the small, focused quake, rocking the yellow moving van hard.

It groaned and heaved over on its side, crushing part of the gate and fence.

She took a deep breath and coughed at the sudden rush of gas fumes and burned oil. The van's engine must have been running when it tipped. She hoped it didn't explode. At least not yet.

Riana kept up the shaking of the earth and dashed the last few yards down the road, straight into the chaos.

The guards couldn't keep their feet. One by one, they hit the ground and struggled to pull themselves into sitting positions. Some gagged from the roiling dirt and smoke. Others fought to wipe their eyes. Black smoke billowed from the van's tailpipe, filling the cold, gray air with even more pungent fumes.

Riana hacked and spit to keep the awful taste of hot oil out of her mouth. She used the cab of the overturned van for balance as she struggled across the twisted piece of gate and fence, still holding her daggers in both hands. The sun was going down. She so didn't want to be at this house after dark, but she pressed ahead.

As she hopped inside the Latch compound, the front door of the brick house burst open. A man with salt-and-pepper hair filled the doorway, one hand on either side of the doorframe to keep his balance despite the rolling of the earth. Riana hesitated at the foot of the steps, looking up at the figure framed by the porch's white columns. Light poured onto the porch from either side of him, highlighting the green smoking jacket and sharp black slacks.

She recognized him from all the newspaper pictures.

Riana couldn't see Davin Latch's eyes clearly in the smoke and evening gloom, but she knew he was staring at her in her leathers, with her daggers in hand. He had to know what she was. He probably knew who she was. Riana wasn't sure why she thought that, but she felt it, deep inside.

He was waiting for me.

She gathered the energy not engaged by the focal earthquake and tried to steel herself against a mental invasion.

Mind-raping bastards.

That's what Andy called Latch and his wife.

Riana's muscles twitched as she readied herself to leap right or left, or to throw a dagger in response to his attack—but no attack came.

Latch turned and walked back into his house without shutting the door.

Riana was so shocked she almost released the earthquake and freed the guards to fill her full of bullets.

Now she *really* didn't want to go into the Latch house.

Someone will die if I cross that threshold. Her gut churned with the force of her Sibyl's instinct. *And it might be me.*

But the same instinct told her Creed was in that house, that he needed her. And she had to stop Raven and Davin Latch at any cost.

Heart racing, daggers forward, Riana ran up the steps.

The moment she cleared the threshold and slammed the door, she let go her hold on the quake outside and gathered back all the earth energy she could wield. She would use it. She wouldn't hesitate. If she felt a risk, she would strike first and deal with the guilt later.

Compared to outside, the big house seemed hot and stuffy and crazily still and quiet.

Lights blazed everywhere, and for a moment, Riana didn't know whether to head up the stairs or down.

Down, her instincts told her.

Down.

Even if she didn't come up again.

The elevator felt too dangerous, so Riana found the door to the steps leading below the ground. It was standing open like an invitation.

Riana hated walking into an obvious trap, but if Latch had wanted her dead, he would have killed her already. The advantage was his. She had to play, or she wouldn't be in the game.

Riana stared at the open door, at the dark entrance to the steps. No lights blazing on the staircase, except for a faint red glow below. She eased over to the door and looked inside.

Nothing.

Blood rushed in her ears, adding sound to the silence. Her face felt hot inside her leather mask.

Where does that damned staircase end? Riana squinted into the blackness, surprised by her inability to see where the stairs terminated. *Hell?*

Or something like it.

At least if she died, she'd die in the earth's embrace.

She felt disoriented, but pushed against the sensation and made herself focus. Senses on high alert, Riana slipped into the stairwell, keeping her footfalls quiet despite the polished hardwood. She descended the first few steps slowly, like a scorpion, with one dagger in front for a quick thrust or parry and one dagger raised over her head for a sudden plunge.

She sensed something watching her from behind.

Riana whirled around, but saw nothing. Heard nothing but the sandpaper rub of her own breathing.

She turned forward and started down again, noting that the paneled walls had no decoration. Not a knickknack, not a picture. The red glow from below bathed the blank wood in eerie, dark tones. Riana's brain seemed to vibrate, and she sensed someone trying to touch her thoughts.

Andy's words rang through her consciousness again.

Mind-raping bastards . . .

"Not this time," Riana whispered, and created a thick shield of earth energy around her thoughts and essence.

For a few moments, the air crackled as if lightning wanted to burst from the shadowy ceiling. Some sort of power shoved and pushed against her shield, then surrendered with a huff.

Riana found herself breathing in shallow gasps. She strained her ears and eyes for any hint of what lay below, but it was her nose that gave her the first clue.

A whiff of sulfur drifted up to meet her.

Riana's throat went dry.

Asmodai.

How many?

Two more steps down, then three, then four.

The red glow grew brighter. The stench of Asmodai got stronger.

A metal door came into view at the bottom of the steps, set into heavy, grooved stone. The door seemed absurdly far away and too small. Riana blinked, fending off a woozy, drunken sensation. She felt like Alice in Wonderland—*after* she drank the wrong potion and grew to colossal size.

Mind-raping bastards . . .

Riana threw more power into the earth energy protecting her mind.

Give it up, assholes. I'm coming through that door.

Her head swam and she almost tumbled the rest of the way down to the mini-door at the bottom of the stairs. Seconds later, her Sibyl's vision cleared, and she saw only ten or so steps remaining, and a normal-sized door. It was metal, yes, and set into grooved stone—but it wasn't tiny and she wasn't huge. Something had been confusing her perceptions, big time.

Did the Legion seek and train general telepaths, or was this mental interference something . . . more?

She thought about Frith Gregory and his dehydration attacks. At the time, she had assumed he was working with water, with an element, but what if he was actually affecting bodily functions? Squeezing cells?

Were these people biosentients?

Once more, Riana had that sense of something behind her.

This time, she turned slowly and took her time studying the distance between herself and the upstairs door.

Again, she saw nothing.

Was this another mind trick? A distraction? A tactic to wear her down?

What if the Legion recruited telepaths who had an affinity for the biological, the way Sibyls had an affinity for natural elements?

Unlike the four elements, however, there were dozens of biological functions. Hundreds, if animal and plant life were included. Biosentients were beyond dangerous.

Cold fingers of fear massaged Riana's spine.

Biosentients kill with thoughts.

Riana had to reach deep into her own courage to turn forward again and take another step toward the metal door marking the end of her descent.

Her better judgment once more insisted she should flee, go get help, but her instincts told her if she did that, she would never see Creed again. At least not alive.

Trust my judgment.

No fear.

No hesitation.

Riana ground her teeth.

Fine.

Now or never, right?

Keeping her daggers poised, she took two powerful strides forward, threw her earth energy into weakening metal and stone, and kicked open the door in front of her.

35

As the metal door at the bottom of the steps burst open from Riana's well-placed kick, the door at the top of the stairs slammed shut.

Riana felt the stifling sensation of elemental locks slamming into place. Their energy weighed like lead against her leathers.

A chamber. I'm in a chamber, and the door completed the lock. Goddess. I can't use my earth energy for anything but personal shielding.

She barely had time to process that there would be no quick escape from this trap, because she stepped into a windowless stone room to find Davin Latch on her left, about fifteen feet away, flanked by five huge, smoking fire Asmodai.

Raven Latch stood to the right, about the same distance from Riana and the door, with Creed-as-*other* directly behind her.

Riana's heart gave a little jump, but the blazing golden creature showed no sign of recognizing her. The *other* seemed preoccupied with the woman beside it, gazing at her like she might control the sun and the movement of the earth.

Raven Latch held up her hand to show Riana she had the signet ring.

It was all Riana could do to keep concentrating on shielding her mind from intrusion. She knew she should be plotting a battle strategy, but all she wanted to do was cry.

The bitch was controlling Creed. She had the ring.

What if, back on Rikers . . .

No. Creed is not a murderer. Absolutely not.

With a flourish, Raven Latch gestured to a spot halfway between her and her husband—to a small, portable cell no bigger than a coffin. Wheels on the bottom, resting on the smooth stone floor. Elementally locked bars. The door was open.

Confused, Riana stared at the coffin-cell, then gazed at Davin Latch.

"It's simple, my dear," he said in his silky politician's voice. "Riana Dumain, right? Creed's little fling. Get in that cage, or die."

When Riana didn't move, he added, "We had to give up the Sibyl we were studying. We don't intend to give you up—or lose you."

The metal door behind Riana slammed shut.

The hairs on the back of her neck stood up.

Something shut that door—not just energy, either.

Someone.

This time, she didn't turn around. She knew she'd see empty air, but she refused to doubt her perceptions. An invisible Asmodai, a friggin' rabbit with a pocket watch who knew how to vanish—someone was standing a few feet away from her. She could feel breath tickling her hair.

"What's behind me?" she asked in a voice so steady it surprised her. Somehow, she managed not to look at Creed. Seeing the *other* slobbering over Raven Latch would only weaken Riana, and she knew it.

Davin Latch smiled at her question. "I'm impressed. Since you asked, I get to brag. My son is behind you."

"That's not possible, Senator." Riana still didn't turn to check behind her. "Jacob is dead, just like your firstborn. You and your wife killed them both."

Raven Latch let out a theatrical sigh. "Transmography is a lost art to the Sibyls, I see. The new Jacob is just as much ours as Creed and Dominic. We *made* them. They're our children."

Dread flowed through Riana like ice water, but she refused to be swept up in the Legion madness. "Dead is dead. You murdered your children, no matter what monsters you built from their blood."

Oh, Goddess. I called Creed a monster.

But the *other* didn't react at all.

Davin Latch laughed at her opinion. In another setting, his laugh might have been rich and engaging, drawing followers the way a light drew moths. To Riana, the sound strained reality, challenged sanity. He lifted his hand to his neck, pulled a chain with a ring from the folds of his smoking jacket, and said, "The lady needs enlightenment, Jacob. Show yourself."

The air around Riana shifted, turned cooler all of a sudden. A bitter, sweet scent assaulted her senses. Cherry bark, or something like it.

"Mullein," she said aloud, naming the herb so often used in perverted rituals.

"I'm impressed again," Davin Latch said. "Now give my son, my beautiful Astaroth, a proper greeting."

An Astaroth? Sweet Goddess. They're just theory. No one has made an Astaroth in modern times.

Have they?

Riana shifted from foot to foot, hoping Latch was as insane as he seemed. Keeping her daggers ready, she turned around.

Her brain went numb at the sight behind her.

He—it—had to be eight feet tall.

More corporeal than the *other*. No shifting like an Asmodai.

For all the world, the Astaroth looked like a huge, naked man with translucent pearly skin, subtle fangs, pointed claws, and two pairs of leathery dragon wings that probably stretched wall to wall when unfolded. Despite the fangs and claws and reptile wings, the thing was almost . . . handsome. Like a fantastical sculpture. The eerily beautiful creature's golden eyes weren't blank like an Asmodai's, either, but they didn't seem as human as the *other*'s.

"Permanent and quite biddable," Latch explained, answering Riana's questions before she asked them, no doubt because he was certain Riana would be dead or his captive in a matter of minutes. "No donor wombs needed, no troublesome childhoods—just an object of power to make the cuts to harvest the blood and a powerful mortar to hold it. We used the dagger and mortar we liberated from the Volgograd collection." He smiled. "Astaroths are much smarter than Asmodai, much less independent than Cursons. And best of all—Jacob, hide yourself."

The Astaroth lowered its head obediently, and vanished.

Riana held tight to her shock, refusing to give Latch the pleasure of her surprise. She made herself turn her back on the Astaroth and face the senator again.

He kept one hand on his necklace with the ring pendant, no doubt the talisman used to control his new demon. With the other, he gestured upward as if to say, *sky's the limit*.

"The perfect weapon," he said. Then, "Jacob, put our guest in the cage."

Riana's gut flipped.

As she felt the big demon's fingers close on her shoulder, reflex took over. She whirled out of its grip, slashed across the empty space behind her, and heard the thing's bellow of pain. It flashed into view, ghostly hands pressed over a rent in its chest.

Raven Latch gave a shriek of fury, but Riana didn't glance in her direction. She spun to her left and hurled a dagger directly at Davin Latch.

His eyes widened as the blade sped toward him without a single midair flip and drove straight into his throat.

Survival instinct forced him to reach up and yank the dagger free, as Riana knew he would. He gurgled, unable to speak because she had sliced straight through his vocal cords.

Blood followed the blade in a wide arc.

Too much blood, pumping with force.

A split second later, Latch dropped the gore-soaked dagger, tried to press his hand to his throat, and tipped sideways, eyes blank as he crashed to the ground.

Immediately, three of the five Asmodai burst into flames and "died" with him.

Thank the Goddess he made a few of those five. Fewer to fight now.

Riana had no time to enjoy her small victory. Raven Latch flashed into view and plowed into Riana's side, knocking her remaining dagger from her hand.

Riana grabbed the bitch's streaked blond hair and did her best to yank half of it out of her head.

They struck the ground, but Riana barely noticed the impact.

Raven Latch screamed obscenities as she jerked off Riana's face mask and threw it aside. They rolled away from the *other,* past the cage, toward the center of the big room. Latch's nails flashed toward Riana's exposed cheeks, but Riana knocked her hands away. Riana had obviously trained for fighting better than her opponent. Once they stopped moving, it was too easy to pull free and roll to her feet in front of Latch.

To Riana's surprise, she didn't try to come after her.

Instead, the woman pushed up on her elbows. She leaned to see around Riana, glared toward the door at the two remaining Asmodai, and shouted, "Kill her. Now."

Riana wheeled to face the demons. She was several feet away from both of her daggers, which were back toward the two monsters. She could reach one that was off to the side, but not both.

Just one. And two Asmodai. Shit!

The Asmodai lumbered toward her.

Riana leaped away from Raven Latch, then took a running jump toward the nearest dagger. She hit the stone floor in a tumble-roll and grabbed the blade before the Asmodai could make a course adjustment.

When she landed on her feet again, she was a few feet from the *other*. It stood there, glowing gold, staring past her, toward Raven Latch.

"Creed, I love you," Riana said, hoping with all her heart he could hear her. "I'm so sorry about what happened— I came here to find you."

The *other*'s posture never changed.

A fireball tore through the air between them and slammed into the stone wall ten feet from her shoulder. Riana winced as the rock cracked from the force. Heat and rock fragments pelted her. She turned away from the haze of stone dust and settled into fighting stance, barely breathing, barely holding on to her panic.

Both Asmodai hurled fire at her, one high and one low.

Riana dived between the hurtling balls of flame, once more moving away from the *other*. A blast of heat nicked her shoulder, burning through the leather bodysuit as if the suit was made of paper.

She had to force the battle. If she waited for the demons to come to her, she'd die.

"Creed!" she yelled over her shoulder as she charged toward the biggest of the two Asmodai. "I need you. Please help me!"

Raven Latch's laughter answered her.

Riana sensed no movement from the *other*, no indication it noticed her plea.

She reached the big Asmodai just as it raised a massive fireball. Riana pulled up short and slashed at its arm.

Missed.

"Your girlfriend wants you, Creed," Raven Latch said as she got to her feet behind Riana, back at the center of the room. "Maybe you should go to her—and smash her head in your palms."

Riana shouted as the Asmodai threw its fire at close range.

She pivoted, but the fireball slammed into her left arm, side, and hip. Scalding heat dug into her skin. Riana cried out from the pain and fell sideways on the stone floor. Breath rushed from her lungs, and for a moment, she had only painful nothingness inside her instead of air.

The Asmodai dropped on top of her like a three-hundred-pound weight.

Riana barely managed to get her dagger up, more reflex than intentional defense, but good enough. Her blade drove into its chest even as heat from its skin burned her through her bodysuit. Its black pit eyes halted inches from her own.

"Creed!" She took in one deep draft of sulfur, burned leather, and melting hair. "Please!"

The dead Asmodai burst into flames.

Riana tried to roll to her side to get up, but the second demon kicked the dagger out of her trembling hand.

It dropped on her and wrapped its hot fingers around her vulnerable throat.

Then it opened its mouth to spit fire in her face. Clouds of sulfur stung her eyes.

It would burn her to death, starting at the top. They liked that, Asmodai.

Riana couldn't breathe. She couldn't hold on to the shred of earth energy she had retained inside the elementally locked chamber, either. Her shielding fell away, leaving her vulnerable to whatever mental attack Raven Latch chose to make.

Sights and sounds swirled around her, making less and less sense as the thing's weight and choke hold kept her from drawing air. The pain in her chest felt like hundreds of daggers striking home.

Creed.

He was there.

The *other*.

It was standing behind the Asmodai, gazing at her with seemingly sightless golden eyes.

Waiting its turn.

He's come to kill me, too.

Hope ebbed from Riana like a tide, hurting more than the burns and the crushing, squeezing throb in her chest. Pressure and bolts of heat exploded through her head, and Riana knew Raven Latch was attacking, too. Pain shot down Riana's left arm and up, up, into her left jaw.

She's stopping my heart. Stopping it . . .

Riana struggled against the Asmodai, but that was useless. Even with her close combat skills, without her earth energy, she couldn't counter its weight when it had her pinned. She was losing consciousness.

Fire roared up the thing's throat.

Riana squeezed her eyes shut.

The weight and heat vanished.

Almost as fast, the crushing pressure left her chest and her heart started a frantic but steady beat.

For a second, she couldn't quite believe her face wasn't melting, that air was flowing into her body, that her heart hadn't exploded into bloody bits.

Riana's eyes flew open with surprise and confusion, just in time to see the *other* pile-drive the fire Asmodai into the stone floor.

The thing's head shattered, and it turned into smoking bits of cloth before the *other* could smash it again.

He . . . saved me.

Her reservoir of hope came flowing right back, and Riana wheezed and choked as she took breath after sweet breath, despite the charred-flesh reek in the air. Her bodysuit hung in tatters, but her burns were manageable for now.

Raven Latch swore from somewhere behind Riana.

"Kill *her,* you fucking idiot!"

The *other* turned toward Riana and gazed down at her.

Riana met its eyes.

This time, instead of no color at all, she saw a hint of onyx and fire, deep and warm and wonderfully Creed.

She caught up the shreds of earth energy trapped inside

the chamber with her and brought them to bear again, shielding herself against further biosentient attack.

A light flashed against the stone wall. She got to her hands and knees and saw Raven Latch holding Creed's signet ring like a wand. Flame played off the gold, spattering the stone wall with bright flashes. Raven Latch shook the ring at the *other*. At Creed.

It's like they're one person. Or one creature.

"You *must* kill her," Raven Latch insisted. "I command it!"

If Riana could have formed words, she would have told Latch a thing or two. Since she didn't have any voice yet, she settled for a quick spring off the stone floor, a fast charge, and a bone-bashing football tackle.

Creed's signet ring went flying as Riana drove Raven Latch into the smooth, hard floor. She hoped all her ribs would snap, but the crack of skull against rock was satisfying enough. The woman drooped beneath her, and Riana got back up and dragged her skinny, unconscious ass straight to the elementally locked cage. It took her a second to fish the cage keys out of the bitch's pants pocket, then she locked Raven Latch up tight in the coffin-sized jail once meant for a Sibyl.

For Riana.

She glanced at Creed-as-*other*. The creature was staring into the far corner of the room, moving a little to the right, then a little to the left, as if keeping itself between Riana and some unseen threat.

The white demon.

The silence of the room hammered against Riana's ears as she turned, strode over to Davin Latch, and took hold of the necklace with the ring pendant he had used to control the new horror he and his wife had created. The Astaroth.

Riana had no idea if the white demon weakened when Davin Latch died, but she figured it didn't. That only happened with Asmodai and lesser demons, according to

Sibyl research. The Astaroth seemed much more stable than a Curson, than Creed, and Creed-as-*other* was still standing. Riana didn't think Creed and the Astaroth—Jacob—would die even if Riana gave in to her burning desire to roll Raven Latch's cage into the elevator, haul it to the fourth floor, and shove the damned thing right off a terrace.

Riana slipped the necklace over Latch's head, held up the talisman, and turned a slow circle on the bloody, soot-streaked floor. She gazed briefly at the *other* as she did. It had relaxed once she took hold of the talisman, and moved to stand near the cage. It was holding the signet ring and studying Raven Latch with wariness and disgust.

He saved me.

"Jacob, I have your talisman," Riana announced. "I am your master now. You will not harm me, my triad, any Sibyl, or any human. Make yourself seen, and stand in the corner nearest the door."

The handsome, ethereal demon-creature winked into view, head down and double-wings drooping as it limped to the location where Riana ordered it to stand. Its hand was still pressed against its chest, which had leaked black fluid onto its—his?—pearl-white skin.

The *other* moved away, and Riana saw it bend down to pick up the signet ring.

He's got it. He's safe.

Relief, fatigue, and pain washed over Riana then.

She almost dropped the talisman, but strong hands caught her from behind and held her gently upright.

Riana turned to find herself in the huge, glowing, golden arms of the *other*.

The creature's touch didn't burn her. It filled her with warmth, with strength. It took the talisman from her hands and slipped it over her head, then once more wrapped her in its arms.

She stared into the *other*'s face and saw Creed's dark eyes gazing at her.

"Will you hurt me?" she whispered.

The *other* shook its head.

No.

The eyes said, *Never.*

"Did you hurt anyone at Rikers Island?"

Again, Creed-as-*other* shook his head. He nodded toward Raven Latch and the Astaroth. When his gaze flickered toward the wounded demon, Riana thought she saw compassion in the *other*'s eyes.

He looked at her again then, and pulled her closer, pressing the length of his massive body along hers. The *other*'s energy seemed to flow into her, around her, and as it did, she felt Creed. She smelled his cedar-mandarin scent.

Her burns stopped burning. Her aches stopped aching. Intense healing energy raced through her body, invigorating her, heating her from singed head to bruised toe.

She heard Creed in her heart, in her mind. Maybe even out loud.

I love you. I will always love you.

Her heart leaped—then broke into pieces.

Something in the way he said it . . .

She looked up at him and saw the truth in his eyes.

Her grip on his warm muscled arms doubled. "No. You can't leave me."

Creed-as-*other* bent down, his dark eyes adoring her and grieving her all at once. His lips brushed hers, sending shocks through her body, making her want him more than ever, in whatever form he chose to take.

I can't stay, said that deep, reverberating voice in her mind and heart. *I can't risk hurting you.*

A sob tore from Riana's throat as she tried desperately to hold on to him. "You're controlling yourself now, damnit! Don't you dare leave me!"

He pushed back from her and pulled free, trapping her hands in his shimmering, warm palms.

After one last, longing look from those dark, dark eyes,

Creed-as-*other* let go her hands, turned away, and barreled through the closed metal door, leaving it warped and crushed on the stone floor.

Riana heard the heavy thunder of his footsteps on the stairs, and felt the shattering of the upstairs door and the elemental lock on the chamber.

Gone.

He was gone.

Despite the fact that every wound on her body had been healed by the *other*'s energy, Riana felt like she was dying. A hollow, empty ache bloomed in her belly, and her skin went cold all over.

Creed was gone.

Creed was gone forever.

She wouldn't survive this loss. She couldn't.

Her knees tried to give out, and she had to use Raven Latch's cage to steady herself.

Feminine shouts and curses rang out upstairs, then more footsteps came hammering down the stairs.

Before Riana could so much as visually locate her daggers, Merilee, Bela Argos, and a bandaged Andy with her neck in a temporary brace burst into the chamber. All had weapons drawn and ready.

Cynda was the first to lower her sword as she surveyed the bloody room, Riana's torn, burned jumpsuit, and Raven Latch in the cage. Then Cynda's eyes landed on the Astaroth, and she raised her blade again.

"Christ on a crutch," Andy grumbled. "What the hell is *that* thing?"

Riana lifted her fingers to the chain and ring pendant around her neck. She let herself feel the joy of seeing her triad again, which gave her the strength to say, "Ladies, meet our new pet demon. His name is Jacob."

"I'm shooting him now," Andy said, but Merilee snatched Andy's gun away from her before she could squeeze off a round.

Riana gave them the short version of what happened in the chamber, and what really happened on Rikers Island, and made Jacob demonstrate his ability to disappear. As she started to order him to reappear, something grabbed the talisman from behind and nearly tore Riana's head right off.

She gagged from the sudden pressure and thrust her fingers between the chain and her neck, snapping the chain to protect her windpipe.

Raven Latch wedged her scrawny arm back inside the bars of the coffin-cage, dragging the talisman, then wrapping it around her fingers.

"Run, Jacob!" Latch shouted to the still-invisible Astaroth in slurred, drunken tones. Her eyes were still closed, and she seemed to go into some kind of trance, muttering phrases in Sumerian.

A swish of air told Riana Jacob had left the room.

The triad raised their weapons, poised to strike Raven Latch.

"Move!" Cynda yelled to Riana, but Riana choked out, "Locked," before they wasted their time bouncing swords, bullets, and arrows off the repelling energy of the elementally bound lead bars.

Raven Latch kept chanting.

Everyone got visibly tense as the air in the room began to change.

Thunder seemed to hit the stairs again, and Riana's heart soared as the *other* came racing back to the chamber. Something struck Cynda in the head. She swore and spun around, then she stooped to pick up the golden object from the stone floor.

The *other* stormed across the floor and yanked the coffin-cage's door right off its hinges.

Before anyone could react, the *other* thrust its massive arms inside the cage, snatched the talisman from Raven Latch with his right hand, and broke her neck with his left.

In the stunned silence that followed, Raven Latch's body fell heavily to the basement floor.

Riana stepped back, horrified.

"Creed?" she whispered.

The *other* threw down the talisman, turned on her and bellowed, looking wild and furious and ready to eat her.

"Stop!" Cynda yelled, holding up what looked like a golden chain. "Don't fucking twitch!"

The *other* went stone still.

Riana didn't think she could move, but she got out of the way when Cynda told her to.

Cynda approached the *other*, ordered it to its knees, then flipped the chain over its big head.

As the chain settled into place, the other began to change into Creed—but, not Creed. Naked, like Creed always was after the transition, yes. With the same gorgeous physique. The same soulful, dark eyes. Longer hair, pulled back in a ponytail that rested like black silk between his powerful shoulders. A jagged scar ran from his *right* shoulder to his elbow.

Riana didn't know whether to sob with disappointment or relief.

She managed not to do either, but just looking at the man made her ache inside.

Creed is gone. He's really gone. How will I ever get over that?

As this mirror-image Creed finished materializing, he dropped to his knees, wrapped his arms around his bare chest, and rasped, "Biosentient. That chant. She would have blown herself up. The cage . . . shrapnel . . ."

"Biosentient?" Bela Argos walked forward and toed Raven Latch's body as if to be sure she was dead. "A few of them can break elemental locks, right?"

Like Creed, Riana thought. *Of course. That's why he can heal, too. He's from the Latch bloodline, just like this man.*

Mirror-Creed nodded. "Raven Latch could split cells like

atoms. That's what—" He took a ragged breath and looked first at Riana, then at Bela, then at Cynda. His gaze remained there, locked with hers. "That's what she was doing with that chant. She would have killed all of you."

"Dominic," Cynda said, giving voice to what Riana had already realized. "You're Creed's twin brother."

"Nick," the man replied. "Sergeant Nick Lowell, OCU special ops. I've been deep-cover with the Legion for fifty-four months. I'd stand up and shake your hand, but I'm naked."

"Well, don't let that stop you," Cynda said without missing a beat. Her lips twitched as she let her eyes slide lower, to the ample package Nick was attempting to conceal with his knees and hands.

Merilee snickered.

Andy let out a colorful string of Southern obscenities.

Bela Argos shook her head and pressed her fingers against her eyes. "What the fuck? Do you people *collect* demon cops?"

Keeping his dark, smoky gaze fixed on Cynda, Nick Lowell said, "We've got to get out of here before the NYPD storms the place. Come on." He stood, careful to keep his hands over his cock. "I'll take you through the service tunnel."

36

They knew I was coming.

Creed elbowed his way through the small, crowded arrival square at Volgograd-Gumrak International Airport. The fact that the Mothers sent someone to meet him both relieved Creed and bothered him at the same time.

When he had started his journey to Russia almost a week before, it took him a whole day and a shitload of cash to get more clothes and a newly minted fake identity from his street contacts, complete with valid passport. He had hidden out in the streets of New York, not daring to go back to his apartment or show his face, for fear of what the security cameras at Rikers Island had captured.

Flying to St. Petersburg blotted out another entire day in the air. Then he had to wait four days to catch one of only two Aeroflot jets scheduled to stop in Volgograd before the week ended.

And, of course, it was already unseasonably cold for fall in southern Russia.

Everyone who spoke English told him that, like he hadn't noticed the record snowfall.

Creed had bought some American-made flannel-lined jeans and a flannel shirt in St. Petersburg, along with three pairs of mittens, three pairs of socks, some boots, a Russian *ushanka* hat with fur earflaps, and a *dublionka* shearling coat—all of which he was wearing. He didn't have any luggage, which was a good thing, because the old guy waiting for him by the Baggage Reclamation entrance seemed way past ready to go. Creed kept his gaze fixed on the strange little man with the beard stubble, the one wearing the traditional black *kosovorotka* shirt and broad-brimmed *kartuz* cap. The shirt reached almost to the knees of the old man's patched, frayed jeans, and the guy's red felt boots looked about three sizes too big.

It was the sign, though, that had caught Creed's attention.

The old man was holding up a rough board with two jagged words painted across the splintering surface. The first word, all in black, was in Russian. Creed had no idea what it meant. The second word, though—that one was unmistakable.

Curson.

Deep in Creed's mind, the *other* gave a grunt of recognition.

Curson. That's what he was. What they were, him and the *other*. Half-human, half-demon, and the Mothers knew it. They were all of one mind about this journey, Creed and the *other*, and obviously, the Mothers, too.

Creed made his way to the old man, stopped, and pointed at the sign. "That's me." He pointed to himself. "Uh, that's us. Curson."

The old man turned his rheumy brown eyes to Creed's face and gave him a slow, probing head-to-toe examination. Then he nodded, turned, and shot off toward the door.

Good thing I didn't have any bags, Creed thought as he ran after the guy.

A few minutes later, Creed found himself careening through the four-hundred-year-old city in a rusty black Chaika convertible. Icy wind blasted into his face, and he had to hold his *ushanka* with both hands to keep from losing it. The old guy seemed to be taking the scenic route, first showing him the Volga River, then various war-related memorials, until he finally pulled to a halt at the foot of Mamayev Hill.

Creed gazed upward to the stunning sight of the Rodina, a steel-and-concrete monument in the shape of a sword-wielding woman almost twice the size of the Statue of Liberty, visible for miles in any direction. The warrior, representing the spirit of Mother Russia herself, was a tribute to the million or more soldiers who died defending Volgograd from Nazi invasion during one of the worst military sieges ever known in human history. In the mound below the Rodina's massive feet lay the reinterred remains of thousands and thousands of soldiers. She guarded them and paid them tribute, with her right arm thrusting a frightening sword up, endlessly up, piercing the cold, gray Russian sky. Her hair and robes were swept back, as if billowing in a steady, relentless wind.

Creed had seen the Rodina in pictures before, as a statement of national pride and perseverance. As a reminder of strength and the incredible losses the Russian people endured during World War II.

Now he saw her differently.

Now he saw a three-hundred-foot Sibyl stamped against an endless foreign sky, glaring down at him, questioning him, daring him.

The old man grunted.

When Creed looked at him, the old man's wide brown eyes held an unmistakable judgment—and a question.

Fool. Are you sure *you want to do this?*

Creed glanced back up Mamayev Hill, to the fierce, omnipresent Sibyl.

He imagined Riana's face, beautiful and loving and so wounded, the way he had seen her when he left her in the Latch basement. His heart ached. He had to do this, even if it killed him. Better dead than living without the woman he loved forever—and someone would have to kill him before he could stay away from her.

He nodded.

The old man had taken him out of Volgograd hours ago, and Creed could have sworn the little bastard drove him in circles a few times to keep him confused and disoriented. He tried to use the Rodina for a reference point, but foggy snowfall and the low afternoon light gradually obscured even her imposing presence.

They had abandoned the bottomed-out convertible at what had to be the old man's small farm—at least Creed hoped it was his farm—in favor of a sled drawn by two massive brown draft horses. Soviet Heavy Draft horses, the old man had told him in broken English. A breed originated in Russia, to weather the harsh demands of their climate.

Creed had never seen horses so huge or single-minded. Their thick muscles rippled as they pulled the sled down a heavily wooded path, deeper into what Creed perceived to be the wilderness of the Russian steppe. He thought they might be going north, and he thought the snow-covered trees might be mostly oak, but he had no real idea.

He couldn't even tell what time of day it was anymore. His watch had stopped working when they entered the woods, and the snowcapped trees blocked most of the natural light. The old man had two candlelit lanterns dangling from the sides of the sled, casting just enough light in front of the horses to keep them moving. Snow fell at a steady pace now, and Creed thought the air was much, much colder. Layers of snow gathered at the sides of the path, stirred along by occasional bursts of wind that sliced through every layer he was wearing. He kept his heavy coat pulled tight around him, and rubbed his hands together. They were icy, despite the three pairs of mittens.

His eyes grew more and more heavy, and Creed wondered if he might be freezing to death. Was that the plan? To run him around in these woods until he turned to ice? Then the Sibyls could haul him off to wherever Dracula lived, right?

Or was that in Romania?

He didn't know for sure. Confusion clouded the images

and thoughts that bounced around in his head. The energy in this place felt ancient. Heavy. Like it wanted to crush him slowly, slowly, until he just didn't exist anymore.

Probably some sort of protection.

The tempting scent of roasted meat drifted through the woods. Spices. The alcoholic tang of hot Russian coffee.

Creed's stomach rumbled.

He sat back in the sled, knowing he should be alert and wary, but that just wasn't possible. The *other* didn't seem able to get agitated, either. Both of them were passive prisoners now, just passengers in the old man's sled.

Creed's eyelids drifted shut as the jog-jog-jog movement of the big draft horses lulled him and pulled him toward those wonderful smells. For a few seconds, he forced his eyes open again, but sleep stalked him like those shadows, the ones slinking closer and closer to the sled, using the snowy oaks for cover.

Dangerous, carnivorous shadows, sliding through the frosty tree trunks.

Are those panthers?

Big cats in the trees . . .

Or were those wolves?

And farther into the trees—was that a castle made out of logs and stone?

For a second Creed thought he saw heavy wooden gates lodged in a carved granite archway. Then the whole castle seemed to rise and turn away from him, settling into the snowy mists so that he couldn't see the door anymore.

Baba Yaga's house, he thought, remembering a tale his grandmother once told him about an old Russian witch with iron teeth, who flew through the sky in her ancient mortar, using her pestle to push and grind, and her broom to sweep the clouds away behind her. Baba Yaga lived in a hut mounted on chicken legs. The hut spun and screeched and screeched and spun, and walked wherever it chose to go. Unwelcome travelers could starve to death just trying to catch the hut, or find its door. And if a poor fool did happen to catch the hut, it had eyes for windows and teeth in its keyholes.

What a place.

Creed tried to stare into the snowy trees, tried to find the castle again, but he saw nothing but snow and shadows.

Maybe it walked off on its chicken legs.

Once more, his eyelids drifted shut.

Baba Yaga, here I come.

Riana's green eyes flashed with passion as she lowered her sensual mouth to his and kissed him.

God, she was warm.

Hot.

He wanted her now.

He wanted her hard and fast and all night, and the next, and next week.

Riana . . .

Creed woke suddenly as a big, slobber-coated tongue swiped across his face again.

He was lying on his back in a clearing, lodged in a mound of snow. The moonlight was so bright Creed had to blink. Ice had crusted around his mouth and nose, partially licked away by the giant gray wolf standing with its forepaws on his chest.

Creed stared into the animal's luminescent yellow eyes and knew better than to move.

Fuck that little bastard of a guide. He drove me out here and dumped me. He was too scared to—

A female figure crossed into his line of sight, coming up behind the wolf like a murderous wraith. She walked with a long, twisted stick that had to be twice as tall as she was. Her brown robes looked frosty in the bright moonlight.

More wolves crowded in around Creed's prone form.

A few growled, low and steady.

Creed couldn't see the face of the woman, or the faces of

any of the dozens more brown-robed women who came silently through the snow to surround him.

The woman with the stick came closer and bent over, showing Creed her wrinkled visage and her wild riot of white hair.

Mother Yana.

The Russian Mother smiled, showing sharp wolves' teeth.

Creed didn't know whether she looked like the wolves, or the wolves looked like her.

Both seemed capable of eating him without a second thought.

"Vat do you vant, Curson?" she asked, her words sending white plumes spiraling into the cold Slavic night.

Creed wondered what would happen if he chose the wrong answer. Would they kill him outright, or just leave him to the snow and the wolves?

He glanced up at the wolf still standing on his chest.

It growled at him, pulling back its lips in a ghastly, lethal smile.

Would it tear out his throat if he spoke?

Guess I'll have to chance it.

"I want Riana," Creed said. "I want permission to marry her, but only if you can give me full control of the *other*." He sucked in a gulp of cold, harsh air. "If you can't do that, I want you to destroy me, and the demon inside me, too. That's the only way to protect her."

Seconds went by, then minutes.

No one spoke or made a sound, not even the wolves.

After another few frozen moments, Mother Yana nodded.

"Fair enough," she said.

Then she cackled as Baba Yaga must have done across the centuries, in the nightmares of countless children.

(37)

Riana sat on the overstuffed sofa in her brownstone, holding her crescent pendant and staring into the mirrors hanging above the big oak table. She and her triad had been back home from the safe house a little over two weeks.

And Creed has been gone more than a month. She sighed. *Thirty-eight days, twelve hours, and about twenty minutes, but who's counting.*

Her heart ached just as much as the day she lost him. If she closed her eyes, she saw him in his *other* form, shimmering in the basement of the Latch house, gazing at her like he would love her forever.

Right before he blasted through the metal door and disappeared.

He wasn't coming back.

Everyone said so, except Nick, who looked so damned much like Creed Riana wanted to kill the man most days. Nick didn't say much of anything about Creed. Nick didn't say much of anything at all. *Brooding* was a kind adjective for the OCU special ops sergeant, who for now had taken up residence in the brownstone. *Arrogant* would fit, too. And if he didn't quit pissing off Cynda on an hourly basis, *perpetually naked* would soon apply. He couldn't have many more leather jackets, or that many spare pairs of jeans.

In the kitchen, Merilee and Cynda were going over a new search vector for Jacob the Astaroth, based on a tip from two Wiccan groups who liked to hold rituals near the Reservoir. From the sweet odor of soy, chicken, and cilantro wafting around the room, Riana figured Cynda and Merilee were spending just as much time coming up with new strategies to get her to eat more.

Merilee thought Riana was losing too much weight "pining over that chickenshit runaway demon-man," or so she said at least four times a day.

Sometimes five.

To Riana's left, over by the front door, OCU officers and a Sibyl ranger group were getting the lowdown on last night's raid on a Legion stronghold in Hell's Kitchen from Captain Sal Freeman, Nick, and Andy. The information obtained from computers, notes, and journals in the Latch house had been quite useful, both in destroying Legion bases within New York City and in mapping out the organization's loose structure and major hot spots across the globe. A series of counterstrikes much like Riana's invasion of the Latch house had taken out some of the leadership, driven the Legion back underground, and made it safe for Sibyls to return to their homes and routines.

Meanwhile, Andy had arranged for Captain Freeman and the OCU to meet the Sibyls. By mutual agreement, the two groups were working together to root out Legion locations, members, accounts, suppliers, and collaborating groups. Similar collaborations were under way with law enforcement groups worldwide.

The brownstone served as an operational center for Manhattan, since the Sibyls couldn't very well hang out at an official police precinct. All the medieval weapons might pose a problem with public relations.

For the first time in a century, the Sibyls felt like they had a foothold in their war with their archfoes. No one had any illusions that they were winning the war to destroy the Legion, but at least there was hope.

Riana let go of her pendant and stared into the oldest, biggest mirror, the one used to reach Motherhouse Russia.

Hope for the Sibyls, at least. Not for her. No matter how

hard she tried, she couldn't seem to muster much energy and joy. The only time she felt a measure of peace was when she was out on patrol with her triad and the officers they worked with every other night. There was no room then for anything but duty, concentration, and long, quiet walks.

Illustrating the opposite of quiet, Merilee and Cynda came banging out of the kitchen carrying a roast beef and avocado sandwich, some soup, a homemade ice cream sundae, a taco, and an egg roll. They placed all of these on the big oak table in front of Riana, then looked at her expectantly.

Riana noticed that Merilee had chocolate fudge all over her black blouse and jeans, and Cynda seemed to be wearing a healthy portion of chicken soup and whipped cream on her white tunic. It took a few seconds, but Riana worked up the muscle coordination to smile at them. "Thanks," she said. "That looks—uh—like a lot of variety."

"Take what you want," Merilee encouraged. "We'll eat the rest."

"Especially the ice cream," Cynda agreed.

Nick crossed into Riana's view, snagged the egg roll, and sat on the edge of the table only a few feet from Riana. Merilee glared at him, and Cynda's expression turned thunderous. Smoke curled dangerously from her palms, and Riana knew Nick's jeans were in serious jeopardy once again.

He didn't seem to care.

Nick just gazed at Riana with his Creed-looking dark eyes, ate half the egg roll in one bite, then held up the rest. "It's good," he announced after he swallowed. "You should make them heat up a few more of these."

"Asshole," Cynda said. "We didn't cook for *you*."

Nick shrugged. "Might as well. She won't eat any of this. Except maybe the soup." He polished off the egg roll, picked up the bowl of soup, and held it toward Riana.

She leaned forward and took it from him, battling a wave of nausea.

Did he have to be Creed's *twin,* for the sake of the Goddess?

Nick kept staring at Riana until she swallowed a spoonful.

Warm. Soothing. A hint of rosemary and thyme. Not as bad as she thought it would be. In fact, the soup was really good.

And Nick was too damned intense.

How was she ever supposed to regain her mental balance with a mirror image of her lover hovering around the brownstone every day?

Andy came around the sofa and claimed the taco, while Merilee got hold of the roast beef and avocado. Cynda, of course, took the ice cream. Riana couldn't help but notice how Andy's gaze tended to drift back to the other side of the room, where Captain Freeman was busy giving out duty assignments to the team of officers and their Sibyl companions, and sending them on their way.

Riana ate another few spoonfuls of soup, beginning to enjoy the buttery, savory scent and the way it seemed to coat her belly with every swallow.

Andy and Sal Freeman.

Now *that* would be an interesting development.

Talk about against all the rules . . .

Rules. I hate rules.

The soup seemed to sour in Riana's mouth.

According to all the rules, she never should have touched Creed, or let him touch her. But if she had it to do all over again, would she give up one kiss? One single second?

Absolutely not.

Riana trusted herself and her own instincts more than ever before. She knew loving Creed had been the right choice, the only choice, even if it cost her more than she could pay.

As the last of the patrol groups left the brownstone, the chimes over the front door rang softly.

Cynda reacted first, shooing Andy and Nick off the oak table, then handing her ice cream to Merilee.

The chimes rang louder.

"It's Motherhouse Russia," Cynda said as she climbed on the table. "They want the channels opened. Someone's coming through."

"Coming through?" Riana put her bowl of soup on the floor beside her chair and stood, concerned. Her heart started to beat a little faster, and she thought about heading for the closet to get their leathers and weapons. Something must be wrong.

Who was coming through?

And why?

The Mothers had been almost silent since the last set of raids on the Legion, and Motherhouse Russia had been quiet for well over a month. Everyone was just too busy archiving, analyzing, planning, and training replacements for the Sibyls who had been slaughtered in the big Legion attack. New York City was still two triads shy of a full complement.

Maybe Motherhouse Russia was finally sending through a novice mortar for the North Bronx trial?

Cynda threw up her hands, and the energy in the brownstone began to dance and spark right along with her. Nick stared up at Cynda, focusing all of his dark intensity on the fire Sibyl as she danced. Captain Freeman came over to stand beside Andy, Nick, and Merilee. He had seen a few communications before, but he had never seen the channels opened.

Riana's heart surged as the room's energy swirled and shifted, lending itself to Cynda and the adepts on the other end of the communication. The big, ancient-looking projective mirror of Motherhouse Russia flickered, then began to glow. Blurred images came into view through a haze of light and fog so thick and white it looked like snow.

A tiny figure stepped forward in the mirror, and Riana recognized Mother Yana. The old woman appeared to be struggling to build enough energy for what she was attempting to transport.

The mirrors of Motherhouse Ireland and Motherhouse Greece winked to life. Riana saw blue-robed women and green-robed women raise their arms to assist Mother Yana through the oldest of channels, Mother to Mother.

What the hell are they trying to send us—a giant dragon?

But it wasn't a dragon. It was a brown-robed, hooded figure, much bigger than most women Riana knew.

The figure moved up beside Mother Yana and held out its very masculine hand.

What in the name of the Goddess?

The Russian Mother grabbed hold of the figure's fingers.

Energy exploded outward in every direction, showering the room with sparks and light and frenetic sparkles. Cynda swore and leaped off the table. Nick caught her and shielded her from a blast of wind and water and earth and fire. Smoke billowed from the Motherhouse mirrors, temporarily blinding everyone.

Riana coughed and rubbed her tearing eyes. Her heart was pounding now and her instincts hummed with the knowledge that she had just witnessed something unique in Sibyl history. She had no idea what—but she knew it was special.

As the smoky haze cleared, Riana saw that the very tall hooded figure in the brown robe was standing on the table in her living room, head bowed, hands clasped inside the sleeves of its robes. The Motherhouse mirrors were still active, with the three oldest Mothers standing forward, hoods down, wide smiles on their faces.

Mother Yana gestured for Riana to come forward and get on the table.

Riana stared at the old woman like she was nuts.

Mother Yana narrowed her eyes and gestured again.

Old habits took over, and Riana complied, moving slowly, staring at the hooded figure every inch of the way. For some reason, she *did* feel drawn to it in ways she couldn't even express. As she got up on the table and faced the mirror open to Motherhouse Russia, Mother Yana rewarded Riana with a wink and nod.

"Permission granted," the old woman said.

"Agreed," the other two Mothers chanted in unison, and the Motherhouse mirrors went dark.

The figure standing an arm's length in front of Riana pushed back its hood.

Riana stared into Creed's handsome face, barely able to believe what she was seeing. She wondered if she had slipped into a trance, or maybe some beautiful dream.

He was a little thinner. Maybe a bit pale.

But Creed was standing on the table in front of her. All she had to do was reach out, and she would touch him.

Goddess. He's here. He came back.

He came back to me.

Riana felt like she was dying and returning to life all at the same time. Her chest throbbed. Her throat tightened. A thousand questions wedged into her mind, but all she wanted to do was hold him. Then slap him for leaving. Then do a lot more than hold him. Her body burned all over at the thought, a fire hotter than any Sibyl could command.

She realized she was laughing like a crazy woman, and covered her mouth.

Creed held up his hands, showing her that he wore no signet ring. Riana was about to tell him that leaving the ring with the Mothers was brilliant, but he parted the front of his robe to show her what looked like a thin golden tattoo pulsing on his muscled chest—a ring around his heart, buried deep in his skin.

"What—what did you do?" she asked, shocked to her depths. "How?"

Creed smiled, then shifted into a much more stable-looking, much brighter golden *other,* without changing height or burning off his robe.

Riana stared at the creature, who was more Creed than demon, with human eyes and human features, though it retained that almost godlike pulsing golden energy.

It's tamed, Riana thought. *Somehow, Creed internalized his talisman, and he's the* other's *master now.*

Creed shifted back to his human form and closed his robe.

"The Mothers melted my ring, locked the molten metal, infused it into a tattoo, then locked the design." He touched his chest. A look of pain flickered across his features, and Riana wondered if he was remembering the process a little too clearly, or if it still hurt. She couldn't imagine the agony. She couldn't believe he'd done that. She couldn't believe he'd had the balls to go to Motherhouse Russia at all.

For me. All for me.

"It was one hell of a ritual." Creed grimaced. "Not to mention that trip through the Russian woods—but I'm in control now. Completely." His smoldering eyes raked over her whole body. "And you're mine, Riana Dumain."

"Was—was that a proposal?" she asked over the murmur of voices around the table. Riana knew Andy, Freeman, Nick, and her triad were all talking at once, trying to get their attention, but she couldn't begin to pay attention to what they were saying.

Creed didn't seem to notice the five other people in the room. He had eyes for Riana and only Riana as he nodded. "Absolutely." He gestured to the mirrors. "You heard the Mothers. I already asked your family for permission and got it. Marry me, Riana."

Riana took a step forward, stopping an inch from Creed. She stared deep into his dark eyes. They seemed more alive, less burdened, and poignantly vulnerable. Open, completely, to her, for her scrutiny.

Here I am, those gorgeous eyes said.

Creed was looking at her like his whole life hinged on her answer to his proposal, and he didn't care if she knew that.

Straightforward about what he wants. So honest. So Creed.

She took a slow, steadying breath, reveling in his familiar masculine scent. Cedar, this time with a breath of snow and ice and untainted air, straight from the Russian woods that had been her home for so many wonderful years.

He came back to me.

Creed raised his hands and caressed her arms. The heat of his touch, the nearness of his lips, made her want to moan.

"Marry me," he said again as he lifted her chin and bent toward her.

Riana melted into him, treasuring the sensation of his strength against her softness. "I'll marry you," she whispered just before his lips pressed against hers and robbed her of rational thought.

He held her so tightly, yet so gently, as if she might be some rare, precious flower he didn't want to crush. Creed's kiss stole her breath, her resistance, and wiped away her last shreds of doubt and fear. His tongue joined with hers, probing, needing to know, asking his questions without words.

Did you wait for me?

Are you still mine?

Will you be mine forever?

She answered each inquiry with her body, with her helpless moans of pleasure.

Yes.

Yes.

Yes.

This was what she wanted, what she needed, and part of what she had been born to experience. This perfect emotion. This wonderful closeness. This incredible man.

She wrapped her arms around his neck, never intending to let go again—except his robe caught fire, and so did the sleeves of her blouse.

Creed released Riana in a hurry and pulled back.

She blotted out the flames with a wave of earth energy as Merilee said, "Cynda, you are *such* a fucking killjoy."

Riana saw Creed's eyes widen as he looked around and realized who had witnessed his return and proposal. Then she saw him break into a boyish smile.

Creed pulled Riana to him and held her with one arm as he said, "Dominic."

From the floor in front of the table, Nick patted out a few glowing cinders on his jeans and grinned back at Creed. "Nice threads," he said, straight-faced, gesturing to the robe.

"Should I kill you?" Creed asked, looking amused and worried at the same time. "All those fucked-up letters you sent, trying to get me to join the Legion—"

"Were on my orders," Freeman interjected, holding up both hands. "He's clean, Creed. Nick is clean."

Freeman went on to give Creed a rundown of Nick's deep-cover assignment. Then the captain explained the new collaborative arrangement between the OCU and the Sibyls. He even started to say something about new rules and fraternization with the warrior women, but Andy stuffed her last bite of taco in Freeman's mouth.

"You owe me," Andy told Creed as Freeman nearly choked and started hopping around from the super-hot sauce Cynda always used when she made Mexican food. "This whole working-without-a-partner routine sucks."

"Am I still your partner?" Creed asked her, obviously surprised.

"What the hell do you think?" Andy narrowed her eyes. "I'm not letting you dump me for some other OCU chump."

Nick shrugged. "And nobody can find anything in the

NYPD policy and procedures forbidding half-demon cops. For now, we're good."

Riana smiled as Creed tightened his grip on her waist. She glanced up at him and followed his gaze to Nick's pants, then to Cynda, who had her arms folded and a major sulk-face in progress.

It didn't take Creed longer than a moment to size up the serious crackle in the air between Nick and Cynda.

Creed whistled long and low, then gave his brother a sympathetic look. "Damn, man. You've got your hands full with that one."

Merilee had to tackle Cynda and drag her into the kitchen to keep her from turning the oak table into a fiery maelstrom.

Andy made a let's-be-sensitive face at Nick, then started herding Freeman and the OCU out the front door.

Nick lingered for a moment, gave Creed a thumbs-up, then bravely headed into the kitchen. Apparently, he wasn't put off by the cursing and shouting, or the clouds of smoke billowing out from under the swinging door.

Riana couldn't help herself. Before the swinging door even settled on its hinges, she pushed open Creed's robe, pressed her face against his chest, and felt the tingle of his shimmering golden tattoo against her cheek.

"Don't ever leave me again, Creed." Her tears dampened his skin. "I love you so, so much. I thought I wasn't going to make it without you."

He snuggled her against him and kissed the top of her head. "I love you, too, honey. I'm never letting you out of my sight if I can help it—and that includes when you run off to fight monsters. This is a joint enterprise now. Triad plus one."

She nodded, then ran her hand down his side, across his lean hip, and back toward the center of his body until she brushed her fingers against his hard, ready cock. Her body responded with a flood of moisture and a round of delicious, eager trembles.

Goddess, she wanted him. She had to have him.

"You stay right here," she murmured into his neck as she palmed his erection through the soft cloth of his robe. "From now on. Here, with me. I'll keep you in the cell if I have to."

His rumble of arousal made her skin tingle.

Creed gently moved her hand away from his cock, then lifted her off the table, cradled her, and held her tight against him. His kiss was tender this time, raw and possessive, but reverent. When he pulled back and gazed at her, she saw the absolute love in his eyes, and his feral, hungry expression turned her insides into liquid heat.

"Who am I to refuse a grown woman's invitation?" he said in that low, body-stroking voice she had waited weeks to hear again.

Cynda, Merilee, and Nick burst out of the kitchen. Cynda and Merilee were arguing over whether or not *they* had to consent to Riana's marriage. Nick, Riana noted, was wisely keeping his mouth shut and just picking up whatever they knocked over as they slugged it out.

Nick gave Creed a run-for-it look.

Riana's heart thumped as Creed jumped down from the table, still carrying her like a bride against his chest. He eased her through the swinging door into the smoking kitchen, then down the steps toward her earthy sanctuary.

Behind them, the argument got louder.

"Sounds like it's getting interesting up there," Riana said just before she kissed his cheek.

"Not half as interesting as it's about to be down here." He paused at the bottom step and gave her a devastating smile. "Bedroom or cell? Your call, honey."

Riana's body buzzed with anticipation, and she licked her lips. "The cell, for starters." She pressed against him harder and ran her nails across the rough stubble on his cheek. "But stop by the bedroom first. Andy gave me some handcuffs, and I've been just dying to try them out with a wickedly handsome demon-man. Any volunteers?"

"You're some kind of psychic, aren't you?" Creed kissed her so hard and so deep Riana laced her fingers through his silky black hair and held on for the wonderful ride.

"Just so you know," he said when he pulled back, leaving her gasping for air and his next kiss and the endless hours of pleasure promised by his smoky black eyes, "I think I have a thing for psychics."

Acknowledgments

Thank you, reader, for your love of books, for your time, and for your interest. I hope I swept you away.

I extend endless thanks to my intrepid critique partners Cheyenne McCray, Tara Donn, and Nelissa Donovan. Quick reads, startling insight, an eye for detail—nobody does it better than you ladies.

Two editors lent their expertise to this work. First, my appreciation to Charlotte Hersher for taking a chance on me, and on this series. To Kate Collins, welcome, welcome, and thank you for everything you've done so far. I'm fortunate to have been blessed with two sharp, witty, and ultra-competent professionals.

Last but definitely not least, thank you to Nancy Yost, without whom this book would not have found such a wonderful home. You've made it fun so far, and kept me from panicking. I owe you lots of chocolate.

Turn the page to catch a sneak peek at

Bound by Flame

the next sizzling novel in the trilogy by
Anna Windsor!

(1)

Cynda knelt behind a dumpster in an alley near Sixty-fifth and Lexington. Her teeth chattered. Smoke rose from her shoulders as she shivered and bumped her sheathed Celtic broadsword against the hulking cop crouched beside her.

Nick didn't react.

Sleet clattered against dumpsters and fire escapes, pelting the top of Cynda's tightly zipped leather face mask. Her toes ached like she had a good case of frostbite, never mind her leather boots, gloves, and bodysuit.

March in New York City *so* sucked.

First chance she got, she would kill Riana and Merilee for having "previous commitments," best friends and sister-Sibyls or not. How could they strand her in a friggin' sleet storm?

The smoke around her face got thicker.

Nick, who in his heart-stopping human hunk form, was a cop, had dragged her into the frigid night to meet with his prize informant. Cynda adjusted the strap of her special glasses and peered through the overlarge lenses. Stupid things reminded her of motorcycle racing goggles, in fetching shades of black rubber and yellow polycarbonate. Highly attractive.

Not.

Probably had icicles hanging from both sides to add to the effect.

But the treated lenses detected sulfur dioxide left behind by demons sent to do the bidding of their Legion masters. So the lenses had become standard issue for Sibyls on patrol all over the world.

Of course, most Sibyls didn't have far-too-sexy cops to babysit. Teaming up with law enforcement was a pain in the ass, even when law enforcement meant the OCU—New York City's low-profile Occult Crimes Unit.

Cynda pulled at her ugly demon-hunting goggles again and wished she could see the sulfur traces without them, the way Nick could.

"Be still and quit smoking," he rumbled. "If he sees you, he'll bolt."

A thousand retorts flashed across Cynda's mind, but she clamped her mouth shut. More heat rushed through her body. It took every bit of willpower she possessed not to set Nick on fire, and her leather bodysuit in the bargain. She'd freeze to death if she burned holes in her clothes—and he'd laugh his ass off, too. At least the sleet was slowing some, and ah, there, yes. Finally stopping.

"Maybe your informant was shining you on," she muttered.

"He's reliable. If Max says he knows something about Legion activity, then he does."

Cynda cut Nick a sideways look, then had to turn her whole head to see him through the goggles.

"The Legion's been quiet for too long." Nick's expression stayed distant, but tension bunched at his eyes. "They haven't left New York like everyone thinks. That's bullshit. I've been on the inside, Cynda. I *know*. We have to find out what the cult's planning before it's too late."

She wanted to argue with Nick just to keep warm, but part of her knew he was right. In the four months she had worked with him, they had busted a slew of Legion houses before cult activity fell off the radar.

Nick knew his stuff.

He had good instincts, almost as good as her own, and

the stirrings in her gut agreed with him. The Legion *wasn't* gone. No way. The zealous freaks were cooking up something extra nasty to gain the upper hand with their ancient enemies, the Sibyls—but what would it be?

Cynda had no idea.

Flames broke out along her gloved fingertips.

She *hated* not knowing. She usually had inklings, at least a hunch about actions to take to protect the Sibyl family she loved more than anything on Earth, but this time, nothing.

Nick had infiltrated the Legion, lived with the murdering maniacs for almost five years, and paid a major price for that, and he had no guesses, either.

Cynda glanced at him again, gradually pulling her fire energy back inside her chilled body. Even in the middle of an ice storm, she could smell his unusual scent of ocean and musk. His chiseled face looked almost exotic in the low light, with his black hair pulled into a ponytail at the nape of his neck. A gold chain, the talisman that controlled his *other*, hung inside the open collar of his black shirt.

The way the chain lay against his skin tempted her to kiss it—or grab it and twist. Hard.

Making Nick's eyes bug out might give her a little satisfaction.

Kissing him—now, that would be satisfaction, too, but if she ever let herself kiss him once, she'd want to do it again. Maybe a lot.

Smoke poured out of her boots.

Not going there. Gotta stop.

Even if Nick did feel some attraction to her—which he had never indicated—Cynda didn't do attachments other than her bond with her Sibyl sisters. She'd learned when she was just a little girl—nobody else was reliable, or worth that risk.

But did Nick's jeans *ever* fit him like a faded blue glove.

No jackets, hats, mittens, or anything to guard against the cold. *It's a discipline,* he had told Cynda more than once. *Mind over matter. A mental thing.*

Yeah.

Most mental things involved straitjackets and locked hospital units, but insane or not, the man was one tasty package. He kept his powerful body in a ready stance, with one big hand on the ground like a football player ready to charge forward. The most striking feature, though, was the way her goggles made his muscular silhouette glow dark red about the edges.

Because he's not completely human.

That little reminder sobered Cynda, but didn't curb her tongue. "Couldn't you at least get an informant who shows up on time?"

"Max does his best." Nick didn't twitch or shift. Totally still. Totally calm. "He's Irish like you, so he follows his own rules."

She let out a cloud of smoke and popped his hip with the flat tip of her broadsword. "What's that supposed to mean?"

Nick didn't answer. His dark eyes stayed focused on the alley's icy darkness with characteristic intensity and single-minded concentration.

"Why would anybody tell you anything?" she mumbled, more to herself than to the big jerk beside her.

"Most people find me charming. Don't know what's the matter with you."

Cynda flicked her fingers and showered his hair with sparks.

Nick rubbed his hand over the dark strands and snuffed the flames without so much as looking at her. He could deflect her elemental powers better than anyone she had ever known, save for Mother Keara.

"You—" she started, but Nick shook his head and cut her off before she could say anything else.

His body tightened.

Cynda swiveled back toward the alley, smoking from more places than she could count.

A tall, thin man made his way slowly through the darkness, fingers trailing along one grimy, icy brick wall. Obviously, he couldn't see in the low light as well as Cynda or Nick, or at least he wanted them to think he couldn't.

Cynda squinted at the man. Blond. About six feet tall, underfed, pock-faced—just the way Nick had described him, except his face seemed badly bruised.

Max Moses, the informant.

Waves of heat rose from his body. Traces of red hung about his tattered overcoat, and his gait hitched and sputtered as he blundered down the alley. Cynda squinted at the red flecks clustered around Max's shoulders and neck. Not enough sulfur traces to equal a demon, no, but weird. And wrong.

"Something's off about him." Cynda's words came out soft against the curtain of smoke shrouding her head.

Nick hushed her with a sharp gesture. "Max drinks. He's a sensitive. Has to block things out."

Then Nick stood and strode away from Cynda's hiding place.

She swore to herself and barely held back a jet of fire. Her hand tightened on the hilt of her sword. Those red streaks almost had a pattern. If they'd been on Max's skin instead of his clothes, they might have been bruises, as if someone—or something—had grabbed Max from behind.

And tried to choke him.

Nick reached Max at the same moment Cynda caught a darker flash of red to her left, farther away, near the mouth of the alley. Her heart rate kicked up and she barely kept back her fire. She blinked, tried to fix on the signal, but couldn't.

What was it?

A spell?

But spells were intricate procedures, requiring tools and setup and patterns, all kinds of props. "Magic" was more elemental science than anything, and elements had to be handled carefully, bound and controlled, or "locked" to channel their power—like the fire, air, water, and earth power locked along the double-edged blade of Cynda's sheathed sword.

She didn't know any paranormal group that could cast random spells in a dark alley.

And now, she didn't see a thing.

Back to dark.

But it still didn't feel right.

She reached out with her pyrosentience—her fire sense—but got nothing back. Her eyes darted to the numerous dumpsters and fire escapes. All dark and quiet and still. All empty.

Screw this.

Cynda rose to her feet and drew her sword, making no sound. Whatever was out there, it could eat steel and explain itself later.

Max remained deep in conversation with Nick, not paying attention, but the red demon residue on his clothing blared at Cynda like a bullhorn.

Didn't Nick feel something off in this situation?

She sensed it, stronger and stronger. Wrongness. Like darkness creeping through the alley, spreading into the city.

The taste in her mouth turned acrid, the way it always did when she was nervous—and she hated being nervous almost as much as she hated being cold. Her eyes strained inside the goggles, searching up, down, left, right.

Where was that streak of red residue?

There.

No wait, there!

On the fire escape nearest Nick, the one just above his left shoulder. A flicker of red. Just a hint, and then it was gone.

Cynda ground her teeth. Her leathers gave at the ankles, and she knew she had burned holes in her fighting suit. Her Sibyl instincts told her this was a creature, some type of being her Sibyl triad hadn't encountered before.

As if in response to her thoughts, malice radiated across the alley. It struck Cynda, pummeled against her like the cold. Now her instincts *shouted* wrongness, and not just in the alley.

Everywhere.

Her pyrosentience swept in all directions. Touching—yet not touching. What the hell was out there?

Her muscles tightened. Her belly burned. Flames surged along her arms, gathered at her hands, but she couldn't throw fire at the thing, whatever it was. It might deflect the heat and fry Nick and Max, if it had the ability to fight elements.

A centering breath . . .

The weight of her sword . . .

Yes.

"Nick!" she shouted. "Heads up!"

His attention snapped to her at the same time she gave a battle cry and launched herself from behind the dumpster. Jerking warmth from the air, building sparks, breathing flames, Cynda ignited her sword. The fierce blaze flared orange, lighting up the end of the alley.

Heart pounding, body seething with heat, she leaped past Nick and his informant. With her free hand, she grabbed the bottom rung of the fire escape. The metal was ice-cold and rough through her glove as she hoisted herself to hang off the edge.

Whatever was there, she'd take it down at the ankles.

She sucked in a breath of cold air as she swept her blazing sword low across the first platform.

Cynda's blade connected with something solid.

Something with powerful protections.

Her swing stopped mid-arc, thrumming, vibrating. Like

banging the blade into a stack of cement bricks. Pain ricocheted up her hand, wrist, and arm. Her teeth slammed together.

The force of the blow ripped her sword from her hand. It clattered against metal as it fell to the fire escape platform, just out of her reach.

Shit!

Red flickered in the air above her head. Just as Cynda lost her grip on the platform, she saw a distinct man-shape wink into reality, and she heard its angry, dangerous howl.

She let out a shriek as she fell backward, fast and hard. Bolts of agony shot through her back and limbs as she slammed ass-first into the ice-crusted pavement. Breath left her in a harsh rush.

Nick shouted as the informant bolted down the alleyway, his footsteps pounding the asphalt as he ran. "Stay down," Nick ordered Cynda as he drew his weapon.

"Bullshit." Heat from her face clouded her goggle-vision as she caught her breath and scrambled to her feet, fire blazing along her shoulders.

Where the hell was the thing she'd just hit?

Let's see if it can eat fire.

She paused as her gaze followed the direction Nick had his weapon pointed.

Aimed at . . . nothing?

Wait. He was training his gun on—

On a bucket of paint?

Thick, white fluid slopped over the side of the bucket that hovered in midair, right in front of Nick.

Cynda blinked. Smoke rose off her cheeks and chin.

The bucket *floated* in the alley. Red flecks covered the handle and bottom in a pattern just like hands. Nick kept his Glock trained on the paint, clearly intending to pump elementally locked bullets into whatever was holding the can.

The paint can didn't stick around to be shot.

It flew upward, above Cynda's head, to the fire escape platform.

She was letting her power build up inside her, trying to get ready for whatever came next, but this was way past wrong.

"Shoot it," she shouted.

"No." Nick held fast. "We don't know what it is."

"Shoot it anyway!" she screeched over the pounding of her heart. Gouts of flame roared from her fingertips. "We'll identify it later!"

Nick snarled something unintelligible, and Cynda hated, hated, hated his years of cop training in the judicious use of deadly force. If he had been a Sibyl, that paint can would have been *so* full of holes already.

When she caught sight of Nick's face, his devastated expression struck her like a blow to her belly.

Nick *never* looked like that.

His hesitation was more than habit. Something was tearing at him, way down deep, and the sight of his pain rattled Cynda completely.

Nick didn't want to shoot the creature.

The paint can jerked sideways. It soared upward, then turned itself upside down. White paint rained from the fire escape.

Cynda lunged sideways to avoid the bath, but paint splattered her leathers, and she barely kept to her feet. Her mind was still spinning from the look on Nick's face. Holes opened in her bodysuit as fire spit forward, lashing out at nothing and everything.

Above her, the spilled paint coalesced on a man-shape frozen in defensive posture—and the man had wings. Two sets of them.

Big wings.